"I SAW HIM GASP, REEL, AND FALL."

WILD WESTERN SCENES
Gihon

WILD WESTERN SCENES:

A NARRATIVE

OF

Adventures in the Western Wilderness,

WHEREIN

THE EXPLOITS OF DANIEL BOONE, THE GREAT AMERICAN PIONEER
ARE PARTICULARLY DESCRIBED

ALSO,

ACCOUNTS OF BEAR, DEER, AND BUFFALO HUNTS—DESPERATE CONFLICTS
WITH THE SAVAGES—WOLF HUNTS—FISHING AND FOWLING
ADVENTURES—ENCOUNTERS WITH SERPENTS, ETC.

NEW STEREOTYPE EDITION, ALTERED, REVISED, AND CORRECTED

BY J. B. JONES.
AUTHOR OF "THE WAR PATH," "ADVENTURES OF A COUNTRY MERCHANT," ETC.

Illustrated with Sixteen Engravings from Original Designs

PHILADELPHIA:
J. B. LIPPINCOTT & CO.
1875.

STEREOTYPED BY L. JOHNSON & CO.
PHILADELPHIA.

PREFACE.

When a work of fiction has reached its fortieth edition, one would suppose the author might congratulate himself upon having contributed something of an imperishable character to the literature of the country. But no such pretensions are asserted for this production, now in its fortieth thousand. Being the first essay of an impetuous youth in a field where giants even have not always successfully contended, it would be a rash assumption to suppose it could receive from those who confer such honors any high award of merit. It has been before the public some fifteen years, and has never been reviewed. Perhaps the forbearance of those who wield the cerebral scalpels may not be further prolonged, and the book remains amenable to the judgment they may be pleased to pronounce.

To that portion of the public who have read with approbation so many thousands of his book, the author may speak with greater confidence. To this class of his friends he may make disclosures and confessions pertaining to the secret history of the "Wild Western Scenes," without the hazard of incurring their displeasure.

Like the hero of his book, the author had his vicissitudes in boyhood, and committed such indiscretions as were incident to one of his years and circumstances, but nevertheless only such as might be readily pardoned by the charitable. Like Glenn, he submitted to a voluntary exile in the wilds of Missouri. Hence the description of scenery is a true picture, and several characters in the scenes were real persons. Many of the occurrences actually transpired in his presence, or had been enacted in the vicinity at no remote period; and the dream of the hero—his visit to the haunted island—was truly a dream of the author's

But the worst miseries of the author were felt when his work was completed; he could get no publisher to examine it. He then purchased an interest in a weekly newspaper, in the columns of which it appeared in consecutive chapters. The subscribers were pleased with it, and desired to possess it in a volume; but still no publisher would undertake it,—the author had no reputation in the literary world. He offered it for fifty dollars, but could find no purchaser at any price. Believing the British booksellers more accommodating, a friend was employed to make a fair copy in manuscript, at a certain number of cents per hundred words. The work was sent to a British publisher, with whom it remained many months, but was returned, accompanied by a note declining to treat for it.

Undeterred by the rebuffs of two worlds, the author had his cherished production published on his own account, and was remunerated by the sale of the whole edition. After the tardy sale of several subsequent editions by houses of limited influence, the book had the good fortune, finally, to fall into the hands of the gigantic establishment whose imprint is now upon its title-page. And now, the author is informed, it is regularly and liberally ordered by the London booksellers, and is sold with an increasing rapidity in almost every section of the Union.

Such are the hazards, the miseries, and sometimes the rewards, of authorship.

J. B. J.

BURLINGTON, N J., *March*, 1856.

CONTENTS.

CHAPTER I.

CHAPTER II.

CHAPTER III.

CHAPTER IV.

CHAPTER V.

CHAPTER VI.

CHAPTER VII.

CHAPTER VIII.

CHAPTER IX.

CHAPTER X.

CHAPTER XI.

CHAPTER XII.

CHAPTER XIII.

CHAPTER XIV.

CHAPTER XV.

CHAPTER XVI.

CHAPTER XVII.

WILD WESTERN SCENES:

A NARRATIVE OF ADVENTURES.

CHAPTER I.

Glenn and Joe—Their horses—A storm—A black stump—A rough tumble—Moaning—Stars—Light—A log fire—Tents, and something to eat—Another stranger, who turns out to be well known—Joe has a snack—He studies revenge against the black stump—Boone proposes a bear hunt.

"Do you see any light yet, Joe?"

"Not the least speck that ever was created, except the lightning, and it's gone before I can turn my head to look at it."

The interrogator, Charles Glenn, reclined musingly in a two-horse wagon, the canvas covering of which served in some measure to protect him from the wind and rain. His servant, Joe Beck, was perched upon one of the horses, his shoulders screwed under the scanty folds of an oil-cloth cape, and his knees drawn nearly up to the pommel of the saddle, to avoid the thumping bushes and briers that occasionally assailed him, as the team plunged along in a stumbling pace. Their pathway, or rather their direction, for there was no beaten road, lay along the northern bank of the "Mad Missouri," some two hundred miles above the St. Louis settlement. It was at a time when there were no white men in those regions save a few trappers, traders, and emigrants, and each new sojourner found it convenient to carry with him a means of shelter, as houses of any description were but few and far between.

Our travellers had been told in the morning, when setting out from a temporary village which consisted of a few families of emigrants, with whom they had sojourned the preceding night, that they could attain the desired point by making the river their guide, should they be at a loss to distinguish the faintly-marked pathway that led in a more direct course to the place of destination. The storm coming up suddenly from the north, and showers of hail accompanying the gusts, caused the poor driver to incline his face to the left, to avoid the peltings that assailed him so frequently; and the drenched horses, similarly influenced, had unconsciously departed far from the right line of march; and now, rather than turn his front again to the pitiless blast, which could be the only means of regaining the road, Joe preferred diverging still farther, until he should find himself on the margin of the river, by which time he hoped the storm would abate. At all events, he thought there would be more safety on the beach, which extended out a hundred paces from the water, among the small switches of cotton-wood that grew thereon, than in the midst of the tall trees of the forest, where a heavy branch was every now and then torn off by the wind, and thrown to the earth with a terrible crash. Occasionally a deafening explosion of thunder would burst overhead; and Joe, prostrating himself on the neck of his horse, would, with his eyes closed and his teeth set, bear it out in silence. He spoke not, save to give an occasional word of command to his team, or a brief reply to a question from his master.

It was an odd spectacle to see such a vehicle trudging along at such an hour, where no carriage had ever passed before. The two young men were odd characters; the horses were oddly matched, one being a little dumpy black pony, and the other a noble white steed; and it was an odd whim which induced Glenn to abandon his comfortable home in Philadelphia, and traverse such inclement wilds. But love can play the "*wild*" with any young man. Yet we will not spoil our narrative by introducing any of it here. Nor could it have been love that induced Joe to share his master's freaks; but rather a rare penchant for the miraculous adventures to be enjoyed in the western wilderness, and the gold which his master often showered upon him with a reckless hand. Joe's forefathers were from the

Isle of Erin, and although he had lost the brogue, ne still retained some of their superstitions.

The wind continued to blow, the wolves howled, the lightning flashed, and the thunder rolled. Ere long the little black pony snorted aloud and paused abruptly.

"What ails you, Pete?" said Joe from his lofty position on the steed, addressing his favourite little pet. "Get along," he continued, striking the animal gently with his whip. But Pete was as immovable and unconscious of the lash as would have been a stone. And the steed seemed likewise to be infected with the pony's stubbornness, after the wagon was brought to a pause.

"Why have you stopped, Joe?" inquired Glen.

"I don't hardly know, sir; but the stupid horses won't budge an inch farther!"

"Very well; we can remain here till morning. Take the harness off, and give them the corn in the box; we can sleep in the wagon till daylight."

"But we have no food for ourselves, sir; and I'm vastly hungry. It can't be much farther to the ferry," continued Joe, vexed at the conduct of the horses.

"Very well; do as you like; drive on, if you desire to do so," said Glenn.

"Get along, you stupid creatures!" cried Joe, applying the lash with some violence. But the horses regarded him no more than blocks would have done. Immediately in front he perceived a dark object that resembled a stump and turning the horses slightly to one side, endeavoured to urge them past it. Still they would not go, but continued to regard the object mentioned with dread, which was manifested by sundry restless pawings and unaccustomed snorts. Joe resolved to ascertain the cause of their alarm, and springing to the ground, moved cautiously in the direction of the dark obstruction, which still seemed to be a blackened stump, about his own height, and a very trifling obstacle, in his opinion, to arrest the progress of his redoubtable team. The darkness was intense, yet he managed to keep his eyes on the dim outlines of the object as he stealthily approached And he stepped as noiselessly as possible, notwithstanding he meditated an encounter with nothing more than an inanimate object. But his imagination was always on the alert, and as he often feared dangers that arose unde finable and indescribable in his mind, it was not without some trepidation that he had separated himself from the horses and groped his way toward the object that had so much terrified his pony. He paused within a few feet of the object, and waited for the next flash of lightning to scrutinize the thing more closely before putting his hand upon it. But no flash came, and he grew tired of standing. He stooped down, so as to bring the upper portion of it in a line with the sky beyond, but still he could not make it out. He ventured still nearer, and stared at it long and steadily, but to no avail: the black mass only was before him, seemingly inanimate, and of a deeper hue than the darkness around.

"I've a notion to try my whip on you," said he, thinking if it should be a human being it would doubtless make a movement. He started back with a momentary conviction that he heard a rush creak under its feet. But as it still maintained its position, he soon concluded the noise to have been only imaginary, and venturing quite close gave it a smart blow with his whip. Instantaneously poor Joe was rolling on the earth, almost insensible, and the dark object disappeared rushing through the bushes into the woods. The noise attracted Glenn, who now approached the scene, and with no little surprise found his servant lying on his face.

"What's the matter, Joe?" demanded he.

"Oh, St. Peter! O preserve me!" exclaimed Joe.

"What has happened? Why do you lie there?"

"Oh, I'm almost killed! Didn't you see him?"

"See what? I can see nothing this dark night but the flying clouds and yonder yellow sheet of water."

"Oh, I've been struck!" said Joe, groaning piteously.

"Struck by what? Has the lightning struck you?"

"No—no! my head is all smashed up—it was a bear."

"Pshaw! get up, and either drive on, or feed the horses," said Glenn with some impatience.

"I call all the saints to witness that it was a wild bear—a great wild bear! I thought it was a stump, but just as I struck it a flash of lightning revealed to my eyes a big black bear standing on his hind feet, grinning at me, and he gave me a blow on the side of the face, which has entirely blinded my left eye, and set my ears to ringing like a thousand bells. Just feel the blood on my face."

A DARK ENCOUNTER.—P. 12.

Glenn actually felt something which might be blood, and really had thought he could distinguish the stump himself when the wagon halted; yet he did not believe that Joe had received the hurt in any other manner than by striking his face against some hard substance which he could not avoid in the darkness.

"You only fancy it was a bear, Joe; so come along back to the horses and drive on. The rain has ceased, and the stars are appearing." Saying this, Glenn led the way to the wagon.

"I'd be willing to swear on the altar that it was a huge bear, and nothing else!" replied Joe, as he mounted and drove on, the horses now evincing no reluctance to proceed. One after another the stars came out and shone in purest brightness as the mists swept away, and ere long the whole canopy of blue was gemmed with twinkling brilliants. The winds soon lulled, and the dense forest on the right reposed from the moaning gale which had disturbed it a short time before; and the waves that had been tossed into foaming ridges now spent their fury on the beach, each lashing the bank more gently than the last, until the power of the gliding current swept them all down the turbid stream. Soon the space between the water and the forest gradually diminished, and seemed to join at a point not far ahead. Joe observed this with some concern, being aware that to meander among the trees at such an hour was impossible. He therefore inclined toward the river, resolved to defer his re-entrance into the forest as long as possible. As he drove on he kept up a continual groaning, with his head hung to one side, as if suffering with the toothache, and occasionally reproaching Pete with some petulance, as if a portion of the blame attached to his sagacious pony.

"Why do you keep up such a howling, Joe? Do you really suffer much pain?" inquired Glenn, annoyed by his man's lamentations.

"It don't hurt as bad as it did—but then to think that I was such a fool as to go right into the beast's clutches, when even Pete had more sense!"

"If it was actually a bear, Joe, you can boast of the thrilling encounter hereafter," said Glenn, in a joking and partly consoling manner.

"But if I have many more such, I fear I shall never get

back to relate them. My face is all swelled—Huzza! yonder is a light, at last! It's on this side of the river, and if we can't get over the ferry to-night, we shall have something to eat on this side, at all events. Ha! ha! ha! I see a living man moving before the fire, as if he were roasting meat." Joe forgot his wound in the joy of an anticipated supper, and whipping the horses into a brisk pace, they soon drew near the encampment, where they discovered numerous persons, male and female, who had been prevented from crossing the river that day, in consequence of the violence of the storm, and had raised their tents at the edge of the woods, preferring to repose thus until the following morning than to venture into the frail ferry-boat while the waves yet ran so high.

There was no habitation in the immediate vicinity, save a rude hovel occupied by Jasper Roughgrove and his ferrymen, which was on the opposite shore in a narrow valley that cleft asunder the otherwise uniform cliff of rocks.

The creaking of the wheels, when the vehicle approached within a few hundred paces of the encampment, attracted the watch-dogs, and their fierce and continued barking drew the attention of the emigrants in the direction indicated. Several men with guns in their hands came out to meet the young travellers.

"We are white men, friends, strangers, lost, benighted, and hungry!" exclaimed Joe, stopping the horses, and addressing the men before he was accosted.

"Come on, then, and eat and rest with us," said they, amused at Joe's exclamations, and leading the way to the encampment.

When they arrived at the edge of the camp, Glenn dismounted from the wagon, and directing Joe to follow when he had taken care of the horses, drew near the huge log fire in company with those who had gone out to meet him. Several tall and spreading elms towered in majesty above, and their clustering leaves, yet partially green, notwithstanding the autumn was midway advanced, were beautifully tinged by the bright light thrown upward from the glaring flames. The view on one side was lost in the dark labyrinth of the moss-grown trunks of the forest. On the other swept the turbid river, bearing downward in its rapid current severed branches, and even whole trees, that had been swept away by the continual falling in of the river bank, for the sandy soil was always subject to the undermining of the impetuous stream. A circle of tents was formed round the fire, constructed of thin poles bent in the shape of an arch, and the ends planted firmly in the earth. These were covered with buffalo skins, which would effectually shield the inmates from the rain; and quantities of leaves, after being carefully dried before the fire, were placed on the ground within, over which were spread buffalo robes with the hair uppermost, and thus in a brief space was completed temporary but not uncomfortable places of repose. The ends of the tents nearest to the fire were open, to admit the heat and a portion of light, that those who desired it might retire during their repast, or engage in pious meditation undisturbed by the more clamorous portion of the company.

Glenn paused when within the circle, and looked with some degree of interest on the admirable arrangement of those independent and hardy people. A majority of the emigrants were seated on logs brought thither for that purpose, and feasting quietly from several large pans and well-filled camp-kettles, which were set out for all in common. They motioned Glenn to partake with them; and although many curious looks were directed toward him, yet he was not annoyed by questions while eating. Joe came in, and following the example of the rest, played his part to perfection, without complaining once of his wound.

The feast was just finished, when the dogs again set up a furious yelping, and ran into the forest. But they returned very quickly, some of them whining with the hurts received from the strangers they encountered so roughly; and presently they were followed by several enormous hounds, and soon after an athletic woodsman was seen approaching. This personage was a tall muscular man, past the middle age, but agile and vigorous in all his motions. He was habited in a buck-skin hunting-shirt, and wore leggins of the same material. Although he was armed with a long knife and heavy rifle, and the expression of his brow and chin indicated an unusual degree of firmness and determination, yet there was an openness and blandness in the expression of his features which won the confidence of the beholder, and instantly dispelled every apprehension of violence. All of the emigrants had either seen or heard of him before, for his name was not only repeated by every tongue in the territory, but was familiar in every State in the Union, and not unknown in many parts of Europe. He was instantly recognised by the emigrants, and crowding round, they gave him a hearty welcome. They led him to a conspicuous seat, and forming a circle about him, were eager to catch every word that might escape his lips, and relied with implicit confidence on every species of information he imparted respecting the dangers and advantages of the locations they were about to visit. Boone had settled some three miles distant from the ferry, among the hills, where his people were engaged in the manufacture of salt. He had selected this place of abode long before the general tide of emigration had reached so far up the Missouri. It was said that he pitched his tent among the barren hills as a security against the intrusion of other men, who, being swayed by a love of wealth, would naturally seek their homes in the rich level prairies. It is true that Boone loved to dwell in solitude. But he was no misanthrope. And now, although questions were asked without number, he answered them with cheerfulness; advised the families what would be necessary to be done when their locations were selected, and even pressingly invited them to remain in his settlement a few days to recover from the fatigue of travel, and promised to accompany them afterward over the river into the rich plains to which they were journeying.

During the brisk conversation that had been kept up for a great length of time, Glenn, unlike the rest of the company, sat at a distance and maintained a strict silence. Occasionally, as some of the extraordinary feats related of the person before him occurred to his memory, he turned his eyes in the direction of the great pioneer, and at each time observed the gaze of the woodsman fixed upon him. Nevertheless his habitual listlessness was not disturbed, and he pursued his peculiar train of reflections. Joe likewise treated the presence of the renowned Indian fighter with apparent unconcern, and being alone in his glory, dived the deeper into the saucepan.

Boone at length advanced to where Glenn was sitting, and after scanning his pale features, and his costly though not exquisitely-fashioned habiliments, thus addressed him:—

"Young man, may I inquire what brings thee to these wilds?"

"I am a freeman," replied Glenn, somewhat haughtily, "and may be influenced by that which brings other men hither."

"Nay, young man, excuse the freedom which all expect to exercise in this comparative wilderness; but I am very sure there is not another emigrant on this side of the Ohio who has been actuated by the same motives that brought thee hither. Others come to fell the forest oak, and till the soil of the prairie, that they may prepare a heritage for their children; but thy soft hands and slender limbs are unequal to the task; nor dost thou seem to have felt the want of this world's goods; and thou bringest no family to provide for. Thou hast committed that which banished thee from society, or found in society that which disgusted thee—speak, which of these?" said Boone, in accents, though not positively commanding, yet they produced a sense of reverence that subdued the rising indignation of Glenn, and looking upon the interrogator as the acknowledged host of the eternal wilds, and himself as a mere guest, who might be required to produce his testimonials of worthiness to associate with nature's most honest of men, he replied with calmness, though with subdued emotion—

"You are right, sir—it was the latter. I had heard that you were happy in the solitude of the mountain-shaded valley, or on the interminable prairies that greet the horizon in the distance, where neither the derision of the proud, the malice of the envious, nor the deceptions of pretended love and friendship, could disturb your peaceful meditations: and from amid the wreck of certain hopes, which I once thought no circumstances could destroy, I rose with a determined though saddened heart, and solemnly vowed to seek such a wilderness, where I could pass a certain number of my days engaging in the pursuits that might be most congenial to my disposition. Already I imagine I experience the happy effects of my resolution. Here the whispers of vituperating foes cannot injure, nor the smiles of those fondly cherished deceive."

"Your hand, young man," said Boone, with an earnestness which convinced Glenn that his tale was not imprudently divulged.

"Ho! what's the matter with *you?*" Boone continued, turning to Joe, who had just arisen from his supper, and was stretching back his shoulders.

"I got a licking from a bear to-night—but I don't mind it much since I've had a snack. But if ever I come across him in the daytime, I'll show him a thing or two," said Joe, with his fists doubled up.

"Pshaw! do you still entertain the ridiculous belief that it was really a bear you encountered?" inquired Glenn, with an incredulous smile.

"I'll swear to it!" replied Joe.

"Let me see your face," remarked Boone, turning him to where there was more light.

"Hollo! don't squeeze it so hard!" cried Joe, as Boone removed some of the coagulated blood that remained or the surface.

"There is no doubt about it—it was a bear, most cer tainly," said Boone; and examining the wound more closely, continued: "Here are the marks of his claws, plain enough: he might easily be captured to-morrow. Who will hunt him with me?"

"I will!" burst from the lips of nearly every one present.

"Huzza—revenge! I'll have revenge, huzza!" cried Joe, throwing round his hat."

"You will join us?" inquired Boone, turning to Glenn.

"Yes," replied Glenn; "I came hither provided with the implements to hunt; and as such is to be principally my occupation during my sojourn in this region, I could not desire a more happy opportunity than the present to make a beginning. And as it is my intention to settle near the ferry on the opposite shore, I am pleased to find that I shall not be far from one whose acquaintance I hoped to make, above all others."

"And you may not find me reluctant to cultivate a social intercourse, notwithstanding men think me a crabbed old misanthrope," replied Boone, pressing the extended hand of Glenn. They then separated for the night, retiring to the tents that had been provided for them.

It was not long before a comparative silence pervaded the scene. The fierce yelpings of the watch-dogs gradually ceased, and the howling wolf was but indistinctly heard in the distance. The katydid and whippoorwill still sang at intervals, and these sounds, as well as the occasional whirlpool that could be heard rising on the surface of the gliding stream, had a soothing influence, and lulled to slumber the wandering mortals who now reclined under the forest trees, far from the homes of their childhood and the graves of their kindred. Glenn gazed from his couch through the branches above at the calm, blue sky, resplendent with twinkling stars; and if a sad reflection, that he thus lay, a lonely being, a thousand miles from those who had been most dear to him, dimmed his eye for an instant with a tear, he still felt a consciousness of innocence within, and resolving to execute his vow in every particular, he too was soon steeped in undisturbed slumber.

CHAPTER II.

Boone hunts the bear—Hounds and terriers—Sneak Punk, the Hatchet-face—Another stump—The high passes—The bear roused—The chase—A sight—A shot—A wound—Joe—His meditations—His friend, the bear—The bear retreats—Joe takes courage—He fires—Immense execution—Sneak—The last struggle—Desperation of the bear—His death—Sneak's puppies—Joe.

By the time the first streaks of gray twilight marked the eastern horizon, Boone, at the head of the party of hunters, set out from the encampment and proceeded down the river in the direction of the place where Joe had been so roughly handled by Bruin. All, with the exception of Glenn and his man, being accustomed to much walking, were on foot. Glenn rode his white steed, and Joe was mounted on his little black pony. The large hounds belonging to Boone, and the curs, spaniels, and terriers of the emigrants were all taken along. As they proceeded down the river, Boone proposed the plan of operations which was to guide their conduct in the chase, and each man was eager to perform his part, whatever it might be. It was arranged that a portion of the company should precede the rest, and cross the level woodland about two miles in width, to a range of hills and perpendicular cliffs that appeared to have once bounded the river, and select such ravines or outlets as in their opinion the bear would be most likely to pass through, if he were indeed still in the flat bottom-land. At these places they were to station themselves with their guns well charged, and either await the coming of the animal or the drivers; the first would be announced by the yelping of the dogs, and the last by the hunters' horns.

Glenn and one or two others remained with Boone to hunt Bruin in his lair, while Joe and the remainder of the company were despatched to the passes among the hills. There was a narrow-featured Vermonter in this party, termed, by his comrades, the Hatchet-face, and, in truth, the extreme thinness of his chest and the slenderness of his limbs might as aptly have been called the hatchet-handle. But, so far from being unfit for the hardy pursuits of a hunter, he was gifted with the activity of a greyhound, and the swiftness and bottom of a race-horse. His name was Sneak Punk, which was always abbreviated to merely Sneak, for his general success in creeping up to the unsuspecting game of whatsoever kind he might be hunting, while others could not meet with such success. He had been striding along some time in silence a short distance in advance of Joe, who, even by dint of sundry kicks and the free use of his whip, could hardly keep pace with him. The rest were a few yards in the rear, and all had maintained a strict silence, implicitly relying on the guidance of Sneak, who, though he had never traversed these woods before, was made perfectly familiar with the course he was to pursue by the instructions of Boone.

Although the light of morning was now apparent above, yet the thick growth of the trees, whose clustering branches mingled in one dense mass overhead, made it still dark and sombre below; and Joe, to divert Sneak from his unconscionable gait, which, in his endeavours to keep up, often subjected him to the rude blows of elastic switches, and many twinges of overhanging grape vines, essayed to engage his companion in conversation.

"I say, Mr. Sneak," observed Joe, with an eager voice, as his pony trotted along rather roughly through the wild gooseberry bushes, and often stumbled over the decayed logs that lay about.

"What do you want, stranger?" replied Sneak, slackening his gait until he fell back alongside of Joe.

"I only wanted to know if you ever killed a bear before," said Joe, drawing an easy breath as Pete fell into a comfortable walk.

"Dod rot it, I hain't killed this one yit," said Sneak.

"I didn't mean any offence," said Joe.

"What makes you think you have given any?"

"Because you said *dod rot it.*"

"I nearly always say so—I've said so so often that I can't help it. But now, as we are on the right footing, I can tell you that I wintered once in Arkansaw, and that's enough to let you know I'm no greenhorn, no how you can fix it. And moreover, I tell you, if old Boone wasn't here hisself, I'd kill this bar as sure as a gun, and my gun is as sure as a streak of lightning run into a barrel of gunpowder;" and as he spoke he threw up his heavy gun and saluted the iron with his lips.

"Is your's a rifle?" inquired Joe, to prolong the conversation, his companion showing symptoms of a disposition to fall into his habit of going ahead again.

"Sartainly! Does anybody, I wonder, expect to do any thing with a shot-gun in sich a place as this?"

"Mine's a shot-gun," said Joe.

"Dod—did you ever kill any thing better than a quail with it?" inquired Sneak, contemptuously.

"I never killed any thing in my life with it—I never shot a gun in all my life before to-night," said Joe.

"Dod, you haven't fired it to-night, to my sartain knowledge."

"I mean I never went a shooting."

"Did you load her yourself?" inquired Sneak, taking hold of the musket and feeling the calibre.

"Yes—but I'm sure I did it right. I put in a handful of powder, and paper on top of it, and then poured in a handful of balls," said Joe.

"Ha! ha! ha! I'll be busted if you don't raise a fuss if you ever get a shot at the bar!" said Sneak, with emphasis.

"That's what I am after."

"Why don't you go ahead?" demanded Sneak, as Joe's pony stopped suddenly, with his ears thrust forward. "Dod! whip him up," continued he, seeing that his companion was intently gazing at some object ahead, and exhibiting as many marks of alarm as Pete. "It's nothing but a stump!" said Sneak, going forwards and kicking the object, which was truly nothing more than he took it to be. Joe then related to him all the particulars of his noctural affair with the supposed stump, previous to his arrival at the camp, and Sneak, with a hearty laugh, admitted that both he and the pony were excusable for inspecting all the stumps they might chance to come across in the dark in future. They now emerged into the open space which was the boundary of the woods, and after clambering up a steep ascent for some minutes, they reached the summit of a tall range of bluffs. From this position the sun could be seen rising over the eastern ridges, but the flat woods that had been traversed still lay in darkness below, and silent as the tomb, save the hooting of owls as they flapped to their hollow habitations in the trees.

The party then dispersed to their coverts under the direction of Sneak, who with a practised eye instantly perceived all the advantageous posts for the men, and the places where the bear would most probably run. Joe had insisted on having his revenge, and begged to be stationed where he would be most likely to get a shot. He was therefore permitted to remain at the head of the ravine they had just ascended, through which a deer path ran, as the most favourable position. After tying Pete some paces in the rear, he came forwards to the verge of the valley and seated himself on a dry rock, where he could see some distance down the path under the tall sumach bushes. He then commenced cogitating how he would act, should Bruin have the hardihood to face him in the daytime.

Boone and his party drew near the spot where the bear had been seen the previous night. The two large hounds, Ringwood and Jowler, kept at their master's heels, being trained to understand and perform all the duties required of them, while the curs and terriers were running helter-skelter far ahead, or striking out into the woods without aim, and always returning without effecting any thing At length the two hounds paused, and scented the earth, giving certain information that they had arrived at the desired point. The curs and terriers had already passed far beyond the spot, being unable to decide any thing by the nose, and always relying on their swiftness in the chase when they should be in sight of the object pursued.

Now, Glenn perceived to what perfection dogs could be trained, and learned, what had been a matter of wonder to him, how Boone could keep up with them in the chase. The hounds set off at a signal from their master, not like an arrow from the bow, but at a moderate pace, ever and anon looking back and pausing until the men came up; while the erratic curs flew hither and thither, chasing every hare and squirrel they could find. As they pursued the trail they occasionally saw the foot-print of the animal, which was broad and deep, indicating one of enormous size. Presently they came to a spot thickly overgrown with spice-wood bushes and prickly vines, where he had made his lair, and from the erect tails of Ringwood and Jowler, and the intense interest they otherwise evinced, it was evident they were fast approaching the presence of Bruin. Ere long, as they ran along with their heads up, for the first time that morning, they commenced yelping in clear and distinct tones, which rang musically far and wide through the woods. The curs relinquished their unprofitable racing round the thickets, attracted by the hounds, and soon learned to keep in the rear, depending on the unerring trailing of the old hunters, as the object of pursuit was not yet in sight. The chase became more animated, and the men quickened their pace as the inspiring notes of the hounds rang out at regular intervals. Glenn soon found he possessed no advantage over those on foot, who were able to run under the branches of the trees, and glide through the thickets with but little difficulty, while the rush of his noble steed was often arrested by the tenacious vines clinging to the bushes abreast, and he was sometimes under the necessity of dismounting to recover his cap or whip.

It was not long before the notes of Ringwood and Jowler suddenly increased in sharpness and quickness, and the curs and terriers, hitherto silent, set up a confused medley of sounds, which reverberated like one continuous scream. They had pounced upon the bear, and from the stationary position of the dogs for a few minutes, indicated by their peculiar baying, it was evident Bruin had turned to survey the enemy, and perhaps to give them battle; but it seemed that their number or noise soon intimidated him, and that he preferred seeking safety in flight. How Boone could possibly know beforehand which way the bear would run, was a mystery to Glenn; but that he often abandoned the direction taken by the dogs, turning off at almost right angles, and still had a sight of him was no less true. No one had yet been near enough to fire with effect. The bear, notwithstanding his many feints and novel demonstrations to get rid of his persecutors, had continued to make towards the hills where the standers were stationed. Boone falling in with Glenn, from whom he had been frequently separated, they continued together some time, following the course of the sounds towards the east.

"This sport is really exciting and noble!" exclaimed Glenn, as the deep and melodious intonations of Ringwood and Jowler fell upon his ear.

"Excellent! excellent!" replied Boone, listening intently, and pausing suddenly, as the discharge of a gun in the direction of the hills sounded through the woods.

"He has reached the standers," remarked Glenn, reining up his steed at Boone's side.

"No; it was one of our men who has not followed him in all his deviations," replied Boone, still marking the notes of the hounds.

"I doubt not our company is sufficiently scattered in every direction through the forest to force him into the hills very speedily, if, indeed, that shot was not fatal," remarked Glenn.

"He is not hurt—perhaps it was not fired at him, but at a bird—nor will he yet leave the woods," said Boone, still listening to the hounds. "He comes!" he exclaimed a moment after, with marks of joy in his face; "he will make a grand circle before quitting the lowland." And now the dogs could be heard more distinctly, as if they were gradually approaching the place from which they first started.

"If you will remain here," continued Boone, "it is quite likely you will have a shot as he makes his final push for the hills."

"Then here will I remain," replied Glenn; and fixing

himself firmly in the saddle, resolved to await the coming of Bruin, having every confidence in the intimation of his friend. Boone selected a position a few hundred paces distant, with a view of permitting Glenn to have the first fire.

The bear took a wide circuit towards the river, pausing at times until the foremost of the dogs came up, which he could easily manage to keep at bay; but when all of them (and the curs did good service now) surrounded him, he found it necessary to set forward again. When he had run as far as the river, and turned once more towards the hills, his course seemed to be in a direct line with Glenn, and the young man's heart fluttered with anticipation as he examined his gun, and turned his horse (which had been accustomed to firearms) in a favourable position to give the enemy a salute as he passed. Nearer they came, the dogs pursuing with redoubled fierceness, their blood heated by the exercise, and their most sanguine passions roused by their frequent severe skirmishes with their huge antagonist. As they approached, the strange and simultaneous yelpings of the curs and terriers resembled an embodied roar, amid which the flute-like notes of Ringwood and Jowler could hardly be heard. Glenn could now distinctly hear the bear rushing like a torrent through the bushes, almost directly towards the place where he was posted, and a moment after it emerged from a dense thicket of hazel, and the noble steed, instead of leaping away with affright, threw back his ears and stood firm, until Glenn fired. Bruin uttered a howl, and halting with a fierce growl, raised himself on his haunches, and displaying his array of white teeth, prepared to assail our hero. Glenn proceeded to reload his rifle with as much expedition as was in his power, though not without some tremor, notwithstanding he was mounted on his tall steed, whose nostrils dilated, and eyes flashing fire, indicated that he was willing to take part in the conflict. The bear was preparing for a dreadful encounter, and on the very eve of springing towards his assailant, when the hounds coming up admonished him to flee his more numerous foes, and turning off, he continued his route towards the hills. Glenn perceived that he had not missed his aim by the blood sprinkled on the bushes, and being ready for another fire, galloped after him. Just when he came in sight, Boone's gun was heard, and Bruin fell, remaining motionless for a moment; but ere Glenn arrived within shooting distance, or Boone could reload, he had risen and again continued his course, as if in defiance of everything that man could do to oppose him.

"Is it possible he still survives!" exclaimed Glenn, joining his companion.

"There is nothing more possible," replied Boone; "but I saw by his limping that your shot had taken effect."

"And I saw him fall when you fired," said Glenn; "but he still runs."

"And he *will* run for some time yet," remarked Boone, "for they are extremely hard to kill, when heated by the pursuit of dogs. But we have done our part, and it now remains for those at the passes to finish the work so well begun."

Joe's imagination had several times worked him into a fury, which had as often subsided in disappointment, during the chase below, every particle of which could be distinctly heard from his position. More than once, when a brisk breeze swept up the valley, he was convinced that his enemy was approaching him, and, every nerve quivering with the expectation of the bear coming in view the next instant, he stood a spectacle of eagerness, with perhaps a small portion of apprehension intermingled. At length, from the frequent deceptions the distance practiced upon him, he grew composed by degrees, and resuming his seat on the stone, with his musket lying across his knees, thus gave vent to his thoughts: "What if an Indian were to pounce upon me while I'm sitting here?" Here he paused, and looked carefully round in every direction. "No!" he continued; "if there were any at this time in the neighbourhood, wouldn't Boone know it? To be sure he would, and here's my gun—I forgot that. Let them come as soon as they please! I wonder if the bear *will* come out here? Suppose he does, what's the danger? Didn't I grapple with him last night? And couldn't I jump on Pete and get away from him! But—pshaw! I keep forgetting my gun—I wish he *would* come, I'd serve him worse than he served me last night! My face feels very sore this morning. There!" he exclaimed, when he heard the fire of Glenn's gun, and the report that succeeded from

Boone's, "they've floored him as dead as a nail, I'll bet. Hang it! I should like to have had a word or two with him myself, to have told him I hadn't forgotten his ugly grin. The men must have known I would stand no chance of killing him when they placed me up here. I should like to know what part of the sport *I've* had—ough!" exclaimed he, his hair standing upright, as he beheld the huge bear, panting and bleeding, coming towards him, and not twenty paces distant!

Bruin had eluded the dogs a few minutes by climbing a bending tree at the mouth of the valley, from which he passed to another, and descending again to the earth, proceeded almost exhausted up the ravine. Joe's eyes grew larger and larger as the monster approached, and when within a few feet of him he uttered a horrible unearthly sound, which attracted the bear, and fearing the fatal aim of man more than the teeth of the dogs, he whirled about, with a determination to fight his way back, in preference to again risking the murderous lead. No sooner was the bear out of sight, and plunging down the dell amid the cries of the dogs, which assailed him on all sides, than Joe bethought him of his gun, and becoming valorous, ran a few steps down the path and fired in the direction of the confused melée. The moment after he discharged his musket, the back part of his head struck the earth, and the gun made two or three end-over-end revolutions up the path behind him. Never, perhaps, was such a rebound from overloading known before. Joe now thought not of the bear, nor looked to see what execution he had done. He thought of his own person, which he found prostrate on the ground. When somewhat recovered from the blow, he rose with his hand pressed to his nose, while the blood ran out between his fingers. "Oh! my goodness!" he exclaimed, seating himself at the root of a pecan tree, and rocking backwards and forwards.

"What's your gun doing up here?" exclaimed Sneak, coming down the path. Joe made no answer, but continued to rock backwards and forwards most dolefully.

"Why don't you speak? Where's the bar?"

"I don't know. Oh!" murmured Joe.

"What's the matter?" inquired Sneak, seeing the copious effusion of blood.

"I shot off that outrageous musket, and it's kicked my nose to pieces! I shall faint!" said Joe, dropping his head between his knees.

"Faint? I never saw a *man* faint!" said Sneak, listening to the chase below.

"Oh! can't you help me to stop this blood?"

"Don't you hear *that*, down there?" replied Sneak, his attention entirely directed to that which was going on in the valley.

"My ears are deafened by that savage gun! I can't hear a bit, hardly! Oh, what shall I do, Mr. Sneak?" continued Joe.

"Dod rot it!" exclaimed Sneak, leaping like a wild buck down the path, and paying no further attention to the piteous lamentations of his comrade.

Ere the bear reached the mouth of the glen, the hunters generally had come up, and poor Bruin found himself hemmed in on all sides. He could not ascend on either hand, the loss of blood having weakened him too much to climb over the almost precipitous rocks, and he made a final stand, determined to sell his life as dearly as possible. The dogs sprang upon him in a body, and it was soon evident that his desperate struggles were not harmless. He grasped one of the curs in his deadly hug, and with his teeth planted in its neck, relinquished not his hold until it fell from his arms a disfigured and lifeless object. He boxed those that were tearing his hams with his ponderous claws, sending them screaming to the right and left. He then stood up on his haunches, with his back against a rock, and with a snarl of defiance resolved never to retreat "from its firm base." Never were blows more rapidly dealt. When attacked on one side, he had no sooner turned to beat down his sanguine foe than he was assailed on the other. Thus he fought alternately from right to left, his mouth gaping open, his tongue hanging out, and his eyes gleaming furiously as if swimming in liquid fire. At times he was charged simultaneously in front and flank, when for an instant the whole group seemed to be one dark writhing mass, uttering a medly of discordant and horrid sounds. But determined to conquer or die on the spot he occupied, Bruin never relaxed his blows, until the bruised and exhausted dogs were forced to withdraw a moment from the combat, and rush into the narrow rivulet. While they lay panting in the water, the bear turned his head back against the rocks, and lapped in the dripping moisture without moving from his position. But he was fast sinking under his wounds: a stream of blood, which constantly issued from his body, and ran down and discoloured the water, indicated that his career was nearly finished. Yet his spirit was not daunted; for while the canine assailants he had withstood so often were bathing preparatory for a renewal of the conflict, Boone and Glenn, who had approached the immediate vicinity, fired, and Bruin, echoing the howl of death as the bullets entered his body, turned his eyes reproachfully towards the men for an instant, and then, with a growl of convulsed, expiring rage, plunged into the water, and, seizing the largest cur, crushed him to death. Ringwood and Jowler, whose sagacity had hitherto led them to keep in some measure aloof, knowing their efforts would be unavailing against so powerful an enemy without the fatal aim of their master, now sprang forward to the rescue, both seizing the prostrate foe by the throat. But he could not be made to relinquish his victim, nor did he make resistance. Boone, advancing at the head of the hunters, (all of whom, with the exception of Joe and Sneak, being there assembled,) with some difficulty prevented his companions from discharging their guns at the dark mass before them. He struck up several of their guns as they were endeavouring to aim at the now motionless bear, fearing that his hounds might suffer by their fire, and stooping down, whence he could distinctly see the pale gums and tongue, as his hounds grappled the neck of the animal, announced the death of Bruin, and the termination of the hunt. The hounds soon abandoned their inanimate victim, and its sinewy limbs relaxing, the devoted cur rolled out a lifeless body.

"How like you this specimen of our wild sports?" inquired Boone, turning to Glenn, as the rest proceeded to skin and dress the bear preparatory for its conveyance to the camp.

"It is exciting, if not terrific and cruel," replied Glenn, musing.

"None could be more eager than yourself in the chase,' said Boone.

"True," replied Glenn; "and notwithstanding the uninitiated may for an instant revolt at the spilling of blood, yet the chase has ever been considered the noblest and the most innocent of sports. The animals hunted are often an evil while running at large, being destructive or dangerous; but even if they were harmless in their nature, they are still necessary or desirable for the support or comfort of man. Blood of a similar value is spilt everywhere without the least compunction. The knife daily pierces the neck of the swine, and the kitchen wench wrings off the head of the fowl while she hums a ditty. This is far better than hunting down our own species on the battle-field, or ruining and being ruined at the gaming-table. I think I shall be content in this region."

"And you will no doubt be an expert hunter, if I have any judgment in such matters," replied Boone.

"I wonder that Joe has not yet made his appearance," remarked Glenn, approaching the bear; "I expected ere this to have seen him triumphing over his fallen enemy."

"What kind of a gun had he?" inquired Boone.

"A large musket," said Glenn, recollecting the enormous explosion that seemed to jar the whole woods like an earthquake; "it must have been Joe who fired—he had certainly overcharged the gun, and I fear it has burst in his hands, which may account for his absence."

"Be not uneasy," replied Boone; "for I can assure you from the peculiar sound it made that it did nothing more than rebound violently; besides, those guns very rarely burst. But here comes Sneak, (I think they call him so,) no doubt having some tidings of your man. It seems he has not been idle. He has a brace of racoons in his hands."

The tall slim form of Sneak was seen coming down the path. Ever and anon he cast his eyes from one hand to the other, regarding with no ordinary interest the dead animals he bore.

"I did not hear him fire," remarked Glenn.

"He may have killed them with stones," said Boone; and as Sneak drew near, he continued, with a smile, "they are nothing more than a brace of his terriers, that doubtless Bruin dispatched, and which may well be spared, notwithstanding Sneak's seeming sorrow."

Sneak approached the place where Boone and Glenn

were standing, with the gravest face that man ever wore. His eyes seemed to be set in his head, for not once did they wink, nor did his lips move for some length of time after he threw down the dogs at the feet of Glenn, although several men addressed him. He stood with his arms folded, and gazed mournfully at his dead dogs.

"The little fellows fought bravely, and covered themselves with glory," said Glenn, much amused at the solemn demeanour of Sneak.

"If there ain't more blood spilt on the strength of it, I wish I may be smashed!" said Sneak, compressing his lips.

"What mean you? what's the matter?" inquired Boone, who best understood what the man was meditating.

"I've got as good a gun as anybody here! And I'll have revenge, or pay!" replied Sneak, turning his eyes on Glenn.

"If your remarks are intended for me," said Glenn, "rely upon it you shall have justice."

"Tell us all about it," said Boone.

"When I heard that fool up the valley shoot off his forty-four pounder, I ran to see what he had done, and when I came near to where he was, his gun was lying up the hill behind him, and he setting down whining like a baby, and a great gore of blood hanging to his nose. I wish it had blowed his head off! I got tired of staying with the tarnation fool, who couldn't tell me a thing, when I heard you shooting, and the horn blowing for the men; and knowing the bar was dead, I started off full tilt. I hadn't gone fifty steps before I began to see where his bullets had spattered the trees and bushes in every direction. Presently I stumbled over these dogs, my own puppies—and there they lay as dead as door nails. I whistled, and they didn't move; I then stooped down to see how the bear had killed 'em, and I found these bullet holes in 'em!" said Sneak, turning their limber bodies over with his foot, until their wounds were uppermost. "I'll be shot if I don't have pay, or revenge!" he continued, with tears in his eyes.

"What were they worth?" demanded Glenn, laughing.

"I was offered two dollars a-piece for 'em as we came through Indiana," replied Sneak.

"Here's the money," said Glenn, handing him the amount. After receiving the cash, Sneak turned away perfectly satisfied, and seemed not to bestow another thought upon his puppies.

This affair had hardly been settled before Joe made his appearance on Pete. He rode slowly along down the path, as dolefully as ever man approached the graveyard. As he drew near, all eyes were fixed upon him. Never were any one's features so much disfigured. His nose was as large as a hen's egg, and as purple as a plum. Still it was not much disproportioned to the rest of his swollen face; and the whole resembled the unearthly phiz of the most bloated gnome that watched over the slumbers of Rip Van Winkle.

CHAPTER III.

Glenn's castle—Mary—Books—A hunt—Joe and Pete—A tumble—An opossum—A shot—Another tumble—A doe—The return—They set out again—A mound—A buffalo—An encounter—Night—Terrific spectacle—Escape—Boone—Sneak—Indians.

Some weeks had passed since the bear hunt. The emigrants had crossed the river, and selected their future homes in the groves that bordered the prairie, some miles distant from the ferry. Glenn, when landed on the south side of the Missouri, took up his abode for a short time with Jasper Roughgrove, the ferryman, while some half dozen men, whose services his gold secured, were building him a novel habitation. And the location was as singular as the construction of his house. It was on a peak that jutted over the river, some three hundred feet high, whence he had a view eight or ten miles down the stream, and across the opposite bottom-land to the hills mentioned in the preceding chapter. The view was obstructed above by a sudden bend of the stream; but on the south, the level prairie ran out as far as the eye could reach, interrupted only by the few young groves that were interspersed at intervals. His house, constructed of heavy stones, was about fifteen feet square, and not more than ten in height. The floor was formed of hewn timbers, the walls covered with a rough coat of lime, and the roof made of heavy boards. However uncouth this abode appeared to the eye of Glenn, yet he had followed the instructions of Boone, (to whom he had fully disclosed his plan, and repeated his odd resolution,) and reared a tenement not only capable of resisting the wintry winds that were to howl around it, but sufficiently firm to withstand the attacks of any foe, whether the wild beast of the forest or the prowling Indian. The door was very narrow and low, being made of a solid rock full six inches in thickness, which required the strength of a man to turn on its hinges, even when the ponderous bolt on the inside was unfastened. There was a small square window on each side containing a single pane of glass, and made to be secured at a moment's warning, by means of thick stone shutters on the inside. The fire-place was ample at the hearth, but the flue through which the smoke escaped was small, and ran in a serpentine direction up through the northern wall; while the ceiling was overlaid with smooth flat stones, fastened down with huge iron spikes, and supported by strong wooden joists. The furniture consisted of a few trunks, (which answered for seats,) two camp beds, four barrels of hard biscuit, a few dishes and cooking utensils, and a quantity of hunting implements. Many times did Joe shake his head in wonderment as this house was preparing for his reception. It seemed to him too much danger was apprehended from without, and it too much resembled a solitary and secure prison, should one be confined within. Nevertheless, he was permitted to adopt his own plan in the construction of a shelter for the horses. And the retention of these animals was some relief to his otherwise gloomy forebodings, when he beheld the erection of his master's suspicious tenement. He superintended the building of a substantial and comfortable stable. He had stalls, a small granary, and a regular rack made for the accommodation of the horses, and procured, with difficulty and no little expense, a supply of provender. The space, including the buildings, which had been cleared of the roots and stones, for the purpose of cultivating a garden, was about one hundred feet in diameter, and enclosed by a circular row of posts driven firmly in the ground, and rising some ten feet above the surface. These were planted so closely together that even a squirrel would have found it difficult to enter without climbing over them. Indeed, Joe had an especial eye to this department, having heard some awful tales of the snakes that somewhat abounded in those regions in the warm seasons.

One corner of the stable, wherein a quantity of straw was placed, was appropriated for the comfort of the dogs, Ringwood and Jowler, which had been presented to Glenn by his obliging friend, after they had exhibited their skill in the bear hunt.

When every thing was completed, preparatory for his removal thither, Glenn dismissed his faithful artisans, bestowing upon them a liberal reward for their labour, and took possession of his castle. But, notwithstanding the strange manner in which he proposed to spend his days, and his habitual grave demeanour and taciturnity, yet his kind tone, when he uttered a request, or ventured a remark, on the transactions passing around him, and his contempt for money, which he squandered with a prodigal hand, had secured for him the good-will of the ferrymen, and the friendship of the surrounding emigrants. But there was one whose esteem had no venal mixture in it. This was Mary, the old ferryman's daughter, a fair-cheeked girl of nineteen, who never neglected an opportunity of performing a kind office for her father's temporary guest; and when he and his man departed for their own tenement, not venturing directly to bestow them on our hero, she presented Joe with divers articles for their amusement and comfort in their secluded abode, among which were sundry live fowls, a pet fawn, and a kitten.

The first few days, after being installed in his solitary home, our hero passed with his books. But he did not realize all the satisfaction he anticipated from his favourite authors in his secluded cell. The scene around him contrasted but ill with the creations of Shakspeare; and if some of the heroes of Scott were identified with the wildest features of nature, he found it impossible to look around him and enjoy the magic of the page at the same time.

Joe employed himself in attending to his horses, feeding the fowls and dogs, and playing with the fawn and kitten.

He alsc practiced loading and shooting his musket, and endeavoured to learn the mode of doing execution on other objects without committing violence on himself.

"Joe," said Glenn, one bright frosty morning, "saddle the horses; we will make an excursion in the prairie, and see what success we can have without the presence and assistance of an experienced hunter. I designed awaiting the visit of Boone, which he promised should take place about this time; but we will venture out without him; if we kill nothing, at least we shall have the satisfaction of doing no harm."

Joe set off towards the stable, smiling at Glenn's joke, and heartily delighted to exchange the monotony of his domestic employment, which was becoming irksome, for the sports of the field, particularly as he was now entirely recovered from the effects of his late disasters, and began to grow weary of wasting his ammunition in firing at a target, when there was an abundance of game in the vicinity.

"Whoop! Ringwood—Jowler!" cried he, leading the horses briskly forth. The dogs came prancing and yelping round him, as well pleased as himself at the prospect of a day's sport; and when Glenn came out they exhibited palpable signs of recognition and eagerness to accompany their new master on his first deer-hunt. Glenn stroked their heads, which were constantly rubbed against his hands, and his caresses were gratefully received by the faithful hounds. He had been instructed by Boone how to manage them, so as either to keep them at his side when he wished to approach the game stealthily, or to send them forth when rapid pursuit was required, and he was now anxious to test their sagacity.

When mounted, the young men set forward in a southern direction, the valley in which the ferryman's cabin was situated on one hand, and one about the same distance above on the other. But the space between them gradually widened as they progressed, and in a few minutes both disappeared entirely, terminating in scarcely perceptible rivulets running slowly down from the high and level prairie. Here Glenn paused to determine what course he should take. The sun shone brightly on the interminable expanse before him, and not a breeze ruffled the long dry grass around, nor disturbed the few sear leaves that yet clung to the diminutive clusters of bushes scattered at long intervals over the prairie. It was a delightful scene. From the high position of our hero, he could distinguish objects miles distant on the plain; and if the landscape was not enlivened by houses and domestic herds, he could at all events here and there behold parties of deer browsing peacefully in the distance. Ringwood and Jowler also saw or scented them, as their attention was pointed in that direction; but so far from marring the sport by prematurely running forward, they knew too well their duty to leave their master, even were the game within a few paces of them, without the word of command.

"I see a deer!" cried Joe, at length, having till then been employed gathering some fine wild grapes from a neighbouring vine.

"I see several," replied Glenn; "but how we are to get within gun shot of them, is the question."

"I see them, too," said Joe, his eyes glistening.

"I have thought of a plan, Joe; whether right or wrong, is not very material, as respects the exercise we are seeking; but I am inclined to believe it is the proper one. It will at all events give you a fair opportunity of killing a deer, as you will have to fire as they run, and the great number of bullets in your musket will make you more certain to do execution than if you fired a rifle. You will proceed to yon thicket, about a thousand yards distant, keeping the bushes all the time between you and the deer. When you arrive at it dismount, and after tying your pony in the bushes where he will be well hid, select a position whence you can see the deer when they run; I think they will go within reach of your fire. I will make a detour beyond them, and approach from the opposite side."

"I'd rather not tie my pony," said Joe.

"Why? he would not leave you, even were he to get loose," replied Glenn.

"I don't think he would—but I'd rather not leave him yet awhile, till I get a little better used to hunting," said Joe, probably thinking there might be some danger to himself on foot in a country where bears, wolves, and panthers were sometimes seen.

"Can you fire while sitting on your pony?" inquired Glenn

Glenn heard a tremendous thumping behind.—P. 37

"I suppose so," said Joe; "though I never thought to try it yet."

"Suppose you try it now, while I watch the deer, and see if what I have been told is true, that the mere report of a gun will not alarm them."

"Well, I will," said Joe. "I think Pete knows as well as the steed, that shooting on him won't hurt him."

"Fire away, then," said Glenn, looking steadfastly at the deer. Joe fired, and none of the deer ran off. Some continued their playful sports, while others browsed along without lifting their heads; in all likelihood the report did not reach them. But Glenn heard a tremendous thumping behind, and on turning round, beheld his man quietly lying on the ground, and the pony standing about ten paces distant, with his head turned towards Joe, his ears thrust forwards, his nostrils distended and snorting, and his little blue eyes ready to burst out of his head.

"How is this, Joe?" inquired Glenn, scarce able to repress a smile at the ridiculous posture of his man.

"I hardly know myself," replied Joe, casting a silly glance at his treacherous pony; and after examining his limbs and finding no injury had been sustained, continued, "I fired as you directed, and when the smoke cleared away, I found myself lying just as you see me here. I don't know how Pete contrived to get from under me, but there he stands, and here I lie."

"Load your gun, and try it again," said Glenn.

"I'd rather not," said Joe.

"Then I will," replied Glenn, whose horsemanship enabled him to retain the saddle in spite of the struggles of Pete, who, after several discharges, submitted and bore it quietly.

Joe then mounted and set out for the designated thicket, while Glenn galloped off in another direction, followed by the hounds.

When Joe arrived at the hazel thicket, he continued in the saddle, and otherwise he would not have been able to see over the prairie for the tall grass which had grown very luxuriantly in that vicinity. There was a path, however, running round the edge of the bushes, which had been made by the deer and other wild animals, and in this he cautiously groped his way, looking out in every direction for the deer. When he had progressed about halfway found, he espied them feeding composedly, about three hundred paces distant, on a slight eminence. There were at least fifteen of them, and some very large ones. Fearful of giving the alarm before Glenn should fire, he shielded himself from view behind a cluster of persimmon bushes, and tasted the ripe and not unpalatable fruit. And here he was destined to win his first trophy as a hunter. While bending down some branches over head, without looking up, an opossum fell upon his hat, knocking it over his eyes, and springing on the neck of Pete, thence leaped to the ground. But before it disappeared Joe had dismounted, and giving it a blow with the butt of his musket it rolled over on its side, with its eyes closed and tongue hanging out, indicating that the stroke had been fatal.

"So much for you!" said Joe, casting a proud look at his victim; and then leaping on his pony, he gazed again at the deer. They seemed to be still entirely unconscious of danger, and several were now lying in the grass with their heads up, and chewing the cud like domestic animals. Joe drew back once more to await the action of Glenn, and turning to look at the opossum, found to his surprise that it had vanished!

"Well, I'm the biggest fool that ever breathed!" said he, recollecting the craftiness imputed to those animals, and searching in vain for his game. "If ever I come across another, he'll not come the 'possum over me, I'll answer for it!" he continued, somewhat vexed. At this juncture Glenn's gun was heard, and Joe observed a majority of the deer leaping affrighted in the direction of his position. The foremost passed within twenty yards of him, and, his limbs trembling with excitement, he drew his gun up to his shoulder and pulled the trigger. It snapped, perhaps fortunately, for his eyes were convulsively closed at the moment; and recovering measurably by the time the next came up, this trial the gun went off, and he found himself once more prostrate on the ground.

"What in the world is the reason you won't stand still!" he exclaimed, rising and seizing the pony by the bit. The only answer Pete made was a snort of unequivocal dissatisfaction. "Plague take your little *hide* of you!" I should have killed that fellow to a certainty, if you hadn't played the fool!" continued he, still addressing his pony while he proceeded to load his gun. When ready for another fire, he mounted again, in quite an ill humour, convinced that all chance of killing a deer was effectually over for the present, when, to his utter astonishment, he beheld the deer he had fired at lying dead before him, and but a few paces distant. With feelings of unmixed delight he galloped to where it lay, and springing to the earth, one moment he whirled round his hat in exultation, and the next caressed Pete, who evinced some repugnance to approach the weltering victim, and snuffed the scent of blood with any other sensation than that of pleasure. Joe discovered that no less than a dozen balls had penetrated the doe's side, (for such it was,) which sufficiently accounted for its immediate and quiet death, that had so effectually deceived him into the belief that his discharge had been harmless. He now blew his horn, which was answered by a blast from Glenn, who soon came up to announce his own success in bringing down the largest buck in the party, and to congratulate his man on his truly remarkable achievement.

An hour was consumed in preparing the deer to be conveyed to the house, and by the time they were safely deposited in our hero's diminutive castle, and the hunters ready to issue forth in quest of more sport, the day was far advanced, and a slight haziness of the atmosphere dimmed in a great measure the lustre of the descending sun.

Animated with their excellent success, they anticipated much more sport, inasmuch as neither themselves nor the hounds (which hitherto were not required to do farther service than to watch one of the deer while the men were engaged with the other) were in the slightest degree fatigued. The hours flew past unnoticed, while the young men proceeded gayly outward from the river in quest of new adventures.

Glenn and his man rode far beyond the scene of their late success without discovering any new object to gratify their undiminished zest for the chase. It seemed that the deer which had escaped had actually given intelligence to the rest of the arrival of a deadly foe in the vicinity, for not one could now be seen in riding several miles. The sun was sinking low and dim in the west, and Glenn was on the eve of turning homeward, when, on emerging from the flat prairie to a slight eminence that he had marked as the boundary of his excursion, he beheld at no great distance an enormous mound, of pyramidical shape, which, from its isolated condition, he could not believe to be the formation of nature. Curious to inspect what he supposed to be a stupendous specimen of the remains of former generations of the aborigines, he resolved to protract his ride and ascend to the summit. The mound was some five hundred feet in diameter at the base, and terminated at a peak about one hundred and fifty feet in height. As our riders ascended, with some difficulty keeping in the saddle, they observed the earth on the sides to be mixed with flint-stones, and many of them apparently having once been cut in the shape of arrow-heads; and in several places where chasms had been formed by heavy showers, they remarked a great many pieces of bones, but so much broken and decayed they could not be certain that they were particles of human skeletons. When they reached the summit, which was not more than twenty feet in width and entirely barren, a magnificent scene burst in view. For ten or fifteen miles round on every side, the eye could discern oval, oblong, and circular groves of various dimensions, scattered over the rich virgin soil. The gentle undulations of the prairie resembled the boundless ocean entranced, as if the long swells had been suddenly abandoned by the wind, and yet remained stationary in their rolling attitude.

"What think you of the view, Joe?" inquired Glenn, after regarding the scene many minutes in silence.

"I've been watching a little speck, way out toward the sun, which keeps bobbing up and down, and gets bigger and bigger," said Joe.

"I mean the prospect around," said Glenn.

"I can't form an opinion, because I can't see the end of it," replied Joe, still intently regarding the object referred to.

"That is an animal of some kind," observed Glenn, marking the object that attracted Joe.

"And a wapper, too; when I first saw it I thought it was a rabbit, and now it's bigger than a deer, and still a mile or two off," said Joe.

"We'll wait a few minutes, and see what it is," replied Glenn, checking his steed, which had proceeded a few steps downward. The object of their attention held its course directly towards them, and as it drew nearer it was easily distinguished to be a very large buffalo, an animal then somewhat rare so near the white man's settlement, and one that our hero had often expressed a wish to see. Its dark shaggy sides, protuberant back and bushy head, were quite perceptible as it careered swiftly onward, seemingly flying from some danger behind.

"Down, Ringwood! Jowler!" exclaimed Glenn, preparing to fire.

"Down, Joe, too," said Joe, slipping down from his pony, preferring not to risk another fall, and likewise preparing to fire.

When the buffalo reached the base of the mound, it saw for the first time the objects above, and halted. It regarded the men with more symptoms of curiosity than alarm, but as it gazed, its distressed pantings indicated that it had been long retreating from some object of dread.

Meantime both guns were discharged, and the contents undoubtedly penetrated the animal's body, for he leapt upright in the air, and on descending, staggered off slowly in a course at right angles from the one which he was first pursuing. Glenn then let the hounds go forth, and soon overtaking the animal, they were speedily forced to act on the defensive; for the enormous foe wheeled round and pursued in turn. Finding the hounds were too cautious and active to fall victims to his sharp horns, he pawed the earth, and uttered the most horrific bellowings. As Glenn and Joe rode by the place where he had stood when they fired, they perceived large quantities of frothy blood, which convinced them that he had received a mortal wound. They rode on and paused within eighty paces of where he now stood, and calling back the baying hounds, again discharged their guns. The buffalo roared most hideously, and making a few plunges towards his assailants, fell on his knees, and the next moment turned over on his side.

"Come back, Joe!" cried Glenn to his man, who had mounted and wheeled when the animal rushed towards them, and was still flying away as fast as his pony could carry him.

"No—never!" replied Joe; "I won't go nigh that awful thing! Don't you see it's getting dark? How'll we ever find the way home again?"

The latter remark startled Glenn, for he had lost all consciousness of the lateness of the hour in the excitement, and to his dismay had also lost all recollection of the direction of his dwelling, and darkness had now overtaken them! While pausing to reflect from which quarter they first approached the mound, the buffalo, to his surprise and no little chagrin, rose up and staggered away, the darkness soon obscuring him from view altogether. Glenn, by a blast of his horn, recalled the dogs, and joining Joe, set off much dispirited, in a course which he feared was not the correct one. Night came upon them suddenly, and before they had gone a mile the darkness was intense. And the breathless calm that had prevailed during the day was now succeeded by fitful winds that howled mournfully over the interminable prairie. Interminable the plain seemed to our benighted riders, for there was still no object to vary the monotony of the cheerless scene, although they had paced briskly, and, as they supposed, far enough to have reached the cliffs of the river. Nor was there even a sound heard as they rode along, save the muffled strokes of their horses' hoofs in the dry grass that covered the earth, the low winds, and an occasional cry of the dogs as they were trodden upon by the horses.

Ere long a change came over the scene. About two-thirds of the distance round the verge of the horizon a faint light appeared, resembling the scene when a dense curtain of clouds hangs over head, and the rays of the morning sun steal under the edge of the thick vapour. But the stars could be seen, and the only appearance of clouds was immediately above the circle of light. In a very few minutes the terrible truth flashed upon the mind of Glenn. The dim light along the horizon was changed to an approaching flame! Columns of smoke could be seen rolling upwards, while the fire beneath imparted a lurid glare to them. The wind blew more fiercely, and the fire approached from almost every quarter with the swiftness of a race horse. The darkened vault above became gradually illuminated with a crimson reflection, and the young man shuddered with the horrid apprehension of being burnt alive! It was madness to proceed in a direction that must inevitably hasten their fate, the fire extending in one unbroken line from left to right, and in front of them; and they turned in a course which seemed to place the greatest distance between them and the furious element. Ever and anon a frightened deer or elk leaped past. The hounds no longer noticed them, but remained close to the horses. The leaping flames came in awful rapidity. The light increased in brilliance, and objects were distinguishable far over the prairie. A red glare could be seen on the sides of the deer as they bounded over the tall, dry grass, which was soon to be no longer a refuge for them. The young men heard a low, continued roar, that increased every moment in loudness, and looking in the direction whence they supposed it proceeded, they observed an immense, dark, moving mass, the nature of which they could not divine, but it threatened to annihilate every thing that opposed it. While gazing at this additional source of danger, the horses, blinded by the surrounding light, plunged into a deep ditch that the rain had washed in the rich soil. Neither men nor horses, fortunately, were injured; and after several ineffectual efforts to extricate themselves, they here resolved to await the coming of the fire. Ringwood and Jowler whined fearfully on the verge of the ditch for an instant, and then sprang in and crouched trembling at the feet of their master. The next instant the dark, thundering mass passed over head, being nothing less than an immense herd of buffalo driven forwards by the flames! The horses bowed their heads as if a thunderbolt was passing. The fire and the heavens were hid from view, and the roar above resembled the rush of mighty waters. When the last animal had sprung over the chasm, Glenn thanked the propitious accident that thus providentially prevented him from being crushed to atoms, and uttered a prayer to Heaven that he might by a like means be rescued from the fiery ordeal that awaited him. It now occurred to him that the accumulation of weeds and grass in the chasm, which saved them from injury when falling in, would prove fatal when the flames arrived! And after groping some distance along the trench, he found the depth diminished, but the fire was not three hundred paces distant! His heart sank within him! But when on the eve of returning to his former position, with a resolution to remove as much of the combustible matter as possible, a gleam of joy spread over his features, as, casting a glance in a contrary direction from that they had recently pursued, he beheld the identical mound he had ascended before dark, and from which his unsteady and erratic riding in the night had fortunately prevented a distant separation. They now led their horses forth, and mounting without delay, whipped forward for life or death. Could the summit of the mound be attained they were in safety—for there the soil was not encumbered with decayed vegetation—and they spurred their animals to the top of their speed. It was a noble sight to see the majestic white steed flying towards the mound with the velocity of the wind, while the diminutive pony miraculously followed in the wake like an inseparable shadow. The careering flames were not far behind; and when the horses gained the summit and Glenn looked back, the fire had reached the base!

"I thank all the saints at once!" exclaimed Joe, dismounting and falling on his knees.

"Thank your pony's legs, also," remarked Glenn, smiling.

"Was there ever such a blessed deliverance!" said Joe, panting.

"Was there ever such a lucky tumble into a ditch!" replied Glenn, with spirits more buoyant than usual.

"Was there ever an old hunter so much deceived!" said a voice a few paces down that side of the cone least exposed to the glare of the fire, and so much in the shadow of the peak that the speaker was not perceived from the position of the young men. But as soon as the words were uttered, Ringwood and Jowler sprang from the horses' heels where they had lain panting, and rushed in the direction of the speaker, whom they accosted with marks of joyful recognition.

"It is Boone!" exclaimed Glenn, leaping from his horse, and running forward to his friend, who was now seen to rise up, and a moment after his horse, that had been prostrate and still, was likewise on his feet.

"Ha! ha! ha! You have played me a fine trick, truly," laughingly remarked Boone, returning their hearty salutations.

"How?" inquired Glenn.

"In the first place, to venture forth before my arrival; in the next to inspire me with the belief that I was on the eve of encountering a brace of Indians. But I will begin at the beginning. When I crossed the river and reached your hut, (which is indeed impregnable,) I was astonished to find you had gone forth to hunt without a guide; and not so much fearing you would be lost, should night overtake you, as apprehending serious danger from the fire, the approach of which I anticipated long before night, from the peculiar complexion of the atmosphere, I set out on your trail, in hopes of overtaking you before the shades of evening set in; but darkness coming on, I could trace you no farther than to this mound. In vain did I endeavour to ascertain which direction you then travelled; but resolving not to abandon the search, I continued cruising about the prairie until the near approach of the fire forced me to retreat hither. It was when urging my horse to his utmost speed that I beheld you and your bear-hunter charging from another direction, and from the partial view, as we were all under whip, (and knowing the Osages were not far off,) I was instantly convinced that you were savages. Arriving first, I made my sagacious horse lie down, and then concealed myself behind his body."

"I am not only rejoiced that we were not the savages yousupposed,(for then Joe and I must have perished in the flames somewhere,) on our own account, but for the sake of the only man who can possibly extricate us from this dilemma," replied Glenn.

"You are somewhat wide of the mark as respects my jeopardy, my lad," said Boone; "for had you been hostile Osages, most assuredly ere this you had both been killed."

"Good gracious!" exclaimed Joe, whose predicament suddenly flashed upon his mind; "for Heaven's sake let us get home as fast as possible! He says the Indians are about! Do let us go, Mr. Glenn; we can travel now out yonder where the grass has all been burnt."

"Pshaw! You seem more alarmed now, Joe, than when there really was danger. Are the Osages truly hostile?" continued Glenn, addressing Boone.

"They are not at war with the whites, as a nation," replied Boone, ever and anon looking towards the only point from which the fire now approached; "but in thin settlements, where they may easily be the strongest party, as roving brigands, they may be considered extremely dangerous. Your man's advice is not bad."

"There! Don't you hear that? Now, *do* let's go home!" continued Joe, with increased alarm.

Fortunately, that portion of the plain over which the scathing element had spent its fury was the direction the party should pursue in retracing their way homeward.

The light dry grass had been soon consumed, and the earth wore a blackened appearance, and was as smooth as if vegetation had never covered the surface. As the party rode briskly along, (and the pony now kept in advance,) the horses' hoofs rattled as loudly on the baked ground as if it were a plank floor. The reflection of the fire in the distance still threw a lurid glare over the extended heath. As the smoke gradually ascended, objects could be discerned at a great distance, and occasionally a half-roasted deer or elk, was seen plunging about, driven to madness by its tortures. And frequently they found the dead bodies of smaller animals that could find no safety in flight.

"What's that?" cried Joe, reining up his pony, and gazing at a huge dark object ahead.

"A prize, to which we are justly entitled!" exclaimed Glenn, riding forward, on discovering it to be the buffalo (now dead) that they had fired upon early in the evening, and which circumstance he was relating to Boone at the moment of the discovery by Joe.

"You have not only been lucky as hunters," said Boone, as they dismounted to inspect the animal, (which was an enormous bull,) "but, what is extraordinary indeed, when you find your fallen game, it is already cooked!"

"Huzza for us!" cried Joe, momentarily forgetting the Indians, in his extravagant joy of having aided in killing the animal, and at the same time leaping astride of it.

"The wolves have been here before us," observed Boone, seeing a large quantity of the buffalo's viscera on the ground, which he supposed had been torn out by those ravenous animals.

"Oh! oh! oh! oh!" exclaimed Joe, leaping up, and running a few steps, and then tumbling down and continuing his cries.

"What has hurt the fellow so badly?" inquired Glenn, walking round from the back of the animal to the front. The words were scarcely uttered before he likewise sprang away, hastily, as he beheld a pronged instrument thrust from the orifice in the body whence the bowels had been extracted!

"Dod! I wonder if it's wolves or Injins!" exclaimed a voice within the cavity of the huge body.

"I've heard that voice before—it must be Sneak's," said Boone, laughing heartily.

Now the buffalo was observed to quiver slightly, and after some exertion to extricate himself, the long snake-like form of the redoubtable "Hatchet-face" came forth and stood erect before the gaping mouth and staring eyes of Joe.

"If I didn't hear a white man speak, I wish I may be singed!" exclaimed Sneak, wiping the moisture from his face, and rolling his eyes round.

"What did you stick that sharp thing in the calf of my leg for?" demanded Joe, shaking his head threateningly and coming forward.

"He! he! he! That's revenge for shooting my pups," replied Sneak.

"But how came you here?" inquired Boone.

"I was taking a hunt"—here Boone interrupted him by asking where his gun was. "I had no gun," said Sneak; and then stooping down and running his arm into the body of the buffalo, he produced a pronged spear, about four feet in length; "this," he continued, "is what I hunted with, and I was hunting after muskrats in the ponds out here, when the fire came like blazes, and like to 'ave ketched me! I dropped all the muskrats I had stuck, and streaked it for about an hour towards the river. But it gained on me like lightning, and I'd 'ave been in a purty fix if I hadn't come across this dead bull. I out with my knife and was into him in less than no time—but split me, if I didn't feel the heat of the fire as I pulled in my feet! I knew the Injins was about, by the buffalo; and the tarnation wolves, too, are always everywhere, and that accounts for my jobbing that feller's leg when he sot down on top of me."

Glenn's laughter at the above narration was arrested by Boone, who placed one hand on his shoulder, and with the other pointed out towards the fire about a mile distant, before which and thrown in relief by the flames could be distinctly discerned the flitting forms of a band of savages! A number were mounted, and others could be seen on foot, and all moving about in various directions round a large herd of buffalo, which occasionally made a stand to resist the foe that harassed them on all sides, but were soon driven forward again by the flames. Now a mounted chief could be seen to ride boldly up within a few paces of the dark mass of animals, and drawing his arrow to the head, discharge it, shaft and all, into the defenceless side of his victim. The enraged animal thus pursued either fell or rushed furiously on its foe; but the skilful savage, by a dexterous turn or sudden leap, seemed to avoid him with ease, and flying round, sent forth another barbed messenger as he careered at full speed.

"As I'm afoot, I'll go ahead!" cried Sneak, starting off at a gait that verified his words.

"Good gracious!" exclaimed Joe, leaping on his pony and whipping after Sneak, while Boone and Glenn followed in a brisk gallop.

CHAPTER IV.

The retreat—Joe makes a mysterious discovery—Mary—A disclosure—Supper—Sleep—A cat—Joe's flint—The watch—Mary—The bush—The attack—Joe's musket again—The repulse—The starting rally—The desperate alternative—Relief.

THE guidance of Sneak was infallible. Ere long the party reached the vicinity of the river, which was indicated by the tall trees and the valleys, and all apprehensions of immediate danger subsiding, they slackened their pace.

Sneak, though not so much distressed as the panting horses, fell back, and entered into conversation with Boone relative to the probable operations of the Indians, while Joe continued some little distance in advance, apparently wrapped in contemplation of the recent scenes that had so much astonished him. When he was within about a hundred paces of his long-wished for home, he thought he saw an object moving about in front of the palisade. He checked his pony for an instant; but convinced that the savages could not possibly have arrived already, he again whipped onward, inclined to believe it to be nothing more than a phantom of the brain. But when he proceeded a few steps farther, his pony stopped suddenly and snorted, while a being, which he could not exactly define, was distinctly seen to rise up and glide swiftly out of view round the inclosure.

"Who's that!" shouted he, and at the same time looking eagerly back at his companions, whose near approach induced him to maintain his position.

"Go on, Joe! What's the matter?" remarked Glenn, the head of his steed having passed over the back of the pony as he stood across the path and blocked up the way.

"I beg to be excused! As sure as I'm alive, I saw an Indian run round towards the gate!" replied Joe.

"Foller me," said Sneak, poising his spear in the air, and advancing.

"Thank Heaven, it's you!" exclaimed the mysterious object, coming forward fearlessly, on hearing the men's voices.

"Dod rot your cowardly skin!" said Sneak, after looking at the approaching form and turning to Joe, "how dare you to be frightened at sich a thing as that—a female woman!"

"It was not me—it was my pony, you great——"

"What?" asked Sneak, sharply, turning abruptly round, as they paused at the gate.

"You great long buffalo tapeworm!" said Joe, alighting on the side of the pony opposite to his quarrelsome companion, and then going forward and opening the gate in silence.

"What brings thee hither at this late hour, Mary?" inquired Glenn, on recognizing the ferryman's daughter.

"Nothing—only—I"—stammered the abashed girl, who had expected only to see our hero and his man.

"Speak out, lass, if you have any thing important to say, remarked Boone, when they entered the inclosure, placing his hand encouragingly on the girl's head.

Mary still hesitated, and Boone was no little puzzled to conjecture rightly what it was she intended to impart; but he was convinced it must be something of no ordinary nature that would induce a maiden of reputed timidity to leave her father's hut at a late hour of the night.

"Now tell me, Mary, what it was you wished to say," remarked Glenn, addressing her in a playful tone, when they were seated in the house, and a lamp suspended against the wall was lighted.

"I did not expect to find Mr. Boone and Sneak with you —and now——"

"What?" inquired Glenn, much moved by her paleness, and the throbbing of her breast, which now seemed to be gradually subsiding.

"Nothing—only you and Joe are both safe now," she replied, with her eyes cast down.

"Were we in danger? How are we safe?" inquired Glenn, regarding her words as highly mysterious.

"Everybody is safe where Mr. Boone is," replied Mary.

"But what was the danger, my pretty lass?" inquired Boone, playfully taking her hand.

"Why Posin, one of father's boatmen——"

"Speak on, lass—I know Posin to be an unfeeling wretch, and a half-blood Indian; but he is also known to be a great coward, and surely no harm could have been feared from him," said Boone.

"But I heard him speaking to himself when I was filling my pitcher at the spring, and he was standing behind some rocks, where he couldn't see me, and didn't think any one was within hearing."

"What said he?" inquired Glenn, impatiently, and much interested in the anticipated disclosure, for he had often remarked the satanic expression of Posin's features.

"These were his words: 'The Osages will be here before to-morrow morning. If Raven, the chief, will go halves with me, I'll tell him how much money the young men have, and help to get it!' Such were his very words!" continued Mary, her dark eyes assuming a brightness, and her voice a boldness unwonted on ordinary occasions, as she proceeded: "He then started off towards the prairie with his rifle, and nobody has seen him since. I told father about it but he wouldn't believe there was any danger; and when night came, he told me not to be uneasy, but to sleep like a good girl. I did lie down, for I never like to disobey my father; but I couldn't sleep, and so I got up and came here to wait till you returned, to tell you all about it."

"Thanks, Mary—I shall never forget your kindness," said Glenn, as much affected by her simplicity and gentleness as at the threatened danger.

"You're a sweet lass; God bless you, Mary!" said Boone, kissing her smooth forehead. "Now run home and go to sleep, child; we will be on our guard. As for you, your father is respected by all the Indians, and therefore your own safety will be best secured under his protection."

"I will accompany you to the hut," said Glenn, as the girl bid them good night, and was about departing.

"Oh no—I'm used to going alone," said Mary, promptly declining the proposition.

"She speaks truly, and it is unnecessary," said Boone, as the maiden bowed and disappeared.

The party then fastened the gate and secured themselves within the stone house. Joe petitioned Glenn to permit him to bring in the dogs, and Sneak seconded the motion, proposing to lie with them before the fire.

After a hearty repast, Boone and Glenn retired to their couches in quest of repose, so much needed after the exercises of the day. Nor was it long before they were steeped in that deep and solemn slumber which throws a mysterious veil over the senses, obscuring from the vision all objects of an unpleasant nature, relieving the mind of the cares that may have pressed heavily upon it during the day, and at the same time by the gentlest process refreshing and reinvigorating the weary faculties for renewed exertion.

Silence brooded over the fireside scene. The lamp threw a dim ray around its small flame unruffled by the confined and motionless air. The fawn was coiled in a sleeping posture under its master's bed, while the kitten purred upon its velvet back. On one side of the hearth lay Sneak, his head pillowed upon one of the hounds, while the other slept against his back. Joe was the only one present who had not fallen under the magic influence of slumber. Hitherto he had yielded to a more powerful impulse—that of the appetite—and he now sat upon a low stool on the corner of the hearth opposite to Sneak, his back leaning against the side of the fireplace, holding in his left hand a pewter platter, and in his right a rib of the deer he had killed, well cooked, which he raised to his mouth occasionally, and sometimes at very long intervals, between the approaches of the sleep which was gradually overpowering him. Once, when his eyelids sank heavily and closed, and the platter rested on his lap, and his right hand, still clenching the savoury bone, fell powerless at his side—Ringwood, in his hard breathing, chanced to snuff up some ashes that caused him to sneeze. Joe started at the sound, and after rolling his eyes round once or twice and finding all right, raised the bone once more to his mouth and set his jaws again in motion.

"Dod, man! are you going to chaw all night?" asked Sneak, awakened by the motion of Ringwood, and looking up at the face of Joe in astonishment.

"I had nothing to eat all day," replied Joe, fishing for a cracker floating in the greasy platter.

"But ain't you a-going to sleep some?" asked Sneak, half unconsciously, the final utterance smothered in a guttural rumble as he again sank back on his canine pillow.

"Yes, when I've got my supper," replied Joe lazily, and indistinctly, with one end of the bone in his mouth. But it was not long before he again nodded, and his hand with the bone in it was once more lowered softly down at his side. He was soon palpably fast asleep. And now the kitten, having finished its nap, came with a noiseless tread to the comfortable fire, humming its low unvaried song; and, rubbing its soft side against the head of Jowler, finally crouched down before the embers, with its feet drawn under it, and its eyes apparently watching the brilliant sparks that ever and anon flew up the chimney. But ere long it scented the well-flavoured viand that dangled in the vicinity, and after casting a glance at the face of Joe, and being satisfied that he was insensible to all external objects, stealthily began to gnaw the end of the bone that rested on the hearth. As long as it had in mind the fear of interruption, it was permitted to feast moderately; but when its ravenous propensity urged it to more active and vigorous operations, Joe once more opened his eyes, and after looking slowly around, but not down, again attempted to raise the rib to his mouth.

"Hello!—augh! scat!" he cried, leaping up violently.

His first impression was that the Indians, about whom he had been dreaming, were upon him; his next that a rattle-snake clung to his finger; and finally, finding it to be the kitten bestowing some scratches on the hand that sought to bereave it of its prize, he uttered the latter exclamation, first in rage; but pleased that his condition was no worse, soon after called the poor frightened pet to him, and with one or two caresses gave it the bone, and then resigned himself to unrestrained slumber.

They were all aroused in the morning by the snorting of the horses without, and the growling and sharp yelping of the hounds within.

"What's the matter with the horses and dogs, Joe?" inquired Glenn, rising from his couch.

"I don't know what ails the foolish things. I know that I fed the horses; and as for Ringwood and Jowler, I'll soon kick them out. Let go my ankle!" exclaimed he, turning to Sneak, who caught hold of him as he rose to approach the door.

"Don't open the door yet," said Boone, who had been listening to the sounds outside, and then continued in an under tone, addressing Glenn: "They are certainly here; but whether or not with an evil intent I am unable to determine."

"Oh goodness! It's the Indians!" exclaimed Joe, yielding to sudden alarm, having momentarily forgotten the anticipated danger when he proposed opening the door.

"Keep your mouth shet!" said Sneak, listening with his ear placed near the floor behind the door.

"How many do you make them out to be?" inquired Boone, when Sneak had occupied his position a few minutes.

"It's all right!" replied Sneak, eagerly; "there is only two or three of 'em, and old Roughgrove's out there talking to 'em! How do you open the door? Let me out!"

The door was opened with reluctance and cautiously by Joe, and Sneak going foremost all the party sallied out into the fresh air. A snow of several inches in depth had fallen, and within the circle enclosed by the palisade not a single track was to be seen. But when the gate was drawn back, several Osage Indians were observed standing a few paces distant with their tomahawks hung in their belts, and instead of exhibiting any symptoms of hostility, they approached smiling, and extended the hand of friendship to the whites.

"How do!" exclaimed the leader, in imperfect English, grasping the hands held out in salutation, while his actions were imitated by the others in silence.

"I'm very well, I thank you," said Joe, bowing and retreating backwards when they accosted him, unwilling to venture his hand within their reach, as Glenn and the rest did.

"Shake hands with them, you silly fellow," said Boone, "or they will think you are an enemy."

"Here, Mr. Osage!" said Joe, his teeth chattering as he extended his hand; and the Indian, perceiving his alarm, squeezed it so tightly for merriment that he was on the eve of crying out; and when liberated, he sprang violently back, much inclined to run away, to their great amusement.

"That is Raven, the chief," remarked Roughgrove to Glenn, pointing to the one that first addressed them, and who was now conversing with Boone, whom he seemed to know, or to have been familiar with his character, from his animated gestures and the excited expression of his features. Sneak stood in silence, a convenient distance apart, apparently gleaning intelligence from the conference. The chief (as are the members of this tribe generally) was extremely dark, tall, athletic, and wore a ferocious aspect, while the few followers with him manifested a curosity to examine the apparel and accoutrements of the whites, but without betraying any signs of an evil disposition.

"Are there not more of them in the vicinity?" inquired Glenn.

"Yes—quite a large party," said Roughgrove; "but Raven said he did not wish to intimidate the whites by showing them, without first extending the hand of friendship himself. They profess to entertain the kindest feeling towards us, and propose through their chiefs to traffic their furs and moccasins for such goods as we may be disposed to give them in return."

"I do not see your oarsman, Posin," remarked Glenn, the disclosure of Mary occurring to him—and then accosted Mary herself, who now joined them with her eyes cast down in apparent bashfulness.

"His absence is a mystery to me," replied the old ferry

man, "though I do not attach the same importance to it that Mary does."

"Father"—uttered his daughter, and pausing in mingled timidity and dread, as if some undefinable forebodings of harm oppressed her.

"I'll be shot if I understand all this to my liking," said Sneak, staring at the great number of moccasin tracks that had been made round the enclosure, which truly indicated that more than the four chiefs present had been prowling there before daylight.

"Hush, Mr. Sneak!" said Joe; "they hear every word you say."

"Jest let me alone a minute," replied Sneak, getting down on his knees and examining the various foot-prints with great minuteness. When he rose he made some signs to Boone, which the others did not comprehend.

At this juncture several other Indians were seen to approach from the valley above, where the party had encamped. These painted visitors likewise came forward with sundry nods and gesticulations of friendship, at the same time exhibiting several furred articles of curious workmanship, and a few precious stones, as samples of what they wished to barter. A short conference then ensued between them and the head chief, which terminated in a pressing invitation for the whites to accompany them to their encampment.

"You may all do as you like—I shall stay here," said Joe, stepping back towards the gate.

"You are a coward, Joe!" said Glenn; "you may remain, however, to prevent them from pilfering any thing while we are away," and he turned towards the Indians for the purpose of accompanying them.

"Stay!" said Mary, in a distinct and startling tone.

"Why should we not go? We are armed, and could as easily withstand an attack in their encampment as elsewhere. If it be their determination to do us harm, their numbers will enable them to accomplish their purpose notwithstanding all the opposition we can offer," said Glenn.

"There is no danger," said Roughgrove, endeavouring to extricate his arm from the grasp of Mary, who strenuously held him back.

"I have a secret for thee, child," said Boone, beckoning the trembling girl to him.

"Oh, what is it? You will not let him—I mean my father, go among them, will you? *You* know that Posin is away—perhaps in some ambush——"

"Hush child!" said Boone, in a low tone, and employing gestures that led the savages to believe he was quieting her fears, while he whispered a message in her ear that had a singular effect. Though very pale, the girl now smiled playfully, and returning to her father, said, in tones so low that no one else could hear, "Father, he says you must instantly cross the river for assistance—I will be safe, under *his* protection, till you return."

"I'll do it!" replied Roughgrove, setting off towards the ferry. But when he departed, the chief evinced much anger, and was only appeased by the assurance that the old ferryman was gone for some article desired by his child, and would return ere long.

The footprint which had so much attracted Sneak was recognized by some peculiar marks to be that of Posin, and when the discovery was communicated to Boone, he at once surmised that danger lurked in the vicinity; and the subsequent impatience on the part of the Indians to urge the whites to visit their camp, convinced him that some foul treachery had been concocted between the half-breed and the savages. He had also caught a glimpse of several armed Indians behind some bushes at no great distance from where he stood, notwithstanding Raven had asserted that the rest of his party were in their encampment; and when the chief grew angry, and almost menacing, on the withdrawal of the old ferryman, he resolved to adopt the surest means of safety without delay. No sooner was the ferry-boat seen to shoot out from the land than Boone motioned the whites to enter the inclosure. As they turned towards the gate, the chief made a movement to intercept them; but Boone drew forth a brace of pistols that had been concealed under his hunting-shirt, one of which he pointed at Raven, and with the other intimidated the rest who had advanced likewise, until his friends were all within the palisade.

Boone did not wish to be the first to shed blood, and in their own language asserted as much to the savages; but

Boone drew forth a brace of pistols that had been concealed under his hunting-shirt, one of which he pointed at Raven, and with the other intimidated the rest who had advanced on himself, until his friends were all within the palisade.—P. 56

at the same time he warned them not to commit any violence in the settlement at their peril. The chief had not thought there would be any necessity for bloodshed so soon, and perhaps not at all, if Glenn could be enticed from his house, while Posin and his comrades might obtain his money.

Nor did he expect to meet with Boone, (renowned among all the tribes for his wisdom and prowess,) much less to be anticipated on the very threshold of the enterprise. His rage grew intense on finding himself outwitted and defied. He drew forth his tomahawk, and though not venturing to throw it, (for he perceived Glenn and Sneak behind, with their guns in readiness to fire,) he shook it threateningly at Boone as he closed the gate, and then strode away sulkily in the direction of the bushes, where some of his followers had been seen partially concealed.

When the gate was secured, the inmates of the little fort crowded about Boone and overwhelmed him with questions.

"Do you think they can get over the posts?" inquired Joe.

"Will they come before father returns?" asked Mary.

"Do you think they will attack us at all?" interrogated Glenn.

"There can be no doubt of it," replied Boone; "but if we do our duty, I think we shall be able to resist them. We must be ready to defend ourselves, at all events—and in the mean time we must watch through the loopholes on every side to prevent a surprise." This was hardly spoken before an arrow whizzed over their heads, and, striking against the stone wall of the house, fell at the feet of Joe.

"Ugh! look at that!" cried he, leaping some ten feet away.

"Go in, child—and the rest to their posts!" remarked Boone, first to Mary, and then addressing the men.

"Yes—*do* go in, Miss!" cried Joe, forcing Mary into the house, where he also seemed determined to remain himself.

"Come out here!" cried Sneak, going to the door.

"Wait till I screw a flint in my musket," said Joe.

"You can see better out here," replied Sneak.

"But I haven't found the flint yet," answered Joe.

"He's a coward!" said Sneak, turning away and going to his post, whence he could watch the valley below.

Boone's station was on the opposite side, in the direction of the supposed encampment of the Indians. But not a savage could now be seen, and the arrow that fell among them had evidently been discharged from a great distance above.

"Shall we fire if any of them come within the range of our guns?" inquired Glenn, from his position on the east, which overlooked the cliff.

"Certainly," replied Boone; "the arrow was their declaration of war, and if they are again seen, it will be in a hostile attitude. Watch close, Sneak!" he cried, as another shaft flew over the palisade from the valley below, and penetrated the wood but a few feet above his head.

"Come out to your post, Joe!" cried Glenn, impatiently.

"I will presently—as soon as I get my gun fixed," replied Joe.

"If you do not come forth instantly, I'll thrust you out of the inclosure!" continued Glenn, somewhat fiercely.

"Here I am," said Joe, coming out, and making an effort to assume a bold bearing: "I'm ready now—I only wanted to fix my gun—who's afraid?" saying which, he strode in a stooping posture to the loophole on the west of the inclosure.

While the whole male force of the garrison was required to act as sentinels, Mary, whose trepidation had been succeeded by deliberate resolution, was busily employed moulding bullets.

An hour passed, and no Indians had yet been seen, although an occasional arrow assured the besieged party that the enemy still remained in the immediate vicinity. They cleared away the snow at their posts, and placing dry straw to stand upon, prepared to continue the watch throughout the day and night. Nor were they to suffer for food; for Mary, though she had not been requested so to do, ere long, to their joyful surprise, came forth with a dinner handsomely provided, which she placed before them with a smile of satisfaction playing on her lips, and entirely unmindful of the shafts that continued to fly overhead, which either pierced the wood and remained stationary, or fell expended and harmless at her feet.

Affairs thus remained till night, when the arrows ceased to fly. There was not a cloud in the heavens, and the moon rose up in purest brightness. A breathless stillness pervaded the air, and no sound for a great length of time could be heard but the hooting of owls on the opposite side of the river, and the howling of wolves in the flats about a mile above.

"I'm not a bit cold—are you?" said Joe, addressing Sneak.

"Dod! keep an eye out!" replied Sneak, in a low tone.

"There's nothing out this way but a bush. But I declare it seems to be bigger and nigher than it was in the day-time," said Joe.

"Don't speak so loud," remarked Boone, crossing to where Joe stood, and looking through at the bush.

"It's nothing but a bush," said Joe.

"Do you wish to kill an Indian?" inquired Boone.

"I wish they were all worms, and I could get my heel on them!" said Joe.

"That would be cruel—but as any execution we may now do, is in our own defence, you may fire at that bush if you like," continued Boone.

"Well," said Joe; and taking deliberate aim, discharged his musket as directed, and was knocked down on his back in the snow by the rebound.

"Plague take the gun!" said he, recovering his feet; "but I remember it had two loads in—I forgot it was charged, and loaded it again. Ha! ha! ha! but what's become of the bush?" he continued jocularly, not thinking he had fired at an Indian.

"Look for yourself," replied Boone.

"Hang me if it ain't gone!" exclaimed Joe.

"Ay, truly it is; but had you hit the mark, it would have fallen. It was rather too far, however, even for your musket," said Boone, returning to his former position.

"You are the poorest marksman that ever I saw, or you'd 'ave killed that red rascal," said Sneak, coming up to Joe, and finding where the bush had been.

"I didn't know it was any thing but a bush—if I'd only known it was an Indian——"

"You be hanged!" replied Sneak, vexed that such a capital opportunity should be lost, and petulantly resuming his own station.

An intense silence succeeded the discharge of Joe's gun, after the tremendous report died away, in successive reverberations up and down the river, and over the low woodland opposite. The owls and wolves were hushed; and as the watchful sentinels cast their eyes over the snow, on which the calm rays of the moon rested in repose, there was not the least indication of the presence of a dangerous foe.

Joe leant against the palisade, holding with one hand the breech of his gun, while the barrel was thrust through the loophole, and seemed to be indulging in a peculiar train of reflections.

"Now, I'd much rather be in Philadelphia," said he, in a voice but little louder than a whisper, and unconscious of giving utterance to his thoughts—"a great deal rather be there—in some comfortable oyster-cellar—than standing out here in the lone wilderness, up to my knees in snow, and expecting every minute to have a poisoned arrow shot through my head. Hang it all! I wonder what pleasure Mr. Glenn can enjoy here? Suppose, now, while I'm standing here thinking, an arrow should dart over the other side, and stick five or six inches into me? I hope they keep a careful look-out. And that reminds me that I ought to keep an eye out myself, for fear some one may be pinked from my side." He applied his eye to the hole, and continued in the same strain: "I don't see a single living thing; maybe they've all gone off. If they have, I'll deserve all the credit, for I'm the only person that shot at them. And I don't think that long hatchet-face Sneak will think that I'm a coward any more. But these savages are strange beings; I had no more idea that the bush hid an Indian than that there's one not ten feet off now, under the snow. And if we hadn't found him out he might have crawled up and shot me in the eye through this hole. I won't hold my eye here all the time!" said he, rising, and to his astonishment Sneak stood at his elbow, whither he had glided softly, his quick ear having caught the hum of Joe's soliloquy, and his curiosity leading him to find out the meaning of the mysterious jargon of his companion-in-arms.

"Of all the men I ever saw you are the dod-rottedest!" exclaimed Sneak, after staring at him a few moments in silent wonderment, and then striding back to his post.

"I should like to hear that sentence parsed, said Joe, looking after him.

The hours wore on in peace, until midnight, when a low chattering, like that of a squirrel, was heard in the valley below; while a shrill whistling, resembling that of quails was distinguished above.

"Come hither!" exclaimed Boone in a whisper to Glenn.

"Do you see any of them?" inquired Glenn, joining his friend.

"Not yet—but we will see enough of them presently. The sounds in the valleys are signals, and they will attack us on these sides. You may abandon your watch on the east, and assist me here."

"And you may come and spell me," said Sneak to Joe.

"I must not desert my post," said Joe.

"If you stay there, you'll be dead sure to be shot!" replied Sneak.

"You don't think they're coming back, do you?" inquired Joe, gliding swiftly to Sneak's side.

"They'll be on us in no time. Is your gun loaded?"

"I declare I have forgotten whether I loaded it again or not!" said Joe.

"You're a purty feller, to watch with an empty gun, now ain't you? Never mind blowing in her—run down a cartridge as quick as you kin; it makes no odds how much you have in; a big noise will do as much good as any thing else," said Sneak, hurriedly, evidently expecting to see the savage enemy every moment, while Joe did his bidding, asserting all the time that he believed his musket was already loaded, and expressing a decided dislike to being kicked over every day from overcharging.

As Boone predicted, but a very short time elapsed before a series of startling and frightful yells were heard below, which were answered by similar horrid sounds above. Joe first ran towards Boone and Glenn, and then sprang back to his place at the side of Sneak, fully convinced there were no means of retreat, and, being effectually cornered, at length evinced an ardent desire to fire. When the yells died away in the distance, a flight of arrows from the north and south poured upon the besieged party. Many of them pierced the outer side of the palisade, while others, flying over, penetrated the opposite timbers, and quivered above the heads of the men; and some rattled against the top of the house, (the snow having melted from the roof,) and fell harmless to the earth.

There having been no shot yet fired in the direction whence the arrows came, (for such was the order of Boone,) the savages, emboldened by the absence of any demonstrations of resistance, and thinking their foes were shut up in the house, or killed by their numberless shafts, charged upon the premises simultaneously from both sides, shooting their arrows and yelling as they came. When they had approached within a hundred paces of the inclosure, Boone and Sneak fired with deadly aim at the foremost of the party, and the next moment Glenn followed the example, while Boone reloaded his gun.

"Now fire!" exclaimed Sneak, shaking Joe by the shoulder, having seen the savages pause when one of their party uttered the death-howl and fell.

"Here goes!" said Joe, pulling the trigger and falling over on his back in the snow from the rebound, for the musket had been truly twice charged.

"Split me if you didn't accidentally throw a handful of bullets among their legs that crack!" said Sneak, observing the now discomfited and retreating Indians, as they endeavoured to bear off their wounded, and then firing on them again himself as they vanished down the valley. The like result was witnessed above, and again in a very short time there was not a savage to be seen.

"What's the matter? Why don't you get up?" asked Sneak turning to Joe, who still remained prostrate on the ground.

"My mouth's bleeding—I don't know but I'm wounded. Didn't an arrow come through the hole when I was shooting?" asked Joe, rising partially up and spitting out a quantity of blood on the snow.

"It was nothing but the gun kicking you like it did in the bear hunt. If it was an arrow you must have swallered it, for I don't see the shaft. But maybe you did—you're sech a gormandizer," said Sneak.

"Hang it all, I don't believe I'm much hurt!" exclaimed Joe, jumping up suddenly. "Get from before the hole!" he continued, ramming down a cartridge hastily, and thrusting out the muzzle of his gun.

"Why don't you blaze away?" asked Sneak, laughing, and observing that he hesitated.

"Why, they're all gone!" cried Joe, joyfully, "and it was my old cannon that swept them off, too."

Once more silence pervaded the scene. Boone, after the repeated solicitations of Mary, partook of another bountiful repast, and the others in turn likewise refreshed themselves, and then resumed the watch.

Nor was it long before the Osages were once more heard to howl like fiends, and the sound had hardly ceased to vibrate through the air before a singular and unexpected assault terrified the besieged party for a moment. This was a shower of *blazing arrows* coming from below, (where all the savages now seemed to be collected,) which ignited the palisade in many places where the snow had fallen off. But the fire was easily extinguished, and all, with the exception of Boone, were disposed to attach but little importance to any further device of the enemy. Boone, on the contrary, was unusually grave, and requested his companions to be on the alert, or they would yet be the victims of the savages.

"I like these kind of arrows the best," said Joe, "for I can see how to dodge them."

"But the wooden slabs can't dodge—dod! they're afire on the outside now!" cried Sneak, truly discovering a flame reaching above the inclosure from without.

"Watch well from the loopholes!" cried Boone, throwing open the gate and rushing out, and running round to where the fire was crackling. "Come, Sneak!—I want your assistance—quick!" he exclaimed, finding the flames making rapid progress.

"Keep your eye skinned now!" said Sneak, as he left Joe alone to watch for the Indians, and ran out to aid in subduing the fire.

The savages could evidently see what was transacting, although unseen themselves, for most of their arrows now seemed to be directed at those without.

"Look sharp!" said Boone to Joe, through the loophole.

"Let me assist!" cried Glenn, imprudently leaving his post in his eagerness to share the danger, and coming out with a spade.

"Go in, my friend—we are sufficient here," said Boone, addressing Glenn.

"Come in! come in! come in!" cried Joe.

"I see no Indians," remarked Boone.

"The house is on fire! Fire! fire! fire!" screamed Joe, falling into his old habit when in the city.

Glenn ran back in this emergency, but when he arrived within the inclosure, he found that this service had been anticipated by Mary, who had quietly thrust her hands into the snow, and with balls thus made, easily extinguished the fire on the roof.

When Boone and Sneak had effected their purpose, they repaired to their former positions, assured that the utmost caution must be observed to prevent a surprise from some unexpected quarter, while their attention was naturally directed to one particular point. But they had hardly resumed their stations before their ears were saluted by the joyful report of rifles in the valley. Relief was at hand. Roughgrove had recrossed the river, with a party of recruits, and fallen upon the rear of the savages, at a moment when success seemed to smile on their sanguinary purpose. Their shouts of exultation at the prospect of firing the premises were now changed to howls of despair, and they fled in all directions. But Roughgrove, aware of the impolicy of pursuit, led his men directly to the gallant little garrison; and the victorious huzzas of his band were answered in like manner by the besieged, who came forth and gave them a cordial welcome. Never, perhaps, when they met, did hand grasp hand more heartily. But Mary, who had hitherto cast aside all the weaker fears of the woman, no sooner beheld her aged father in safety than she rushed into his arms and fainted on his breast.

CHAPTER V.

A strange excursion—A fairy scene—Joe is puzzled and frightened—A wonderful discovery—Navigation of the upper regions—A crash—No bones broken.

SEVERAL weeks had elapsed since the incidents recorded in the last chapter. The repulse of the Osages was succeeded by the arrival of a war-party of Pawnees, and a deadly feud existing between these tribes, the latter readily joined the whites, and speedily chased the enemy far beyond the settlements. Boone had returned to his family on the other side of the river; and Sneak, having made peace with Joe, had likewise withdrawn to his own domicil, to pursue his avocations of hunting and trapping in solitude.

Glenn sat before a blazing fire in his little castle, his left hand clasping a closed book he had been reading, while his dextral elbow was resting on the rude arm of a chair which he had constructed and cushioned with furs, and his palm supported his chin. He thus sat silently, looking steadfastly through one of the little square windows at the snow-encrusted branches of the trees beyond the inclosure, and apparently indulging a pleasing train of reflections.

Joe, on the contrary, was engaged in boisterous and mirthful exercise on the deep and frozen snow without. He was playing with the kitten, the fawn, and the hounds, and occasionally ran into the stable to caress the horses.

At length, with no other object than a dreamy impulse to wander among the wild scenes in the vicinity, Glenn started up, and donning a warm overcoat and seizing his rifle, set out along the cliff up the river, (a direction which he had never yet traversed,) accompanied by Joe, who seemed to look upon his master's pale composed face, and determined though gentle motions, with curiosity, if not mystery.

"Why do you stare at me so often?" inquired Glenn, pausing, after they had walked some distance in silence.

"Because I don't know what you're after," replied Joe

"You'll see what I'm after," said Glenn, setting forward, and continuing his course along the cliff.

A snow of several feet in depth rested on the earth, and the sun that shone forth at noon had melted the surface so frequently, that the freezing nights which had as often succeeded had formed an icy incrustation quite strong enough to bear the weight of a man. Though it was a dreary waste, yet Glenn gleaned a satisfaction in casting his eyes around where his glance beheld no one striving to oppress his fellow being that he might acquire riches and power, to be again snatched from his grasp by others, but a peaceful scene, fresh from the hand of God, and unmarred by the workmanship of meaner creatures. The broad river far below was covered with a massy plate of ice, and the snow that rested upon it gave it the appearance of an immense plain, rather than an incrusted surface of the most perturbed and erratic stream in the world. The geese and other fowl that wandered over the frozen surface in quest of their native element, from the great distance down, seemed to be no larger than sparrows.

Ere long, Glenn and his man reached the valley above, and commenced a descent through the timber in a diagonal direction, that would conduct them, after numerous windings, to the edge of the frozen stream, along which a narrow pathway ran northward about a mile. Glenn paused at an abrupt angle in his descent, after having proceeded a few paces through the undergrowth, and stood long in wonderment and admiration, gazing at the scene that suddenly burst in view. His towering position overlooked the whole valley. The ten thousand trees beneath, and their ten million branches and twigs all completely clothed in crystal—while not the slightest breeze was stirring—presented a view of fairyland, such as flits across the vision in dreams, that the memory fain would cling to, but which is lost in the real and conflicting transactions of returning day. The noonday sun was momentarily veiled by a listless cloud, which seemed to be stationary in the heavens, as if designed to enhance the effect of the beauty below, that outvied in brightness even the usual light above. Not a squirrel was seen to leap from bough to bough, nor a bird to flit across the opening between the lofty trees; but all was stillness, silence, and beauty. As Glenn stood entranced, Joe seemed to be more struck with the operation of the enchantment on his companion's features and attitude, than with any effect from the same source experienced on himself.

"Ain't you going down to the bottom of the valley?" asked Joe.

"It is a scene such as is beheld by infants in their slumbers, when they dream of paradise!" said Glenn, paying no attention to Joe, his eyes immovably riveted on the innumerable sprigs of alabaster which pointed out in every direction in profuse clusters, while his pale lips seemed to move mechanically, and his brow expressed a mournful serenity, as if entertaining a regret that he should ever be separated from the pearly labyrinths before him, amid which he would delight to wander forever.

"I think you must be dreaming yourself," said Joe, staring at him.

"How composed is every object!" continued Glenn; "such must be the abode of angels and departed spirits, who are not permitted longer to behold the strifes of earth and its contaminations, but rove continually with noiseless tread, or on self-poised wing, through devious and delightful paths, surrounded by sedges of silver embroidery, and shielded above by mazy fretwork spangled with diamonds, or gliding without effort through the pure and buoyant air, from bower to bower of crystal——"

"Ugh—talking of the icy trees makes me chilly!" said Joe.

"With life everlasting and unchangeable!" continued Glenn, after a momentary pause from the interruption of his man, which he only noticed by a significant motion of the hand for him to be silent.

"But I wouldn't like the eternal *frost-work*," said Joe.

"Pshaw!" replied Glenn, pursuing his way downwards. When they reached the bottom of the valley, they were yet a hundred paces distant from its junction with the river, which was obscured by the many intervening trees that grew along the frozen rivulet. Here Glenn again paused to contemplate the scene. The hills that rose abruptly on either hand, and the thick intertwining branches above, combined to produce a dusky aspect scarce less dim than twilight. Glenn folded his arms composedly, and looked thoughtfully round, as if indulging the delightful fancies engendered when wandering forth on a summer's pleasant evening. "There seems to be a supernatural influence pervading the air to-day," he said, in a low tone, "for I sometimes imagine that flitting spirits become partially visible. On the pendent icicles and jewelled twigs, methinks I sometimes behold for an instant the prismatic rays of elfins' eyes——"

"Don't believe it," said Joe; "or if it is so, they are weeping at the cold, and will soon be frozen up."

"And at each sudden turn," continued Glenn, "they seem to linger an instant in view, and then vanish sportively, as if amused at the expense of impotent mortals."

"I can't hear 'em laugh," said Joe.

"And then," continued Glenn, "although beyond human consciousness, there may be heavenly sounds in the air—the melody of aërial harps and fairy voices—to which our ears may be sealed, when, perchance, our vicinity to their presence may inspire the peculiar sensation I now experience."

"I heard a heap of curious sounds one warm sunshiny morning," said Joe; "but when I asked an old fellow jogging along the same road what they meant, he said the day before had been so cold when the stage-driver went by that his wind froze as it came out of the bugle, and was just then thawing."

"If such beings do exist," continued Glenn, paying no attention to Joe, "it would delight me to commune with them face to face."

"I see a buck's head!" cried Joe, looking down the dell, where the object he mentioned was distinctly observable amid a cluster of spicewood bushes, whence a slight jingling sound proceeded as the animal plucked the nutritious buds bent down by the innumerable icicles.

"Why should not the sylvan gods"—continued Glenn.

"Hush! I'm going to fire!" said Joe.

"Why should they not resort hither," said Glenn, unmindful of Joe, "where no meaner beings abide?"

Joe fired, and Glenn started in astonishment, as if he had had no intimation of his companion's intention.

"Hang it all! Isn't he going to die, I wonder?" said Joe, after the buck had made one or two plunges in the snow, his sharp hoofs piercing through the crust or the surface, and with much struggling extricated himself and stood trembling, and looked imploringly at his foe.

"What in the world are you about?" exclaimed Glenn, casting a listless glance at the deer, and then staring his companion in the face.

"Whip me if there was any lead in the gun!" said Joe. "I drew the bullets out yesterday, and forgot to put them in again. But no matter—he can't run through the snow—I'll kill him with the butt of my musket."

"Move not, at your peril!" said Glenn, authoritatively, when Joe was about to rush on the defenceless buck.

"I do believe you are out of your head!" said Joe, staring Glenn in the face, and glancing at the tempting prize, alternately.

"At such an hour—in such an elysian place as this—no blood shall be spilled. It were profanity to discolor these pearly walks with clotted gore."

"The deuce take the pearls, say I!" said Joe.

"Perhaps," continued Glenn, "a god may have put on the semblance of a stag to tempt us."

"And hang me, if I wouldn't pretty soon spoil his physiognomy, if you would only say the word!" said Joe, shaking his head sullenly at the buck.

"Come," said Glenn, sternly; and, leading the way, he passed within a few feet of the terrified animal without turning his head aside, and directed his steps down the valley towards the river. Joe said nothing when opposite the buck, awed by the impressive tone and mysterious bearing of his master; but he grinned defiance at him, and resolved to embrace the first opportunity to steal out alone, and fully gratify his revenge; for such was the feeling he now harboured against the animal.

When they reached the margin of the river, they wandered along the narrow path that turned to the left, and continued up the stream, with the ice but a few feet distant on one hand, and the precipitous acclivity of rocks on the other. They maintained a brisk pace for about thirty minutes, when the range of cliffs terminating abruptly, they entered a low flat forest.

"*Now*, what do you say to my firing?" exclaimed Joe, staring at an enormous wolf, a short distance on the left.

that seemed to be tearing the flesh from the carcass of a deer.

"You must not fire," replied Glenn, viewing the scene with no interest.

"Why not? If the deer's a sylvan god, the wolf's sure to be a black devil, and it's a duty to take the god's part," said Joe.

"No!" replied Glenn, still striding on.

"Where are you going to, I should like to know? I hope you haven't any idea of going closer to the haunted island!" said Joe, following reluctantly.

"What haunted island?" asked Glenn.

"Why that one right ahead of us!" replied Joe, pointing to a small island a few hundred paces distant.

"Who says it is haunted?" demanded Glenn.

"Why, everybody in the country *knows* it's haunted. Didn't you hear Miss Mary telling all about it?"

"What did she tell about it?"

"That several years ago a man flew up the river riding on a black cloud of smoke, and after scaring all the Indians and everybody else away, took up his abode in yonder island. Not a soul, from that day to this, has ever been nearer to it than we are now. But strange sights have been seen there. Once a great big swan, as large as our house, was seen to come out of the willows and leap into the water After seeing it paddle about an hour or two in every direction, an old beaver trapper and deer hunter took it into his head that it was nothing more than a water-fowl of some large species; and resolving to have a crack at it anyhow, he crept behind the rocks at the end of the cliff, and blazed away when it swam past the next time. Mercy on us! when he fired, they say the thing turned his head towards him, and came at him in a straight line, and as fast as lightning, blowing sparks of fire out of its nostrils, while the poor man stood stock still, spell-bound, until it seized upon him, and he has never been heard of since."

"Nothing more?" asked Glenn, lightly, and smiling.

"Good gracious! what more would you want? But there *was* more; for the very next day, when the people were looking at the island from a distance, and wondering what had been the fate of old Odell, another large bird came out. But this was like an eagle, and instead of going into the water, it flew up into the air, and kept going higher and higher, until it was no bigger than a sparrow, and soon vanished altogether! I declare we are too near the island now, Mr. Glenn; let us go back; we have gone far enough!" said Joe, beseechingly, his own tale having roused all the terrors which his nature was capable of harboring.

Glenn seemed to pay no attention to what his companion was saying, but strode onward directly towards the island.

"Mr. Glenn!" continued Joe, stepping ahead, and facing him by turning round. "Oh, sir! you don't certainly intend to venture any closer to that fatal spot?"

"Pshaw!" replied Glenn, pushing him aside, and continuing on. When they were opposite the island, Joe, whose alarm had almost deprived him of the power of motion, was now struck with horror as he beheld his master pause, and then descend to the ice, and walk deliberately to the haunted ground! When Glenn reached the bank, he turned to his pale and shivering companion, and motioned him to follow.

"Oh, Heaven! we'll never be seen any more!" cried Joe, between his chattering teeth.

"Come on, Joe! I'll take care of you," said Glenn, encouragingly, as his man hesitated in doubt when midway on the ice.

"The holy saints preserve me!" said Joe, gliding over, quaking with fear, and clinging to Glenn's hand.

They walked up a gentle ascent from the water's edge, whence Glenn expected to see nothing more than a surface of snow, and the dense growth of young timber incident to such a place. But what was his surprise on beholding, in the midst of the island, and obscured from view to the surrounding country by an almost impenetrable grove of young willows, a round chimney-top rising over a high circular granite wall! Nothing daunted, he continued his steps directly towards the mysterious dwelling, notwithstanding the protestations and prayers of Joe. When they drew near, a thin slightly coloured vapor could be distinguished ascending from the chimney, indicating that the tenement was certainly inhabited. When they reached the wall, they pursued their way round it until they found a small iron gate

"Rap there, Joe," said Glenn. Joe only turned his head, and looked at him in silence.

"Knock," continued Glenn.

"Oh!" exclaimed Joe, falling on his knees. "If ever you were prevailed on not to do any thing you were doing, let me this one time persuade you to leave this place."

"Knock!" repeated Glenn, emphatically. Joe struck the gate several blows with his knuckles, but so gently that he could not hear them himself. Glenn seemed to grow angry, and seizing his man's musket, was in the act of applying the end of it violently, when the gate flew open at one spring, and a hoary porter stood bowing and beckoning before him.

"Do not enter!" cried Joe, throwing his arms around Glenn.

"It is too late, now—you have knocked, and it is opened unto you—your mission must be accomplished before you turn back. Mine is not yet effected—I am the one who dared to face the magic swan—and like me, all who come hither must remain until it shall be the pleasure of the fire-wizard to release them," said the old attendant.

"Lead me to this fire-wizard!" said Glenn, firmly, stepping into the inclosure. When they entered, the gate closed after them without any apparent agency of the old hunter, and with such force that Joe sprang several feet forward.

"Oh, goodness! we are nothing but poor rats in the trap, now!" exclaimed he.

"I pledged myself for your safety, and will keep my word," said Glenn.

"But what will the wizard care about your veracity?" asked Joe.

"Follow!" said the old porter, leading the way towards the house. After passing several small buildings, Glenn found himself in a spacious area, over which were scattered various and strange implements, and divers nondescript machines. Some half dozen men were also observed, their sleeves rolled up, and intently plying the chisel, the file and other tools. These men cast a momentary and sullen glance at the visitors, like convicts in the penitentiary, and resumed their labours in silence. The party soon arrived at the door of the main building, when the old porter entered alone, and after remaining a few moments within, came forth and announced his readiness to conduct our hero into the presence of the fire-wizard. Glenn motioned him to lead on, and after following through a short hall, and turning into a large chamber, the mysterious lord of the island was confronted, reclining before them on a couch of furs. He appeared to be an emaciated and decrepit old man, his long white beard extending down to his breast; and when he motioned our hero to a seat, his hand seemed to tremble with feebleness. Yet there was something in his eye that indicated no ordinary spirit, and instantly impressed Glenn with the respect that he conceived to be due to superior genius; for notwithstanding all the miraculous things told of the fire-wizard, he rightly conjectured the personage before him to be nothing more than a human being, a recluse, perhaps, and, like himself, seeking in solitude the enjoyments which (for peculiar reasons) could not be found among mankind.

"What brings thee hither?" demanded the aged man, after a few minutes' silence, during which his brilliant eyes were closely fixed upon the composed features of Glenn.

"That which induced thee to seek such a solitary abode," replied our hero.

"Have you no fears?" continued the old man.

"None!" replied Glenn, firmly.

"Give me your hand!" exclaimed the old man; "you are the only being that ever confronted the fire-wizard without feeling terror—and for those who know not fear there is no danger. Instead of a menial, or a victim, I will make you my companion."

"Thank him, Mr. Glenn," whispered Joe, "and perhaps he won't hurt us."

"I am seeking amusement," said Glenn; "and as long as I am pleased, it matters not with whom or where shall be my abode. But the moment I desire it, I will go hence."

The fire-wizard motioned the attendant to withdraw, who instantly obeyed, leading Joe out at the same time, the poor fellow evincing great reluctance to be separated from Glenn.

"Before exhibiting to you the mysterious objects which have acquired for me the name of magician," said the old man, "I will briefly give you my history. I was, in youth, what they termed an idle dreamer—ever on the alert for new discoveries—and was more laughed at than encouraged in my pursuit of rare inventions. More than fifty years ago I ascertained that steam might be made to propel machinery. I attempted to explain the principles of this discovery to my fellow-men, and to convince them of the vast benefits that might result from it. I was not heeded —nay, I was insulted by their indifference—and made a solemn vow that its advantages should never be reaped through my instrumentality. In secret I constructed a small steamboat, and having placed on board such materials as might be required, and secured the assistance of a requisite number of artisans, I came hither, resolved to prosocute my experiments to my own satisfaction in solitude, where the taunts of skeptics could not reach me. Follow, and you shall behold what has been the result of my unrestrained researches." The old man arose, and conducted our hero across the yard to a curtained shelter on one side of the inclosure.

"La! if that ain't its foot!" exclaimed Joe, who joined our hero, and observing a large foot, resembling in shape that of the swan, under the folds of the curtain, while the old wizard paused a moment before unveiling the curious object. It was as Joe surmised: when the canvas was withdrawn, an artificial swan of monstrous dimensions, though perfect in all its proportions, was revealed to their wondering gaze. A little beyond, another curtain was drawn aside, and an eagle, holding in its beak a bloody crown, and in its talons a silken banner of stripes and stars, stood before them in the attitude of springing up in the air.

"Which will you try first?" demanded the fire-wizard, while a proud smile played on his lips.

"Can *either* of them be set in motion by your art?" asked Glenn.

"Both!" exclaimed the wizard. "If you will tarry till the ice is gone, the swan shall rush through the strongest current as swiftly as the wild horse careers over the prairie; or the eagle shall even now dart beyond the clouds, and transport you in a few brief hours to where you will see the briny waves rolling against the distant Atlantic coast!"

Glenn was incredulous, and his unbelief was betrayed by a smile, in spite of his efforts to the contrary.

"Bring hither a lamp!" said the wizard to the attendant and was quickly obeyed.

"Oh, don't make him mad! He's going to do something now!" whispered Joe to Glenn. The wizard touched a spring; the breast of the eagle flew open, and within could be seen polished wheels and other portions of a complicated machinery. The old man next applied the blaze of the lamp to some spirits within, and in a very few minutes particles of steam could be seen to escape from the eagle's nostrils. The wizard touched another spring, and the enormous bird strode out and paused in the centre of the area.

"If you would behold the home of your youth, be it whithersoever it may, so that you name it, follow me, and your eyes shall gaze upon that spot within a few hours," said the sage, as the wings of the stupendous eagle slowly unfolded, and rising to a horizontal position, uncovered a transparency in the side of the chest, through which could be seen a gorgeous couch within, sufficiently ample to contain two men, and separate from the fire and machinery by a partition of isinglass.

"Come!" exclaimed the sage, opening the tortoise-shell door under the wing, and stepping into the couch.

"Don't do any such thing!" said Joe.

"Ha! ha! ha! Do you think it can fly, Joe?" remarked Glenn, laughing.

"It *will* fly!" said the old man, emphatically; "and I charge you to be prepared to ascend beyond the clouds, if you have the courage to occupy a portion of my couch."

"Though I cannot believe it will rise at your bidding," replied Glenn, "yet, should it do so, I must be permitted to regard you as being only flesh and blood, and as such, I do not hesitate to venture as much as another mortal will;" saying which, our hero seated himself beside the reputed fire-wizard.

The old man closed the door, and drawing forth a small compass (his companion intimating the course,) adjusted several screws within convenient reach, accordingly; he then pressed a small lever with his foot, and the wings, after quivering a moment, flapped quickly, and the great eagle darted almost perpendicularly up in the air, and was beyond the reach of vision in a very few seconds!

When a certain height was attained, the wizard turned the bird in the course indicated by his companion.

"What think you now of the fire-wizard!" demanded the sage, with an air of triumph.

"Still that he is a man—but a great one—and this, the perfection of his art, the greatest extent the Supreme Being has permitted the mind of a man to attain!" replied Glenn, gazing in admiration at the countries far below, which he was passing with the velocity of a hurricane.

"And still you fear not!" demanded the wizard.

"And shall not!" replied Glenn, "so long as your features are composed." The old man pressed his hand and smiled.

"Yonder is St. Louis!" cried Glenn, running his eye along the valley of the Missouri, down to its confluence with the Mississippi; and a short distance beyond, descried the town in question, though it did not seem to be larger than one ordinary mansion, with its garden and customary appendages.

"We are far above the reach of vision from the earth," said the wizard, bounding forward to endeavour to regulate a part of the machinery that had for some time attracted his attention, and which Glenn believed to be not altogether right, from the abrupt movement of his companion.

"How far above the earth are we?' asked Glenn.

"About twenty-five miles—but should this screw give way, it may be less very speedily!" exclaimed the old man, almost incoherently, and applying all his strength to the loosened screw to keep it in its place.

"Let me assist!" exclaimed Glenn, springing forward.

"It's gone!" cried the old man; "you have knocked it out! we are falling—crushed!"

"That's just what I expected," said Joe, addressing the fawn, which had been playing with the dogs, and at length ran against Glenn's chair so violently as to push it over

"Oh! oh! oh!" exclaimed Glenn.

"Goodness! Are you hurt?" asked Joe.

"Is it possible? Am I alive, and *here?*" exclaimed Glenn, staring wildly round, and doubting his own identity.

"Well, I never heard a dead man talk, as I know of,

before; and as to our being *here*, if your own eyes don't convince you, I'll swear to it," said Joe.

"Did I not go up to the island this morning?" inquired Glenn.

"No," said Joe.

"Did you not accompany me, and fire at the buck?" interrogated Glenn, resuming his seat.

"No—I'll be hanged if I did!" said Joe somewhat warmly.

"What have I been doing all day?"

"You've been sitting there fast asleep, and I presume you were dreaming."

"Thank Heaven, it was but a dream!" exclaimed Glenn, laughing.

"A dream?" responded Joe, sitting down on his stool, and soliciting Glenn to relate it to him. Glenn complied, and the narration was nothing more than what the incredulous reader has been staring at all this time. But we will make amends.

CHAPTER VI.

A hunt—A deer taken—The hounds—Joe makes a horrid discovery—Sneak—The exhumation.

"It beats all the dreams I ever heard," said Joe, feeling his right shoulder with his left hand.

"Why do you feel your shoulder, Joe?" asked Glenn, smilling, as he recollected the many times his man had suffered by the rebound of his musket, and diverted at the grave and thoughtful expression of his features.

"It *was* a dream, wasn't it?" asked Joe, with simplicity, still examining his shoulder.

"But you know there was no lead in the gun, and it could not rebound with much violence," said Glenn.

"I'll soon see all about it," exclaimed Joe, springing up and running to his gun. After a careful examination he returned to his stool beside the fire, and sat some minutes, with the musket lying across his knees, and his chin in his hand, plunged in profound meditation on the imaginary incidents which had just been related to him. Had the dream been an ordinary one, and he not an actor in it, it might have passed swiftly from his memory; but inasmuch as the conduct imputed to him was so natural, and the expressions he was made to utter so characteristic, he could not but regard it as a vision far more significant and important than a mere freak of the brain during a moment of slumber.

"What are you studying about?" interrogated Glenn.

"I can't understand it," replied Joe, shaking his head.

"Neither can the most renowned philosopher," said Glenn; "but you can tell whether your musket has been discharged."

"It hasn't been fired," said Joe. "But what distresses me is, that there should be only a charge of powder in it, just as you stated, and when I drew out the shot you were fast asleep. You must have heard me say I intended to do it."

"Not that I remember," said Glenn.

"Then there must be a wizard about, sure enough," said Joe, and he crossed himself.

"Suppose we take our guns and walk out in the direction mentioned?" said Glenn; "I feel the want of exercise after my sleep, and have some curiosity to test the accuracy of my dream by comparing the things described with the real objects on the island."

"Not for the world!" cried Joe, lifting both hands imploringly; "but I will gladly go anywhere else, just to see if the bushes are as beautiful as you thought they were, and if the deer can't run on the snow-crust as well as the dogs."

"Come on, then—I care not which course we go," said Glenn, taking up his gun, and leading the way out of the inclosure.

They pursued a westerly course until they reached nearly to the edge of the prairie, when they paused in the midst of a cluster of hazel bushes, to admire the beauty of the novel scene. The description had been perfect. Even Glenn surveyed the emblazonry of magic "frost work" around him with some misgivings as to the fallacy of his vision. Joe stared at his master with a curious and ludicrous expression.

"I am not dreaming now, Joe," said he, with a smile.

"How do you know?" asked Joe.

"That's well put," said Glenn; "indeed, I am very sure that many of my lively and spirited friends in Philadelphia and New York, could they but see me, would swear that I have been dreaming every day for the last three months. However, I have not now the same reverence for the sylvan gods I was so much inclined to worship in my last sleep; and, moreover, I am the first to see the deer this time. Yonder it stands. It is not a buck, though; capture it as soon as you please."

"Where is it?" exclaimed Joe, his superstition vanishing as he anticipated some sport; and, gliding quickly to Glenn's side, he beheld, under the branches of a low scrubby oak tree, the head and ears of a large doe. It was intently watching our pedestrians, and stood motionless in the ambush, on which it vainly relied to obscure it from the eyes of an enemy.

"You must not fire," said Glenn, placing his hand on the shoulder of Joe. Joe lowered his musket reluctantly, and turning his eyes to his master, seemed inclined to relapse into the belief that all was not right and natural in their proceedings.

"Now go to it," said Glenn, gently taking the gun from Joe.

"I'd rather not," said Joe.

"Why? A doe cannot hurt you—it has no horns."

"I don't fear it—I'm only afraid it will run away," said Joe, eager to secure the prize.

"Try it, at all events; if it should run very fast, I think I shall be able to arrest its career with the gun," said Glenn, who prepared to fire, provided the deer was likely to escape the clutches of Joe.

"Here goes!" cried Joe, leaping through the small bushes towards the covert. The deer moved not until Joe reached within a few feet of it, when, making a mighty spring, it bounded over the head of its assailant, and its sharp feet running through the icy surface of the snow, penetrated so far down, from the force of its weight, that it was unable to escape. It now lay quite still, with its large blue eyes turned imploringly to its foe. Joe seized it by the hind feet, and exultingly exclaimed that the prize was safely his own. The trembling and unresisting animal appeared to be as perfectly submissive as a sheep in the hands of the shearer.

"You have it, sure enough!" said Glenn, coming up and viewing the scene with interest.

"Lash me if I haven't!" said Joe, much excited. "Have you got any sort of a string about you?"

"No."

"Please cut down a hickory withe, and peel the bark off for me, while I hold its legs."

Glenn drew out his hunting knife, but paused when in the act of executing his man's request, and turning, with a smile playing upon his lip, said—

"Perhaps, Joe, this is but another dream; and if so, it is folly to give ourselves any unnecessary trouble."

"Lash me if it ain't reality!" replied Joe, as the deer at length began to struggle violently.

Extricating its feet from his grasp, the doe bestowed a well directed kick on its foe's head, which tumbled him over on his back. The animal then sprang up, but aware there was no chance of escape by running, faced about and plied its bony head so furiously against Joe's breast and sides that he was forced to scamper away with all possible expedition.

"Has it bruised you, Joe? If so, this is certainly no dream," remarked Glenn.

"Oh, goodness! I'm battered almost to a jelly. I'll take my oath there's no dreaming about this. Let me go after Ringwood and Jowler."

"It would be too cruel to let the hounds tear the poor thing," said Glenn; "but after you have bound its feet together, you may bring out one of the horses and a sled, and convey it home unhurt."

"The horses can't go in this deep snow," said Joe.

"True, I forgot that. Take your musket and shoot it," said Glenn, turning away, not wishing to witness the death of the deer.

"I d rather take him prisoner," said Joe, lowering his

musket after taking a long aim. "I can drag it on the sled myself."

"Then go for it," said Glenn; "and you may bring the hounds along; I will exercise them a little after that fox which keeps such a chattering in the next grove. But first let us secure the deer."

Joe charged upon the doe once more, and when it aimed another blow at him, he threw himself under its body, and the animal falling over on its side, the combined efforts of the men sufficed to bind its feet. Joe then went to the house for the hounds and the sled, and Glenn leant against the oak, awaiting his return. It was not long before the hounds arrived, which was soon succeeded by the approach of Joe with the sled. Ringwood and Jowler evinced palpable signs of delight on beholding the bound captive, but their training was so perfect that they showed no disposition to molest it without the orders of their master. One word from Glenn, and the deer would have been instantly torn in pieces; but it was exempt from danger as long as that word was withheld.

Joe soon came up, and in a very few minutes the doe was laid upon the sled. When he was in the act of starting homewards with his novel burden, the hounds, contrary to their usual practice, refused to accompany Glenn to the thicket north of their position, where the fox was still heard, and strangely seemed inclined to run in a contrary direction. And what was equally remarkable, while snuffing the air towards the south, they gave utterance to repeated fierce growls. Joe was utterly astonished, and Glenn was fast losing the equanimity of his temper.

"There's something more than common down there; see how Ringwood bristles up on the back," said Joe.

"Run there with the hounds, and see what it is," said Glenn.

"And I'll take my musket, too," said Joe, striding in the direction indicated, with the hounds at his heels and his musket on his shoulder.

When he reached a narrow rivulet about one hundred paces distant, that gradually widened and deepened until it formed the valley in which the ferry-house was situated a half mile below, he paused and suffered the hounds to lead the way. They ran a short distance up the ravine and halted at the edge of a small thicket, and commenced barking very fiercely as they scented the air under the bushes.

"I'll bet it's another bear," said Joe, putting a fresh priming in the pan of his musket, and proceeding after the hounds. "If it is a bear, ought I to fool with him by myself?" said he, pausing at the edge of the thicket. "I might get my other ear boxed," he continued, "and it's not such a pleasant thing to be knocked down by the heavy fist of a big black bear. If I don't trouble him, he'll be sure to let me alone. What if I call the dogs off, and go back? But what tale can I manufacture to tell Mr. Glenn? Pshaw! What should I fear, with such a musket as this in my hand? I can't help it. I really believe I *am* a little touched with cowardice! I'm sorry for it, but I can't help it. It was born with me, and it's not my fault. Confound it! I *will* screw up courage enough to see what it is, anyhow." Saying this, he strode forward desperately, and urging the hounds onward, followed closely in the rear in a stooping posture, under the hazel bushes.

In a very few moments Joe reached the head of the ravine, but to his astonishment and no little satisfaction, he beheld nothing but a shelving rock, from under which a spring of clear smoking water flowed, and a large bank of snow which had drifted around it, but through which the gurgling stream had forced its way. Yet the mystery was not solved. Ringwood and Jowler continued to growl and yelp still more furiously, running round the embankment of snow repeatedly, and ever and anon snuffing its icy surface.

"Whip me if I can figure out this," said Joe; "what in the world do the dogs keep sticking their noses in that snow for? There can't be a bear in it, surely. I've a notion to shoot into it. No I won't. I'll do this, though," and drawing out his long knife he thrust it up to the handle in the place which seemed the most to attract the hounds.

"Freeze me if it hasn't gone into something besides the snow!" exclaimed he, conscious that the steel had penetrated some firm substance below the frozen snow-crust. "What the deuce is it?" he continued, pulling out the knife and examining it. "Ha! blood, by jingo!" he cried, springing up; "but it can't be a living bear, or it would have moved; and if it had moved, the stab would have killed it. I *won't* be afraid!" said he, again plunging his knife into it. "It don't move yet—it must be dead—why, it's frozen. Pshaw! any thing would freeze here, in less than an hour. I'll soon see what it is." Saying this, he knelt down on the embankment, and commenced digging the snow away with all his might. The dogs crouched down beside him, growling and whining alternately, and otherwise exhibiting symptoms of restlessness and distress.

"Be still, poor Ringwood, I'm coming to him; I see something dark, but there's no hair on it. Ugh! hallo! Oh goodness! St. Peter! Ugh! ugh! ugh!" cried he, springing up, his face as pale as the snow, his hair standing upright, his chin fallen, and his eyes almost straining out of their sockets. Without taking his gun, or putting on his hat, he ran through the bushes like a frightened antelope, leaping over ditches like a fox-chaser, tearing through opposing grape vines, and not pausing until his course was suddenly arrested by Glenn, who seized him by the skirt of the coat, and hurled him on his back beside the sled on which the deer was bound.

"What is the matter?" demanded Glenn.

Joe panted painfully, and was unable to answer.

"What ails you, I say?" repeated Glenn in a loud voice.

"Peter"—panted Joe.

"Do you mean the pony?"

"St. Peter!" ejaculated Joe.

"Well, what of St. Peter?"

"Oh, let me be off!" cried he, endeavouring to scramble to his feet. But he was most effectually prevented. For no sooner had he turned over on his hands and knees, than Glenn leaped astride of him.

"Now, if you *will* go, you shall carry me on your back, and I will pelt the secret out of you with my heels, as we travel!"

"Just let me get in the house and fasten the door, and I will tell you every word," said Joe imploringly.

"Tell me now, or you shall remain in the snow all day long!" said Glenn, with a hand grasping each side of Joe's neck.

"Oh, what shall I do? I can't speak!" yelled Joe, crying outright, the large tear-drops falling from his nose and chin.

"You have not lost your voice, I should say, at all events," replied Glenn, somewhat touched with pity at his man's unequivocal distress, though he could scarce restrain his laughter when he viewed his grotesque posture. "What has become of your musket and hat?" he added.

"I left them both there," said Joe, gradually becoming composed under the weight of his master.

"Where?" asked Glenn.

"At the cave-spring."

"Well, what made you leave them there?"

"Just get off my back and I'll tell you. I'm getting over it now; I'm going to be mad instead of frightened," said Joe, with real composure.

"Get up, then; but I won't trust you yet. You must still suffer me to hold your collar," said Glenn.

"If you go to the cave-spring you will see a sight!"

"What kind of a sight?"

"Such a sight as I never dreamed of before!"

"Then it has been nothing but a dream *this time*, after all your foolery?"

"No, I'll be shot if there was any dreaming about it," replied Joe; and he related every thing up to the horrid discovery which caused him to retreat so precipitately, and then paused, as if dreading to revert to the subject.

"What did you find there? Was it any thing that could injure you?"

"No," said Joe, shaking his head solemnly.

"Why did you run, then?" demanded Glenn, impatiently.

"The truth is, I don't know myself, now I reflect about it. But I'd rather not tell what I saw just yet. I was pretty considerably alarmed, wasn't I?"

"Ridiculous! I will not be trifled with in this manner Tell me instantly what you saw!" said Glenn, his vexation and anger overcoming his usual indulgent nature.

"I'll tell you now—it was a——Didn't you see them bushes move?" asked Joe, staring wildly at a clump of sumach bushes a few paces distant.

"What was it you saw at the cave-spring!" shouted Glenn, his face turning red.

"I—I"—responded Joe, his eyes still fixed on the bushes. "It was a——Ugh!"—cried he, starting, as he beheld the little thicket open, and a tall man rise up, holding in his hand a bunch of dead muskrats.

"Dod speak on—I want to hear what it was—I've been laying here all this time waiting to know what great thing it was that skeered you so much. I never laughed so in all my life as I did when he got a-straddle of you. I was coming up to the sled, when I saw you streaking it through the vines and briers, and then I squatted down awhile to see what would turn up next."

"Ha! ha! ha! is it you, Sneak? I thought you was an Indian! Come on, I'll tell now. *It was a man's moccasin!*" said Joe, in a low, mysterious tone.

"And you ran in that manner from an old moccasin!" said Glenn, reproachfully.

"But there was a *foot* in it!" continued Joe.

"A *he* man's foot?" inquired Sneak, quickly turning to Joe.

"How could I tell whether it was a he man's foot, or a female woman's, as you call them?" replied Joe.

"Are you sure it was a human being's foot?" demanded Glenn.

"Well, I never saw any other animal but a man wear a buckskin moccasin!" replied Joe.

"An Irishman can't tell any thing right, nohow you can fix it," said Sneak.

"They can't tell how you make wooden nutmegs," retorted Joe.

'Come," said Glenn, "we will go and examine for ourselves."

The party set off in a brisk walk, and soon reached the scene of Joe's alarm. Sure enough, there was the moccasin, and a man's foot in it!

"It's somebody, after all," said Sneak, giving the frozen foot a kick.

"Ain't you ashamed to do that?" said Joe, knitting his brows.

"He's nothing more than a stone, now. Why didn't he holler when you stuck your knife into him?" replied Sneak.

"Dig him up, that we may see who he is," said Glenn.

"I'd rather not touch him," said Joe.

"You're a fool!" said Sneak. "Stand off, and let me

at him—I'll soon see who he is." Sneak threw down his muskrats, and with his spear and knife soon extricated the body, which he handled as unceremoniously as he would have done a log of wood. "Dod rot your skin!" he exclaimed, when he brushed the snow from the man's face. He then threw down the body with great violence.

"Oh don't!" cried Joe, while the cold chills ran up his back.

"Who is it?" asked Glenn.

"It's that copper-snake, traitor, skunk, water-dog, lizard-hawk, horned frog ——"

"Who do you mean?" interrupted Glenn.

"*Posin*, the maliverous rascal who collogued with the Injins to murder us all! I'm glad he got his dose—and if he was alive now, I'd make him swaller at least two foot of my spear," said Sneak.

"'Twas me—I killed him—look at the buck-shot holes in his back!" exclaimed Joe, now recovering from his excitement and affright.

"Yes, and you're a nice chap, ain't you, to run like flugins from a dead man that you killed yourself!" said Sneak.

"How did I know that I killed him?" retorted Joe.

"Any fool might know he was dead," replied Sneak.

"I'll pay you for this, some of these times," said Joe.

"How shall we bury him?" asked Glenn.

"That can be done real easy," said Sneak, taking hold of the dead man's leg and dragging him along on the snow like a sled.

"What are you going to do with him?" demanded Glenn.

"I'm a going to cut a hole in the ice on the river, and push him under," said Sneak.

"You shall do no such thing!" said Glenn, firmly; "he must be buried in the earth."

"Just as you say," said Sneak, submissively, throwing down the leg.

"Run home and bring the spades, Joe," said Glenn, "and call for the ferrymen to assist us."

"And I'll take the sled along and leave it in the yard," said Joe, starting in the direction of the deer and calling the hounds after him.

"Let the hounds remain," said Glenn. "I am resolved to have my fox-hunt." Joe soon disappeared.

"If you want to hunt, you can go on; Roughgrove and me will bury this robber," said Sneak.

"Be it so," said Glenn; "but remember that you are not to put him in the river, nor must you commit any indecent outrage upon his person. Let his body return to the earth—his soul is already in the hands of Him who created it."

'That's as true as gospel," said Sneak; "and I would rather be froze in this snow than to have his hot berth in the t'other world. I don't feel a bit mad at him now—he's paying for his black dagiverous conduct hard enough by this time, I'll be bound. I say, Mr. Glenn, it'll be rather late when we get through with this job—will there be any vacant room at your fireside to-night?"

"Certainly, and something to eat—you will be welcome, provided you don't quarrel too much with Joe," replied Glenn.

"Oh, Joe and me understand each other—the more we quarrel the more we love one another. We'll never fight—do you mind that—for he's a coward for one thing, and I won't corner him too close, because he's broad-shouldered enough to *lick me*, if he was to take it into his head to fight."

Glenn called the hounds after him and set out in quest of the fox, and Sneak turned to the dead body and mused in silence.

CHAPTER VII.

Boone—The interment—Startling intelligence—Indians about—A skunk —Thrilling fears—Boone's device.

Ere long Joe was on his way back to tne cave-spring, with several spades on his shoulder, accompanied by Boone, (who had just crossed the river on a visit to Glenn,) and Roughgrove, with his two oarsmen.

"Is Glenn at the spring with Sneak?" asked Boone, in a very thoughtful and grave manner.

"Yes, sir, I left him there, and I now hear him with the hounds chasing a fox," replied Joe, in true native style.

"If he is with the hounds, he is certainly not at the spring," remarked Roughgrove.

"I meant that he was there, or *thereabouts*," replied Joe.

"Who found the dead man?" inquired Boone.

"I did—that is, when the dogs scented him—and it almost frightened me when I dug out his foot," said Joe.

"No doubt!" observed Boone.

The party now moved along in silence, still permitting Joe to lead the way, until they suddenly emerged from the thicket in the immediate vicinity of the spring, when an unexpected scene attracted their notice. Sneak was composedly seated on the body of the dead man, and very deliberately searching his pockets!

"Well! that beats all the mean actions I ever beheld before!" said Joe, pausing and staring indignantly at Sneak.

"You're a fool!" replied Sneak.

'What for? because I wouldn't rob the dead?" retorted Joe.

"Do you call this robbing the dead? Hain't this traitor stoled this lump of gold from the Injins?" said Sneak, displaying a rough piece of the precious metal about the size of a crow's egg.

"Is it gold?" asked Joe, with some anxiety.

"Sartainly it is," answered Sneak, handing it to him to be examined; "and what good could come of burying it agin? I'll leave it to Mr. Boone to say if I ain't right in taking it myself."

"Oh, any thing worth this much ought to be taken," said Joe, depositing the lump of gold in his pocket.

"See here, my chap," said Sneak, rising up and casting a furious glance at him, "if you don't mean to hand that out again, one or the t'other of us must be put in the ground with the traitorious Posin—and if it is to be you, it'll be a purty thing for it to be said that you brought a spade to bury yourself with."

"Didn't I find the body?" said Joe.

"But burn me if you found the gold," said Sneak.

"Shall I decide the matter?" interposed Roughgrove.

"I'm willing," said Sneak.

"And so am I," replied Joe.

"Then give it to me, and I'll cut it in two, and give a half to each of you," said Roughgrove.

The decision was final; and seizing the spades, Joe, Sneak, and the oarsmen began to prepare a resting-place for the dead body. Boone continued silent, with his eyes steadfastly gazing at the earth which the workmen began to throw up.

"Posin's done ferrying now," said Dan Rudder, one of the defunct's old companions in the service of Roughgrove.

"No he ain't," said Sneak, throwing up a spadeful of flint stones.

"I'll keep some of these for my musket," said Joe.

"Why ain't he?" demanded Dan.

"Because he's got to cross the river—the river—what do they call it?—the river Poles," said Sneak.

"Styx, you dunce," said Joe.

"Well, 'twas only a slip of the tongue—what's the difference between poles and sticks?"

"*You* never read any thing about it; you only heard somebody say so," said Joe, pausing to listen to the hounds that ever and anon yelped in the vicinity.

"If I didn't, I don't believe the man that wrote that book ever crossed, or even had a squint at the river himself," replied Sneak.

"Whereabouts is the river?" asked Dan.

"In the lower regions," said Joe, striking his spade against a hard substance.

"What's that you're scraping the dirt off of?" asked Sneak.

"Oh, my goodness!" cried Joe, leaping out of the grave.

"Let it remain!" said Boone, in a commanding tone, looking in and discovering a skull; "I once buried a friend here—he was shot down at my side by the Indians."

"Fill up the hole agin! Posin shan't lay on top of any of your friends!" exclaimed Sneak, likewise leaping out of the grave.

"It matters not—but do as you please," said Boone, turning away and marking the distressed yelping of the hounds, which indicated, from some unusual cause, that they did not enjoy the chase as much as was their wont.

"Split me if he shan't be buried somewhere else, if I have to dig the hole myself," said Sneak, filling up the grave.

"I'll stick by you, Sneak," said Dan.

"Dan and me 'll finish the job; all the rest of you may go off," said Sneak, releasing the rest of the party from any further participation in the depositing of the remains of Posin in the earth.

"Glenn does not yet understand Ringwood and Jowler," said Boone, still listening to the chase.

"I never heard the dogs bark that way before until to-day," said Joe; "only that night when we killed the buffalo."

"Something besides the buffalo caused them to do it then," replied Boone.

"Yes, indeed—they must have known the fire was coming—but the fire can't come now."

'Sneak," said Boone, "when you are done here, come to Mr. Glenn's house."

"I will, as soon as I go to my muskrat trap out at the lake and get my rifle."

"Be in a hurry," said Boone; and turning towards the chase, he uttered a "Ya-ho!" and instantly the hounds were hushed.

'Dod!" exclaimed Sneak, staring a moment at Boone, while his large eyes seemed to increase in size, and then rolling up his sleeves, he delved away with extraordinary dispatch.

In a very short space of time, Ringwood and Jowler rushed from the thicket, and leaping up against the breast of their old master, evinced a positive happiness in once more beholding him. They were soon followed by Glenn, who dashed briskly through the thicket to see who it was that caused his hounds to abandon him so unceremoniously. No sooner did he discover his aged friend than he ran forward and grasped his hand.

"I thought not of you, and yet I could think of no one else who might thus entice my noble hounds away. Return with me, and we will have the fox in a few minutes—he is now nearly exhausted," said Glenn.

"Molest him not," said Boone. "Did you not observe how reluctantly the hounds chased him?"

"I did; what was the cause of it?" asked Glenn.

"The breeze is tainted with the scent of Indians!" whispered Boone.

"Again thou art my preserver!" said Glenn, in a low tone.

"I came to give you intelligence that the Osages would probably be upon you in a few days," said Boone; "but I did not think they were really in the neighbourhood until I heard your unerring hounds. Col. Cooper, of my settlement, made an excursion southward some ten days ago to explore a region he had never visited; but observing a large war-party at a distance, coming hitherward, he retreated precipitately, and reached home this morning. Excessive fatigue and illness prevented him from accompanying me over the river; and what is worse, nearly every man in our settlement is at present more than a hundred miles up the river, trapping beaver. If we are attacked to-night, or even within a day or two, we have nothing to depend upon but our own force to defend ourselves."

"Should it be so, I doubt not we will be able to withstand them as successfully as we did before," said Glenn.

"Let us go with Roughgrove to his house, and take his daughter and his effects to your little fortress," said Boone, joining the old ferryman, whom a single word sufficed to apprize of the state of affairs.

"I must prepare for the worst, now," said Roughgrove; "they will never forget or forgive the part I acted on the night of their defeat."

Boone, Glenn, and Roughgrove proceeded down the valley, while Joe seemed disposed to loiter, undetermined what to engage in, having cast an occasional curious glance at Boone and his master when engaged in their low conversation, and rightly conjecturing that "something wrong was in the wind," as he expressed it.

"Why don't you go home?" asked Sneak, rolling the dead body into the grave, and dashing the mingled earth and snow remorselessly upon it.

"I'll go when I'm ready," replied Joe; "but I should like to know what all that whispering and nodding was about."

"I can tell you," said Dan; but his speech was suddenly arrested by a sign from Sneak.

"I wish you would tell me," continued Joe, manifesting no little uneasiness.

"Have you got a plenty to eat at your house?" asked Sneak.

"To be sure we have," said Joe; "now tell me what's in the wind."

"If I was to tell you, I bet you'd be frightened half to death," remarked Sneak, driving down a headstone, having filled up the grave.

"No! no—I—indeed but I wouldn't, though!" said Joe, trembling at every joint, the true cause, for the first time, occurring to him. "Ain't it Indians, Mr. Sneak?"

"Don't call me *Mister* agin, if you please. There are more moccasins than the one you found in these parts, that's all."

"I'll go home and tell Mr. Glenn!" said Joe, whirling round quickly.

"Dod rot your cowardly hide of you!" said Sneak, staring at him contemptuously; "now don't you *know* he knowed it before you did?"

"Yes—but I was going home to tell him that some bullets must be run—that's what I meant."

"Don't you think he knows that as well as you do?" continued Sneak.

"But I—I *must* go!" exclaimed Joe, starting in a half run, with the hounds (which had been forgotten by their master) following at his heels.

"Let me have the hounds, to go after my gun—the red skins might waylay me, if I go alone, in spite of all my cunning woodcraft," said Sneak.

"Go back!" cried Joe, to the hounds. They instantly obeyed, and the next moment Joe was scampering homeward with all the speed of which his legs were capable.

When he reached the house, his fears were by no means allayed on beholding the most valuable articles of Roughgrove's dwelling already removed thither, and the ferryman himself, his daughter, Boone and Glenn, assembled in consultation within the inclosure. Joe closed the gate hurriedly after him, and bolted it on the inside.

"Why did you shut the gate? Open it again," said Glenn.

"Ain't we besieged again? ain't the Indians all around

us, ready to rush in and take our scalps?" said Joe, obeying the command reluctantly.

"They will not trouble us before night," said Roughgrove.

"No, we need not fear them before night," remarked Boone, whose continued thoughtful aspect impressed Glenn with the belief that he apprehended more than the usual horrors of Indian warfare during the impending attack.

"They will burn father's house, but that is nothing compared to what I fear will be his own fate!" murmured Mary, dejectedly.

"We can soon build him another," said Glenn, moved by the evident distress of the pale girl; "and I. am very sure that my little stone castle will suffice to preserve not only your father and yourself, but all who take shelter in it, from personal injury. So, cheer up, Mary."

"Oh, I will not complain; it pained me most when I first heard they were coming once more; I will soon be calm again, and just as composed when they are shooting at us, as I was the other time. But *you* will be in a great deal more danger than you were that night. Yet Boone is with us again—he *must* save us," said Mary.

"Why do you think there will be more danger, Mary?" asked Glenn.

"Yes, why do you think so?" interposed Joe, much interested in the reply.

"Because the snow is so deep and so firm, they will leap over the palisade, if there be a great many of them," replied Mary. Glenn felt a chill shoot through his breast, for this fact had not before occurred to him.

"Oh, goodness!—let us all go to work and shovel it away on the outside," cried Joe, running about in quest of the spades. "Oh, St. Peter!" he continued, "the spades are out at the cave-spring!"

"Run and bring them," said Glenn.

"Never—not for the world! They'd take my scalp to a certainty before I could get back again," replied Joe, trembling all over.

"There is no danger yet," said Roughgrove, the deep snow having occurred to him at the first announcement of the threatened attack, and produced many painful fears in his breast, which caused a sadness to rest upon his time worn features; "but," he continued, "it would not be in our power to remove the snow in two whole days, and a few hours only are left us to prepare for the worst."

"Let them come within the inclosure," said Glenn, "and even then they cannot harm us. The walls of my house are made of stone, and so is the ceiling; they can only burn the roof—I do not think they can harm our persons. We have food enough to last for months, and there is no likelihood of the siege lasting a single week."

"I'll make sure of the deer," muttered Joe; and before any one could interpose, he struck off the head of the doe with an axe, as it still lay bound upon the sled. And he was brandishing the reeking steel over the neck of the fawn, that stood by, looking on innocently, when a cry from Mary arrested the blow.

"If you injure a hair of Mary's gift," said Glenn, in anger, "you shall suffer as severe a fate yourself."

"Pardon me," said Joe to Mary; "I was excited—I didn't hardly know what I was doing. I thought as we were going to be pent up by the Indians, for goodness only knows how long, that we'd better provide enough food to keep from starving. I love the fawn as well as you do, and Mr. Glenn loves it because you gave it to him; but its natural to prefer our own lives to the lives of dumb animals."

"I forgive you," said Mary, playing with the silken ears of the pet.

"Say no more about it," said Glenn; "but as you are so anxious to be well provided with comforts, if we are besieged, there is one thing I had forgotten, that is absolutely necessary for our existence, which you can procure."

"What is it? Be quick, for we havn't a moment to lose," said Joe.

"Water," replied Glenn.

"That's a fact—but—its way off at the spring, by the ferry," said Joe, disliking the idea of exposing himself without the inclosure.

"True, yet it must be had. If you can get it nearer to us, you are at liberty to do so," said Glenn.

"Here comes Sneak," said Mary; "he will assist you."

Sneak readily agreed to the proposition, and he and Joe set out, each with a large bucket, while the rest of the party, with the exception of Boone (who desired to be left alone,) retired within the house.

When Sneak and Joe were filling their buckets at the spring the second time, the hounds (which attended them at Joe's special request) commenced barking.

"What's that?" cried Joe, dashing his bucket, water and all, in Sneak's lap, and running ten or fifteen feet up the hill.

"Dod rot your cowardly heart!" exclaimed Sneak, rising up and shaking the cold water from his clothes; "if I don't pay you for this, I wish I may be shot!"

"I thought it was the Indians," said Joe, still staring at the small thicket of briers, where the hounds were yet growling and bounding about in a singular manner.

"I'll see what it is and then pay you for this ducking," said Sneak, walking briskly to the edge of the thicket, while the water trickled down over his moccasins.

"What is it?" cried Joe, leaping farther up the ascent with great trepidation, as he saw the hounds run out of the bushes as if pursued, and even Sneak retreating a few paces. But what seemed very unaccountable was a *smile* on Sneak's elongated features.

"What in the world can it be?" repeated Joe.

"Ha! ha! ha! if that ain't a purty thing to skeer a full-grown man into fits!" said Sneak, retreating yet farther from the thicket.

"What makes *you* back out, then?" inquired Joe. The hounds now ran to the men, and the next moment a small animal, not larger than a rabbit, of a dark colour, with long white stripes from the nose to the tail, made its appearance, and moved slowly toward the spring. Sneak ran up the hill beyond the position occupied by Joe, maintaining all the time a most provoking smile.

"Who's scared into fits now, I should like to know?" retorted Joe.

"I wish I had my gun," said Sneak.

"Hang me, if I'm afraid of that little thing," said Joe. Still the hounds ran round, yelping, but never venturing within thirty feet of the animal.

"I'll be whipped if I understand all this!" said Joe, in utter astonishment, looking at Sneak, and then at the hounds.

"Why don't you *run?*" cried Sneak, as the animal continued to advance.

"I believe you're making fun of me," said Joe; "that little thing can't hurt anybody. Its a pretty little pet, and I've a notion to catch it."

"What are you talking about? You know you're afraid of it," said Sneak, tauntingly.

"I'll show you," said Joe, springing upon the animal. The polecat (for such it was) gave its assailant a taste of its quality in a twinkling. Joe grasped his nose with both hands and wheeled away with all possible expedition, while the animal pursued its course towards the river.

"My goodness, I've got it all over my coat!" exclaimed Joe, rolling on the snow in agony.

"Didn't I say I'd pay you for spilling the cold water on me?" cried Sneak, in a convulsion of laughter.

"Why didn't you tell me, *you rascal?*" cried Joe, flushed in the face, and forgetting the Indians in his increasing anger.

"Oh, I'll laugh myself sore—ha! ha! ha!" continued Sneak, sitting down on the snow, and laughing obstreperously.

"You long, lopsided scoundrel, you. My Irish blood is up now," said Joe, rushing towards Sneak with a resolution to fight.

"I'll be whipt if you tech me with them hands," said Sneak, running away.

"Oh, what shall I do?" cried Joe, sinking down, his rage suddenly subdued by his sickening condition.

"If you'll say all's square betwixt us, I'll tell you what to do. If you don't do something right quick, they won't let you sleep in the house for a month."

"Well. Now tell me quick!"

"Pull off your coat before it soaks through."

"I didn't think of that," said Joe, obeying with alacrity, and shivering in the cold air.

"Now twist a stick into it, so you can carry it up to the house, without touching it with your hands, that is, if none of it got on 'em," continued Sneak.

"There ain't a bit anywhere else but on the shoulder of my coat,' said Joe, acting according to Sneak's instructions. Filling their buckets, they at length started towards the house, Joe holding a bucket in one hand, and a long pole, on which dangled his coat, in the other. When they entered, the company involuntarily started; and Glenn, losing all control over his temper, hurled a book at his man's head, and commanded him not to venture in his presence again until he could by some means dispense with his horrid odor.

"Foller me," said Sneak, leading the way to the stable, and taking with him one of the spades he had brought in from the burial; "now," he continued, when they were with the horses, "dig a hole at this end of the stall, and bury your coat. If you hadn't took it in the house, like a dunce, they'd never 'ave known any thing about it."

"Oh, my goodness! I'm sick!" said Joe, urging the spade in the earth with his foot, and betraying unequivocal signs of indisposition. However, the garment was soon covered up, and the annoyance abated.

But no sooner was Joe well out of this difficulty, than the dread of the tomahawk and scalping knife returned in greater force than ever.

Boone remained taciturn, his clear, eagle-eye scanning the palisade, and the direction from which the savages would be most likely to come.

Joe approached the renowned pioneer for the purpose of asking his opinion respecting the chances of escaping with life from the expected struggle, but was deterred by his serious and commanding glance. But soon a singular change came over his stern features, and as sudden as strange. His countenance assumed an air of triumph, and a half-formed smile played upon his lip. His meditations had doubtless resulted in the resolution to adopt some decisive course, which, in his opinion, would insure the safety of the little garrison. His brow had been watched by the inmates of the house, and, hailing the change with joy, they came forth to ascertain more certainly their fate.

"How much powder have you, my young friend?" asked Boone.

"Five kegs," answered Glenn, promptly.

"Then we are safe!" said Boone, in a pleasant and affable manner, which imparted confidence to the whole party.

"I thought—I almost *knew* that we were safe, with *you* among us," said Mary, playing with Boone's hand.

"But you must not venture out of the house as much as you did before, my lass, when arrows begin to fly," replied Boone, kissing the maiden's forehead.

"But I'll mould your bullets, and get supper for you," said Mary.

"That's a good child," said Roughgrove; "go in, now, and set about your task."

Mary bowed to her father, and glided away. The men then clustered round Boone, to hear the plan that was to avail them in their present difficulty.

"In times of peril," said Boone, "my knowledge of the Indian character has always served me. I first reflect what I would do were I myself a savage; and, in taking measures to provide against the things which I imagine would be done by myself, I have never yet been disappointed. The Indians will not rashly rush upon us, and expose themselves to our bullets, as they storm the palisade. Had they the resolution to do this, not one of us would escape alive, for they would tear down the house. It is a very large war party, and they could begin at the top and before morning remove every stone. But they shall not touch one of them ——"

"I'm so glad!" ejaculated Joe.

"Hush your jaw!" said Sneak.

"They will be divided into two parties," continued Boone; "one party will attack us from the west with their arrows, keeping at a respectful distance from our guns, while the other will force a passage to the palisade from the east without being seen, for they will come under the snow! We must instantly plant a keg of powder, on the outside of the inclosure, and blow them up when they come. Joe, bring out a keg of powder, and also the fishing rods I saw in the house. The latter must be joined together, and a communication opened through them. They must be filled with powder and one end placed in the keg, while the other reaches the inclosure, passing through an auger hole. You all understand now what is to be done—let us go to work—we have no time to spare."

It was not long before every thing was executed according to the directions of Boone, and at nightfall each man was stationed at a loophole, with gun in hand, awaiting the coming of the savages.

CHAPTER VIII.

Night—Sagacity of the hounds—Reflection—The sneaking savages—Joe's disaster—The approach of the foe under the snow—The silent watch.

THE night was beautiful. The moon sailed through a cloudless sky, and the north wind, which had whistled loudly among the branches of the trees in the valley at the close of day, was hushed, and a perfect calm pervaded the scene.

"What're you leaving your post for?" asked Sneak, as Joe suddenly abandoned his watch on the west side of the inclosure, and tripped across to Roughgrove.

"Mr. Roughgrove—Mr. Roughgrove," said Joe, in a low tone.

"Well, what do you want with me?" responded the old ferryman.

"I wanted to tell you that your two oarsmen are forgotten, and to ask you if we hadn't better call to them to come up here, where they'll be out of danger?"

"They are *not* forgotten," said Roughgrove; "I sent them over the river to procure assistance, if possible."

"Thank you. I'm glad they're out of danger. I couldn't rest till I found out something about them," said Joe, retiring; but instead of resuming his watch, he slipped into the house.

"He's at his old tricks agin," said Sneak, when he observed him stealthily enter the door. "Come out, I say!" he continued, in a loud voice.

"What is the matter?" interrogated Glenn, from his station on the north.

"Why, that feller's crept into the house agin,' replied Sneak.

"Well, but he's come out again," said Joe, reappearing, and walking reluctantly to his loophole.

"What did you go in for?" demanded Glenn.

"I just wanted to tell Miss Mary that the two oarsmen that helped us to bury Posin were gone over the river, and were safe."

"Did she ask for this information?" inquired Glenn.

"No, not exactly," responded Joe; "but I thought if I was uneasy about the young men myself, that she, being more delicate than a man, must be considerably distressed."

"A mere subterfuge! See that you do not leave your post in future, under any circumstances, without permission to do so."

"I won't," replied Joe, peering through his loophole.

Matters remained quiet for a great length of time, and Glenn began to hope that even Boone had been mistaken. But Boone himself had no doubts upon the subject. Yet he seemed far more affable and cheerful than he did before the plan of resistance was formed in his mind. Occasionally he would walk round from post to post, and after scanning the aspect without, direct the sentinels to observe closely certain points, trees or bushes, where he thought the enemy might first be seen. He never hinted once that there was a possibility of escaping an attack, and the little party felt that the only alternative was to watch with diligence and act with vigor and resolution when assailed.

"Do you think they are now in this immediate neighbourhood?" inquired Glenn.

"They are not far off, I imagine," replied Boone; and calling the hounds from the stable, he continued, "I can show you in which quarter they are." The hounds well understood their old master. At his bidding they snuffed the air, and whining in a peculiar manner, with their heads turned towards the west, the vicinity of the savages was not only made manifest, but their location positively pointed out.

"I was not aware, before, of the inestimable value of your gift," said Glenn, gazing at the hounds, and completely convinced that their conduct was an unerring indication of the presence of the foe.

"Eh! Ringwood!" exclaimed Boone, observing that his favorite hound now pointed his nose in a northern direction and uttered a low growl. "Indeed!" he continued, "they have got in motion since we have been observing the hounds. I was not mistaken. Even while we were speaking they divided their strength. One party is even now moving round to the east, and at a given signal the other will attack us on the west, precisely as I predicted. See! Ringwood turns gradually."

"And you think the greatest danger is to be apprehended from those on the east?" said Glenn.

"Yes," said Boone, "for the others cannot approach near enough to do much injury without exposing themselves to great peril."

"But how can you ascertain that they will cut a passage under the snow, and the precise direction in which they will come?"

"Because," said Boone, "we are situated near the cliff on the east, to the summit of which they can climb, without being exposed to our fire, and thence it is likewise the shortest distance they can find to cut a passage to us under the snow. Mark Ringwood!" he continued, as the hound having made a semicircle from the point first noticed, became at length stationary, and crouching down on the earth, (where the snow had been cleared away at Boone's post,) growled more angrily than before, but so low he could not have been heard twenty paces distant.

"This is strange—very strange," said Glenn.

A sound resembling the cry of an owl was heard in the direction of the cliff. It was answered on the west apparently by the shrill howl of a wolf.

"The signal!" said Boone. "Now let us be on the alert,' he continued, "and I think we will surprise *them*, both on and under the snow. Let no one fire without first consulting me, even should they venture within the range of your guns."

The party resumed their respective stations, and once more not a sound of any description was heard for a considerable length of time. Roughgrove was at the side of Boone, and the other three men were posted as before described. The hounds had been sent back to their lair in the stable. Not a motion, animate or inanimate, save the occasional shooting of the stars in the begemmed firmament, could be observed.

While Glenn rested upon his gun, attracted ever and anon by the twinkling host above, a throng of unwonted memories crowded upon him. He thought of his guileless youth; the uncontaminated days of enjoyment ere he had mingled with the designing and heartless associates who strove to entice him from the path of virtue; of the hopes of budding manhood; of ambitious schemes to win a name by great and honourable deeds; of parents, kindred, home; of *her*, who had been the angel of all his dreams of paradise below: and then he contemplated his present condition, and notwithstanding his resolution was unabated, yet in spite of all his struggles, a tear bedewed his cheek. He felt that his fate was hard, but he *knew* that his course was proper, and he resolved to fulfil his vow. But with his sadness, gloomy forebodings, and deep and unusual thoughts obtruded. In the scene of death and carnage that was about to ensue, it occurred to him more than once that it might be his lot to fall. This was a painful thought. He was brave in conflict, and would not have hesitated to rush reckless into the midst of danger; but he was calm now, and the thought of death was appalling. He would have preferred to die on a nobler field, if he were to fall in battle. He did not wish to die in his *youth*, to be cut off, without accomplishing the many ends he had so often meditated, and without reaping a few of the sweets of life as the reward of his voluntary sacrifice. He also desired to appear once more in the busy and detracting world, to vindicate the character that might have been unjustly aspersed, to reward the true friendship of those whose confidence had never been shaken, and to rebuke, perhaps forgive, the enemies who had recklessly pursued him. But another, and yet a more stirring and important thought obtruded upon his reflections. It was one he had never seriously considered before, and it now operated upon him with irresistible power. It was a thought of things *beyond* the grave. The stillness of midnight, the million stars above him, the blue eternal expanse through which they were distributed --the repose of the invisible winds, that late had howled around him—the never-ceasing flow of the ice-bound stream before him, and the continual change of hill and valley—now desolate, and clothed in frosty vestments, and anon teeming with verdure and variegated beauty—constrained him to acknowledge in the secret portals of his breast that there was a great, ever-existing Creator. He then called to mind the many impressive lessons of a pious mother, which he had subsequently disregarded. He remembered the things she had read to him in the book of books—the words of prayer she taught him to utter every eve, ere he closed his eyes in slumber—and he *now* repeated that humble petition with all the fervency of a chastened spirit. He felt truly convinced of the fallacy of setting the heart and the affections altogether on the things of this world, where mortals are only permitted to abide but a brief space; and a hearty repentance of past errors, and a firm resolve to obey the requisitions of the Omnipotent in future, were in that hour conceived and engraven indelibly upon his heart.

"Mr. Boone—Mr. Boone—Mr. Boone!" cried Joe, softly.

"Dod! don't make sich a fuss," said Sneak.

"Be silent," whispered Boone, gliding to Joe, and gazing out on the snow, where he beheld about twenty savages standing erect and motionless, not eighty paces distant.

"I came within an ace of shooting," said Joe, "before I thought of what you had said. I pulled the trigger with all my might before I remembered that you said I musn't shoot till you told me, but as good luck would have it, my musket wasn't cocked." Boone went to each of the other loopholes, and after scrutinizing every side very closely, he directed Sneak and Glenn to abandon their posts and join him at Joe's stand, for the purpose of discharging a deadly volley at the unsuspecting foe.

"Does it not seem cruel to spill blood in this manner?" whispered Glenn, when he viewed the statue-like forms of the unconscious Indians.

"Had you witnessed the barbarous deeds that *I* have seen *them* perform—had you beheld the innocent babe ruthlessly butchered—your children—your friends maimed, tomahawked, scalped, *burned* before your eyes—could you know the hellish horrors they are *now* meditating—you would not entertain much pity for them," said Boone, in a low tone, evidently moved by terrible memories, the precise nature of which the one addressed could not understand But Glenn's scruples vanished, and as a matter of necessity he determined to submit without reserve to the guidance of his experienced friend.

"I should like to know how them yaller rascals got up here so close without being eyed sooner," said Sneak to Joe.

"That's what's been puzzling me, ever since I first saw them," said Joe, in scarce audible tones.

"Split me if you havn't been asleep," said Sneak.

"No indeed I havn't," said Joe. "I'll declare," he continued, looking out, "I never should have thought of *that.* I see now, well enough, how they got there without my seeing them. They've got a great big ball of snow, half as high as a man's head, and they've been rolling it all the time, and creeping along behind it. They're all standing before it now, and just as I looked one moved his leg, and then I saw what it was. This beats the old boy himself. It's a mercy they didn't come all the way and shoot me in the eye!"

"Hush!" said Boone. "They must have heard something, or supposed they did, or else your neglect would have been fatal to you ere this. They are now waiting to ascertain whether they were mistaken or not. Move not, and speak no more, until I order you."

"I won't," said Joe, still gazing at the erect dark forms.

"See how many there is—can't you count 'em?" said Sneak, in a whisper, leaning against Joe, and slyly taking a cartridge from his belt, slipped it in the muzzle of the musket which was standing against the palisade.

"What 're you doing with my gun?" asked Joe, in a very low tone, as he happened to turn his head and see Sneak take his hand away from the muzzle of the musket.

"Nothing—I was only feeling the size of the bore. It's big enough to kick down a cow."

"What are you tittering about? you think it's a going to kick me again, but you're mistaken—it ain't got two loads in this time."

"Didn't Mr. Boone jest tell you to keep quiet?" said Sneak.

"Don't you speak—then I won't," responded Joe.

The moon had not yet reached the meridian, and the dark shadow of the house reaching to the palisade on the west, prevented the Indians from observing the movements of the whites through the many slight apertures in the inclosure, but through which the besieged party could easily observe them.

After a long pause, during which neither party had uttered a word or betrayed animation by the least movement, Glenn felt the weight of a hand laid gently on his shoulder, and turning beheld Mary at his side. Without a motion of the lips, she placed in his hand some bullets she had moulded, and then passing on to the other men, gave each a like quantity.

"Retire, now, my lass," said Boone; and when she returned to the house, he continued, addressing Glenn—"If they do not move one way or the other very soon, we will give them a broadside where they are."

"And we could do execution at this distance," observed Glenn.

"I'd be dead sure to kill one, I know I would," said Sneak.

"Let me see if I could take aim," said Joe, deliberately pointing his musket through the loophole. The musket had inadvertently been cocked, and left in that condition, and no sooner did Joe's finger gently press upon the trigger, than it went off, making an astounding report, and veiling the whole party in an immense cloud of smoke.

"Who did that?" cried Boone, stamping with vexation

"Was that you, Joe?" demanded Glenn.

Joe made no answer.

"Oh, dod! my mouth's smashed all to pieces!" said Sneak, crawling up from a prostrate position, caused by the rebound of the musket, for he was looking over Joe's shoulder when the gun went off.

"Where's Joe?" inquired Glenn, pushing Sneak aside.

"He's dead, I guess—I believe the gun's busted," said Sneak.

"Now, sir! why did you fire?" cried Glenn, somewhat passionately, stumbling against Joe, and seizing him by the collar. No answer was made, for poor Joe's neck was limber enough, and he quite insensible.

"He's dead in yearnest, jest as I told you," said Sneak; "for that gun kicked him on the shoulder hard enough to kill a cow—and the hind side of his head struck my tooth hard enough to've kilt a horse. He's broke one of my upper fore-teeth smack in two."

"Every man to his post!" exclaimed Boone, as a shower of arrows rattled about the premises.

Sneak now occupied Joe's station, and the first glance in the direction of the savages sufficed to determine him how to act. Perhaps no one ever discharged a rifle more rapidly than he did. And a brisk and well-directed fire was kept up for some length of time, likewise, by the rest of the besieged.

It was, perhaps, a fortunate thing that Joe *did* fire without orders, and without any intention of doing so himself. It seemed that the savages had been meditating a desperate rush upon the fort, notwithstanding Boone's prediction; for no sooner did Joe fire, than they hastily retreated a short distance, scattering in every direction, and, without a moment's consultation, again appeared, advancing rapidly from every quarter. It was evident that this plan had been preconcerted among them; and had all fired, instead of Joe only, they might easily have scaled the palisade before the guns could have been reloaded. Neither had the besiegers been aware of the strength of the garrison. But they were soon made to understand that they had more than Glenn and his man to contend against. The discharges followed in such quick succession that they paused, when but a moment more would have placed them within the inclosure. But several of them being wounded, and Boone and Glenn still doing execution with their pistols, the discomfited enemy made a precipitate retreat. An occasional flight of arrows continued to assail the besieged, but they came from a great distance, for the Indians were not long in scampering beyond the range of the loopholes.

When Glenn could no longer see any of the dark forms of the enemy, he turned round to contemplate the sad condition of Joe. Joe was sitting up, with his hands locked round his knees.

"Well, split me in two!" cried Sneak, staring at his companion.

"What's the matter, Sneak?" asked Joe, with much simplicity.

"That's a purty question for *you* to ask, after laying there for dead this half-hour almost."

"Have the Indians been here?" asked Joe, staring round wildly.

"Hain't you heard us shooting?"

"My goodness," cried Joe, springing up. "Oh! am I wounded? say!" he continued, evincing the most lively alarm.

"Well, if this don't beat every thing that ever I saw in all my life, I wish I may be shot!" said Sneak.

"What is it?" asked Joe, his senses yet wandering.

"Jest feel the back of your head," said Sneak. Joe put his hand to the place indicated, and winced under the pain of the touch. He then looked at his hand, and beholding a quantity of clotted blood upon it, fell down suddenly on the snow.

"What's the matter now?" asked Glenn, who had seen his man sitting up, and came swiftly to him when he fell.

"I'm a dead man!" said Joe, mournfully.

"That's a lie!" said Sneak.

"What ails you, Joe?" asked Glenn, his tone much softened.

"I'm dying—oh! I'm shot through the head!"

"Don't believe him, Mr. Glenn—I'll be smashed if its any thing but my tooth," said Sneak.

"Oh—I'm dying!" continued Joe, pressing his hand against his head, while the pain and loss of blood actually produced a faintness, and his voice became very weak.

"Are you really much hurt?" continued Glenn, stooping down, and feeling his pulse.

"It's all over!" muttered Joe. "I'm going fast. Sancte Petre!—Pater noster, qui es in cœlis, sanctificeter nomen tuum; adveniat regnum tu——"

Here Joe's voice failed, and, falling into a syncope, Glenn and Sneak lifted him up and carried him into the house.

"Is he shot?" exclaimed Mary, instantly producing some lint and bandages which she had prepared in anticipation of such an event.

"I fear he has received a serious hurt," said Glenn, aiding Mary, who had proceeded at once to bind up the wound.

"I'll be split if he's shot!" said Sneak, going out and returning to his post. Glenn did likewise when he saw the first indications of returning consciousness in his man; and

Mary was left alone to restore and nurse poor Joe. But he could not have been in better hands.

"I should like to know something about them curious words the feller was speaking when he keeled over," said Sneak, as he looked out at the now quiet scene from the loophole, and mused over the events of the night. "I begin to believe that the feller's a going to die. I don't believe any man could talk so, if he wasn't dying."

"Have you seen any of them lately?" inquired Boone, coming to Sneak's post and running his eye along the horizon through the loophole.

"Not a one," replied Sneak, "except that feller laying out yander by the snowball."

"He's dead," said Boone, "and he is the only one that we are sure of having killed to-night. But many are wounded."

"And smash me if Joe didn't kill that one when his musket went off before he was ready," said Sneak.

"Yes, I saw him fall when Joe fired; and that accident was, after all, a fortunate thing for us," continued Boone.

"But I'm sorry for poor Joe," said Sneak.

"Pshaw!" said Boone; "he'll be well again in an hour."

"No, he's a gone chicken."

"Why do you think so?"

"Didn't he say so himself? and didn't he gabble out a whole parcel of purgatory talk? He's as sure gone as a stuck pig, I tell you," continued Sneak.

"He will eat as hearty a breakfast to-morrow morning as ever he did in his life," said Boone. "But let us attend to the business in hand. I hardly think we will be annoyed any more from this quarter, unless yonder dead Indian was a chief, and then it is more than probable they will try to steal him away. However, you may remain here. I, alone, can manage the others."

"Which others?" inquired Sneak.

"Those under the snow," replied Boone; "they are now within twenty paces of the palisade."

"You don't say so?" said Sneak, cocking his gun.

"I have been listening to them cutting through the snow a long while, and it will be a half hour yet before I spring the mine," said Boone.

"I hope it will kill 'em all!" said Sneak.

"Watch close, and perhaps *you* will kill one yet from this loophole," said Boone, returning to his post, where the slow-match was exposed through the palisade near the ground; and Roughgrove stood by, holding a pistol, charged with powder only, in readiness to fire the train when Boone should give the word of command.

Boone applied his ear to a crevice between the timbers near the earth, where the snow had been cleared away. After remaining in this position a few moments, he beckoned Glenn to him.

"Place your ear against this crevice," said Boone.

"It is not the Indians I hear, certainly!" remarked Glenn. The sounds resembled the ticking of a large clock, differing only in their greater rapidity than the strokes of seconds.

"Most certainly it is nothing else," replied Boone.

"But how do they produce such singular sounds? Is it the trampling of feet?" continued Glenn.

"It is the sound of many tomahawks cutting a passage," replied Boone.

"But what disposition do they make of the snow, when it is cut loose."

"A portion of them dig, while the rest convey the loose snow out and cast it down the cliff."

While the above conversation was going on, a colloquy of a different nature transpired within the house. Joe, after recovering from his second temporary insensibility, had sunk into a gentle doze, which lasted many minutes. Mary had bathed his face repeatedly with sundry restoratives, and likewise administered a cordial that she had brought from her father's house, which seemed to have a most astonishing somniferous effect. When the contents of the bottle were exhausted, she sat silently by, watching Joe's apparent slumber, and felt rejoiced that her patient promised a speedy recovery. Once, after she had been gazing at the fawn, (that had been suffered to occupy a place near the wall, where it was now coiled up and sleeping,) on turning her eyes towards the face of Joe, she imagined for a moment that she saw him close his eyelids quickly. But calling him softly and receiving no answer, she concluded it was a mere fancy, and again resigned herself to her lonely watch. When she had been sitting thus some minutes, watching him patiently, she observed his eyes open slowly, and quickly smack to again, when he found that she was looking at him. But a moment after, conscious that his wakefulness was discovered, he opened them boldly, and found himself possessed of a full recollection of all the incidents of the night up to his disaster.

"Have they whipt all the Indians away that were standing out on the snow, Miss Mary?"

"Yes, long ago—and none have been seen, but the one you killed, for some time," she replied, encouragingly.

"Did I kill one sure enough?" asked Joe, while his eyes sparkled exceedingly.

"Yes, indeed," replied she; "and I heard Mr. Boone say he was glad it happened, and that the accident was, after all, a fortunate thing for us."

"*Accident!*" iterated Joe; "who says it was an accident?"

"Wasn't it an accident?" asked the simple girl.

"No, indeed!" replied Joe. "But," he continued, "have they blown up the other Indians yet?"

"Not yet—but I heard them say they would do it very soon. They can be heard digging under the snow now, very plainly," said Mary.

"Indeed!" said Joe, with no little terror depicted in his face. "I wish you'd go and ask Mr. Boone if he thinks you'll be entirely safe, if you please, Miss Mary," said Joe beseechingly.

"I will," responded Mary, rising to depart.

"And if they ask how I am," continued Joe, "please say I am a great deal better, but too weak yet to go out."

Mary did his bidding; and when she returned, what was her astonishment to find her patient running briskly across the room from the cupboard, with a whole roasted prairie-hen in one hand, or at least the body of it, while he tore away the breast with his teeth, and some half dozen crackers in the other! In vain did he attempt to conceal them under the covering of his bed, into which he jumped as quickly as possible. Guilt was manifest in his averted look, his trembling hand, and his greasy mouth! Mary gazed in silent wonder. Joe cowered under her glance a few moments, until the irresistible flavour of the fowl overcame him, and then his jaws were again set in motion.

"I fear that eating will injure you," remarked Mary, at length.

"Never fear," replied Joe. "When a sick person has a good appetite, it's a sure sign he's getting better."

"If you think so you can eat as much as you please," said Mary; "and you needn't hide any thing from me."

Joe felt a degree of shame in being so palpably detected, but his appetite soon got the better of his scruples, and he gratified the demands of his stomach without reserve.

"But what did Mr. Boone say?" asked he, peeping out.

"He says he thinks there is no danger. But the Indians are now within a few feet of the palisade, and the explosion is about to take place."

CHAPTER IX.

Sneak skills a sow that "was not all a swine"—The breathless suspense —The match in readiness—Joe's cool demeanour—The match ignited —Explosion of the mine—Defeat of the savages—The captive—His liberation—The repose—The kitten—Morning.

"DON'T you think I know who you are, and what you're after?" said Sneak, as he observed a large black sow, or what seemed to be one, rambling about on the snow within a hundred paces of him. "If that ain't *my* sow! She's gone, that's dead sure; and if I don't pepper the red rascal that killed her I wish I may be split. That Indian 'll find I'm not such a fool as he took me for. Just wait till he gits close enough. I ain't to be deceived by my own sow's dead skin, with a great big Osage in it, nohow you can fix it." Sneak's conjecture was right. The Indian that Joe had killed was a chief, and the apparent sow was nothing more than a savage enveloped in a swine's skin. The Indian, after reconnoitering the premises with some deliberation, evidently believed that his stratagem was successful, and at length moved in the direction of his dead comrade, with the manifest intention of bearing the body away.

"I'll let you have it now!" said Sneak, firing his rifle, when the seeming sow began to drag the fallen chief from the field. The discharge took effect; the savage sprang upright and endeavoured to retreat in the manner that nature designed him to run; but he did not go more than a dozen paces before he sank down and expired.

"That's tit for tat, for killing my sow," said Sneak, gazing at his postrate foe.

"Come here, Sneak," said Boone, from the opposite side of the inclosure.

"There was but one, and I fixed him," said Sneak, when they asked him how many of the enemy were in view when he fired.

"They heard the gun," said Glenn, applying his ear to the chink, and remarking that the Indians had suddenly ceased to work under the snow.

"Be quiet," said Boone; "they will begin again in a minute or two."

"They're at it a'ready," said Sneak, a moment after, and very soon they were heard again, more distinctly than ever, cutting away with increased rapidity.

"Suppose the match does not burn?" observed Glenn, in tones betraying a fearful apprehension.

"In such an event," said Boone, "we must retreat into the house, and fasten the door without a moment's delay. But I do not much fear any such failure, for the dampness of the snow cannot so soon have penetrated through the dry reeds to the powder. Still we should be prepared—therefore, as there is no necessity that more than one of us should be here now, and as I am that man, withdraw, all of you, within the house, and remain there until your ears and eyes shall dictate what course to pursue." Boone's command was promptly obeyed, and when they reached the house and looked back, (the door was kept open,) they beheld the renowned pioneer standing erect, holding a pistol in his right hand (which he pointed at the cotton that connected with a train of powder running along a short plank to the reed that reached the buried keg,) while the moon, now midway in the heavens, "and beautifully bright," revealed the stern and determined expression of his pa-

brow and fixed lip. Thus he stood many minutes, and they seemed hours to those who gazed upon the breathless scene from the house. Not a sound was heard, save the rapid ticking of tomahawks under the snow outside of the inclosure, or the occasional hasty remark of those who were looking on in painful and thrilling suspense. Once Boone bowed his head and listened an instant to the operations of the savages, and when he rose erect again, the party looking on confidently expected he would fire the train. But the fatal moment had not yet arrived. Still he pointed the pistol at the combustible matter, and his eye glanced along the barrel; but he maintained a statue-like stillness, as if awaiting some preconcerted signal.

"Why don't he fire?" inquired Glenn, in a whisper.

"It is not quite time yet," responded Roughgrove.

"Dod! they'll crawl up presently, and jump over the fence," said Sneak.

"Oh, goodness! I wish he'd shoot!" said Joe, in low, sepulchral tones, his head thrust between Sneak's legs, whither he had crawled unobserved, and was now peering out at the scene.

"Who are you?" exclaimed Sneak, leaping away from Joe's bandaged head, which he did not recognize at the first glance.

"It's nobody but me," said Joe, turning his face upward, that his friend might not suppose him an enemy.

"Well, what are you doing here? I thought you was a dying."

"I'm a good deal better, but I'm too weak to do any thing yet," said Joe, in piteous tones, as he looked fearfully at Boone, and listened to the strokes of the Indians without, which became louder and louder.

"Stand back a little," said Boone to those in the doorway, "that I may enter when I fire—the match may burn more briskly than I anticipated."

A passage was opened for him to enter. He pulled the trigger—the pistol missed fire—he deliberately poured in fresh priming from his horn, and once more taking aim, the pistol was discharged, and, running to the house, and entering a little beyond the threshold, he paused, and turned to behold the realization of his hopes. The light combustible matter flashed up brightly, and the blaze ran along the ground a moment in the direction of the end of the reed: but at the instant when all expected to see the powder ignited, the flames seemed to die away, and the darkness which succeeded impressed them with the fear that the damp snow had, indeed, defeated their purpose.

"Split me if it *shan't* go off!" cried Sneak, running out with a torch in his hand, that he snatched from the fire-place. When he reached the trench that had been dug along the palisade, and in which the slow match was placed, he looked down but once, and dashing his fire-brand behind him, sprang back to the house, with all the celerity of which he was capable. "Dod!" said he, "it's burning yet, but we couldn't see it from here. It'll set the powder off in less than no time!"

"I trust it will!" said Boone, with much anxiety. And truly the crisis had arrived, beyond which, if it were delayed a single minute, it would be too late! The *voices* of the Indians could now be heard, and the sounds of the tomahawks had ceased. They were evidently on the eve of breaking through the icy barrier, and rushing upon their victims. Boone, with a composed but livid brow, placed his hand upon the ponderous door, for the purpose of retreating within, and barring out the ruthless assailants. The rest instinctively imitated his motions, but at the same time their eyes were yet riveted on the dimly burning match. A small flash was observed to illumine the trench—another and a larger one succeeded! The first train of powder was ignited—the Indians were bursting through the snow-crust with direful yells—the blaze ran quickly along the plank—it reached the end of the reed—a shrill whizzing sound succeeded—a sharp crash under the snow—and then all was involved in a tremendous chaotic explosion! An enormous circular cloud of smoke enveloped the scene for a moment, and then could be seen tomahawks, bows, and arrows, and even *savages*, sailing through the air. The moon was darkened for the space of several minutes, during which time immense quantities of snow poured down from above. The startling report seemed to rend both the earth and the heavens, and rumbled far up and down the valley of the Missouri, like the deep bellowing of a coruscant thunder-cloud, and died away in successive vibrations until it finally resembled the partially suppressed growling of an angry lion.

When the inmates of the house sallied forth, the scene was again quiet. After clearing away the enormous masses of snow from the palisade, they looked out from the inclosure through the loophole on the east, and all was stillness and silence. But the view was changed. Instead of the level and smooth surface, they now beheld a concave formation of snow, beginning at the earth, which was laid bare where the powder had been deposited, and widening, upward and outward, till the ring of the extreme angle reached a height of fifteen or twenty feet, and measured a circumference of fifty paces. But they did not discover a single dead body. On the contrary, they soon distinguished the sounds of the savages afar off, in fiendish and fearful yells, as they retreated in great precipitation.

"Dod! none of 'em's killed!" exclaimed Sneak, looking about in disappointment.

"Hang it all, how could they expect to kill any, without putting in some lead?" replied Joe, standing at his elbow, and evincing no symptoms of illness.

"What're *you* a doing out here? You'd better go in and finish dying," said Sneak.

"No, I thank you," said Joe; "my time's not come yet; and when it does come, I'll know what to do without your instructions. I'm well now—I never felt better in my life, only when I was eating."

"Go to the horses, Joe, and see if they have suffered any injury," said Glenn. "I don't believe a single Indian was killed by the explosion," he continued, addressing Boone.

"The snow may have preserved them," replied Boone; "and yet," he continued, "I am sure I saw some of them flying up in the air."

"I saw them too," said Glenn, "but I have known instances of the kind, when powder-mills have blown up, where men were thrown a considerable distance without being much injured."

"It answered our purpose, at all events," said Boone, "for now, no inducement whatever can ever bring them back"

"If I were sure of that," replied Glenn, "I would not regret the bloodless result of the explosion."

"You may rely upon it implicitly," said Boone; "for it was a surprise they can never understand, and they will attach to it some superstitious interpretation, which will most effectually prevent them from meditating another attack."

"Goodness gracious alive!" exclaimed Joe, nimbly springing past Boone and Glenn, and rushing into the house.

"What can be the matter with the fellow, now?" exclaimed Glenn.

"He was alarmed at something in the stable—see what it is, Sneak," said Boone.

"I've got you, have I? Dod! come out here!" exclaimed Sneak, when he had been in the stable a few moments.

"Who are you talking to?" asked Glenn.

"A venimirous Osage smutty-face!" said Sneak, stepping out of the stable door backwards, and dragging an Indian after him by the ears.

"What is that?" demanded Glenn, staring at the singular object before him. The question was by no means an unnatural one, for no being in the human shape ever seemed less like a man. The unresisting and bewildered savage looked wildly round, displaying a face as black as if he had just risen from the bottom of some infernal lake. His tattered buckskin garments had shared the same fate in the explosion; his eyebrows, and the hair of his head were singed and crisped; and, altogether he might easily have passed for one of Pluto's scullions. He did not make resistance when Sneak led him forth, seeming to anticipate nothing else than an instantaneous and cruel death, and was apparently resigned to his fate. He doubtless imagined that escape and longer life were utterly impossible, inasmuch as, to his comprehension, he was in the grasp of evil spirits. If he had asked himself *how* he came thither, it could not have occurred to him that any other means than the agency of a supernatural power threw him into the hands of the foe.

"I thought I saw one of them plunging through the air over the inclosure," said Boone, smiling.

"Hanged if I didn't think so too," said Joe, who had at length returned to gaze at the captive, when he ascertained that he was entirely meek and inoffensive.

"Have you got over your fright already?" asked Sneak.

"What fright?" demanded Joe, with affected surprise.

"Now, *can* you say you weren't skeered?"

"Ha! ha! ha! I believe you really thought I *was* frightened. Why, you dunce, you! I only ran in to to tell Miss Mary about it."

"Now go to bed. Don't speak to me agin to night," said Sneak, indignantly.

"I'll go and get something to eat," said Joe, retreating into the house.

"Tell Roughgrove to come here," said Boone, speaking to Joe.

"I will," said Joe, vanishing through the door.

When the old ferryman came out, Boone requested him (he being the most familiar with the Osage language,) to ask the savage by what means he was enabled to get inside of the inclosure. Roughgrove did his bidding; and the Indian replied that the Great Spirit *threw* him over the palisade, because he once killed a friend of Boone's at the cave-spring, and was now attempting to kill another.

"Why did you wish to kill us?" asked Roughgrove.

The Indian said it was because they thought Glenn had a great deal of money, many fire weapons, and powder and bullets, which they (the savages) wanted.

"Was it *right* to rob the white man of these things, and then to murder him?" continued Roughgrove.

The savage replied that the prophet (Raven) had told the war-party it was right. Besides, they came a long and painful journey to get (Glenn's) goods, and had suffered much with cold in digging under the snow; several of their party had been killed and wounded, and he thought they had a good right to every thing they could get.

"Did the whites ever go to your village to rob and murder?" inquired the old ferryman.

The Indian assumed a proud look, and replied that they *had*. He said that the buffalo, the bear, the deer, and the beaver—the eternal prairies and forests—the rivers, the air and the sky, all belonged to the red men. That the whites had not been *invited* to come among them, but they had intruded upon their lands, stolen their game, and killed their warriors. Yet, he said, the Indians did not hate Boone, and would not have attacked the premises that night, if they had known he was there.

"Why do they not hate Boone? He has killed more of them than any one else in this region," continued Roughgrove.

The Indian said that Boone was a great prophet, and was loved by the Great Spirit.

"Will the war-party return hither to-night?" asked Roughgrove.

The Indian answered in the negative; and added that they would never attack that place again, because the Great Spirit had fought against them.

Boone requested Roughgrove to ask what would be done with the false prophet who had advised them to make the attack.

The savage frowned fiercely, and replied that he would be tied to a tree, and shot through the heart a hundred times.

"What do you think we intend to do to *you?*" asked Roughgrove.

The savage said he would be skinned alive and put under the ice in the river, or burned to death by a slow fire. He said he was ready to die.

"I'll be shot if he isn't a spunky fellow!" said Sneak.

"Do you desire such a fate?" continued the old ferry man.

"The Indian looked at him with surprise, and answered without hesitation that he *did*—and then insisted upon being killed immediately.

"Would you attempt to injure the white man again if we were not to kill you?"

The Indian smiled, but made no answer.

"I am in earnest," continued Roughgrove, "and wish to know what you would do if we spared your life."

The Indian said such talk was only trifling, and again insisted upon being dispatched.

After a short consultation with Boone and Glenn, Roughgrove repeated his question.

The savage replied that he did not believe it possible for him to escape immediate death—but if he were not killed, he could never think of hurting any of those, who saved him, afterwards. Yet he stated very frankly that he would kill and rob any *other* pale-faces he might meet with.

"Let me blow his brains out," said Sneak, throwing his gun up to his shoulder. The Indian understood the movement, if not the words, and turning towards him, presented a full front, without quailing.

"He speaks the truth," said Boone; "he would never injure any of us himself, nor permit any of his tribe to do it, so far as his influence extended. Yet he will die rather than make a promise not to molest others. His word may be strictly relied upon. It is not fear that extorts the promise never to war against us—it would be his gratitude for sparing his life. Take down your gun, Sneak. Let us decide upon his fate. I am in favour of liberating him."

"And I," said Glenn.

"And I," said Roughgrove.

"I vote for killing him," said Sneak.

"Hanged if I don't, too," said Joe, who had been listening from the door.

"Spare him," said Mary, who came out, and saw what was passing.

"We have the majority, Mary," said Glenn; "and when innocence pleads, the generous hand is stayed."

Roughgrove motioned the savage to follow, and he led him to the gate. The prisoner did not understand what was to be done. He evidently supposed that his captors were about to slay him, and he looked up, as he thought, the last time, at the moon and the stars, and his lips moved in deep and silent adoration.

Roughgrove opened the gate, and the savage followed him out, composedly awaiting his fate. But seeing no indication of violence, and calling to mind the many wild joys of his roving youth, and the horrors of a sudden death, he spoke not, yet his brilliant eyes were dimmed for a moment with tears. His deep gaze seemed to implore mercy at the hands of his captors. He would not utter a petition that his life might be spared, yet his breast heaved to rove free again over the flowery prairies, to bathe in the clear waters of running streams, to inhale the balmy air of midsummer morning, to chase the panting deer upon the dizzy peak, and to hail once more the bright smiles of his timid bride in the forest-shadowed glen.

"Go! thou art free!" said Roughgrove.

The Indian stared in doubt, and looked reproachfully at the guns in the hands of his captors, as if he thought they were only mocking him with hopes of freedom, when it was their intention to shoot him down the moment he should think his life was truly spared.

"Go! we will not harm thee!" repeated Roughgrove.

"And take this," said Mary, placing some food in his yielding hand.

The Indian gazed upon the maiden's face. His features, by a magical transition, now beamed with confidence and hope. Mary was in tears—not tears of pity for his impending death, but a gush of generous emotion that his life was spared. The savage read her heart—he knew that the white woman never intercedes in vain, and that no victim falls when sanctified by her tears. He clasped her hand and pressed it to his lips; and then turning away in silence, set off in a stately and deliberate pace towards the west. He looked not back to see if a treacherous gun was pointed at him. He knew that the maiden had not trifled with him. He knew that she would not mock a dying man with bread. He neither looked back nor quickened his step. And so he vanished from view in the valley.

"Dod! he's gone! We ought to've had his sculp!" said Sneak, betraying serious mortification.

"We must give it up, though—we were in the minority," said Joe, satisfied with the decision.

"In the what?" asked Sneak.

"In the minority," said Joe.

"Let's go in the house and git something to eat," said Sneak.

"Hang me if I ain't willing to be with you there," said Joe.

The whole party entered the house to partake of a collation prepared by the dainty hands of Mary. Mary had frequently insisted upon serving them with refreshments during the night, but hitherto all her persuasions had been unavailing, for the dangers that beset them on every hand had banished all other thoughts than those of determined defensive operations.

He clasped her hand, and pressed it to his lips.—P. 120.

Boone was so certain that nothing farther was to be apprehended from the enemy, that he dispensed with the sentinels at the loopholes. He relied upon Ringwood and Jowler to guard them through the remainder of the night; and when a hearty meal was eaten he directed his gallant little band to enjoy their wonted repose.

Ere long Mary slumbered quietly beside her father, while Boone and Glenn occupied the remaining couch. Sneak was seated on a low stool, near the blazing fire, and Joe sat in Glenn's large arm chair, on the opposite side of the hearth. The fawn and the kitten were coiled close together in the centre of the room.

Save the grinding jaws of Sneak and Joe, a death-like silence reigned. Occasionally, when Sneak lifted his eyes from the pewter platter that lay upon his knees, and glanced at the bandages on his companion's head, his jaws would cease to move for a few moments, during which he gazed in astonishment at the ravenous propensity of the invalid. But not being inclined to converse or remonstrate, he endeavoured to get through with his supper with as much expedition as possible, that he might enjoy all the comforts of refreshing sleep. Yet he was often on the eve of picking a quarrel with Joe, when he suffered a sudden twinge from his broken tooth, while striving to tear the firmer portion of the venison from the bone. But when he reflected upon his peculiar participation in the occurrence which had caused him so justly to suffer, he repressed his rising anger and proceeded with his labour of eating.

Joe, on the other hand, discussed his savoury dish with unalloyed satisfaction; yet he, too, paused occasionally, and fixing his eyes upon the glaring fire, seemed plunged in the deepest thought. But he did not glance at his companion. At these brief intervals he was apparently reflecting upon the incidents of the night. One thing in particular puzzled him; he could not, for the life of him, conceive how his musket rebounded with such violence, when he was positively certain that he had put but one charge in it, and that only a moderate one. He was sometimes inclined to think the blow he received on the head was dealt by Sneak; but when he reflected it would be unnatural for one man to strike another with his *teeth*, and that Sneak had likewise sustained a serious injury at the same time, his conjectures were entirely at fault.

"What are you a thinking about so hard?" asked Sneak.

"I'm trying to think how I got that blow on the back of my head," said Joe, turning half abstractedly to Sneak.

"Yes, and I'd like to know how you come to mash my mouth so dod-rottedly," said Sneak, in well-affected ill nature.

"Hang it, Sneak, you know well enough that I wouldn't do such a thing on purpose, when I was obliged to almost knock out my own brains to do it," said Joe, apologetically.

"If I hadn't thought of that," replied Sneak, "I don't know but I should 've shot you through when I got up."

"And I should never have blamed you for it," said Joe, "if it had been done on purpose. Does it hurt you much now?"

"Don't you see how its bleeding?"

"That's gravy running out of your mouth, ain't it?"

"Yes, but its bloody a little," said Sneak, licking his lips.

"I shall have to sit up and sleep," said Joe; "for my head's so sore I can't lie down."

"I'm a going to lay my head on this stool and sleep; and I'm getting so drowsy I can't set much longer," said Sneak.

"And all 'll be square between us, about breaking your tooth, won't it?"

"Yes, I can't bear malice," said Sneak, shaking Joe's extended hand.

"Oh me!" said Joe, "I shan't be able to doze a bit, hardly, for trying to study out how the old musket came to kick me so."

"I've got a notion to tell you, jest to see if you'll sleep any better, then."

"Do you know?" asked Joe, quickly; "if you do, I'll thank you with all my heart to tell me?"

"Dod! if I don't!" said Sneak; "but all's square betwixt us?"

"Yes, if you're willing."

"Well, don't you remember when I told you to count

the Indians standing out there, I leant agin you to look over your shoulder? I stole a cartrich out of your shot-bag then, and slipt it in the muzzle of your musket. Don't you know it was leaning agin the post?"

Joe turned round and looked Sneak full in the face for several moments, without uttering a word.

"When it went off," continued Sneak, "it made the tremendousest crack I ever heard in all my life, except when the keg of powder busted."

"You confounded, blasted rascal you!" exclaimed Joe, doubling up his fists, and preparing to assault his friend.

"Now don't go to waking up the folks!" said Sneak.

"I'll be hanged if I hain't got a great notion to wear out the iron poker over your head!" continued Joe, his eyes gleaming with rage

"Look at my tooth," said Sneak, grinning in such manner that the remaining fragment of the member named could be distinctly seen. The ludicrous expression of his features was such as constrained Joe to smile, and his enmity vanished instantaneously.

"I believe you got the worst of the bargain, after all," said Joe, falling back in his chair and laughing quite heartily.

"You know," continued Sneak, "I didn't mean it to turn out as bad as it did. I jest thought it would kick you over in the snow, and not hurt you any, hardly."

"Well, let's say no more about it," said Joe; "but when you do any thing of that kind hereafter, pause and reflect on the consequences, and forbear."

"I'll keep my mouth out of the way next time," said Sneak; "and now, as all's square betwixt us, s'pose we agree about how we are to do with them dead Indians. S'pose we go halves with all the things they've got?"

"No, I'll be hanged if I do!" said Joe quickly. "The one I shot was a chief, and he's sure to have some gold about him."

"Yes, but you know you'd never a killed him if it hadn't been for me."

"But if it hadn't been for you I wouldn't have got hurt," replied Joe, reproachfully.

"Well, I don't care much about the chief—the one I killed maybe took all his silver and gold before I shot him.

Anyhow, I know I can find something out there in the snow where they were blowed up," said Sneak, arranging a buffalo robe on the hearth and lying down.

"And we must hereafter let each other alone, Sneak," said Joe, "for the fact is, we are both too much for one another in our tricks."

"I'm willing," replied Sneak, lazily, as his eyes gradually closed.

Joe placed his dish on the shelf over the fireplace, and folding his arms, and leaning back in his great chair, likewise closed his eyes.

But a few moments sufficed to place them both in the land of dreams. And now the silence was intense. Even the consuming logs of wood seemed to sink by degrees into huge livid coals, without emitting the least sparkling sound. The embers threw a dim glare over the scene, such as Queen Mab delights in when she leads her fairy train through the chambers of sleeping mortals. A sweet smile rested upon the lips of Mary. A loved form flitted athwart her visions. Roughgrove's features wore a grave but placid cast. Boone's face was as passionless and calm as if he were a stranger to terrific strife. Perils could now make no impression on him. There was sadness on the damp brow of Glenn, and a tear was stealing through the corner of his lids. A scene of woe, or the crush of cherished hopes, was passing before his entranced vision. Sneak, ever and anon grasped the empty air, and motioned his arm, as if in the midst of deadly conflict. And Joe, though his bruised face betrayed not his cast of thought, still evinced a participation in the ideal transactions of the night, by the frequent involuntary motions of his body, and repeated endeavours to avoid visionary dangers.

The kitten lay upon the soft neck of the fawn, and at intervals resumed its low, humming song, which had more than once been hushed in perfect repose. At a late hour, or rather an early one, just ere the first faint ray of morning appeared in the distant east, puss purred rather harshly on the silken ears of its companion, and its sharp claws producing a stinging sensation, the fawn shook its head violently, and threw its little bed-fellow rather rudely several feet away. The kitten, instead of being angry, fell into a merry mood, and began to frisk about in divers directions, first running under the bed, then springing upon some diminutive object on the floor as it would upon a mouse, and finally pricking again the ear of the fawn. The fawn then rose up, and creeping gently about the room, touched the cheeks or hands of the slumbering inmates with its velvet tongue, but so softly that none were awakened The kitten, no longer able to annoy its companion by its mischievous pranks, now paced up to the fire and commenced playing with a dangling string attached to Joe's moccasin. Once it jumped up with such force against his foot that he jerked it quickly several inches away. But this only diverted puss the more. Instead of being content with the palpable demonstration thus effected, it followed up the advantage gained by applying both its claws and teeth to the foot. While it confined its operations to the stout buckskin, but little impression was made; but when it came in contact with the ankle, which was only covered with a yarn stocking, the result was entirely different.

"Ugh! Confound the fire!" exclaimed Joe, giving a tremendous kick, which dashed puss most violently into Sneak's face.

"Hey! Dod! What is it?" cried Sneak, tearing the kitten (whose briery nails had penetrated the skin of his nose) away, and throwing it across the room. "I say! did you do that?" continued Sneak, wiping the blood from his nose with his sleeve, and addressing Joe, who kept his eyes fast closed, though almost bursting with suppressed laughter, and pretending to be steeped in earnest slumber. "I won't stand this!" said Sneak, smarting with his wounds, and striking the chair in which Joe sat with his foot. "Now," continued Sneak, "if you done that, jest say so, that's all."

"Did what?" asked Joe, opening his eyes suddenly.

"Why, throwed that ere pestiverous cat on me!" said Sneak.

"No. Goodness! is there a pole-cat in here?" exclaimed Joe, in such well-counterfeited tones of anxiety and alarm, that the real encounter occurring to Sneak, and his pain being now somewhat abated, he gave vent to a hearty fit of laughter, which awoke every person in the house,

CHAPTER X.

The lead removed—The wolves on the river—The wolf hunt—Gumfœtid—Joe's incredulity—His conviction—His surprise—His predicament—His narrow escape.

WHEN Sneak opened the door, the sun had risen and was shining brightly. In a moment the inmates of the house were stirring. The horses neighed in the stable for their accustomed food and water, and when Joe hastened to them, he embraced the neck of each, in testimony of his joy that they were once more saved from the hands of the Indians. The hounds pranced round Boone and Glenn, manifesting their delight in being relieved of the presence of the enemy. The gate was thrown open, and the scene of the explosion minutely examined. Fortunately the channel cut under the snow by the savages ran a few feet apart from the powder, or the whole of them must inevitably have perished. As it was, not a single one lost his life, though many were blown up in the air to a considerable height. Joe and Sneak found only a few spears, knives, and tomahawks, that had been abandoned by the savages; and then they repaired to the west side of the inclosure, where the two dead Indians were still lying. They had scarce commenced searching their victims for booty, when a solitary Indian was seen approaching from the upper valley.

"We hain't got our guns!" exclaimed Sneak, pulling out his knife.

"I'll get mine!" cried Joe, running away with all his might.

"What's the matter?" inquired Boone, smiling, who had also seen the approaching Indian, and was walking to where the dead savages lay, accompanied by Glenn and Roughgrove, when he met Joe running swiftly towards the house

They had scarce commenced searching their victims for booty, when a solitary Indian was seen approaching from the upper valley.—P. 126.

"Hang me, if the Indians ain't coming back again," replied Joe.

"There is but one, and he has a white flag," said Boone, who had discovered a small rag attached to a pole borne by the Indian.

"What can he want?" inquired Glenn.

"He wants permission to bury the dead," replied Roughgrove.

"He's the very rascal we let loose last night," said Sneak.

This was true. Although the singed savage had removed some of the black marks produced by the explosion, yet so many palpable traces of that event were still exhibited on his person, there could be no doubt of his identity.

The Indian came for the purpose mentioned by Roughgrove, and his request was granted. He made a sign to a comrade he had left some distance behind, who, in a very few minutes, was seen to approach in a hasty though timorous pace.

"Don't go to shooting out here!" exclaimed Sneak, hearing a clicking sound, and the next moment observing Joe pointing his musket through the loophole nearly in a line with the spot where he stood.

"Come in! come in! come in!" cried Joe.

"Put your gun away, and be silent," said Glenn.

"I'll be silent," replied Joe, "but I'd rather stand here and watch awhile. If they ain't going to hurt any of us, it'll do no harm; and if they *do* try to kill any of you, it may do some good."

When the second Indian arrived, he seized the body of the savage enveloped in the swine-skin, (knowing that permission to do so had been obtained by his comrade,) and bore him away with great expedition, manifesting no inclination whatever to tarry at a place which had been so fatal to his brethren. But the other had every confidence in the mercy of the whites, and lingered some length of time, gazing at the corpse before him, as if hesitating whether to bear it away.

"Why do you not take him up?" inquired Roughgrove.

The Indian said it was the false prophet Raven, and that he hardly deserved to be buried.

Sneak turned the dead Indian over, (he had been lying

on his face,) and he was instantly recognized by the whole party.

"I'm glad its him," said Sneak.

"I think we will have peace now," said Boone, "for Raven has ever been the most blood-thirsty chief of the tribe."

"Where is the war-party encamped? When do they return to their own country?" asked Roughgrove.

The Indian replied that they were encamped in a small grove on the border of the prairie, where they intended to bury their brothers, and then it was their intention to set out immediately for their villages. He added that one of their tribe, whom they had left at home, arrived that morning with intelligence that a war-party of Pawnees had invaded their territories, and it was necessary for them to hasten back with all possible dispatch to defend their wives and children.

Glenn asked Boone how the Indians managed to sleep in the cold prairie; and, Roughgrove repeating the inquiry to the savage, they were informed that the war-party carried with them a long but very light sled, in the shape of a canoe, to which was tied a rope made of buckskins, by which they pulled it along on the snow with great swiftness. This kept them warm with exercise through the day. A quantity of furs and buffalo skins were packed in the canoe that served to keep them warm at night.

"Mr. Roughgrove! Mr. Roughgrove!" cried Joe, from his loophole.

"What do you want with me?" responded the old man.

"Why, Miss Mary's gone down to your house to see if the Indians have been there, and they may be there now, perhaps."

"There's no danger now, you blockhead," replied Roughgrove.

"Keep your mouth shet!" said Sneak.

"Your mouth's mashed—recollect who did it," retorted Joe.

The savage at length lifted up the dead body, and set off at a brisk pace towards the prairie. The party then returned to the house and partook of a plenteous repast that had been provided by Mary.

When the breakfast was over, they repaired to the cliff,

to examine the place where the Indians had first penetrated the snow. They had commenced operations at the very brow of the cliff, on a shelving rock, to attain which, without being seen from the garrison, they must have crawled on their hands and knees a considerable distance. Below could be seen an immense heap of snow, which had been thrown down from the place of entrance, just as Boone had described.

"Jest look yander!" cried Sneak, pointing up the river. The scene was a remarkable one. They beheld a very small deer (the lightness of which enabled it to run on the snow that covered the ice with great fleetness, without breaking through the crust,) chased about on the river by a pack of wolves! These hungry animals had evidently been racing after it a great length of time, from the distressed appearance of the poor victim, and, having driven it upon the ice, they seemed resolved to prevent it from ever again entering the thickets. The plan they adopted was systematic, and worthy the imitation of biped hunters. They dispersed in various directions, and formed themselves in a circle of about a half mile in diameter, hemming the deer in on all sides, while only one or two of their number at a time chased it. Round and round it ran; and though its pursuers were left far in the rear, yet it remained entirely surrounded by the enemy. Occasionally, when a chasing wolf became exhausted, one of the guards (abandoning his post) would enter the ring, and, not being fatigued, was able to carry on the pursuit with redoubled vigour. Thus the chase was kept up with increasing fierceness by means of a succession of fresh wolves, until the poor deer finally sank down and surrendered its life. The voracious pack then rushed from their stations indiscriminately, and coming in contact immediately over their prey, a most frightful contest ensued among them. Horrific yells and screams could be heard by the men as they looked on from their distant position. At times the wolves were so closely jumbled together that nothing could be distinguished but one black, heaving, and echoing mass. But the struggle was soon over. In a very few moments they became quiet, and started off in a comparatively peaceful manner towards the island, whence their prize had been driven, in quest of others. When they abandoned the spot where their victim had fallen, not so much as a bone remained.

"That's making a clean business of it!" said Sneak.

"Its no such thing!" said Joe; "it's a nasty trick to swallow hide, bones, and bowels, in that manner."

"Its clean for wolves," said Sneak.

"Oh, may be you're part wolf," said Joe.

"Now, none of your gab, or I'll play some other trick on you, worse than that at the spring."

"You be hanged," retorted Joe; "I'll give you leave to do it when you get a chance the next time."

"It is a great pity that the deer are subject to such destruction," remarked Glenn.

"The wolves we saw are all on yonder island," said Boone, "and if you are disposed to have a hunt, I have no doubt we might kill some of them."

"We are entirely dependent upon the deer for animal food," said Roughgrove; "and if we could only surround that party of wolves as they did the deer, we might do the settlement much good serviee."

"I go in for it," said Sneak.

"I'd rather wait a day or two, till the Indians have gone clean off," said Joe.

"There is nothing to fear from them now," said Boone, "unless something they might steal should fall in their way. But it will not require an hour to rout the wolves on the little island."

"Then let us hasten and get our guns, and be upon them before they leave it," said Glenn.

They returned to the house, and were all soon equipped for the onslaught, except Joe, who made no preparation whatever.

"Get ready, Joe," said Glenn; "your redoubtable musket will do good service."

"I'd rather not," said Joe; "I'm hardly well enough to walk so far. I'll take care of Miss Mary. I wonder what's become of her? Mr. Roughgrove, Miss Mary hasn't come back yet!"

"Yes she has," replied the old ferryman; "I saw her bring this frozen flower up, while we were standing on the cliff, and she has only returned for the other pots. I hear her singing down the valley now," he added, after stepping to the gate and listening a moment.

"Have you any gum fetid?" asked Boone, addressing Glenn.

"I've got lots of it," interposed Joe, "that I brought along for the horses, because an old man at St. Louis told me they would never die so long as I kept a lump of it in the rack."

"What use do you make of it?" asked Glenn.

"The scent of it will at any time collect the wolves," said Boone, directing Joe to bring it along.

The party set out at a brisk pace, Joe with the rest, for it was necessary to station the men at as many points as possible. Boone, Roughgrove, and Glenn, when they reached the upper valley, descended to the river, while Sneak and Joe were directed to station themselves on the main-land opposite the upper and lower ends of the island. The party of three advanced towards the island on the ice, and Sneak and Joe pursued their way in a parallel direction through the narrow skirt of woods that bordered the range of bluffs.

Ere long the two on land descended from their high position and entered a densely-timbered bottom, the upper part of which (a half mile distant) was only separated from the island by a very narrow channel.

Here, for the first time that day, the thought that the island he was approaching was the haunted one of Glenn's dream occurred to Joe, and he paused suddenly.

"What are you stopping for?" asked Sneak.

"Because"—Joe hesitated, positively ashamed to tell the reason; and after a moment's reflection he was impressed with a thorough conviction that his apprehensions and scruples were ridiculous.

"Don't you hear me?" continued Sneak.

"I was thinking about going back for the dogs," said Joe.

"Yes, and they would be torn to bits in a little less than no time," said Sneak.

"Come on, then," said Joe, setting forward again, and dismissing all fears of the fire-wizard from his mind.

"Let me see how much asafœtida you've got," said Sneak, after they had walked a few moments in silence

"Here it is," said Joe, unwrapping a paper containing several ounces; "but hang me, if that ain't rather too strong a joke of Mr. Boone's about its collecting the wolves. I can't believe that."

"Did you ever hear of Mr. Boone's telling a lie?" asked Sneak.

"No, I never did, and that's a fact," said Joe; "but I'm afraid he's got into a scrape this time—Jingo! look yonder!" he continued, throwing his musket up to his face, and pointing it at a very large black wolf that stood in the path before them.

"Don't shoot! I put two loads in your gun," cried Sneak, hastily.

"Confound your long-necked gourd-head, I say!" said Joe, throwing down the muzzle of his musket in an instant, and the next moment the wolf disappeared among the tall bushes. "Why, hang me, if you didn't tell a lie!" continued Joe, running down his ramrod.

"Don't I know it?" replied Sneak. "I jest said so to keep you from shooting; becaise if you had shot, you'd 'ave skeered all the other wolves away, and we wouldn't 'ave killed any."

"It's well you didn't put in another cartridge," said Joe, "for I wish I may be smashed if I stand this kicking business any longer."

"Now, I guess you'll believe there's something in the asafœtida, after all! and the wolves 'll come all round you and won't go off for shooting at 'em, if you'll only rub it on the soles of your boots.

"I'll try it!" said Joe, suiting the action to the word, and then striding onward, and looking in every direction for the wolves.

"You'll have to tree, if they come too thick."

"Pshaw!" replied Joe, "you can't scare me in that way. I don't believe a hat full of it would make them stand and be shot at."

They were now opposite the island. Joe selected a position even with the upper end of it, and Sneak remained below. Boone, after stationing Roughgrove and Glenn to the best advantage, walked out to the main-land, and taking some of the gum fetid in Joe's possession, returned to the island; and, ere long, he, Roughgrove, and Glenn were heard discharging their guns with great rapidity, and the cries of the wolves attested that they were labouring with effect. But none of the beleaguered animals had yet retreated from the scene of destruction. On the contrary, several were seen to run across from the main-land and join those on the island. Presently Sneak commenced a brisk fire There seemed to be a whole army of wolves congregated in the vicinity. Joe at first laughed, and then became confused and puzzled. He anxiously desired to make the roar of his musket join the melée; but at times he thought the ravenous enemy rather too numerous for him to be in perfect safety. The firing on the island continued without abatement. Sneak's gun was likewise still heard at regular intervals, and what seemed an extraordinary matter to Joe was that Sneak should yell out something or other about the "asafœtida," and "moccasin tracks," after every discharge. Joe was not long idle. He soon saw a huge black wolf trotting along the little deer path he had just traversed, with its nose down to the ground. A moment after, another, and then a third, were seen pursuing the same course, some distance behind. Joe became uneasy. His first impulse was to scamper over to the island: but, when he thought of the jeers and jests that would ensue from Sneak, he resolved to stand his ground. When the foremost wolf had approached within thirty paces of him, he leveled his musket and fired. The wolf uttered a fierce howl and expired.

"Hang me, if I haven't floored you, any how," said he, exultingly, as he proceeded to reload his gun with as much expedition as possible. But the other wolves, so far from being alarmed at the fate of their comrade, seemed to quicken their pace towards the position of Joe. "Slash me, if there ain't too many of them!" ejaculated Joe, as he perceived several others, and all advancing upon him. "I'll settle your hash, by jing!" he continued, firing at the foremost one, which was not twenty paces distant. The leaden contents of the musket entered its breast, and it fell dead without a growl. Still the others advanced. Joe had no time to charge his gun again.

"I'll make tracks!" said he, starting toward the frozen channel that separated him from the island. But he had not gone ten paces before he discovered two enormous wolves approaching from *that* direction. "I'll cut dirt back again!" he continued, whirling suddenly around, and rushing back to his stand, where he stood not a moment, but sprang up in a tree, and after attaining a large limb that put out from the trunk, some fifteen feet above the snow, paused, and pantingly surveyed his assailants. There were now no less than twenty wolves in sight, and several were at the root of the tree yelping at him! "I'll be hanged if I half like this," said he. "Snap me, if I don't begin to believe that the asafœtida does charm them, after all. Confound Sneak! he's always getting me into some hobble or other! Now, if it wasn't for this tree, I'd be in a nice fix. Hang it! all the wolves in the world are broke loose to-day, surely—where the mischief could they all have come from? Just hear the men, how they are shooting! And they are killing the wild black dogs every crack—but still they won't back out! I'll blaze away at 'em again!" Saying this, he reloaded his musket as quickly as his peculiar position would allow, and, for the purpose of ridding himself as soon as possible of his disagreeable visitors, he poured in an additional charge of buckshot. "Now," he continued, "what if the gun should fly out of my hands? I'd be in a pretty condition then! I wouldn't mind the kick at all, if I was only on dry land—but if the gun should kick me over here, I'd tumble right down into their mouths! I wish I'd thought of that before I rammed down the wadding. I havn't got my screw along, or I might draw out the load again. I'll not shoot at all. I'll just watch till somebody comes and scares them away. Ugh! you black rascal! what 're you staring up here for?" he continued, looking down at the largest wolf, which was standing upright against the tree, and tearing the bark away furiously with his long teeth. The number of Joe's enemies continued to increase. There were now perhaps twenty under the tree. And still the firing on the island was kept up, though not so incessantly as at first, which inspired Joe with a hope that they would either kill all the wolves in their vicinity very soon or force them to join his flock under the tree, when the men would surely come to his relief. Sneak's fire abated somewhat, likewise, and Joe's reliance upon having their aid in a very short time caused his fears to subside in a great measure.

"If you're so crazy after asafœtida," said he, looking down at the fiercely staring animals again, "I'll give you a taste, just to see what you'll do." He took a small portion of the gum which he had retained, and rubbed it over a piece of paper that he found in his pocket. He then dropped the paper in their midst. They sprang upon it simultaneously, and in an instant it vanished, Joe knew not whither. "Hang me, if I couldn't pepper a half-dozen at a shot when they all rush up together so close, if I wasn't afraid of being kicked down. I'll be teetotally smashed if I don't fix and try it, any how!" said he, pulling out a strong leather string from his pocket, one end of which he attached firmly to a small limb of the tree, and the other he tied as tightly round the wrist of his left arm. He then pulled out his bandanna, and likewise made his musket fast to a bough. "Now, my snapping beauties," he continued, "I'm mistaken if I don't give you a dose of blue pills that 'll do your business in short order." Saying this, he tore off another piece of paper, and rubbing on the gum, dropped it down as near as possible to the spot where he wished the wolves to cluster together. No sooner did it fall than the whole gang sprang upon it, and he fired with precision in their midst. Joe did not look to see what execution was done. He was dangling in the air and whirling round and round at a rapid rate, like a malefactor suspended from the gallows, with the exception that his neck did not suffer, and he cried out most lustily for assistance. When the cloud of smoke that enveloped him cleared away a little, and he became better acquainted with his critical situation, his yells increased in rapidity and violence. His condition was truly perilous. The small bough to which he had attached himself had not sufficient strength to bear him up when his feet slipped from the larger one below, and it was now bent down a considerable distance, and that too in a divergent direction from his recent foothold, and unfortunately there was no limb of the tree of any strength within his reach. His legs hung within six feet of the surface of the snow. The discharge had killed four or five of the wolves, but, undismayed, the remainder assailed him the more furiously. The most active of them could easily spring as far up as his feet! Never was terror more strongly depicted in the human face than it was displayed in Joe's when he saw the whole pack rushing towards him! They sprang up with fearful snarls and yells. Joe yelled likewise, and doubled his knees up to his chin. They missed his feet by several inches, and were borne out fifteen or twenty feet to one side by the impetus of the leap. It was by a mighty effort that he thus avoided them, and no sooner had they passed under him than his legs again dangled downward. In a moment they whirled round and were again rushing at their victim. Once more Joe screamed, and drew up his legs while they passed under him. "Help! help! for God's sake!" cried he, when they whirled round again. His cry was heard. Several sharp reports resounded from the river bank, a few paces on the east. Three or four of the wolves howled and fell. The rest hesitated, their eyes glistening, and fixed on Joe's suspended boots. "Come quick! for Heaven's sake! I can't pull up my legs any more!" cried Joe. This was true, for his strength was fast failing. The guns were again discharged with deadly effect, and all but one of the largest of the wolves precipitately ran off, and disappeared among the bushes.

"Jerk up your leg! that feller's a going to take one of your feet along with him, if he kin!" cried Sneak. Joe saw the wolf charging upon him, but he was altogether unable to avoid it in the manner he had done before. It was now only a few feet distant, its mouth open, displaying a frightful set of teeth, and springing towards him. Finding it impossible to prevent a collision, Joe resolved to sell his foot as dearly as possible. As much as he was able, he bent up his knee-joints, and when his assailant came, he bestowed his heels upon his head with all his might. The wolf was stunned, and fell under the blow.

"Take that!" cried Sneak, running up and plunging his knife into the animal's side. The wolf groaned and died.

"Ha! ha! ha! you were born to be hanged," said Roughgrove, coming forward with Boone and Glenn, and laughing heartily.

"He has been hung," said Boone.

"And almost quartered," said Glenn.

They sprang up with fearful snarls and yells. Joe yelled likewise, and doubled his knees up to his chin.—P. 136.

"Oh, goodness! Jump up here, Sneak, and cut me loose," said Joe, beseechingly.

"There's no danger of you ever dying," said Sneak.

"Oh, please don't laugh at me, Sneak, but cut me down; that's a good fellow. The string is beginning to cut my wrist like fury!"

"How did you git in such a fix?" continued Sneak.

"Oh, hang it, Sneak, just get me out of the fix, and I'll tell you all about it."

"It's hung *now*—didn't you say 'hang it, Sneak?'" continued Sneak.

"Oh, come, now," continued Joe; "if you were in this way, don't you think I'd help you?"

"Cut him down, Sneak," said Boone; and in a twinkling Sneak was up in the tree, and the string was severed. Joe came down with great force, his feet foremost, and running through the snow-crust to a great depth.

"I wish some of you would help me out of this," said he, after struggling some time in vain to extricate himself.

"You'll want me to carry you home next, I s'pose," said Sneak, assisting him up. Joe made no reply; but as soon as he could cut the string away from his wrist, seized Sneak by the throat, hurled him on his back, and springing upon him, a violent struggle ensued for a few moments before they could be separated.

"What do you mean?" exclaimed Glenn, dragging Joe away from his prostrate victim.

"What did you do that for?" asked Sneak, rising up and brushing the snow from his head and face, his fall having broken the icy surface.

"You rascal, you! I'll show you what for!" cried Joe, endeavouring to get at him again.

"Joe!" said Glenn, "if you attempt any further violence, you shall not remain another day under my roof!"

"He boxed my ear like thunder!" said Sneak; "I didn't think the fellow had so much pluck in him! I like him better now than ever I did. Give us your paw, Joe." Joe shook hands with him reluctantly, and then wiped a flood of tears from his face.

"He told me to put some asafetida on my boots, and said I could then kill more wolves," said Joe; "and it came within an ace of making them kill me."

"It was very wrong to do so, Sneak," said Boone, "and the boxing you got for it was not amiss."

"I believe I think so myself," said Sneak. "But it did make him kill more wolves after all—jest look at 'em all around here!"

Joe soon recovered entirely from the effects of his swing, his fright, and his anger, and looked with something like satisfaction on his many trophies lying round him; and when he disengaged his musket from the bough of the tree, he regarded it with affection.

They moved homeward, entirely content with the result of the excursion. Boone explained the reason why so many of the wolves were congregated about the island. He stated that the vines and bushes on which the deer feed in the winter were abundant and nutritious in the low lands along the river, and that great numbers of them repaired thither at that season of the year. The wolves of course followed them, and having now destroyed all the large deer in the vicinity of the island, and the small ones being enabled to run on the snow-crust, they found it necessary to muster in the chase as great a number as possible, and thus prevent their prey from escaping to the prairies. He said that the wolves preferred the timber, being enabled to make more comfortable lairs and dens among the fallen trees than out in the cold prairies. But their guns had wrought a fearful destruction among them. Perhaps three-fourths of them fell.

The party soon reached Glenn's house. As they entered the inclosure, they were surprised to see Ringwood running wildly about, whining and snarling and tearing the snow to pieces with his teeth. Jowler was more composed, but a low, mournful whine issued continuously from his mouth.

"Dod! what's the dogs been after?" ejaculated Sneak.

"Go in, Joe, and ask Mary what it means," said Rough grove.

"I'd rather not—the house may be full of Indians," replied Joe, relapsing into his natural cowardice.

"Mary," said Roughgrove, approaching the door and calling affectionately. Receiving no reply, the old man entered and called again. A silence succeeded. Roughgrove reappeared a moment after, with a changed countenance. Boone gazed at his pale features, and asked the cause of his distress by a look, not a word.

"She's gone! gone! gone!" exclaimed Roughgrove, covering his face with both hands.

Boone made no answer, but turning his face in the direction of the southern valley, he called upon the name of Mary three times, in clear and loud tones. He listened for her reply, in a motionless attitude, several minutes. But no reply came. Now a change came over *his* features. It was a ferocity from which even the blood-thirsty savages would have fled in horror!

"My eternal curse upon them! They have seized her! I have been deceived! I will have vengeance!" said he, in a low, determined tone.

"Will they kill her, or keep her for a ransom?" inquired Glenn, in extreme and painful excitement.

"A ransom," said Boone; "but they shall pay the weight of the silver they demand in blood!"

"May Heaven guard her!" said Roughgrove, in piteous agony.

"Cheer up—we will get her again," said Boone; and then giving some hasty directions, preparations were made for pursuit.

CHAPTER XI.

Mary—Her meditations—Her capture—Her sad condition—Her mental sufferings—Her escape—Her recapture.

WHEN the men departed for the island in quest of the wolves, Mary was singing over her neglected flowers, at her father's house in the valley, and her clear ringing notes were distinctly heard by the whole party. After they were gone she continued her song, and lingered long over every faded leaf and withered blossom, with no thought of danger whatever, and none of pain, save the regret that her long cherished plants had been forgotten in the consternation of the previous day, and had fallen victims to the frost-king. But nothing had been touched by the savages. The domestic fowls clustered about her, and received their food from her hands as usual. The fawn was with her, and evinced the delight afforded by the occasional caress bestowed upon it, by frequently skipping sportively around her. Mary was happy. Her wants were few, and she knew not that there was such a thing as a malicious enemy in the world, save the wild savage. Her thoughts were as pure as the morning dew, and all her delights were the results of innocence. She had never harmed any one, and her guileless heart never conceived the possibility of suffering ill at the hands of others. She smiled when the beautiful fawn touched her hand with its velvet tongue, and a tear dimmed her eye for an instant when she looked upon her stricken rose.

While looking at one of the homely shelves in a corner of the deserted house, Mary accidentally espied a small volume of poems, the gift of Glenn, that had been neglected. She seized it eagerly, and after turning over the pages the fiftieth time, and humming over many of the songs, she paused suddenly, and lifting her eyes to the bright sunbeams that streamed through the window, long remained in a listless attitude. Something unusual had startled her simple meditations. At first a shade of painful concern seemed to pass across her brow, and then glancing quickly at the book she still held in her hand, a sweet smile animated her lips. But again and again, ever and anon, the abstracted gaze was repeated, and as often succeeded by the smile when her eyes fell upon the volume. Did her thoughts dwell upon the giver of that book? Undoubtedly. Did she love Glenn? This she knew not herself, but she would have died for him! She was ignorant of the terms courtship, love, and marriage. But nature had given her a heart abounding with noble and generous impulses.

At length she drew her shawl closely round her shoulders, and, closing the door of the hut, was in the act of returning up the hill, when she was startled by the furious and sudden barking of the hounds, which she had left confined in the inclosure on the cliff. She paused, and looked steadily in every direction, and was not able to discover, or even conjecture, what it was that had roused the hounds. Yet an undefinable fear seized upon her. The fawn at her side likewise partook of the agitation, for the hair stood upright on its back, and it often snuffed the air with great violence, producing, at each time, a shrill, unnatural sound.

Mary started briskly up the path, determined to shut herself up in Glenn's house until her father returned from the island. When she had proceeded about twenty paces, and was just passing a dense thicket of hazel that bordered the narrow path, she heard a slight rustling on the left, and the next moment she was clasped in the arms of a brawny savage!

"Oh me! who are you?" demanded she, struggling to disengage herself, and unable to see the swarthy features of her captor, who stood behind her. No answer being made, she cast her eyes downwards, and beheld the colour of the arms that encircled her. "Father! Mr. Glenn! Mr. Boone!" she exclaimed, struggling violently. Her efforts were unavailing, and, overcome with exhaustion and affright, she fainted on the Indian's breast. The savage then lifted her on his shoulder, ran down to the rivulet that flowed through the valley, and fled outwards to the prairie. When he reached the cave-spring, a confederate, who had been waiting for him, seized the burden and bore it onwards, in a westerly direction, with increased rapidity. Thus they continued the retreat, bearing the insensible maiden alternately, until they came to a small grove some distance out in the prairie, when they slackened their pace, and, after creeping a short time under the pendent boughs of the trees, halted in the camp of the war-party.

The Indians gathered round the pale captive, some with rage and deadly passions marked upon their faces, and others with expressions of triumph and satisfaction. They now made preparations for departing. Mary was wrapped in a large buffalo robe, enveloping her body and face, and placed in the snow-canoe. The party then deposited their tomahawks and other cumbersome articles at the feet of their captive, and, grasping the leather rope attached to the canoe, set off rapidly in a southerly direction.

Ere long, Mary partially awoke from her state of insensibility, when all was dark and strange to her confused senses. She pulled aside the long hair of the buffalo skin that obscured her face, and looked out from her narrow place of confinement. The blue heavens alone met her view above. The incident of the seizure was indistinct in her memory, and she could not surmise the nature of her present condition. She turned hastily on her side, and the occasional bush she espied in the vicinity indicated that she was rushing along by some means with an almost inconceivable rapidity. She could scarce believe it was reality. How she came thither, and how she was propelled over the snow, for several moments were matters of incomprehensible mystery to the trembling girl. At first, she endeavoured to persuade herself that it was a dream; but, having a consciousness that some terrible thing had actually occurred, all the painful fears of which the mind is capable were put in active operation. The suspense was soon dispelled. Hearing human voices ahead, and not readily comprehending the language, she hastily rose on her elbow. The party of Indians dragging her fleetly over the smooth prairie met her chilled view. But she was now comparatively collected and calm. Instantly her true condition wa apparent. She watched the swarthy forms some moment in silence, meditating the means of escape. Presently one of the savages turned partly round, and she sank back to escape his observation. Again she rose up a few inches, and their faces were all turned away from her. She gradually acquired resolution to encounter any hardship or peril that might be the means of effecting her escape. But what plan was she to adopt? The almost interminable plain of which she was in the midst afforded no hiding-place. Then, the speed of the flying snow-canoe, were she to leap out, would not only produce a hurtful collision with the hard snow-crust, but certainly cause her detection The poor girl's heart sank within her, and, for a time, she reclined submissively in the canoe, and gave way to a flood of tears. She thought of her gray-haired father, and a piercing agony thrilled through her breast. And she thought, too, of others—of Boone, of *Glenn*, and her pangs were hopelessly poignant. Thus she lay for several long hours, a prey to grief and despair. But some pitying angel hovered over her, and kindly lessened her sufferings. By degrees, her mind became possessed of the power of deliberate and rational reflection; and she was inspired with

The savage rushed upon her, entwined his left hand in her flowing hair, and, waving his tomahawk aloft with the other, was in the act of sinking the steel in the fair forehead before him, when the blow was arrested by a mere stripling, who came up at the head of the rest of the Indians.—P. 142.

the belief that the savages only designed to exact a heavy contribution from the whites by her capture, and would then surrender her up without outrage or injury. Another hope, likewise, sprang up in her breast: it was, that the Indian she had been instrumental in releasing from captivity might protect her person, and, perhaps restore her to her father. She also felt convinced that Boone and Glenn would join her father in the pursuit, and she entertained a lively hope that they would overtake her. But, again, when she looked out on the surface of the snow, and beheld the rapidity of the savages' pace, this hope was entertained but for a moment. She then resolved to make an effort herself to escape. If she was not successful, it would, at all events, retard the progress of her captors, and she might also ascertain, with some degree of certainty, their purposes with regard to her fate. She rose as softly as possible and sprang upon the snow. The Indians, as she feared, instantly felt the diminution of weight, and halted so abruptly that every one of them was prostrated on the slippery snow-crust. Mary endeavoured to take advantage of this occurrence, and, springing quickly to her feet, fled rapidly in the opposite direction. But before she had run many minutes, she heard the savages in close pursuit and gaining upon her at every step. It was useless to fly. She turned her head, and beheld the whole party within a few paces of her. The foremost was a tall athletic savage, bearing in his hand a tomahawk he had snatched from the snow-canoe, and wearing a demoniac scowl on his lip. Mary scanned his face and then turned her eyes to heaven. She felt that her end was near, and she breathed a prayer taught her by her buried mother. The savage rushed upon her, entwining his left hand in her flowing hair, and waving his tomahawk aloft with the other, was in the act of sinking the steel in the fair forehead before him, when the blow was arrested by a mere stripling, who came up at the head of the rest of the Indians. The Herculean savage whirled round and scowled passionately at the youth. The young Indian (the chief just elected in the place of Raven) regarded him a moment with gleaming eyes, and a determined expression of feature, and then with much dignity motioned him away. The huge savage was strangely submissive in a moment, and obeyed without a murmur. Mary was conducted back to the snow-canoe by the young chief, who led her by the hand, while the rest walked behind. Once the young warrior turned and looked searchingly in the face of his fair prize, and she returned the gaze with an instantaneous conviction that no personal harm was intended her. The chief was not half so dark as the rest of his tribe, and his countenance was open, generous, and noble. (It may seem improbable to the unthinking reader that a timid and alarmed maiden should be able to read the character of a foe by his features under such circumstances. But those very circumstances tended to produce such acuteness. And this is not only the case with human beings, but even with dumb brutes—for, at the moment they are about to be assailed, they invariably and instinctively look the assailant in the eye, mercy being the only remaining hope.) Again the young warrior turned to behold his captive's face, and Mary was in tears. He paused abruptly, and, after gazing some moments in silence and deep thought, resumed his pace. When they reached the snow-canoe, and while in the act of lifting his captive into her couch, the young chief observed for the first time a massive ring of curious workmanship on her finger (the glove she had hitherto worn being partially torn from her hand in the recent struggle,) and seemed to regard it with much interest. Mary saw that his eyes were rivetted on the jewel, and notwithstanding it possessed a hallowed value in having been worn by her mother, yet she felt that she could resign it to the one who had saved her life, and whose noble bearing, so different from that of the rest, promised to shield her from future harm. But he neither asked it as a gift nor tore it from her, but turned away in silence, and ordered the party to proceed. The command was instantly obeyed.

There was another Indian that had attracted the notice of Mary—one who studiously avoided her glance by constantly enveloping his face in his hairy robe whenever she turned towards him. This he continued to do until she was again seated in the snow-canoe, and the order was given to proceed on the journey. He then lingered behind the rest, and throwing aside his mask, she saw before her the savage that had been thrown within the inclosure by the explosion He pointed to the north, the direction of her home, and, by sundry signs and grimaces, made Mary understand that he had not been a party to her capture, and that he would endeavour to effect her escape. He then joined the others, and the poor girl was once more coursing over the prairie more rapidly than ever.

There was now mingled with the captive maiden's thoughts another subject of contemplation. It was the young chief. His image seemed to be familiar to her dreamy visions, and she often thought that they had really met before. But when or where, her memory failed to designate. She was glad to find herself so unexpectedly under the protection of one so brave and generous, and she hoped when her father and his friends should overtake them, he might not be hurt in the conflict that must inevitably ensue.

The Indians long continued their flight in silence. Scarce a word was uttered, until the sun was sinking low in the west. And then Mary heard them speaking about the place of encampment; for her frequent intercourse with the savages, before the arrival of Glenn in the vicinity, had enabled her, as well as her father, to acquire an imperfect knowledge of their language. But they still swept onward, without any diminution of speed. The chief had probably objected to their making a halt by a shake of the head, for Mary did not hear him reply to those who desired to stop.

When the shades of night fell around, and the broad red face of the moon peeped over the eastern horizon, the party still careered over the prairie. More than thirty miles had been traversed. The Indian is more distinguished for bottom than speed, and has been known to pursue a victim, or fly in the retreat, more than twenty-four hours without resting. But this band had suffered much from fatigue before they set out with their captive. The attempt to surprise the fort had cost them both blood and labour, and when the moon had risen midway up in the heavens, they again became clamorous for food and rest. The chief then told them to turn from their course, and in a few minutes Mary saw that they were approaching a grove of towering trees. Ere long they halted under an enormous beech, whose spreading and clustering branches not only greatly obscured the light from above, but had in a great measure prevented the snow from covering the earth at its roots. It was not long before a fire was struck, and the savages having scattered in every direction in quest of dry wood and bark, in a very short space of time a large bright blaze flashed up in their midst, around which they spread their buffalo robes and commenced preparing their venison. Each one cooked for himself, save the chief, who was provided proportionably by all. He offered Mary a part of his food, but she declined it. He then proffered to lift her from the snow-canoe, and place her nearer the fire. This too she declined, stating that she was warm enough. She was likewise influenced in this determination by the gestures of the Indian whom she had befriended the preceding night, who sat by in apparent unconcern, but at every opportunity, by looks and signs, endeavoured to cheer and encourage the captive maiden.

After a hearty repast the savages, with the exception of the chief, rolled themselves in their warm, hairy robes before the glowing fire, and were soon steeped in profound slumber. The chief long reclined in a half-recumbent attitude on the couch that had been prepared for him, and fixing his eyes on the glaring flame, and sometimes on the pale sad features of Mary, seemed to be under the influence of deep and painful meditations. At times his features assumed a ferocity that caused Mary to start and tremble; but at others they wore a mournful expression, and ever and anon a tear rose up and glistened in his eye. Thus he sat for more than an hour after all the rest were sunk in motionless slumber. Finally his bedecked head, adorned with a profusion of rich and rare feathers, sunk by degrees on the rude pillow, and he too was soon wandering in the land of dreams.

But sleep brooded not upon the watchful lids of Mary. She gazed in silence at the wild savage scene before her. The uncouth beings who had so recently hooted and yelled like sanguinary demons, with intent to slay and pillage, around her father, her friends and herself, now lay motionless, though free and still hostile, within a few feet of her, and she was their captive! She thought of her humble but peaceful home, and sighed bitterly. And she thought, too, of her distressed friends, and she was the more distressed from the consciousness that they sympathized with her sufferings. Poor girl! She looked at the dark brows and compressed lips of her captors as the fitful flashes of the flames threw a bright ray upon them, and, in despite of the many hopes she had entertained, she was horror-stricken to contemplate the reality of her sad predicament.

At a late and solemn hour, the Indian who had been the captive the night before, suddenly ceased his snoring, which had been heard without intermission for a great length of time; and when Mary instinctively cast her eyes towards him, she was surprised to see him gently and slowly raise his head. He enjoined silence by placing his hand upon his mouth. After carefully disengaging himself from his comrades, he crept quietly away, and soon vanished entirely from sight on the northern side of the spreading beech. Mary expected he would soon return and assist her to escape. Although she was aware of the hardships and perils that would attend her flight, yet the thought of again meeting her friends was enough to nerve her for the undertaking, and she waited with anxious impatience the coming of her rescuer. But he came not. She could attribute no other design in his conduct but that of effecting her escape, and yet he neither came for her nor beckoned her away. She had reposed confidence in his promise, for she knew that the Indian, savage as he was, rarely forfeited his word; but when gratitude inspired a pledge, she could not believe that he would use deceit. The fire was now burning quite low, and its waning light scarce cast a beam upon the branches over head. It was evidently not far from morning, and every hope of present escape entirely fled from her bosom. But just as she was yielding to despair, she saw the Indian returning in a stealthy pace, bearing some dark object in his arms. He glided to her side, and beckoned her to leave the snow-canoe, and also to take with her all the robes with which she had been enveloped. She did his bidding, and then he carefully deposited the burden he bore in the place she had just occupied. A portion of the object becoming unwrapped, Mary discovered it to be a huge mass of snow, resembling, in some respects, a human form. and the Indian's stratagem was at once apparent to her Relinquishing herself to his guidance, she was led noiselessly through the bushes about a hundred paces distant from the fire, to a large fallen tree that had yielded to some furious storm, when her conductor paused. He pointed to a spot where a curve caused the huge trunk to rise about a foot from the present surface, under which was a round hole cut through the drifted snow down to the earth, and in which were deposited several buffalo robes, and so arranged that a person could repose within without coming in contact with the frozen element around. Mary looked down, and then at her companion, to ascertain his intentions. He spoke to her in a low tone, enough of which she comprehended to understand that he desired her to descend into the pit without delay. She obeyed, and when he had carefully folded the robes and divers furs about her body, he stepped a few paces to one side, and gently lifting up a round lid of snow crust, placed it over the aperture. It had been so smoothly cut, and fitted with such precision when replaced, that no one would have been able to discover that an incision had been made. He then bade Mary a "Dud by" in bad English, and set off in a run in a northern direction for the purpose of joining the whites.

Long and interminable seemed Mary's confinement to her, but she was entirely comfortable in her hiding-place, as respected her body. Yet many dreadful apprehensions oppressed her still. She feared that the Indians would soon ascertain that she had left the canoe, and return and discover her place of concealment. At times she thought of the wild beasts prowling around, and feared they would devour her before assistance came. But the most harrowing fear was that the friendly Indian would abandon her to her fate or perhaps be *killed*, without making known her locality and helpless condition! Thus was she a prey to painful apprehensions and worrying reflections, until from exhaustion she sank into an unquiet and troubled slumber.

With the first light of morning, the war-party sprang to their feet, and hastily dispatching a slight repast, they set out on their journey with renewed animation and increased rapidity. Before starting, the chief called to Mary, and again offered some food; but no reply being returned, or motion discovered under the robe which he imagined enveloped her, he supposed she was sleeping, and directed the party to select the most even route when they emerged in the prairie, that she might as much as possible enjoy her repose.

The Indian who had planned and executed the escape of Mary, with the well-devised cunning for which the race is proverbial, had told his companions that he would rise before day and pursue the same direction they were going in advance of them, and endeavour to kill a deer for their next night's meal. Thus his absence created no suspicion. and the party continued their precipitate retreat.

But, about noon, after casting many glances back at the supposed form of the captive reclining peacefully in the snow-canoe, the chief, with much excitement, betrayed by his looks, which seemed to be mingled with an apprehension that she was dead, abruptly ordered the party to halt. He sprang to the canoe, and convulsively tearing away the skins discovered only the roll of snow! He at first compressed his lips in momentary rage, and then burst into a fit of irrepressible laughter. But the rest raved and stamped, and uttered direful imprecations and threats of vengeance. Immediately they were aware of the treachery of the absent Indian, and resolved with one voice that his blood should be an atonement for the act. Their thoughts had dwelt too fondly on the shining gold they were to get in exchange for the maiden, for them ever to forgive the recreant brother who had snatched the prize from them. The chief soon recovered his usual grave expression, and partook in some measure the general disappointment and chagrin. His motives were not of the same mercenary cast which actuated his tribe, nor did he condemn the conduct of the one who had rescued the maid, being aware of the clemency extended him when in the power of the enemy; but the thought of being outwitted and thwarted roused his anger, and he determined to recover the lost captive, if possible.

The snow was quickly thrown out, and the war-party adjusted their weapons, with the expectation of encountering the whites; and then whirling about they retraced their steps even more swiftly than they had been advancing. Just as the night was setting in, they came in sight of the grove where they had encamped. They slackened their pace, and looking eagerly forward, seemed to think it not improbable that the whites had arrived in the vicinity, and might be lying in ambush awaiting their return in search of the maid. They then abandoned the canoe, after having concealed it under some low bushes, and entered the grove in a stooping and watchful posture. Ere long the chief attained the immediate neighbourhood of the spreading tree, and with an arrow drawn to its head, crept within a few paces of the spot where he had lain the preceding night. His party were mostly a few feet in the rear, while a few were approaching in the same manner from the opposite direction. Hearing no sound whatever, he rose up slowly, and with an "Ugh" of disappointment, strode carelessly across the silent and untenanted place of encampment.

Vexation and anger were expressed by the savages in being thus disappointed. They hoped to wreak their vengeance on the whites, and had resolved to recapture the maiden. Where they expected to find them, the scene was silent and desolate. And they now sauntered about under the trees in the partial light of the moon that struggled through the matted branches, threatening in the most horrid manner the one who had thus baffled them. Some struck their tomahawks into the trunks of trees, while others brandished their knives, and uttered direful yells. The young chief stood in silence, with his arms folded on his breast. A small ray of light that fell upon his face exhibited a meditative brow, and features expressing both firmness and determination. He had said that the captive should be regained, and his followers ever and anon regarded his thoughtful attitude with the confidence that his decision would accelerate the accomplishment of their desires. Long he remained thus, motionless and dignified, and no one dared to address him. [He had been elected chief by acclamation, after the death of Raven. He was not an Osage by birth, but had been captured from one of the neighbouring tribes (the Pawnee) when only six years old. His bravery, as he grew up, had elicited the admiration of the whole tribe, and it had long been settled that he should succeed Raven. His cómplexion was many degrees lighter than that of the Osages, or even that of the Pawnees, and had it not been for the paint and stains with which the warriors decorate their faces, he might have passed, if properly attired, for an American. When taken in battle he was saved from the torture by a young Indian maiden. She procured his release, and he refused to return to his own nation. He said that he was no Pawnee, and when asked to what nation he belonged, he either could not or would not reply, but said he was satisfied to hunt and fight with any tribe, and if the chief would give him his daughter (the one that saved his life,) he would be an Osage. It was done, and his brave exploits soon won for him the title of the "Young Eagle."]

The young chief called one of the oldest of the party, who was standing a few paces distant absorbed in thought, to his side, and after a short conference the old savage prostrated himself on the snow, and endeavoured like a hound to scent the tracks of his recreant brother. At first he met with no success, but when making a wide circuit round the premises, still applying his nose to the ground occasionally, and minutely examining the bushes, he paused abruptly, and announced to the party that he had found the precise direction taken by the maid and her deliverer. Instantly they all clustered round him, evincing the most intense interest. Some smelt the surface of the snow, and others examined the bushes. Small twigs, not larger than pins, were picked up and closely scrutinized. They well knew that any one passing through the frozen and clustered bushes must inevitably sever some of the twigs and buds. Their progress was slow, but unerring. The course they pursued was the direction taken by Mary and her rescuer. It was not long before they arrived within a few feet of the place of the maiden's concealment. But now they were at fault. There were no bushes immediately around the fallen tree. They paused, the chief in the van, with their bows and arrows and tomahawks in readiness for instant use. They knew that the maiden could not return to her friends on foot, or the treacherous savage be able to bear her far on his shoulder. They thought that one or both must be concealed somewhere in the neighbourhood, and the fallen tree, were it hollow, was the place most likely to be selected for that purpose. After scanning the fallen trunk a few minutes in silence, and discovering nothing to realize their hopes, they uttered a terrific yell, and commenced striking their tomahawks in the wood, and ripping up the bark in quest of some hiding-place. But their search was in vain. The fallen trunk was sound and solid throughout, and the young chief sat down on it within three paces of

Mary! Others, in passing about, frequently trod on the very verge of the concealed pit.

Mary was awakened by the yell but knew not that the sound came from her enemies. The Indian had told her that he would soon return, and her heart now fluttered with the hope that her father and her friends were at hand. Yet she prudently determined not to rush from her concealment until she was better assured of the fact. She did not think the savages would suspect that she was hid under the snow, but yet she thought it very strange that her father did not come to her at once. Several minutes had elapsed since she had been startled by the sounds in the immediate vicinity. She heard the tramp of men almost directly over her head, and the strokes against the fallen trunk. She was several times on the eve of rising up, but was as often withheld by some mysterious impulse. She endeavoured to reflect calmly, but still she could not, by any mode of conjecture realize the probability of her foes having returned and traced her thither. Yet an undefinable fear still possessed her, and she endeavoured with patience to await the pleasure of her friends. But when the chief seated himself in her vicinity, and fell into one of his fits of abstraction, and the whole party became comparatively still and hushed, the poor girl's suspense was almost insufferable. She knew that human beings were all around her, and yet her situation was truly pitiable and lonely. She felt assured that if the war party had returned in pursuit of her, the same means which enabled them to trace their victim to the fallen trunk would likewise have sufficed to indicate her hiding-place. Then why should she hesitate? The yells that awakened her had not been heard distinctly, and under the circumstances she could not believe that she was surrounded by savages. On the other hand, if they were her friends, why did they not relieve her? Now a sudden, but, alas! erroneous thought occurred to her. She was persuaded that they were her friends, but that the friendly Indian was not with them—he had perhaps directed them where she could be found, and then returned to his home. Might not her friends, at that moment, be anxiously searching for her? Would not one word suffice to dispel their solicitude, and restore the lost one to their arms? She resolved to speak. Bowing down her head slightly, so that her precise location might not instantly be ascertained, she uttered in a soft voice the word "FATHER!" The chief sprang from his seat, and the party was instantly in commotion. Some of the savages looked above, among the twining branches, and some shot their arrows in the snow, but fortunately not in the direction of Mary, while others ran about in every direction, examining all the large trees in the vicinity. The chief was amazed and utterly confounded. He drew not forth an arrow, nor brandished a tomahawk. While he thus stood, and the rest of the party were moving hurriedly about a few paces distant, Mary again repeated the word "FATHER!" As suddenly as if by enchantment every savage was paralyzed. Each stood as devoid of animation as a statue. For many moments an intense silence reigned, as if naught existed there but the cheerless forest trees. Slowly, at length, the tomahawk was returned to the belt, and the arrow to the quiver. No longer was a desire to spill blood manifested. The dusky children of the forest attributed to the mysterious sound a supernatural agency. They believed it was a voice from the perennial hunting-grounds. Humbly they bowed their heads, and whispered devotions to the Great Spirit. The young chief alone stood erect. He gazed at the round moon above him, and sighs burst from his breast, and burning tears ran down his stained cheek. Impatiently, by a motion of the hand, he directed the savages to leave him, and when they withdrew he resumed his seat on the fallen trunk, and reclined his brow upon his hand. One of the long feathers that decked his head waved forward, after he had been seated thus a few minutes, and when his eye rested upon it he started up wildly, and tearing it away, trampled it under his feet. At that instant the same "FATHER!" was again heard. The young chief fell upon his knees, and, while he panted convulsively, said, in ENGLISH, "*Father! Mother! I'm your poor William—you loved me much—where are you? Oh tell me—I will come to you—I want to see you!*" He then fell prostrate and groaned piteously. "Father! oh! where are you? Whose voice was that?" said Mary, breaking through the slight incrustation that obscured her, and leaping from her covert.

The young chief sprang from the earth—gazed a moment at the maid—spoke rapidly and loudly in the language of his tribe to his party, who were now at the place of encampment, seated by the fire they had kindled—and then, seizing his tomahawk, was in the act of hurling it at Mary, when the yells of the war-party and the ringing discharges of firearms arrested his steel when brandished in the air. The white men had arrived! The young chief seized Mary by her long flowing hair—again prepared to level the fatal blow—when she turned her face upwards, and he again hesitated. Discharges in quick succession, and nearer than before, still rang in his ears. Mary strove not to escape. Nor did the Indian strike. The whites were heard rushing through the bushes—the chief seized the trembling girl in his arms—a bullet whizzed by his head—but, unmindful of danger, he vanished among the dark bushes with his burden.

CHAPTER XII.

Joe's indisposition—His cure—Sneak's reformation—The pursuit—The captive Indian—Approach to the encampment of the savages—Joe's illness again—The surprise—The terrific encounter—Rescue of Mary—Capture of the young chief—The return.

WE return to the white men. The grief of Roughgrove, and of all the party, when it was ascertained beyond a doubt that Mary had been carried off by the savages, was deep and poignant. The aged ferryman sat silent and alone, and would not be comforted, while the rest made the necessary arrangements to pursue the foe. The sled was so altered that blankets, buffalo robes, and a small quantity of food could be taken in it. Bullets were moulded and the guns put in order. Joe was ordered to give the horses water, and place a large quantity of provender within their reach. The hounds were fed and then led back to their kennel, and Glenn announced, after Roughgrove declared his determination to go along, that Ringwood and Jowler alone would be left to guard the premises.

"My goodness!" said Joe, when he understood that he was expected to make one of the pursuing party, "I can't go! My head's so sore, and aches so bad, I couldn't go ten miles before I'd have to give up. Let me stay, Mr. Glenn, and take care of the house."

"Do you forget that *Mary* is in the hands of the Indians? Would you hesitate even to *die*, while striving to rescue a poor, innocent, helpless maiden? For shame!" replied Glenn.

"I'd spill my heart's blood for her," said Joe, "if it would do any good. But you know how I was crippled last night, and I didn't sleep a bit afterwards, hardly."

"Dod"—commenced Sneak.

"Joe," said Boone, "from the vigorous manner in which you fought the wolves, I am induced to believe that your present scruples are not well founded. We will need every man we can obtain."

"Oh, I wouldn't mind it at all," said Joe, "if it wasn't that you're a going to start right off now. If I only had a little sleep——"

"You shall have it," said Boone. Both Glenn and Roughgrove looked inquiringly at the speaker. "We will not start to-night," continued he. "It would be useless. We could not overtake them, and if we did, it would cause them to put Mary to death, that they might escape our vengeance the more easily. I have duly considered the matter. We must rest here to-night, and rise refreshed in the morning. We will then set out on their trail, and I solemnly pledge my word never to return without bringing the poor child back unharmed."

"I *hope* my head 'll be well by morning," said Joe.

"I *know* it will be well enough," said Glenn; "so you need entertain no hope of being left behind."

"Now, Sneak a word with you," said Boone. "I think you would do almost *any thing* for my sake——"

"If I wouldn't, I wish I may be dod——"

"Stop!" continued Boone, interrupting him.

"Jest ax me to cut off my little finger," said Sneak, "and if I don't do it, I wish I may be dod——"

"Stop!" again interposed Boone. "My first request is one that poor *Mary* asked me to make. I know it will be a severe trial."

"Name it," cried Sneak, "and if it's to job out ou of my eyes, dod rot me if I don't do it!"

"*Hear* me," continued Boone; "she desired me to ask you not to use that ugly word *dod-rot* any more."

"Hay!" exclaimed Sneak, his eyes dilating, and his mouth falling wide open.

"I know it will be a hard matter," said Boone; "but Mary thinks you have a good and brave heart, and she says you are the only one among us that uses bad words."

"I'd go my death for that gal, or any other female woman in the settlement, any day of my life. And as she wants me to swaller them words, that was born with me, dod—I mean, I wish I may be—*indeed*, I'll be starved to death if I don't do it! only when I'm raven mad at something, and then I can't help it."

"Very well," said Boone. "Now I have a request of my own to make——"

"Sing it out! dod—no—nothing! I didn't say it—but I'll *do* what you want me to," said Sneak.

"I think *you* will not suffer for the want of sleep," continued Boone; "and I wish you to go out and get as many of the neighbours to join us as possible. You can go to three or four houses by midnight, sleep a little, and meet us here, or in the prairie, in the morning."

"I shall cut stick—if I don't I wish I may be do—I—*indeed* I will!" and before he ceased speaking he was rushing through the gate.

The little party then took a hasty repast, and, throwing themselves on the couches, endeavoured to sleep. Boone and Joe were soon wrapped in slumber; but neither Roughgrove nor Glenn, for a great length of time, could find repose.

"Strive to be composed, my friend; all will be well," said Glenn, when the disconsolate old ferryman gave vent to numerous heart-rending sighs.

"If you only knew"—commenced Roughgrove, in reply, and the words he was about to utter died upon his lips.

"I can well imagine the extent of your bereavement," said Glenn; "but at the same time I am sure she will be returned to you unharmed."

"It was not Mary alone I alluded to," said Roughgrove;

"but to lose two children—all that we had—so cruelly—Oh! may we all meet in heaven!"

"Then you had *two* childen, and lost them both? I never heard the other mentioned," said Glenn, now evincing a most lively interest in the subject.

"No—it was my request that it should never be mentioned. Mary and he were twins—only six years old, when he was lost. I wished Mary to forget entirely that she ever had a brother—it could do no good for her to know it, and would distress her. But now, Heavenly Father! both are gone!" added the old man, in tears.

"Was he, too, taken by the Indians? the Osages?" inquired Glenn.

"No," said Roughgrove. "He had been playing on the margin of the river, and we were compelled to believe that he fell in the stream and was drowned—at a time when no eye was upon him. Mary was near at hand, but she did not see him fall, nor could she tell how he disappeared. His poor mother believed that an Indian stole him away. But the only Indians then in the neighbourhood were the Pawnees, and they were at that time friendly. He was surely drowned. If the Pawnees had taken him, they would soon have proposed a ransom. Yet his mother continually charged them with the deed. In her dreams she ever saw him among the savages. In all her thoughts it was the same. She pined away—she never knew a happy moment afterwards—and when she died, the same belief was uttered in her last words. I am now alone!" The old man covered his face with his hands, and sobbed audibly.

"Bear with patience and resignation," said Glenn, "the dispensations of an all-wise Providence. All may yet be well. The son, whom you thought lost forever, may be living, and possibly reclaimed, and Mary shall be restored, if human efforts can accomplish it. Cheer up. Many a happy day may still be reserved for you."

"Oh! my dear young friend! if you but knew *all!*" said Roughgrove.

"Do I not now know all?" asked Glenn.

"No," replied the old man; "but the rest must remain a secret—it should, perhaps, be buried in my breast forever! I will now strive to sleep." They ceased to speak, and silence reigned till morning.

Joe was roused from his couch in the morning by a tremendous "Ya-hoy!" outside of the inclosure.

"Run and open the gate," said Glenn.

"I'd rather not," said Joe, rubbing his eyes.

"Why?" asked Glenn.

"Hang it, it's the Indians again!" replied Joe, seizing his musket.

"It is Sneak and his men," observed Boone, when another shout was uttered.

"Hang me, if I don't have a peep at 'em first, anyhow," said Joe, approaching the gate cautiously, and peering through a small crevice.

"Ya-hoo!" repeated those without.

"Who are you? why don't you speak out?" said Joe, still unable to see their faces.

"Dod—I mean—plague take it! Joe, is Mr. Boone standing there with you?" asked Sneak.

"No," replied Joe, opening the gate.

"Then dod *rot* your hide! why didn't you let us in?" said Sneak, rushing through the gate, and followed by five of the neighbours.

"Why, Sneak, how could I tell that you wern't Indians?" said Joe.

"You be dod—never mind!" continued Sneak, shaking his head, and passing to where Boone stood, near the house.

"I am glad to see you all," said Boone, extending his hand to each of the hardy pioneers. "But let us not waste a moment's time. I see you are all armed. Seize hold of the sled-rope, and let us be off." The command was instantly obeyed, and the party were soon passing out of the inclosure. The gate was scarce fastened before another "Ya-hoo!" came from the valley below, and a moment after they were joined by Col. Cooper and Dan. The other oarsman had been sent up the river for reinforcements, and Col. Cooper and Dan having heard the great explosion, finally resolved to cross over the river, and not await the arrival of the trappers.

The party now amounted to twelve, and no time was lost in commencing the march, or rather the chase; for when they reached the prairie and found the trail of the snow-canoe, their progress equalled that of the savages. But they had not gone far before Joe was taken suddenly ill, and begged to be permitted to return.

"I declare I can hardly hold my head up!" said he still holding on to the rope, and keeping pace with the rest, though his head hung down.

"'Possomin'—dod—I mean he's jest 'possomin'," said Sneak.

"No, indeed I ain't—plague it, don't *you* say any thing, Sneak," Joe, added, in an undertone.

"I am something of a physician," said Boone, whose quick ear had caught the words addressed to Sneak. "Let me feel your pulse," he added, ordering the party to halt, and turning to Joe, whose wrist he seized.

"I feel something better," said Joe, alarmed at the mys terious and severe expression of Boone's face.

"I hope you will be entirely well in *two minutes*," said Boone; "and when it will not be necessary to apply my remedy."

"I'm about well now," said Joe: "I think I can go ahead."

"I believe your pulse is good now; and I think you will hardly have another attack to-day. If you do, just let me know it."

"Oh, now I feel perfectly well," responded Joe; and, seizing the rope, they were all soon again flying along on the trail of the savages.

A little before noon, while casting his eyes along the dim horizon in advance, Sneak abruptly paused, causing the rest to do likewise, and exclaimed, "Dod rot it."

"What's the matter, Sneak? Remember the promise you made," said Boone.

"Oh," replied Sneak, "in sich an extronary case as this, I can't help saying that word yet awhile. But look yander!" he continued, pointing to a slight eminence a great distance in advance.

"True!" said Boone, "that is an Indian—but it is the only one hereabouts."

"He is coming to meet us," said Glenn.

"Yes! my goodness! he's looking at us now," cried Joe, retreating a few steps.

"If there are more of them watching us," said Col. Cooper, "they are somewhere in our rear."

"Oh! we're surrounded!" cried Joe, leaping forward again.

"Come on," said Boone; "we'll soon learn what he wants with us."

When they were within a few hundred yards of the solitary Indian, they again halted, and Joe ran to the sled and seized his musket, which he cocked and threw up to his shoulder.

"Take down your gun!" said Boone; "that is the Indian whose life we spared. I was not deceived in his integrity. He was not the one that stole away Mary. I doubt not he brings intelligence of her."

"God grant she may still be unharmed!" said Roughgrove, advancing to meet the Indian, who, being now within gunshot, raised his small white flag. "Tell me! tell me all about her!" exclaimed Roughgrove, in the Osage language, when he met the Indian. When the Indian informed him of the condition of Mary, the old man could not repress his raptures, his gratitude, or his tears. "She's safe! she's safe! Heaven be praised!" he exclaimed, turning to his companions, who now came up, and experienced almost as much joy at the announcement as himself.

"Hang me, if you ain't a right clever fellow," said Joe, shaking the Indian's hand quite heartily. "Now," he continued, when all the particulars of Mary's escape were made known, "there won't be any use in fighting; we can just get Miss Mary out of the snow, and then go home again."

"You don't know—keep your mouth shet—dod—," said Sneak, suppressing the last word.

"We are not sure of that," said Boone; "on the contrary, I think it is very probable we shall have fighting yet. When the war-party discover the deception, (as they must have done ere this,) they will retrace their steps. If it was early in the day when they ascertained that the captive had escaped, we may expect to see them very soon. If it was late, we will find them in the grove where they encamped. In either event we must expect to fight—and fight hard, too—for they outnumber us considerably."

Joe sighed, but said nothing.

"Are you getting ill again?" inquired Boone.

"No—I was only blowing—I got a little tired," said Joe, in scarce articulate tones.

"And I feel weak—very weak—but it is with joy!" said Roughgrove.

"And I have observed it, too," said Boone. "Get in the sled; we will pull you along till your strength returns."

"I will be able to use my gun when I meet the foe," said the old man, getting into the sled.

The party set forward again, guided by the Indian, and in high spirits. The consciousness that Mary was in safety removed a weight from the breasts of all; and, as they ran along, many a light jest and pleasant repartee lessened the weariness of the march. Even Joe smiled once or twice when Boone, in a mock heroic manner alluded to his exploits among the wolves.

"Blast me," said Joe, when Sneak mentioned a few cases of equivocal courage as an offset to Boone's compliments, "blast me, if I haven't killed more Indians than any of you, since I have been in this plagued country."

"True—that is, your musket has," said Boone.

"Joe can fight sometimes," said Glenn, smiling.

"I'll be hanged if I haven't always fought, when there was any fighting going on," said Joe, reproachfully.

"Yes, and he'll fight again, as manfully as any of us," said Boone.

"Dod—why, what are you holding back for so hard?" said Sneak, remarking that Joe at that instant seemed to be much excited, and, instead of going forward, actually brought the whole party to a moderate walk by his counter exertion.

"What do you mean?" asked Glenn.

"Are you going to be ill?" asked Boone.

"No, goodness, no! Only listen to me a minute. An idea struck me, which I thought it was my duty to tell. I thought this Indian might be deceiving us. Suppose he leads us right into an ambush when we're talking and laughing, and thinking there's no danger.

"Dod—you're a cowardly fool!" said Sneak.

"I have likewise a remedy for interruptions—I advise you not to stop again," said Boone, when Joe once more started forward.

Just as night was setting in, the party came in sight of the grove where Mary was concealed. They slackened their pace and drew near the dark woods quite cautiously. When they entered the edge of the grove, they heard the war-party utter the yell which had awakened Mary. It was fully understood by Boone, and the friendly Indian assured them from the sound, that the Osages had just returned, and were at that moment leaving the encampment on his trail. But he stated that they could not find the pale-faced maiden. And he suggested to the whites a plan of attack, which was to station themselves near the place where he had emerged from the grove, after hiding Mary; so that when they followed on his trail they could thus be surprised without difficulty. This advice was adopted by Boone. The Indian then asked permission to depart, saying he had paid the white men for sparing his life.

"Oh no!" cried Joe, when Roughgrove interpreted the Indian's request, "keep him as a hostage—he may be cheating us."

"I do not see the impropriety of Joe's remark this time," said Glenn.

"Ask him where he will go, if we suffer him to depart," said Boone. To Roughgrove's interrogation, the Indian made a passionate reply. He said the white men were liars. They were now quits. Still the white men were not satisfied. He had risked his life (and would probably be tortured) to pay back the white men's kindness. But they would not believe his words. He was willing to die now. The white men might shoot him. He would as willingly die as live. If suffered to depart, it was his intention to steal his squaw away from the tribe, and join the Pawnees. He would never be an Osage again.

"Go!" said Boone, perceiving by a ray of moonlight that reached the Indian's face through the clustering branches of the trees above, that he was in tears. The savage, without speaking another word, leaped out into the prairie, and from the circuitous direction he pursued, it was manifest that nothing could be further from his desire than to fall in with the war-party.

Boone directed the sled to be abandoned, and, obedient to his will, the party entered a small covert in the imme diate vicinity of the spot where their guide said he had emerged from the grove on his return to meet the whites Here the party long remained esconced, silent and listening, and expecting every moment to see the foe. At length Boone grew impatient, and concluding they would encamp that night under the spreading tree, (the locality of which he was familiar with,) he resolved to advance and surprise them. He was strengthened in this determination by the repeated and painful surmises of Roughgrove respecting Mary's piteous condition. Glenn, and the rest, with perhaps one or two exceptions, likewise seemed disposed to make an instantaneous termination of the torturing suspense respecting the fate of the poor girl.

Boone and Sneak led the way. The party were compelled to proceed with the utmost caution. Sometimes they were forced to crawl many paces on their hands and knees under the pendent snow-covered bushes. They drew near the spreading tree. A fire was burning under it, the flickering rays of which could be occasionally seen glimmering through the branches. A stick was heard to break a little distance on one side, and Boone and Sneak sank down on the snow, and whispered to the rest to follow their example. It was done without a repetition of the order. Joe was the hindmost of all, but after lying a few minutes in silence, he crept softly forward, trembling all the while. When he reached the side of Boone, the aged woodman did not chide him, but simply pointed his finger towards a small decayed log a few paces distant. Joe looked but a moment, and then pulling his hat over his eyes, laid down flat on his face, in silence and submission. An Indian was seated on the log, and very composedly cutting off the dry bark with his tomahawk. Once or twice he paused and remained a moment in a listening attitude. But probably thinking the sounds he heard (if he heard any) proceeded from some comrade like himself in quest of fuel, he continued to cut away, until an armful was obtained, and then very deliberately arose and walked with an almost noiseless step to the fire, which was not more than fifty yards distant. Boone rose softly and whispered the rest to follow. He was promptly obeyed by all except Joe.

"Come, sir! prepare your musket to fire," said Boone,

stooping down to Joe, who still remained apparently frozen to the snow-crust.

"Oh! I'm so sick!" replied Joe.

"If you do not keep with us, you will lose your scalp to a certainty," said Boone. Joe was well in a second. The party were now about midway between the fallen trunk where Mary was concealed, and the great encampment-tree. Boone rose erect for an instant, and beheld the former, and the single Indian (the chief) who was there. One of the Indians again started out from the fire, in the direction of the whites for more fuel. Boone once more passed the word for his little band to lie down. The tall savage came within a few feet of them. His tomahawk accidentally fell from his hand, and in his endeavour to catch it, he knocked it within a few feet of Sneak's head. He stepped carelessly aside, and stooped down for it. A strangling and gushing sound was heard, and falling prostrate, he died without a groan. Sneak had nearly severed his head from his body at one blow with his hunting-knife.

At this juncture Mary sprang from her hiding-place. Her voice reached the ears of her father, but before he could run to her assistance, the chief's loud tones rang through the forest. Boone and the rest sprang forward, and fired upon the savages under the spreading tree. At the second discharge the Indians gave way, and while Col. Cooper, the oarsmen, and the neighbours that had joined the party in the morning, pursued the flying foe, Boone and the remainder ran towards the fallen trunk where Mary had been concealed, but approaching in different directions. Glenn was the first to rush upon the chief, and it was his ball that whizzed so near the Indian's head when he bore away the shrieking maiden. The rest only fired in the direction of the log, not thinking that Mary had left her covert. They soon met at the fallen tree, under which was the pit, all except Glenn, who sprang forward in pursuit of the chief, and Sneak, who had made a wide circuit for the purpose of reaching the scene of action from an opposite direction, entirely regardless of the danger of being shot by his friends.

"She's gone! she's gone!" exclaimed Roughgrove, looking aghast at the vacated pit under the fallen trunk.

"But we will have her yet," said Boone, as he heard

"It is your father, my poor child!" said Roughgrave, pressing the girl to his heart.—P. 165.

Glenn discharge a pistol a few paces apart in the bushes. The report was followed by a yell, not from the chief, but Sneak, and the next moment the rifle of the latter was likewise heard. Still the Indian was not dispatched, for the instant afterwards his tomahawk, which was hurled without effect, came sailing over the bushes, and penetrated a tree hard by, some fifteen or twenty feet above the earth, where it entered the wood with such force that it remained firmly fixed. Now succeeded a struggle—a violent blow was heard—the fall of the Indian, and all was comparatively still. A minute afterwards, Sneak emerged from the thicket, bearing the inanimate body of Mary in his arms, and followed by Glenn.

"Is she dead? Oh, she's dead!" cried Roughgrove, snatching her from the arms of Sneak.

"She has only fainted!" exclaimed Glenn, examining the body of the pale girl, and finding no wounds.

"She is recovering!" said Boone, feeling her pulse.

"God be praised!" exclaimed Roughgrove, when returning animation was manifest.

"Oh! I know you won't kill me! For pity's sake spare me!" said Mary.

"It is your father, my poor child!" said Roughgrove, pressing the girl to his heart.

"It is! it is!" cried the happy girl, clinging rapturously to the old man's neck, and then, seizing the hands of the rest, she seemed to be half wild with delight.

"Dod—I—I mean that none of the black noctilerous savages shall ever hurt you as long as Sneak lives," said Sneak, looking down at his gun, which had been broken off at the breech.

"How did you break that?" asked Boone.

"I broke it over the yaller feller's head," said he, "and I'd do it agin, before he should hurt Miss Mary, if it *is* the only one I've got."

"I have an extra rifle at home," said Glenn, "which shall be yours, as a reward for your gallant conduct."

"Where is the chief? Is he dead?" asked Mary.

"If he ain't dead, his head's harder than my gun, that's all," said Sneak.

"Oh, I'm so sorry!" said Mary.

"Why, my child?" asked Roughgrove.

"Because," said Mary, "he's a good-hearted Indian, and never would have harmed me. When he heard you coming, and raised his tomahawk to kill me, I looked in his face, and he could not strike, for there were tears in his eyes! I know he never would have thought of killing me, when calm, for he treated me very kindly before I escaped."

"Maybe he ain't dead—I'll go and see," said Sneak, repairing to the late scene of conflict. When he arrived he found the young chief sitting upright, having been only stunned; a gold band that confined his head-dress prevented the blow from fracturing his skull. He was now unresisting and sullen. Sneak made him rise up, and after binding his hands behind him with a strong cord, led him forth.

"You did not intend to kill me, did you?" asked Mary, in soothing tones. The chief regarded her not, but looked steadfastly downwards.

"He don't understand you, Mary," said Boone.

"Oh, yes he does," continued Mary; "and he can speak our language, too, for I heard him talking, and thought it was you, and that was the reason why I came out of the pit." Roughgrove addressed him in his own language, but with no better success. The captured chief resolved not to plead for his life. He would make no reply whatever to their questions, but still gazed downwards in reckless sullenness.

"What shall we do with him?" asked Glenn, when the rest of the party, (with the exception of Joe,) who had chased the savages far away, came up and stared at the prisoner.

"Let us set him free!" said Roughgrove.

"Kill him!" cried several.

"No!" exclaimed Mary, "what do *you* say, Mr. Boone?"

"It would be useless to kill him," said Boone.

"Let him go, then," said Glenn.

"No!" said Boone.

"Why?" asked Glenn.

"Because," replied Boone, "he is a chief, and we may make him the means of securing the settlement against future attacks. We will confine him in your garrison as a hostage, and send some friendly Indian to the Osages announcing his capture, and informing them that his life wil be spared provided they keep away from the settlement for a certain length of time, at the expiration of which he shall be restored to them."

"I am glad of that," said Mary, "for I don't believe he is a bad Indian. We will treat him kindly, and then I think he will always be our friend."

"Take him along, and bind him fast in the sled, Sneak," said Boone; "but see that you do not injure him in the least."

"I will. Oh, me and him are purty good friends now. Gee-whoa-haw," continued he, taking hold of the string behind, and endeavouring to drive the silent captive like an ox. The young chief whirled round indignantly, and with such force as to send Sneak sprawling several paces to one side. He rose amid the laughter that ensued, and remembering the words of Boone, conducted his prisoner away in a more respectful manner.

"Where's Joe?" at length inquired Glenn, seeing that he alone was missing.

"Oh! I'm afraid he's dead," said Mary

"If he is, I shall mourn his loss many a day," said Glenn; "for with all his defects, I would not be without him for the world."

"Give yourself no uneasiness," said Boone; "for he is as well at this moment as you or I."

"I hope so," said Glenn; "but I have not seen him since we first fired at the Indians."

"Let us repair to that spot, and there we will find him, for I saw him fall down when he discharged his musket. I venture to say he has not moved an inch since."

The party repaired to the place mentioned, and there they found him, sure enough, lying quite still on his face beside the Indian that Sneak had killed.

"He *is* dead!" said Glenn, after calling to him and re ceiving no answer.

"We'll soon see," said Boone, turning him over on his back. "I will open a vein in his arm."

"Bring a torch from the fire," said Col. Cooper to one of the men.

"Oh!" sighed Joe, lifting his hands to his head.

"I thought he would soon come to life again," said Boone, examining his face with the torch that was brought, and then laughing outright. The spectacle was ludicrous in the extreme. Joe was besmeared with blood, and, when he opened his eyes and stared at the flaming light, he resembled some sanguinary demon.

"Where in the world did all this blood come from?" exclaimed Glenn.

"I'm recovered now," said Joe, rising up and assuming an air of importance.

"What have you been doing?" asked Glenn.

"I've been doing as much as any of you, I'll be bound," replied Joe, very gravely.

"Well, what have you done?" repeated Glenn.

"I've been fighting the last half hour, as hard as anybody ever fought in this world. Only look at the stabs in that Indian!" said he, pointing to the savage.

"Why, you scoundrel! Sneak killed this Indian," said Glenn.

"Sneak thought he did," replied Joe, "but he only wounded him. After a while he got up and clinched me by the throat, and we had it over and over on the snow, till we both got so exhausted we couldn't do any thing. When we rested, we went at it again, and it hasn't been five minutes since I stuck my knife in his breast. When he fell, I stuck him four or five times, and then fainted myself."

"Here is a wound in the savage's breast," said Glenn.

"But here's another in the throat," said Boone, showing where the arteries had been severed by Sneak.

"Joe," said Glenn, "you must abandon this habit of lying, if indeed it is not a portion of your nature."

"Hang it all, I ain't lying—I know Sneak did cut his throat, but he didn't cut it deep—I cut it deeper, myself, after the Indian got up again!" persisted he.

The party hastily glanced at the four or five dead savages under the trees, that had fallen victims to their fire, and then returned to the sled. Mary was placed beside the captive chief, and they set out on their return, well satisfied with the result of the expedition.

CHAPTER XIII.

The return—The young chief in confinement—Joe's fun—His reward—The ring—A discovery—William's recognition—Memories of childhood—A scene—Roughgrove's history—The children's parentage.

THE party on their return did not travel so rapidly as they had advanced. They moreover halted in a grove which they espied about midnight, and finding a spreading tree that had entirely shielded a small space of ground from the snow, they kindled a fire, arranged their robes, and reposed a few hours. The captive chief was still sullen and unresisting. He was suffered to recline in the sled enveloped in skins, with his hands and feet yet bound, and an extra cord passed round his body, the end of which Sneak held in his hand while he slept. When daylight appeared, they set forward again in a moderate pace, and arrived at Glenn's domicil at evening twilight. The neighbours that Sneak had enlisted departed for their homes, and Boone and Col. Cooper, after bidding our hero, Roughgrove, and Mary, a hearty adieu, without entering the inclosure, recrossed the river to their own settlement.

The remainder of the party, except the oarsmen, accepted Glenn's invitation to remain with him till morning. When the gate was thrown open, the faithful hounds manifested great delight to behold their master again, and also Mary, for they pranced so much in the path before them that it was almost impossible to walk. They barked in ecstasy The poor fawn had been forgotten, neglected, and had suffered much for food. Mary placed her arm round its neck and wept. Glenn ordered Joe, who was in the stable caressing the horses, to feed the drooping pet instantly.

The party then entered the house, leading in the chief, and soon after Sneak had a bright fire blazing on the hearth.

The food that remained from the last repast amply sufficed, the captive refusing to partake with them, and Joe having dined during the last twelve miles of the journey on the way.

"How we'll be able to keep this Indian here, when we go out, I should like to know," said Joe, regarding the manly and symmetrical form of the young chief, who was now unbound, and sat silent and thoughtful by the fire.

"I think he ought to be killed," said Sneak.

"Oh, no!" said Mary; "he is not bad like the other Indians." The Indian, for the first time since his capture, raised his head while she spoke, and looked searchingly in her face. "Oh!" continued Mary, thinking of the horrors of savage warfare, and bursting into tears, "you will never attempt to kill any of us again, will you?"

"No!" said the chief, in a low but distinct tone. Every one in the house but Mary started.

"You understand our language, do you? Then why did you not answer my questions?" asked Roughgrove, turning to the captive. The young chief made no answer, but sat with his arms folded, and still regarding the features of Mary.

"He's a perfect fool!" said Sneak.

"He's a snake in the grass, and 'll bite some of us some of these times, before we know any thing about it," said Joe.

"Be silent," said Glenn. "If the hope that fills my breast should be realized, the young chief will cause more rejoicing than sorrowing among us. The wisdom of Providence surpasses all human understanding. Events that bear a frightful import to the limited comprehensions of mortals, may nevertheless be fraught with inestimable blessings. Even the circumstance of your capture, Mary, however distressing at the time to yourself and to all your friends, may some day be looked upon as a happy and fortunate occurrence."

"I hope so," said Mary.

"God is great—is present everywhere, and governs every thing—let us always submit to his just decrees without murmuring," said the old ferryman, his eyes brightening with fervent devotion.

"They've a notion to preach a little, I believe," whispered Sneak to Joe.

"Let 'em go ahead, then," replied Joe, who was busily engaged with a long switch, that he occasionally thrust in the fire, and when the end was burnt to a coal, slyly applied it to the heel of the young chief's moccasin.

"You'd better not let him ketch you at that," said Sneak.

"He'll think its a tick biting him—I want to see if the Indians scratch like other people," said Joe.

Mary, being so requested by her father, began to relate every thing that transpired up to her rescue, while she was in the possession of the savages. The Indian riveted his eyes upon her during the recital, and seemed to mark every word. Whether he understood all she said, or was enchanted with her soft and musical tones, could not be ascertained; but the listeners more than once observed with astonishment his gleaming eyes, his attentive attitude, and the intense interest exhibited in his face. It was during a moment when he was thus absorbed that he suddenly sprang erect. Joe threw down his switch, convulsed with internal laughter. Sneak leaned back against the wall, and while he grinned at the amusing scene, seemed curious to know what would be the result. Mary paused, and Glenn inquired the cause of the interruption.

"Its nothing, hardly," said Sneak: "only a spark of fire got agin the Indian's foot. He ain't as good pluck as the other one we had—he could stand burning at the stake without flinching."

"Did either of you *place* the fire against his foot?" demanded Glenn, in something like anger. But before he could receive an answer, the young chief, who had whirled round furiously, and cast a fierce look at his tormentor, relaxing his knit brows into an expression of contempt, very deliberately took hold of Joe's ear, and turning on his heel like a pivot, forced him to make many circles round him on the floor.

"Let go my ear!" roared Joe, pacing round in pain.

"Hold your holt, my snarvilerous yaller prairie dog!" cried Sneak, inexpressibly amused.

"Let go my ear, I say!" cried Joe, still trotting round, with both hands grasping the Indian's wrist. "Mr. Glenn! Mr. Glenn!" continued Joe, "he's pinching a hole through my ear! Shoot him down, shoot him down. there's my gun, standing against the wall—but its not loaded! Take my knife—oh, he's tearing my ear off!" When the Indian thought he was sufficiently punished, he led him back to his seat, and relinquished his hold. He then resumed his own seat, and composedly turning his eyes to Mary, seemed to desire her to proceed with the narration. She did so, but when she spoke of her attempt to escape in the prairie, of the young chief's noble conduct, and his admiration of her ring (and she pulled off her glove and exhibited it as she spoke,) he again rose from his seat, and walking, apparently unconsciously, to where she reclined upon her father's knees, fixed his eyes upon the jewel in a most mysterious manner. He no longer dwelt upon the maiden's sweet tones. He did nothing but gaze at the ring.

"He's got a notion to steal that ring!" said Joe, with a sneer.

"Shet your mouth!" said Sneak, observing that Mary looked reproachfully at Joe, and paused.

"Don't talk that way, Joe!" said the offended girl. "If he wanted it, why did he not take it when I was his prisoner? I will freely let him have it now," she continued, slipping it off from her finger.

"No! keep it, child—it is a family ring," said Roughgrove.

"I will lend it to him—I know he will give it me again," she continued, placing it in the extended hand of the young chief, who thanked her with his eyes, and resumed his seat. He now seemed to disregard every thing that was said or done, and only gazed at the ring, which he held first in one hand and then in the other, with the sparkling diamond uppermost. Sometimes he would press his forehead with his hand and cover his eyes, and then gaze at the ring again. Then staring wildly around, and slightly starting, he would bite his fingers to ascertain whether the scene was reality or a dream. Finally, giving vent to a piteous sigh, while a tear ran down his stained cheek, he placed his elbows upon his knees, and, bending forward, seemed to muse over some event of the past, which the jewel before him had called to remembrance.

Glenn narrowly watched every look and motion of the young chief, and when Mary finished the account of her capture, he introduced the subject of the lost child, Mary's brother, that Roughgrove had spoken about before starting in pursuit of the war-party.

"I can remember him!" said Mary, "and mother, too—they are both in heaven now—poor brother! poor mother!"

The young chief raised his head quickly, and staring at the maiden's face, seemed to regard her tears and her features with an interest similar to that of a child when it beholds a rare and curious toy.

"Has it not occurred to you," said Glenn, addressing Roughgrove, "that this young chief might possibly be your own son?"

"No!" replied the old man, promptly, and partially rising, "*he* my son—*he* Mary's brother—and once in the act of plunging the tomahawk——"

"But, father," interrupted Mary, "he would never have harmed me—I know he would not—for every time he looked me in the face he seemed to pity me, and sometimes he almost wept to think I was away from my friends, among savages, cold and distressed. But I don't think he can be my brother—my little brother I used to love so much—yet I could never think how he should have fallen in the river without my knowing it. Sometimes I remember it all as if it were yesterday. He was hunting wild violets——"

"Oh! oh!" screamed the young chief, springing from his seat towards Mary. Fear, pain, apprehension, joy and affection, all seemed to be mingled in his heaving breast.

"He's crazy, dod"——the word died upon Sneak's lip.

"I should like to know who burnt his foot then," said Joe.

"Silence! both of you," said Glenn.

"What does he mean?" at length asked Roughgrove, staring at the young chief.

"Let us be patient, and see," said Glenn.

Ere long the Indian turned his eyes slowly downward, and resumed his seat mournfully and in silence.

"Oh!" said Mary, "if he *is* my poor brother, my heart will burst to see him thus—a wild savage."

"How old are you, Mary?" asked Glenn.

"Nineteen," said she.

"Your brother, then, has been lost thirteen years. He may yet be restored to you—re-taught our manners and speech—bless his aged father's declining years, and merit his sister's affection."

"Oh! Mr. Glenn! is he then alive? is this he?" cried Mary.

"No, child!" said Roughgrove, "do not think of such a thing, for you will be most bitterly disappointed. Your brother was *white*—look at this Indian's dark face!"

Glenn approached the chief, extending his hand in a friendly manner. It was frankly grasped. He then gently drew the furs aside and exposed the young man's shoulder. It was as white as his own! Roughgrove, Mary, and all, looked on in wonder. The young chief regarded it with singular emotions himself. He seemed to associate it in some manner with the ring he held, for he glanced from one to the other alternately.

"Did Mary wear that ring before the child was lost?" asked Glenn.

"No," replied Roughgrove, "but her mother did."

"I believe he is your son!" said Glenn. "Mary," he continued, "have you any trinkets or toys you used to play with?"

"Yes. Oh, let me get them!" she replied, and running to a corner of the room where her father's chests and trunks had been placed, she produced a small drum and a brass toy cannon. "He used to play with these from morning till night," she continued, placing them on the floor. She had not taken her hand away from them, before the young chief sprang to her side and cried out—

"They're mine! they're mine! they're William's!"

"What was the child's name?" asked Glenn, quickly.

"William! William!" cried Mary. "It is my brother! it is my poor brother William!" and without a moment's hesitation she threw her arms round his neck, and sobbed upon his breast!

"The poor, poor child!" said Roughgrove, in tremulous tones, embracing them both, his eyes filled with tears.

"Sister! sister!" said the youth, gazing in partial bewilderment at Mary.

"Brother, brother! I am your sister!" said Mary, in tones of thrilling tenderness.

"But mother! where's mother?" asked the youth. The father and sister bowed their heads in silence. The youth, after clinging fondly to Mary a few minutes, started up abruptly and looked amazed, as if waking from a sweet dream to the reality of his recent dreadful condition.

"Brother, why do you look so coldly at us? Why don't you press us to your heart?" said Mary, still clinging to him. The youth's features gradually assumed a grave and haughty cast, and, turning away, he walked to the stool he had occupied, and sat down in silence.

"I will win him from the Indians," said Mary, running after him, and sitting down at his side.

"Ugh!" exclaimed the youth in displeasure, and moved a short distance away.

"He's not true grit—I 'most wish I had killed him," said Sneak.

"Yes, and pinch me if I don't burn him again, if I get a chance," said Joe.

"Silence!" said Glenn, sternly. For many minutes not a word was spoken. At length Mary, who had been sobbing, raised her head and looked tenderly in the face of her brother. Still he regarded her with indifference. She then seized the toy-drum, which with the other articles had been thrust out of view, and placed them before him. When his eyes rested upon them; the severe and wild expressions of his features again relaxed. The young war-chief was a child again. He abandoned his seat and sat down on the floor beside his sister. Looking her guilelessly in the face, an innocent and boyish smile played upon his lips.

"You won't go away again and leave your poor sister; will you, William?" said Mary.

"No, indeed. And when the Indians come we'll run away and go to mother, won't we, Mary?" said the youth, in a complete abandonment of time and condition.

"He *is* restored—restored at last!" exclaimed Roughgrove, walking across the room to where the brother and sister sat. The youth sprang to his feet, and darted a look of defiance at him. "Oh! wretched man that I am! the murderous savages have converted the gentle lamb into a wolf!" Roughgrove then repeated his words to the youth in the Osage language. The youth replied in the same language, his eyes flashing indignantly. He said it was not true; that the red man was great and noble, and the pale face was a beast—and added that he had another tomahawk and bows and arrows in his own country, and might see the day when this insult would be terribly resented. The old man sank down on his rude seat, and gave way to excruciating grief.

"Brother William!" cried Mary, tapping the drum. The youth cast down his eyes to where she sat, and their fierceness vanished in a twinkling. She placed the toy in his possession, and rose to bring some other plaything she remembered.

"Sister, don't go—I'll tell mother!" cried the youth, in infantile earnestness.

"I'll come back presently, brother," said Mary, tripping across the room and searching a trunk.

"Make haste—but I'm not afraid—I'll frighten all the Indians away." Saying this, he rattled the drum as rapidly as possible.

"See what I've got, brother," said Mary, returning with a juvenile book, and sitting down close at his side. He thrust the drum away, and, laughing heartily, placed his arm round his sister and said: "Mother's got *my* book; but you'll let me look at yours, won't you, sister?"

"Yes that I will, brother—see, this is the little old woman, and there's her dog——"

"Yes, and there's the peddler," cried the youth, pointing at the picture.

"Now can't you read it, brother?"

"To be sure I can—let me read:

"'There was a little woman
As I have heard tell,
She went to market
Her eggs for to sell.'

See! there she goes, with a basket on her arm and a cane in her hand."

"Yes, and here she is again on this side, fast asleep, and her basket of eggs sitting by her," said Mary; "now let me read the next:

"'She went to market,
All on a market day,
And she fell asleep
On the king's highway.'"

Now do you read about the peddler, brother. Mother used to say there was a naughty word in it."

"I will," cried the youth, eagerly; but he paused and looked steadfastly at the picture before him.

"Why don't you read?" asked Mary, endeavouring to confine his thoughts to the childish employment.

"That's a pretty *skin*, ain't it?" said he, pointing to the red shawl painted on the picture.

"*Skin!*" said Mary; "why, that's her shawl, brother."

"I'll steal one for my squaw," said he.

"*Steal*, brother!" said the trembling girl.

"No I won't, either, sister—don't you know mother says we must never steal, nor tell stories, nor say bad words."

"That's right, brother. But you haven't got an ugly *squaw*, have you?"

"No indeed, sister, that I haven't!"

"I thought you wouldn't have any thing to do with the ugly squaws."

"That I wouldn't—mine's a pretty one."

"Oh, heaven!" cried the weeping girl, throwing herself on her brother's bosom. He kissed her, and strove to comfort her, and turned to the book and continued to turn over the leaves, while Mary sat by in sadness, but ever and anon replying to his childish questions, and still striving to keep him thus diverted.

"Have you any of the clothes you wore when he was a child?" asked Glenn, addressing Roughgrove.

"Yes," replied the old man; and seizing upon the thought, he unlocked the trunk that contained them, and put them on.

"Where's mother?" suddenly asked the young chief.

"Oh, she's dead!" said Mary.

"Dead? I know better!" said he, emphatically.

"Indeed she is, brother," repeated Mary, in tears.

"When did she die?" he continued, in a musing attitude.

"A long time ago—when you were away," said she.

"I wasn't gone away long, was I?" he asked, with much simplicity.

"Oh, very long—we thought you were dead."

"He was a very bad Indian to steal me away without asking mother. But where's father? Is he dead, too?"

he continued, lifting his eyes and beholding Roughgrove attired in a suit of velvet, and wearing broad silver knee buckles. "Father! father!" he cried, eagerly clasping the old man in his arms.

"My poor boy, I will be your father still!" said Roughgrove.

"I know you will," said the youth, "for you always loved me a great deal, and now that my poor mother's dead, I'm sure you will love sister and me more than ever."

"Indeed I will, poor child! But you must not go back to the naughty savages any more."

The youth gazed round in silence, and made no reply. He was evidently awakening to a consciousness of his condition. A frown of horror darkened his brow as he contemplated the scenes of his wild abode among the Indians; and, when he contrasted his recent mode of life with the Elysian days of his childhood, now fresh in his memory, mingled emotions of regret, fear, and bliss seemed to be contending in his bosom. A cold dampness settled upon his forehead, his limbs trembled violently, and distressful sighs issued from his heaving breast. Gradually he sank down on a couch at his side, and closed his eyes.

When some minutes had elapsed, during which a deathlike silence was maintained, Mary approached lightly to where her father stood, and inquired if her brother was ill.

"No," said Roughgrove, in a whisper; "he only sleeps; but it is a very sound slumber."

"Now let us take off his Indian dress," said Glenn, "and put on him some of my clothes." This was speedily effected, and without awaking the youth, whose senses were benumbed, as if by some powerful opiate.

"Now, Mary," said Roughgrove, "you must likewise have repose. You are almost exhausted in body and mind. Sleep at your brother's side, if you will, poor girl." Mary laid her head on William's pillow, and was soon in a deep slumber.

For several moments Roughgrove stood lost in thought, gazing alternately at the reposing brother and sister, and Glenn. He looked also at Sneak and Joe reclining by the fire; both were fast asleep. He then resumed his seat, and motioned Glenn to do likewise. He bowed his head a brief length of time in silence, apparently recalling to mind some occurrence of more than ordinary import.

"My young friend," said he, at length, while he placed his withered hand upon Glenn's knee, "do you remember that I said there was *another* secret connected with my family?"

"Distinctly," replied Glenn; "and I have since felt so much anxiety to be acquainted with it that I have several times been on the eve of asking you to gratify my curiosity; but thinking it might be impertinent, I have forborne. It has more than once occurred to me that your condition in life must have been different from what it now is."

"It has been different—far different. I will tell you all. I am a native of England—a younger brother, of an ancient and honourable family, but much decayed in fortune. I was educated for the ministry. Our residence was on the Thames, a few miles distant from London, and I was early entered in one of the institutions of the great city. While attending college, it was my practice twice a month to visit my father's mansion on foot. I was fond of solitary musings, and the exercise was beneficial to my weak frame. It was during one of those excursions that I rescued a young lady from the rude assaults of two ruffians. After a brief struggle, they fled. I turned to the one I had so opportunely served, and was struck with her unparalleled beauty. Young; a form of symmetrical loveliness; dark, languishing eyes, a smooth forehead of lily purity, and auburn hair flowing in glossy ringlets—it was not strange that an impression should be made on the heart of a young student. She thanked me for my generous interposition in such sweet and musical tones, that every word thrilled pleasantly through my breast. She prevailed upon me to accompany her to her mother's cottage, but a few hundred paces distant; and during our walk thither, she hung confidingly on my arm. Her aged mother overwhelmed me with expressions of gratitude. She mildly chid her daughter for wandering so far away in quest of flowers, and then withdrawing, left us alone. Again my eyes met those of the blushing maiden—but it is useless to dwell upon the particulars of our mutual passion. Suffice it to say that she was the only child of her widowed mother, in moderate but independent circumstances, and being hitherto secluded from the society of the other sex, soon conceived (for my visits were frequent) an affection as ardent as my own. At length I apprized my father of the attachment, and asked his consent to our union. He refused to sanction the alliance in the most positive terms, and commanded me never to mention the subject again. He said that I was poor, and that he would not consent to my marriage with any other than an heiress. I returned to London, resolved to disobey his injunction, for I felt that my happiness entirely depended upon my union with the lovely Juliet. But I had never yet definitely expressed my desire to her. Yet there could be no doubt from her smiles that my wishes would willingly be acceded to. I determined to arrange every thing at our next interview, and a few weeks afterwards I repaired to the cottage for that purpose. Instead of meeting me with her ever blissful face, I found my Juliet in tears! She was alone; but in the adjoining chamber I heard a man's voice, and feared that it was my father. I was mistaken. Juliet soon brushed away her tears, and informed me that she had been *again* assailed by the same ruffians, and on the lawn within sight of the cottage. She said that the gentleman in the next room was her deliverer. I seized her hand, and when about to propose a plan to secure her against such annoyances for ever, her mother entered and introduced the stranger to me. His name was Nicholson, and he stated that he was a partner in a large banking establishment in Lombard Street. He was past the bloom of youth, but still his fine clothes and his reputed wealth were displeasing to me. I was especially chagrined at the marked attention shown him by Juliet's mother. And my annoyance was increased by the frequent lascivious glances he cast at the maiden. The more I marked him, the more was my uneasiness. It soon occurred to me that I had seen him before! He resembled a person I had seen driving rapidly along the highway in a chariot, on the morning that I first beheld my Juliet. But my recollection of his features was indistinct. There was a condescending suavity in his manners, and sometimes a positive and commanding tone in his conversation, that almost roused my enmity in spite of my peaceful calling and friendly disposition. It was my intention to remain at the cottage, and propose to Juliet after he had departed. But my purpose was defeated, for he declared his intention to enjoy the country air till evening, and I returned, disappointed and dispirited, to the city.

"A few days afterwards I visited the cottage again. What was my surprise and vexation to behold Mr. Nicholson there! He was seated, with his patronizing smile, between Juliet and her mother, and presenting them various richly bound books, jewels, &c., which seemed to me to be received with much gratification. I was welcomed with the usual frankness and pleasure by Juliet, but I thought her mother's reception was less cordial, and Mr. Nicholson regarded me with manifest indifference. I made an ineffectual effort at vivacity, and after an hour's stay, during which my remarks gradually narrowed down to monosyllables, (while Mr. Nicholson became excessively loquacious,) I rose to depart. Juliet made an endeavour to accompany me to the door, where I hoped to be assured of her true affection for me by her own lips, but some pointed inquiry (I do not now recollect what) from Nicholson, which was seconded in a positive manner by her mother, arrested her steps, and while she hesitated, I bad her adieu, and departed for the city, resolved never to see her again.

"It was about a month after the above occurrence that my resolution gave way, and I was again on the road to the cottage, with my mind made up to forgive and forget every thing that had offended me, and to offer my hand where my heart seemed to be already irrevocably fixed. When I entered who should I see but the eternal thwarter of my happiness, the ever-present Nicholson! But horror! he was now the wedded lord of Juliet! The ceremony was just over. There were but two or three strangers present besides the clergyman. Bride, groom, guests, and all were hateful to my sight. The minister, particularly, I thought had a demoniac face, similar to that of one of the ruffians who had tested the quality of my cane. Juliet cast a look at me with more of sadness than joy in it. She offered me her hand in silent salutation, and it trembled in my grasp. The deed was done. Pity for the maiden who had been thus sacrificed to secure a superabundance of wealth which could never be enjoyed, and sorrow at my own forlorn condition, weighed heavily, oh, how heavily!

on my heart. I returned to my lonely and desolate lodgings without a malicious feeling for the one who had robbed me of every hope of earthly enjoyment. I prayed that he might make Juliet happy.

"But, alas! her happiness was of short duration. Scarce six months had passed before Mr. Nicholson began to neglect his youthful and confiding bride. She had still remained at her mother's cottage, while, as she stated, his establishment was being fitted up in town for their reception. He at first drove out to the cottage every evening; but soon afterwards fell into the habit of visiting his bride only two or three times a week. He neither carried her into society nor brought home any visitors. Yet he seemed to possess immense wealth, and bestowed it upon Juliet with a liberal, nay, profuse hand. My young friend, what kind of a character do you suppose this Mr. Nicholson to have been?" said the old man, pausing, and turning to Glenn, who had been listening to the narrative with marked attention.

"He was an impostor—a gambler," replied Glenn, promptly.

"He *was* an impostor! but no adventurous gambler, as you suppose. I will proceed. About seven months after his marriage, he abandoned Juliet altogether! Yet he did not forget her entirely. He may have felt remorse for the ruin he had wrought—or perhaps a slight degree of affection for his unborn ——; and costly presents, and many considerable sums of money, were sent by him to the cottage. But neither the aged mother nor the deserted wife found the consolation they desired in his prodigal gifts. They sent me a note, informing me of their distressful condition, and requesting me to ascertain the locality of Mr. Nicholson's establishment, and, if possible, to find out the cause of his unnatural conduct. I did all in my power to accomplish what they desired. I repaired to the cottage, unable to give the least intelligence of Mr. Nicholson. I had not been able to find any one who had ever heard of him. Juliet became almost frantic. She determined to seek him herself. At her urgent solicitation, I accompanied her to the city in an open curricle. A pitying Providence soon terminated her insupportable suspense. While we were driving through Hyde Park, we were forcibly stopped to permit, among the throng, the passage of a splendid equipage. The approaching carriage was likewise an open one. Juliet glanced at the inmates, and uttering a wild piercing shriek, fainted in my arms. I looked, and saw her quondam husband! He was decked in the magnificent insignia of ROYALTY. Nobles were bowing, high-born ladies smiling, and the multitude shouted, 'There comes his royal highness, the Prince of ——'

"Man cannot punish him," continued Roughgrove, "but God can. HE will deal justly, both with the proud and the oppressed. But to return. He saw Juliet. A few minutes after the gorgeous retinue swept past, one of the prince's attendants came with a note. Juliet was insensible. I took it from the messenger's hand, and started when I looked the villain in the face. He had been the parson! He smiled at the recognition! I hurled my cane at his head, and hastened back to the cottage with a physician in attendance. Juliet soon recovered from her swoon. But a frenzied desperation was manifest in her pale features. I left her in her mother's charge, and returned in agony to my lodgings. That night a raging fever seized upon my brain, and for months I was the victim of excruciating disease. When convalescent, but still confined to my room, I chanced to run my eye over one of the daily papers, and was petrified to see the name of Mrs. Nicholson, in the first article that attracted my attention, in connection with an attempt upon the life of the king! She had been seized with a fit of temporary insanity, and driving to town, sought her betrayer with the intention of shedding his blood. She waited at the gate of St. James's palace until a carriage drove up in which she expected to find the prince. It was the king—yet she did not discover her error until the blow was made. The steel did not perform its office, as you are aware from the history of England, in which this event is recorded. The king humanely pardoned her on the spot. A single word she uttered acquainted him with her history, and her piteous looks made an extraordinary impression on his mind. He too, had, perhaps, sported with innocent beauty. And now the spectre of the weeping maniac haunted his visions. Soon he became one himself. The name of Juliet fortunately was not published in the journals. It was by some means incorrectly stated that the woman who attacked the king was named *Margaret* Nicholson, and so it remains on the page of history.

"As soon as I was able to leave my chamber, I repaired to the cottage. Juliet was a *mother*. Reason had returned, and she strove to submit with Christian humility to her pitiable lot. She received me with the same sweet smile that had formerly beamed on her guileless face. Her mother, the promoter of the fancied advantageous alliance, now seemed to suffer most They both clung to me as their only remaining friend, and in truth I learned that all other friends had forsaken them. I looked upon the deceived, outraged, but still innocent Juliet, with pity. Her little cherub twins ——"

"Twins!" echoed Glenn.

"Ay, twins," replied Roughgrove, "and they lie behind you now, side by side, on yonder bed."

Glenn turned and gazed a moment in silence on the sleeping forms of William and Mary.

"Her poor little ones excited my compassion. They were not blamable for their father's crime, nor could they enjoy the advantages of his exalted station. They were without a protector in the world. Juliet's mother was fast sinking under the calamity she had herself in a great measure wrought. My heart melted when I contemplated the sad condition of the only female I had ever loved. It was not long before the fires of affection again gleamed brightly in my breast. Juliet had committed no crime, either in the eyes of man or God. She did not intend to err. She had acted in good faith. She had never designed to transgress either the laws of earth or heaven, and although the disguised prince did not wholly possess her heart, yet she deemed it a duty to be governed by the advice of her parent. These things I explained to her, and when her conscience was appeased by the facts which I demonstrated, her peace in some measure returned, but she was still subject to occasional melancholy reflections. Perhaps she thought of me—how my heart had suffered (for, young as I was, the occurrence brought premature gray hairs; and even now, although my head is white, I have seen but little more than forty years)—and how happy we might have travelled life's journey together. I seized such a moment to renew my proposals. She declined, but declined in tears. I returned to the city with the intention to repeat the offer the next time we met. Not many weeks elapsed before her aged mother was consigned to the tomb. Poor Juliet's condition was now immeasurably lamentable. She had neither friend nor protector. I again urged my suit, and was successful. But she required of me a promise to retire from the world for ever. I cheerfully agreed, for I was disgusted with the vanity and wickedness of my species. We came hither. You know the rest."

When Roughgrove ceased speaking, the night was far advanced, and a perfect silence reigned. Without uttering another word, he and Glenn rose from their seats, and repairing to the remaining unoccupied couch, ere long yielded to the influence of tranquil slumber.

CHAPTER XIV.

William's illness—Sneak's strange house—Joe's courage—The bee hunt—Joe and Sneak captured by the Indians—Their sad condition—Preparations to burn them alive—Their miraculous escape.

JUST before the dawn of day, Roughgrove and Glenn were awakened by Mary. She was weeping at the bedside of William.

"What's the matter, child?" asked Roughgrove, rising up and lighting the lamp.

"Poor brother!" said she, and her utterance failed her.

"He has a raging fever!" said Glenn, who had approached the bed and placed his hand upon the young man's temples.

"True—and I fear it will be fatal!" said Roughgrove, in alarm, as he held the unresisting wrist of the panting youth.

"Fear not," said Glenn; "God directs all things. This violent illness, too, may in the end be a blessing. Let us do all in our power to restore him to health, and leave the rest to Him. I was once an ardent student of medicine, and the knowledge I acquired may be of some avail."

"I will pray for his recovery," said Mary, bowing down at the foot of the bed.

"Dod—I mean—Joe, it's most daylight," said Sneak, rising up and rubbing his eyes.

"Well, what if it is? what are you waking me up for?" replied Joe, turning over on his rude pallet.

"Why, I'm going home."

"Well, clear out then."

"But you'll have to get up and shut the gate after me."

"Plague take it all, I believe you're just trying to spoil my nap!" said Joe, much vexed.

"No I ain't, Joe; I'm in earnest, indeed I am," continued Sneak; "bekaise I hain't been inside of my house, now, for three or four days, and who knows but the dod—I mean the—Indians have been there and stole all my muskrat skins?"

"If they have, then there's no use in looking for them now."

"If they have, dod—I mean, *burn* me if I don't foller em to the other end of creation but I'll have 'em back agin. But I ain't much afeard that they saw my house—they might rub agin it without knowing it was a house."

"That's a pretty tale," said Joe, now thoroughly awakened, and staring incredulously in his companion's face.

"It's a fact."

"Whereabouts is your house?"

"Why, it's in the second valley we crossed when we went after the wolves on the island."

"Then your skins are gone," said Joe, "for the Indians have been in that valley."

"I know they was there well enough," said Sneak; "but didn't I say they couldn't find the house, even if they was to scratch their backs agin it?"

"What kind of a house is it?"

"'Spose you come along and see," said Sneak, groping about in the dim twilight for his cap, and the gun Glenn had given him.

"I *should* like to see it, just out of curiosity," replied Joe

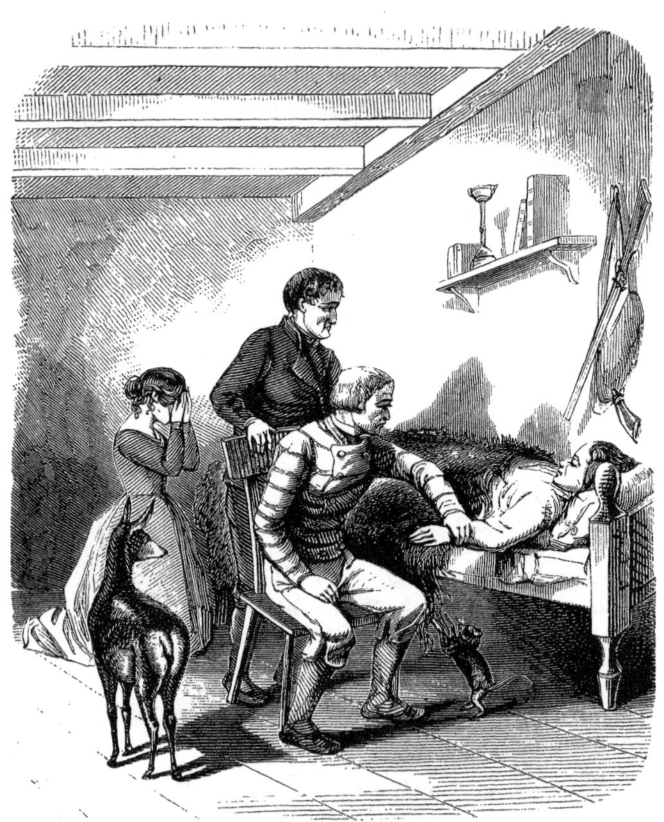

"I will pray for his recovery," said Mary, bowing down at the foot of the bed.—P. 186.

"Then go along with Sneak," said Glenn, who approached the fire to prepare some medicine; "it is necessary that every thing should be quiet and still here."

"If you'll help me to feed and water the horses, Sneak, I'll go home with you," said Joe. Sneak readily agreed to the proposition, and by the time it was quite light, and yet before the sun rose, the labour was accomplished, and they set out together for the designated valley. Their course was somewhat different from that pursued when in quest of the wolves, for Sneak's habitation was about midway between the river and the prairie, and they diverged in a westerly direction. But their progress was slow During the night there had been a change in the atmosphere, and a constant breeze from the south had in a great measure softened the snow-crust, so that our pedestrians frequently broke through.

"This is not the most agreeable walking I ever saw," said Joe, breaking through and tumbling down on his face.

"That's jest as much like swimming as walking," said Sneak, smiling at the blunder of his companion.

"Smash it, Sneak," continued Joe, rising up with some difficulty, "I don't half like this breaking-through business."

"You must walk lighter, and then you won't break through," said Sneak; "tread soft like I do, and put your feet down flat. I hain't broke in once"——But before the sentence was uttered, Sneak had broken through himself, and stood half-submerged in the snow.

"Ha! ha! ha! you musn't count your chickens before they're hatched," said Joe, laughing; "but you may score one, now you have broken the shell."

"I got in that time," said Sneak, now winding through the bushes with much caution, as if it were truly in his power to diminish the weight of his body by a peculiar mode of walking.

"This thaw 'll be good for one thing, any how," said Joe, after they had progressed some time in silence.

"What's that?" asked Sneak.

"Why, it 'll keep the Indians away; they can't travel through the slush when the crust is melted off."

"That's as true as print," replied Sneak; and if none

of 'em follered us back to the settlement, we needn't look for 'em agin till spring."

"I wonder if any of them *did* follow us?" asked Joe, pausing abruptly.

"How can anybody tell till they see 'em?" replied Sneak. "What're you stopping for?"

"I'm going back," said Joe.

"Dod—you're a fool—that's jest what you are. Hain't we got our guns? and if there *is* any about, ain't they in the bushes close to Mr. Glenn's house? and hain't we passed through 'em long ago? But I don't keer any thing about your cowardly company—go back, if you want to," said Sneak, striding onward.

"Sneak, don't go so fast. I haven't any notion of going back," said Joe, springing nimbly to his companion's side.

"I believe you're afeard to go back by yourself," said Sneak, laughing heartily.

"Pshaw, Sneak, I don't think any of 'em followed us, do you?" continued Joe, peering at the bushes and trees in the valley, which they were entering.

"No," said Sneak; "I only wanted to skeer you a bit."

"I've killed too many savages to be scared by them now," said Joe, carelessly striding onward.

"What was you a going back for, if you wasn't skeered?"

"I wonder what always makes you think I'm frightened when I talk of going into the house! Sneak, you're *always* mistaken. I wasn't thinking about myself—I only wanted to put Mr. Glenn on his guard."

"Then what made you tell that wapper for, the other night, about cutting that Indian's throat?"

"How do you know it was a wapper?" asked Joe, somewhat embarrassed by Sneak's home-thrust.

"Bekaise, don't I know that I cut his juggler-vein myself? Didn't the blood gush all over me? and didn't he fall down dead before he had time to holler?" continued Sneak, with much warmth and earnestness.

"Sneak," said Joe, "I've no doubt you thought he was dead—but then you must know it's nearly as hard to kill a man as a cat. You might have been mistaken; every body is liable to be deceived—even a person's eyes deceive him sometimes. I don't pretend to say that I haven't been mistaken before now, myself. It *may* be possible that I was mistaken about the Indian as well as you—I might have just *thought* I saw him move. But I was there longer than you, and the inference is that I didn't stand as good a chance to be deceived."

"Well, I can't answer all that," said Sneak; "but I'll swear I felt my knife grit agin his neck-bone."

Joe did not desire to pursue the subject any further, and they proceeded on their way in silence, ever and anon breaking through the snow-crust. The atmosphere became still more temperate when the bright sun beamed over the horizon. Drops of water trickled down from the snow-covered branches of the trees, and a few birds flitted overhead, and uttered imperfect lays.

"Here we are," said Sneak, halting in the midst of a clump of enormous sycamore trees, over whose roots a sparkling rivulet glided with a gurgling sound.

"I know we're here," said Joe; "but what are you stopping *here* for?"

"Here's where I live," replied Sneak, with a comical smile playing on his lips.

"But where's your house?" asked Joe.

"Didn't I say you couldn't find it, even if you was to rub your back agin it?"

"I know I'm not rubbing against your house now," replied Joe, turning round and looking up in the huge tree he had been leaning against.

"But you have been leaning agin my house," continued Sneak, amused at the incredulous face of his companion.

"I know better," persisted Joe; "this big sycamore is the only thing I've leant against since we started."

"Jest foller me, and I'll show you something," said Sneak, stepping round to the opposite side of the tree, where the ascent on the north rose abruptly from the roots. Here he removed a thin flat stone of about four feet in height, that stood in a vertical position against the tree.

"You don't live in there, Sneak, surely; why that looks like a wolf's den," said Joe, perceiving a dark yawning aperture, and that the immense tree was but a mere shell

"Keep at my heels," said Sneak, stooping down and crawling into the tree.

"I'd rather not," said Joe; "there may be a bear in it."

Soon a clicking sound was heard within, and the next moment Joe perceived the flickering rays of a small lamp that Sneak held in his hand, illuminating the sombre recesses of the novel habitation.

"Why don't you come in?" asked Sneak.

"Sneak, how do you know there ain't a bear up in the hollow?" asked Joe, crawling in timidly and endeavouring to peer through the darkness far above, where even the rays of the lamp could not penetrate.

"I wonder if you think I'd let a bear sleep in my house," continued Sneak, searching among a number of boxes and rude shelves, to see if any thing had been molested during his absence. Finding every thing safe, he handed Joe a stool, and began to kindle a fire in a small stone furnace. Joe sat down in silence, and looked about in astonishment. And the scene was enough to excite the wonder of an Irishman. The interior of the tree was full eight feet in diameter, while the eye was lost above in undeveloped regions. Below, there was a surface of smooth stones, which were comfortably carpeted over with buffalo robes. At one side was a diminutive fireplace, or furnace, constructed of three flat stones about three inches in thickness. The largest was laid horizontally on the ground, and the others placed upright on it, and attached to a clay chimney, that was by some means confined to the interior side of the tree, and ran upward until it was lost in the darkness. After gazing in amazement several minutes at this strange contrivance, Joe exclaimed:

"Sneak, I don't understand this! Where does that smoke go to?"

"Go out doors and see if you can't see," replied Sneak, placing more fuel on the blazing fire.

"Go out of the *hole* you mean to say," said Joe, creeping out.

"You may call it jest what you like," said Sneak; "but I'll be switched if many folks lives in *higher* houses than I does."

"Well, I'll declare!" cried Joe.

"What ails you now?" asked Sneak, thrusting his head out of the aperture, and regarding the surprise of Joe with much satisfaction.

"Why, I see the smoke pouring out of a hole in a *limb*

not much bigger than my thigh!" cried Joe. This was true. Sneak had mounted up in the tree before building his chimney, and finding a hollow bough that communicated directly with the main trunk, had cut through into the cavity, and thus made a vent for the escape of the smoke.

"Come in now, and get something to eat," said Sneak. This was an invitation that Joe was never known to decline. After casting another admiring glance at the blue vapour that issued from the bough some ninety feet from the ground, he passed through the cavity with alacrity.

"Where are you?" cried Joe, upon entering and looking round in vain for his host, who had vanished in a most inexplicable manner. Joe stared in astonishment. The lighted lamp remained on a box, that was designed for the breakfast-table, and on which there was in truth an abundance of dried venison and smoking potatoes. But where was Sneak?

"Sneak, what's become of you?" continued Joe, eagerly listening for a reply, and anxiously scanning the tempting repast set before him. "I know you're at some of your tricks," he added, and sitting down at the table, commenced in no indifferent manner to discuss the savoury venison and potatoes.

"I'm only up stairs," cried Sneak, in the darkness above; and throwing down a rope made of hides, the upper end of which was fastened to the tree within, he soon followed, slipping briskly down, and without delay sprang to Joe's assistance.

When the meal was finished, or rather, when every thing set before them had vanished, Sneak rose up and thrust his long neck out of the aperture.

"What are you looking at?" asked Joe.

"I'm looking at the warm sun shining agin yonder side of the hill," said Sneak; "how'd you like to go a bee-hunting?"

"A bee-hunting!" iterated Joe. "I wonder if you think we could find a bee at this season of the year? and I should like to know what it'd be worth when we found it."

"Plague take the bee—I mean the *honey*—don't you like wild honey?" continued Sneak.

"Yes," said Joe; "but how can you find any when there's such a snow as this on the ground?"

"When there's a snow, that's the time to find 'em," said Sneak; "peticuly when the sun shines warm. Jest come out here and look," he continued, stepping along, and followed by Joe; "don't you see yander big stooping limb?"

"Yes," replied Joe, gazing at the bough pointed out.

"Well," continued Sneak, "there's a bee's nest in that. Look here," he added, picking from the snow several dead bees that had been thrown from the hive; "now this is the way with all wild bees (but these are tame, for they live in my house), for when there comes a warm day they're sartin as fate to throw out the dead ones, and we can find where they are as easy as any thing in the world."

"Sneak, my mouth's watering—suppose we take the axe and go and hunt for some honey."

"Let's be off, then," said Sneak, getting his axe, and preparing to place the stone against the tree.

"Stop, Sneak," said Joe; "let me get my gun before you shut the *door*."

"I guess we'd better leave our guns, and then we won't be so apt to break through," replied Sneak, closing up the aperture.

"The bees won't sting us, will they?" asked Joe, turning to his companion when they had attained the high-timbered ridge that ran parallel with the valley.

"If you chaw 'em in your mouth they will," replied Sneak, striding along under the trees with his head bent down, and minutely examining every small dark object he found lying on the surface of the snow.

"I know that as well as you do," continued Joe, "because that would thaw them."

"Well, if they're froze, how *kin* they sting you?"

"You needn't be so snappish," replied Joe. "I just asked for information. I know as well as anybody they're frozen or torpid."

"Or what?" asked Sneak.

"Torpid," said Joe.

"I'll try to 'member that word," continued Sneak, peeping under a spreading oak that was surrounded by a dense hazel thicket.

"Do," continued Joe, contemptuously, "and if you'll

only recollect all you hear me say, you may get a tolerable education after a while."

"I'll be shivered if this ain't the edication I wan't," said Sneak, turning round with one or two dead bees in his hand, that he had found near the root of the tree.

"Huzza!" cried Joe, "we'll have a mess of honey now. I see the hole where they are—its in a limb, and we won't have to cut down the tree," and before Sneak could interpose, Joe mounted up among the branches, and asked for the axe, saying he would have the bough off in five minutes. Sneak gave it to him, and when he reached the place, (which was not more than fifteen feet from the ground,) he commenced cutting away with great eagerness. The cavity was large, and in a few minutes the bough began to give way. In spite of Sneak's gesticulations and grimaces below, Joe did not bethink him that one of his feet still rested on the bough beyond the place where he was cutting, but continued to ply the axe with increasing rapidity. Presently the bough, axe, and Joe, all fell together. Sneak was convulsed with laughter. Joe sprang to his feet, and after feeling his limbs and ribs, announced that no bones were broken, and laughed very heartily himself. They began to split open the severed bough without loss of time. But just when they were in the act of lifting out the honeycomb, four stalwart savages rose softly from the bushes behind, and springing nimbly forward, seized them both before they could make any resistance. The surprised couple yelled and struggled to no purpose. Their hands were soon bound behind them, and they were driven forward hastily in a southerly direction.

"Oh! for goodness sake, Mr. Chief, please let me go home, and I'll pay you whatever you ask!" said Joe, to the tallest of the savages.

The Indian, if he did not understand his captive's words, seemed to comprehend his terrors, and was much diverted at his ludicrous expression of features.

"Oh pray! good Mr. Chief——"

"Keep your mouth shet! They'll never git through torturing us, if you let 'em know you're afraid," said Sneak.

"That's just what I want," said Joe; "I don't want them to ever quit torturing us—because they'll never quit till we're both dead. But as long as they laugh at me, they'll be sure to let me live."

Ere long, the savages with their captives, entered the dense grove where Mary had been taken, before they set out with her over the prairie. But it was evidently not their intention to conduct their present prisoners to their villages, and demand a ransom for them. Nor were they prepared to convey them away in the same dignified and comfortable manner, over the snow-clad plains. They anticipated a gratification of a different nature. They had been disappointed in all their attempts to obtain booty from the whites. The maid they had taken had been recaptured, and their chief was in the possession of the enemy. These, to say nothing of the loss of a score of their brethren by the fire-weapons of the white men, stimulated them with unerring precision to compass the destruction of their prisoners. Blood only could satiate their vengeful feelings. And the greater and longer the sufferings of their victims the more exquisite would be the luxury of revenge. And this caused them to smile with positive delight when they witnessed the painful terrors of poor Joe.

When they reached their place of encampment, which was in the midst of a cluster of small slim trees that encircled an old spreading oak of huge dimensions, the savages made their prisoners stand with their backs against two saplings that grew some fifteen paces apart. They were compelled to face each other, that they might witness every thing that transpired. Their arms were bound round the trees behind them, and a cord was likewise passed round their legs to confine them more securely. The savages then seemed to consult about the manner of despatching them. The oldest and most experienced, by his hasty gestures and impatient replies, appeared to insist on their instantaneous death. And from his frequent glances northward, through the trees, he doubtless feared some interruption, or dreaded the arrival of an enemy that might inflict an ample retaliation. During a long pause, while the Indians seemed to hesitate, and the old crafty savage drew his steel tomahawk from his belt, Sneak sighed deeply, and said, in rather mournful tones—

"The jig's up with us, Joe. If I was only loose seven seconds, you wouldn't ketch me dying like a coon here

JOE AND SNEAK IN DIFFICULTY.—P. 194.

agin a tree." Joe made no other response than a blubbering sound, while the tears ran down and dropped briskly from his chin.

The savages gave vent to a burst of laughter when they beheld the agony of fear that possessed their captive. The three that were in favour of the slow torture now turned a deaf ear to the old warrior, and advanced to Joe. They held the palms of their hands under his chin, and caught the tears as they fell. They then stroked his head gently, and appeared to sympathize with the sufferer.

"Mr. Indian, if you'll let me go, I'll give you my gun and twenty dollars," said Joe, appealing most piteously to the one that placed his hand on his head. The Indian seemed to understand him, and held his hand out for the money, while a demoniac smile played on his dark lips.

"Just untie my h nds," said Joe, endeavouring to look behind, "and I'll go right straight home and get them."

"You rascal—you want to run away," replied the old Indian, who not only understood Joe's language, but could himself speak English imperfectly.

"Upon my sacred word and honour, I won't!" replied Joe.

"You lie!" said the savage, bestowing a severe smack on Joe's face.

"Oh, Lord! Come now, Mr. Indian, that hurts!"

"No—don't hurt—only kill musketer," replied the savage, laughing heartily, and striking his prisoner on the other side of the face.

"Oh! hang your skin!" cried Joe, endeavouring to break away, "if ever I get you in my power, I'll smash——" Here his sudden courage evaporated, and again the tears filled his eyes.

"Poor fellow!" said the savage, patting his victim on the head. "How much you give for him?" he continued, poir ting to Sneak.

"If you'll only let *me* go, I'll give you every thing I've got in the world. He don't want to live as bad as I do, and I'll give you as much for me alone as I will for both."

"You're a purty white man, now, ain't you?" said Sneak. "But its all the same. My chance is jest as good as your'n They're only fooling you, jest to laugh. I've made up my mind to die, and I ain't a going to make any fun for 'em. And you might as well say your prayers fust as last; they're only playing with you now like a cat with a mice."

The old Indian moved towards Sneak, followed by the others.

"How much you give?" asked the savage.

"Not a coon's tail," replied Sneak, with firmness.

"Now how much?" continued the Indian, slapping the thin lank cheek of his prisoner.

"Not a dod-rotted cent! Now jest take your tomahawk and split my skull open as quick as you kin!" said Sneak; and he bowed down his head to receive the fatal blow.

"You brave rascal," said the Indian, looking his captive in the eye, and hesitating whether to practice his petty annoyances any further. At length they turned again to Joe.

"That wasn't fair, Sneak," cried Joe, when the savages abandoned his fellow-prisoner; "you ought to have kept them away from me as long as I did from you."

"I'm gitting sick of this tanterlizing business," said Sneak. "I want 'em to git through the job, without any more fooling about it. If you wasn't sich a coward, they'd let you alone, and kill us at once."

"I don't want them to kill us—I'd rather they'd do any thing in the world than to kill us," replied Joe.

"Me won't hurt you," said the old savage, again placing his hand on Joe's head; but instead of gently patting it, he wound a lock of hair round one of his fingers, and with a sudden jerk tore it out by the roots.

"Oh, my gracious! Oh, St. Peter! Oh, Lord! Mr. Indian, I beg and pray of you not to do that any more. If you'll only untie me, I'll get down on my knees to you," exclaimed poor Joe.

"Poor fellow, me won't hurt him any more—poor head!" said the Indian, tearing off another lock.

"Oh! oh! goodness gracious. *Dear* Mr. Indian, don't do that! You can have no idea how bad it hurts—I can't stand it. I'll faint presently!" said Joe, trembling at every joint.

"You're a fool," said Sneak, "to mind 'em that way. If you wasn't to notice 'em, they wouldn't do it. See how they're laughing at you."

"Oh, Sneak, I can't help it, to save my life, indeed I can't. Oh, my good Lord, what would I give to be away from here!" said Joe, his eyes fit to burst from their sockets.

"I've killed many a deer in a minit—it don't hurt a man to die more than a deer. I wish the snarvilerous copper-skinned rascals would git through quick!" said Sneak.

"Me try you agin," said the savage, again going to Sneak.

"Well, now, what're you a going to do? I'm not afraid of you!" said Sneak, grinding his teeth.

"Me rub your head," said the savage, seizing a tuft of hair and tearing it out.

"Take some more," said Sneak, bowing down his head.

"A little more," iterated the savage, grasping a handful, which, with much exertion, he severed from the head, and left the white skin exposed to view.

"Won't you have some more?" continued Sneak, without evincing the least pain. "Jest take as much as you please; if you tear it off till my head's as bald as an egg, I won't beg you to let me alone."

"You brave fellow—won't pull your hair any more," said the chief.

"You be dod rot!" said Sneak, contemptuously.

"You mighty brave, shake hands!" continued the laughing savage, holding his hand out in mockery.

"If you'll untie my foot a minit, I'll bet I kick some of the ribs out of your body. Why don't you knock our brains out, and be done at once, you black wolves you!" said Sneak.

"Oh, Sneak! for my sake—your poor friend's sake, don't put such an idea as that into their heads!" said Joe, imploringly.

"You're a purty friend, ain't you? You'd give so *much* to ransom me! They aint a going to quit us without killin' us, and I want it all over jest as soon as it kin be done."

"Oh, no, Sneak! Maybe they'll take pity on us and spare our lives," said Joe, assuming a most entreating look as the savage once more approached him.

"You make good big Osage; you come with us, if we let you live?" demanded the old Indian.

"I pledge you my most sacred word and honour I will!"

"You run away, you rascal," said the savage, plucking another tuft of hair from Joe's head.

"I'll be hanged if I stand this any longer!" said Joe, striving to break the cord that confined him.

"Don't notice the black cowards," said Sneak.

"How can I help noticing them, when they're pulling out my hair by the roots!" said Joe.

"Look where they pulled mine out," said Sneak, turning that part of his head in view which had been made literally bald.

"Didn't it hurt you?" asked Joe.

"Sartinly it did," said Sneak, "but I grinned and bore it. And now I wish they'd pull it all off, and then my sculp wouldn't do 'em any good."

"That's a fact," said Joe. "Here, Mr. Osage," he continued, "pull as much hair off the top of my head as you want." The savages, instead of paying any attention to him, seemed to be attracted by some distant sound. They stooped down and placed their ears near the earth, and listened intently for some time. At length they sprang up, and then ensued another dispute among them about the manner in which the prisoners should be disposed of. The old savage was yet in favour of tomahawking the captives and retreating without delay. But the others would not consent to it. They were not satisfied with the small amount of suffering yet endured by the prisoners. They were resolved to glut their savage vengeance. And the prisoners now observed that all traces of mirth had vanished from their faces. Their eyes gleamed with fiendish fury, and drawing forth their glittering tomahawks, they vanished in the thicket, and were soon heard chopping off the small boughs of the trees.

"What are they doing Sneak?" asked Joe.

"Don't you know what they're doing? ain't they cutting wood as fast as they kin?" replied Sneak.

"Well, I'm not sorry for that," said Joe, "because its almost dark, and I'm getting chilly. If they'd only give me something to eat, I'd feel a heap more comfortable."

"You varasherous fool you, they're cutting wood to burn us up with. Oh, I wish I was loose!"

"Oh, goodness gracious!" cried Joe, "I never thought of that! Oh, I'm gone!"

"Are you?" cried Sneak, eagerly; "I'd like to be off too, and we'd give them a race for it yit."

"Oh! Sneak, I mean I'm ruined, lost for ever! Oh! St. Peter, pity my helpless condition!"

"Don't think about pity now," said Sneak; "nothing of that sort is going to do us any good. We must git loose from these trees and run for it, or we'll be roasted like wild turkeys in less than an hour. I've got one hand loose!"

"So have I almost!" cried Joe, struggling violently.

"One of 'em's coming!—shove your hand back, and pertend like you're fast, till he goes away agin!" said Sneak, in a hurried undertone.

The savage emerged from the bushes the next moment, and after depositing an armful of billets of wood at the feet of Joe, and walking round behind the prisoners to see if they were still secure, returned for more fuel.

"Now work for your life!" said Sneak, extricating his wrist from the cord, and striving to get his feet loose.

"Hang it, Sneak, I can't get my hand out, though the string's quite loose! Make haste, Sneak, and come and help me," said Joe, in a tone that indicated his earnestness.

"Let every man look out for himself," replied Sneak, tugging away at the cord that bound his feet to the tree.

"Oh, Sneak, don't leave me here, to be burnt by myself!" said Joe.

"You wouldn't promise to give any thing to ransom me, a while ago—I'll cut stick as quick as I kin."

"Oh, Sneak, I can't untie my hands! If you wont help me, I'll call the Indians." But Joe was saved the trouble. He had scarce uttered the word when all four of the Indians suddenly appeared, and throwing down their wood, proceeded with much haste to put their horrid purpose in execution. They heaped up the fagots around their victims, until they reached half way to their chins, and when all was ready, they paused, before applying the fire, to enjoy the terrors of their captives.

"You cold—me make some fire to warm--huh." said

the old Indian, addressing Joe, while the others looked on with unmixed satisfaction.

"Oh! my dear Mr. Osage, if you only knew how much money you'd lose by killing me, I know you'd let me go!' said Joe, in tremulous but supplicating tones.

"You lie—you got no money," replied the savage; and, stooping down, he began to split some dry wood into very small pieces to kindle with. Joe looked on in despair, and seemed to anticipate a blister from every splinter he saw. It was different with Sneak. Almost hid by the wood heaped around him, he embraced every opportunity, when the eyes of the savages were turned away, to endeavour to extricate himself from the cords that bound him to the tree. Hope had not yet forsaken him, and he resolved to struggle to the last. When the old savage had split off a large quantity of splinters and chips, he gathered them up and began to arrange them in various parts of the pile of green timber preparatory for a simultaneous ignition. While he was thus engaged, Sneak remained motionless, and assumed a stoical expression of features. But when he turned to Joe, Sneak again began to tug at the cord.

"Oh pray, Mr. Indian!" exclaimed Joe, when he saw the savage carefully placing the combustible matter in all the crevices of the pile around him—"just only let me off this time, and I'll be your best friend all the rest of your life."

"Me warm you little—don't cry—poor fellow!" replied the Indian, striking a light with flint and steel.

"Oh, Sneak, if you've got a knife, run here and cut me loose, before I'm burnt to death!" said Joe, in the most heart-moving manner.

"Keep your mouth shet!" said Sneak; "jest wait till they go to put some fire here, and I'll show you a thing or two," he continued, pouring a handful of *powder* among the dry splinters. The effect of the explosion when the Indians attempted to surprise Glenn's premises occurring to Sneak, and recollecting that he had a quantity of powder in his pockets, he resolved in his extremity to try its virtue on this occasion.

"But they're going to burn me first! Oh, Lord!" exclaimed Joe, as he beheld the savage applying the fire to the splinters near his feet.

"Don't say nor do nothing—jest wait till they come tc

me," said Sneak, with great composure. "Do you jest keep your mouth shet—it'll be a long while a kindling—it won't begin to burn your legs for an hour."

"Oh, goodness gracious! My knees begin to feel warm now. Oh, pray have mercy on me, good Mr. Osage!" cried Joe, before the flame was as large as his hand, and yet full three feet distant from him. The greater portion of the fagots being green, the fire made very slow progress, and it was necessary for the savages to procure a constant supply of dry splinters to prevent it from going out.

At length, after the combustible material had burned out, and been replenished several times, the more substantial billets of Joe's pile began to ignite slowly, and the old Indian then took up a flaming brand and moved towards Sneak.

"Come on! you snarvilerous rattlesnake you, I'll show you sights presently!" said Sneak.

"You brave fellow—me burn you *quick*," said the savage, applying the torch, and, stooping down, placed his face within a few inches of the crackling blaze, and began to blow it gently. Sneak twisted his head round the tree as far as possible, and the next moment the powder exploded, throwing down the pile of wood, and dashing the savage several paces distant violently on the ground, and blackening and scorching his face and hair in a terrible manner. The other Indians instantly prostrated themselves on their faces, and uttered the most doleful lamentations. Thus they remained a few minutes, evidently impressed with the belief that the Great Spirit had interfered to prevent the destruction of the prisoners. Hastily gathering up their arms, they fled precipitately in the direction of their distant home, and their yells of disappointment and defeat rang in the ears of their captives until they died away in the distance.

"Sneak! make haste! they may come back again!" said Joe.

"They've tied my feet so tight I'm afraid I can't undo it in a hurry," replied Sneak, endeavouring to break the cord by thrusting a stick (that he had slipped from the pile to knock out the brains of one of the Indians should his gunpowder plot not succeed,) between it and the tree, and forcing it out until the pain produced became insuffer able. By this means the cord was loosened gradually, and moving it a little higher up where the muscles had not yet been bruised, he repeated the process. In this manner he laboured with certain but tardy success. But while he was thus engaged, Joe's predicament became each moment more critical. The wood being by this time pretty well seasoned, began to burn more freely. The blaze was making formidable advances, and the heat was becoming intolerable.

"For heaven's sake, Sneak!" cried Joe, "make haste and come here, or I'll be roasted alive!"

"Wait till I get away from my own tree," replied Sneak.

"Oh Lord! I can't wait a minute more! My shins are getting blistered!" cried Joe, writhing under the heat of the blaze, which now reached within a few inches of him, and increased in magnitude with awful rapidity.

"Well, if you won't wait till I git there, just go ahead yourself," said Sneak, at last extricating his feet by a violent effort, and hopping to Joe's assistance, with some difficulty, for his nether limbs were considerably bruised.

"Hang it, Sneak, pull these burning sticks away from my knees!" said Joe, his face flushed with pain.

"I'll be bursted with powder, if you didn't like to git into a purty tight fix," said Sneak, dashing down the consuming billets of wood.

"Now, Sneak, cut me loose, and then let's run home as soon as possible."

"I hain't got my knife with me, or I wouldn't 'ave been so long gitting loose myself," said Sneak, slowly untying Joe's hands.

"My goodness, how my arms ache!" said Joe, when his hands were released. "Now, Sneak, undo my feet, and then we'll be off in a hurry."

"I'll be slit if your feet ain't tied like mine was, in sich a hard knot that no mortal being can git it undone. I'll take a chunk, and burn the tarnation string in two," said Sneak, applying the fire.

"Take care you don't burn *me*," said Joe, looking at the operation with much concern.

Sneak's plan of severing his companion's bonds was

successful. Joe sprang in delight from his place of confinement, and, without uttering another word, or pausing a single moment, the liberated companions retreated from the grove with all possible expedition.

CHAPTER XV.

Glenn's History.

THE young chief, or rather the restored youth, awoke in a few days from the delirium into which the fever had plunged him, to a state of convalescence and a consciousness of his altered condition. He now uttered with earnest tenderness the endearing terms of "sister" and "father," when he addressed Mary and Roughgrove. He spoke freely of the many things he had witnessed while living with the Indians, expressing his abhorrence of their habits and nature, and declared it was his intention never to have any further intercourse with them. He promised, when he should be able to leave his bed, to read and study with Mary and Glenn, until he had made amends for the neglect of his education. These symptoms, and the tractable disposition accompanying them, caused Mary and Roughgrove to rejoice over the return of the long-lost youth, and to bow in humble thankfulness to the Disposer of events for the singular and providential circumstances attending his restoration.

Joe had arrived in due course of time, (which was brief,) after his almost miraculous escape from the savages and the flames, and told his story with various embellishments. The Indians were hunted the next day by Sneak and a few of the neighbours, but they had doubtless abandoned the settlement, for no traces of them remained after their mysterious flight from the grove.

A few mild days, during which frequent showers had fallen, had in a great measure removed the snow from the earth. And Joe having soon forgotten his late perilous adventure, amused himself with the horses. He resolved to make some amends for their long confinement in the stable, and to effect it he galloped them several hours each day over the grounds in the vicinity. The hounds, too, seemed delighted to place their feet once more on the bare earth, and they were permitted to accompany the horses in all their excursions.

One night, when William, Mary, and Joe were all quietly sleeping, Roughgrove took occasion to express his gratitude to Glenn for the many and important services rendered his family.

"Whatever good may have attended my efforts," said Glenn, "you may rest assured that I have been amply repaid in the satisfaction enjoyed myself."

"I am sure of it!" exclaimed Roughgrove; "and it was a conviction that you harboured such sentiments that induced me to confide in you, and to disclose things which I intended should remain for ever locked within my own breast."

"Your confidence shall not be abused," said Glenn; and to prove that I am not averse to an exchange of secrets, if you will listen to my recital, I will endeavour briefly to give you a sketch of *my* history."

"I will listen attentively, my young friend, even were it as sad a tale as mine, which can hardly be the case," said Roughgrove, drawing his chair close to Glenn's side, and placing more fuel on the fire.

"Would to Heaven it had not been!" said Glenn, after reclining his head on his hands a few minutes, and recalling transactions which he could have wished to be blotted from his memory for ever. "I am a native of New York," he continued, heaving a sigh and folding his arms, "and was left an orphan at a very early age. My father was once reputed one of the wealthiest merchants in Broadway; but repeated and enormous losses, necessarily inexplicable to one of my age, suddenly reduced him to comparative poverty. Neither he nor my mother survived the blow many months, and before I was ten years old, I was left (with the exception of an uncle in Philadelphia) alone in the world, possessed of only a few hundred dollars. My uncle placed me with an eminent physician, who had been my father's friend, after my education was completed. He told me that he was rich, and would see that I should not suffer for means until I had acquired a profession, which, with energy and diligence, would enable me to procure an honourable support. But he informed me that he had a family of his own, and that I must not depend upon his assistance further than to accomplish a profession.

"It was during my studies, and when about seventeen years old, that my misfortunes began. My preceptor had another student, named Henry Wold, several years my senior, whose parents were wealthy. Wold and I entertained the highest esteem for each other. But our circumstances being different, I could not indulge in all the excesses of extravagance that he did, but made better progress in my studies. He attended all the gay parties and fashionable places of amusement, while I seldom spent an evening from home. He was tall, manly, and possessed of regular and beautiful features—these, with his unlimited wealth, made him a welcome guest in every circle, and extremely popular with the ladies.

"One Sabbath morning, while sitting in church, (which I attended regularly,) I was struck with the appearance of a stranger in an opposite pew across the aisle that belonged to a family with whom I was on the most intimate terms. The stranger was the most beautiful young lady I ever beheld. Dark, languishing eyes, glossy ringlets, pale, smooth forehead—oh! I will not describe her—let it suffice that she was an angel in my eyes! It was impossible to remove my gaze from her, and I fancied that she sometimes returned an approving glance. Before the service was over, I was delighted to observe that she whispered something to Mrs. Arras, (the name of the lady whose pew she was in,) for this assured me that they were acquainted, and that I might obtain some information about the fair being who had made such a sudden and deep impression on my heart, and perhaps procure an introduction to her. When I retired to my couch that night, it was not to sleep. The image of the fair stranger haunted my restless and imperfect slumbers. Nor could I study by day, for my thoughts wandered continually from the page to the same bright vision. Such was my condition throughout the week. The next Sunday I found her seated in the same pew. Our eyes met, and a slight blush that mantled her fair face encouraged me to hope that she might likewise have bestowed some thoughts on me during the preceding week. It was in vain that I uttered the responses during the service, or knelt down when the clergyman offered up his prayers. I could think of nothing but the angelic stranger. I resolved that another week should not pass without my calling at Mrs. Arras's. But my object was obtained sooner than I expected. When the congregation was dismissed, Mrs. Arras beckoned me across the aisle to her.

"'Charles,' whispered she, 'don't you want an introduction to my niece? I saw your eyes riveted on her several times.'

"'I—if you please,' I replied, with feelings of mingled delight and embarrassment.

"'Laura,' she continued, turning to the young lady who lingered behind, but seemed to be conscious of what was passing, 'let me introduce you to my young friend, Charles Glenn.' The bland and accomplished Mrs. Arras then moved onward, while I attended at the side of Laura, and continued with her until I assisted her up the marble steps of her aunt's stately mansion.

"I then bowed, and strode rapidly onward, I knew not whither, (completely bewildered with the enchanting spell that the fair Laura had thrown over me,) until I reached the extremity of Broadway, and found myself in Castle Garden, gazing like a very maniac at the bright water below me. I wandered about alone, enjoying the exhilarating fancies of my teeming brain, until the sun sunk beneath the horizon, and the bright stars twinkled in the blue vault above. Oh! the thoughts, the hopes, the bliss of that hour! The dark curtain that veils the rankling corruptions of mortality had not yet been lifted before my staring eyes, and I felt as one gazing at a beautiful world, and regarded the fair maid as the angel destined to unfold all its brilliance to my vision, and to hold the chalice to my lips while I sipped the nectar of perennial felicity. Alas, that such moments are brief! They fly like the dreams of a startled slumberer, and when they vanish once, they are gone forever!

"Without calling at my lodgings for the usual refreshments, I hovered about the mansion of Mrs. Arras till lights were gleaming in the parlour, and then entered. Laura received me with a smile, and the complaisant matron gave me an encouraging welcome.

"'You are pale this evening, Mr. Glenn,' said Mrs. Ar ras, in a good-humoured, though bantering manner. 'Are you subject to sudden attacks of illness?'

"'I assure you I never enjoyed better health in my life, and feel no symptoms of indisposition whatever,' I replied, but at that moment I chanced to gaze at a mirror, and was startled at my haggard appearance. But when Mrs Arras withdrew, (which she did soon after my arrival,) the affable and lovely Laura banished every thought of my condition. My wan cheek was soon animated with the flush of unbounded admiration, and my sunken eye sparkled with the effervescence of enraptured delight. Deep and ineradicable passion was engendering in my bosom. And from the pleasure indicated in the glitter of Laura's lustrous eyes, the exquisite smile that dwelt upon her coral lips, and the gentle though unconscious swellings of her breast, a conviction thrilled through my soul that my sudden affection was reciprocated. Hours flew like minutes, and I was surprised by the clock striking ONE before it occurred to me that it was time to depart. Again I traversed the streets at that solemn hour, insensible to every feeling, and regardless of every object but the flaming torch lit up in my heart and the seraphic image of Laura. At length I was warned by the scrutinizing gaze of a watchman to repair to my lodgings. But my pillow afforded no rest. All night long I pondered on the exhilarating events of the day. Many were the endearing accents that escaped my lips as I addressed in fancy my beloved Laura. I resolved to declare my passion ere many weeks should pass. I began to settle in my mind the plans of life, and then, for the first time, the future presented a dark spot to my view. I was poor! Laura was rich and her family proud and aristocratic. Her father was a distinguished judge. And the most high-born and haughty of the land would doubtless (if they had not already) sigh at her feet! I sprang upright on my couch when this discordant thought passed across my mind. But the next moment I was consoled with the belief that I already possessed her heart. And with a determination to have her, in spite of every obstacle, should this be the case, I sank back through weariness, and was soon steeped in deep, though unquiet slumber.

"The two next succeeding Sundays I attended Laura to church. The evenings of both days, and nearly all the intervening ones, I was with her at the mansion of Mrs. Arras. But the evening of the last Sunday was to me a memorable one. That evening I opened all my heart to Laura, and found that every pulsation met a responding throb in hers—such, at least, I believed to be the case—and so she asserted. During the short time she remained in New York, I was her accredited lover, and ever, when together, the attachment she manifested was as ardent as mine. Indeed, at times, her passion seemed unbounded, and I was more than once tempted to propose a clandestine and immediate union. I was the more inclined to this, inasmuch as her father (who had now returned from a trip to Washington) began to regard my visits with displeasure. But he soon passed on to Boston to attend to the duties of his office, and again I had unrestrained access to Laura. But I am dwelling too long on this part of my story.

"One day Henry Wold, my fellow-student, inquired the cause of the palpable change in my bearing and disposition. Would that my lips had been sealed to him forever! I knew that he was honest and generous by nature, but I knew not to what extent his dissolute habits (gradually acquired by having ample means, and yielding by degrees to the temptations of vice) had perverted his good qualities. I told him of my love, and while describing the charms of Laura, I was pleased to attribute the interest he evinced at the recital to his disinterested friendship for me, without the thought that *he* could be captivated himself with the bare description. He begged me to introduce him. This, too, gratified my pride, for I knew he would admire her. The perfect form, rare beauty, intelligence, and wealth of Wold did not startle an apprehension in my breast. But I knew not—alas! who can know?—the impulses that govern woman. Wold accompanied me that night to Mrs. Arras's. He seated himself at Laura's side, and poured forth a flood of flattery. They smiled in unison and returned glance for glance. Wold exhibited his fine person and exerted all his captivating powers of intellect. Laura scanned the one and listened attentively to the other. Still I sat by in satisfaction, and strove to repress every rising fear that my supremacy in Laura's heart might be endangered. That evening, as we returned homeward, in answer to my questions, Wold stated that my 'intended' was *pretty enough* for any young man, and would, without doubt, make a *very good wife.* So far from exhibiting the extravagant admiration I expected, he seemed to speak of the object of my adoration with comparative indifference. But a few evenings afterwards, I found him with Laura when I arrived! I started back on beholding them seated on the same sofa as I entered the parlour. Mrs. Arras was present, and wore a thoughtful expression of features. Laura smiled on me, but I thought it was not a happy smile. It did not render me happy. Wold bowed familiarly, and made some witty remark about taking time by the forelock. I sat down in silence, with a compressed lip, and an icy chillness in my breast. An embarrassing pause ensued. At length Mrs. Arras rose, and opening a folding-door, beckoned me into the adjoining room. After we had been seated a few moments, during which her brow assumed a more grave and thoughtful cast, she observed—

"'You seem to be excited to-night, Charles.'

"'I have cause to be so,' I replied.

"'I cannot deny it,' said she, 'when I consider every thing that has transpired. You doubtless have an attachment for Laura—I have *seen* it—and I confess it was and *would* be with my goodwill had I control of the matter. I was acquainted with your family, and acted with the best of motives when I permitted, perhaps encouraged, the intimacy. But I thought not of the austere and passionate nature of my brother-in-law. Neither did I think that any man could object to your addresses to his daughter. But I was mistaken. Judge —— has written that your interviews with Laura must terminate.'

"'Has he given any reason why?' I asked, in tremulous tones.

"'Yes,' she replied, 'but such as mortify me as much as they must pain you. He says that your fortune and family connections are not sufficient to permit the alliance. Oh, I implore you not to suppose these to be my sentiments. I know your family is devoid of ignoble stain, and that your fortune was once second to none. Had I the disposal of Laura's hand it should be yours!'

"'I believe it, Mrs. Arras!' said I. 'But do you not think these objections of Judge —— may be overcome?'

"'Alas, never!' she replied; 'he is immovable when any thing of moment is decided in his mind.'

"'But,' I continued, while the pulsations of my heart were distinctly audible, 'what says Laura?'

"'Would I had been spared this question! You saw her a few minutes since. HE who sees all things knows how my heart ached while I sat by. I can only tell you she had just finished reading her father's letter when Mr. Wold was announced. Spare me, now, I beseech you!' I folded my arms and gazed, I know not how long, at the flame ascending from the hearth. Oh! the agony described of the dying were bliss to that moment. What could I think or do? I sat like one whose heart has been rudely torn from his breast, and who was yet debarred the relief of death. Existence to me at that moment was a hell, and my sufferings were those of the damned! I thank God I have survived them.

"I was aroused from my lethargy by hearing the street door close after Wold, and I desired Mrs. Arras to permit me to have an interview with Laura alone. It was granted, and I was soon in the presence of the lovely maid. She was aware of my perturbation and its cause. She sat with her eyes cast down in silence. I looked upon her form and her features of perfect beauty, and oh! what tongue can describe the mingled and contending emotions that convulsed my breast! I repressed every violent or boisterous inclination of my spirits, however, and taking her unresisting hand, sat down in sorrow at her side.

"'Laura,' said I, with difficulty finding utterance, 'do we thus part, and for ever?' She made no answer, but gazed steadfastly at the rich carpet, while her face, though somewhat paler than usual, betrayed no change of muscle.

"'Laura,' I repeated, in tones more distinct, 'are we *now* to part, and *for ever?*'

"'Father says so,' she replied. Her hand fell from my grasp. The unmoved, *indifferent* manner of her reply froze my blood in my veins! I again stared at her composed features in astonishment allied to contempt.

"'But what do *you* say?' I asked, with a bluntness that startled her.

"'Father knows best, perhaps!' she replied, turning her eyes to mine, I thought, with calmness.

"'Laura,' said I, again taking her hand, for I was once more subdued by her beauty, 'I love you with my whole soul, and must continue to love you. Ay, were you even to spurn me with your foot, so indissolubly have my affections grown to your image, that my bleeding heart would turn in adoration to the smiter. And I fondly hoped and believed that the passion was returned—indeed, I had your assurance of the fact; nay, think not I design to reproach you. It were bootless, had I the heart to do it. Be assured that were you not only cruel to me, but steeped in crime and guilty of injustice to the whole human race, I would still be your friend were all others to forsake you. Deem me never your foe, or capable of ever becoming such. May heaven bless you! We part—but, under *any* circumstances, should adverse fortune overtake you and I can be of service, I beg you not to hesitate to apply to me. You will find me still your friend. I will not attempt to reverse the decision which you have made. However humiliating and poignant the thought may be that I was unconsciously the means of introducing the *object* that influenced your decision, yet I will not murmur, neither will I become *his* enemy, for your sake. I hope you will be happy. I pray that heaven may incline your heart to be true and *constant* to Wold.'

"'I hope so,' said she in a low tone.

"'Laura,' said I, rising, 'you confess, then, that Wold possesses your love?'

"'Yes,' said she; 'but I cannot help it!'

"'Farewell!' said I, kissing her yielding hand, and turning deliberately away, though with the sensation of one stunned by a thunderbolt. I returned home, and threw myself like a loathsome carcass upon my couch. I could not even think. My mind seemed like some untenanted recess in the unfathomable depths below. Instantaneous death, and even eternal perdition afterwards, could have presented no new horrors then. It was haply the design of Providence that the thought of self-destruction should not occur to me. With the means in my reach, I would in all probability have rushed, uncalled and unprepared, into the presence of an offended Creator.

"A fever and delirium, such as possessed the poor youth lying there, ensued. Under the kind care of my preceptor, my malady abated in a few weeks; and, as I recovered, a change took place in my sentiments regarding the events that produced my illness. My pride rose up to my relief, and I resolved to overcome the effects of my disappointment. Yet my heart melted in tenderness when I recalled the blissful moments I had known with Laura. But I determined to prosecute my plans of life as if no such occurrence had transpired.

"A few days after bidding Laura adieu, she returned to Boston, accompanied by Wold. Wold obtained his diploma while I was writhing with disease. Even the loss of my degrée was now borne with patience and resignation. I forgave Wold, and implored him to make Laura happy. He promised faithfully to do so when on the eve of setting out with her. I did not desire to see her myself, but sent my forgiveness and blessing.

"In a few months my diploma was obtained, and I commenced the practice under the most favourable circumstances. My late preceptor was now my partner. Nearly a year elapsed before Wold returned to New York. But a rumor preceded him which again opened all the fountains of bitterness in my heart. It was said (and only two or three were possessed of the secret) that he had betrayed and ruined the lovely Laura! I sought him, to ascertain from his own lips if he had truly committed the act imputed to him. I resolved to avenge her! But Wold avoided me. I could not obtain his ear, and all my notes to him remained unanswered. Despairing of getting an immediate answer from him, I repaired to Mrs. Arras. Her house was in gloom and sorrow. When she appeared, my heart sank within me to behold her sad and mournful brow. She pressed my extended hand, while a flood of tears gushed from her eyes.

"I knew by the disconsolate aspect of the aunt that the niece had been dragged down from her high estate of virtue, fortune, and fame. I sat down, and bowed my head in sorrow many minutes before the first word was spoken. I still loved Laura. What could I say? how begin?

"'It is true!' I at length exclaimed, rising up, and pac

ing the floor rapidly, while many a tear ran down my cheek.

"'Alas! it is too true,' iterated Mrs. Arras.

"'The black-hearted villain!' I continued.

"'Ah, Mr. Glenn, her fate would have been different, if your addresses had not been so cruelly spurned! God knows I was not to blame!' said she.

"'No, Mrs. Arras,' said I; 'had your will been done, I had not been made miserable by the bereavement, nor the beautiful, the innocent—the—Laura, with all her errors, dishonoured, ruined, crushed! But the betrayer, the viper that stung her, still breathes. I loved her—I love her yet—and I will be her avenger!' Saying this, I rushed away, heedless of the matron's half-uttered entreaties to remain and to desist from my plan of vengeance.

"There was a young student of my acquaintance, a brave, chivalrous, noble Virginian, to whom I imparted Laura's sad story. He frankly agreed with me that the venomous reptile in the human shape that could beguile an unsuspecting and lovely girl to minister to his unhallowed desires, and then, without hesitation or remorse, abandon her to the dark, despairing shades of a frowning world, while he crawled on to insinuate his poison into the breasts of new victims, should be pursued, hunted down, and exterminated. Yet there was but one way for me to punish Wold. The ignominy of the act, and the indignation of a virtuous community were to him matters of indifference. The circle in which he moved would smile at the misfortune of his victim, and applaud his address, were the affair published. I resolved that he should answer it to me alone. I had sworn in my heart to be Laura's avenger.

"I penned a message which was delivered by my young Virginian friend in person. Wold said he had no quarrel with me, and strove to evade the subject. He sent me a note, demanding wherein he had ever wronged me, and stating that he was ready and willing to *explain* any thing that might have offended me. I returned his note, with a line on the same sheet, informing him that I was the friend of Laura; and that he must either meet me in the manner indicated in my message, or I would publicly brand him as a dastardly scoundrel. He bit his lip, and referred my friend to one of his companions in iniquity, a Mr. Knabb, who lived by the *profession* of cards and dice. It was arranged that we should meet on one of the islands near the city, and that it should be the next morning. This was what I desired, and I had urged my friend to effect as speedy a consummation of the affair as possible. All the tumult and perturbation that raged in my bosom on parting with Laura had returned, and the throbbing of my brain was almost insufferable. It was with difficulty that my young friend prevailed upon me to embrace the few intermediate hours before the meeting to practice with the pistol. I heeded not his declaration that Wold was an excellent shot, because I felt convinced that justice was on my side. I thought that the criminal must inevitably fall. However, I consented to practice a little to quiet his importunity Truly, it seemed that his urgent solicitation was reasonable enough, for the first fire my ball was several feet wide of the mark. I had never fired a pistol before in my life. But there was no quivering of nerve, no misgiving as to my fate; for notwithstanding I was aware of being a novice, yet I entertained a conviction, a presentiment, that the destroyer of my Laura's innocence would fall beneath my hand. The next fire I did better, and soon learned to strike the centre.

"We were all on the ground at the hour appointed. While the seconds were arranging the necessary preliminaries, Wold, finding that my eyes rested steadily upon him, endeavoured to intimidate me. There was a bush some thirty paces distant, from which a slim, solitary sprout ran up several feet above the rest of the branches. He gazed an instant at it while I was marking him, and then raised his pistol, and fired in the direction. The sprout fell. Turning, his eyes met mine, while a slight smile was visible on his lip. The effect did not realize his hopes. I looked upon the act with such cold indifference that he at first betrayed surprise at my calmness, and then exhibited palpable signs of trepidation himself. He beckoned Knabb to him, and, after a brief conference in a low tone, his second returned to my friend, and inquired if no amends, no reconciliation, could avert the exchange of shots. My friend reported his words to me, and my reply was that nothing but the restitution of the maiden's honour—instant marriage—would be satisfaction. Wold protested—marriage was utterly impossible under existing circumstances—but he would do any thing else. But nothing else would answer; and I insisted on proceeding to business without further delay. Wold heard me, and became pale. When we were placed at our respective stations, and while the final arrangements were being adjusted, I thought his replies to his friend's observations betrayed much alarm. But there was no retreat. I was never calmer in my life, I even smiled when my careful friend told me that he had detected and prevented a concerted plan that would have given Wold the advantage. The word was given. Wold's ball struck the earth before me, and threw some sand in my face. Mine entered the seducer's side! I saw him gasp, reel, and fall, while the blood gushed out on the beach. My friend hurried me away, and paused not until he had placed me in a stage just starting for Philadelphia. I clasped his hand in silence, and the next moment the horses plunged away at the crack of the driver's whip, and we were soon far on the road. Reflection ere long convinced me that I had been guilty of an unjustifiable act. If it was no crime in the estimation of men, it was certainly a grievous transgression in the eyes of God! I then trembled. The bleeding form and reproachful stare of Wold haunted my vision when the darkness set in. Oh, the errors, in act and deed, of an impetuous youth thrown upon the world with no considerate friend to advise him! The pity I felt for Laura was soon forgotten in the horrible thought that I was a MURDERER! Oh, the anguish of that night! Why did I not leave Wold to the judgment of an offended God? Why did I not permit him to suffer the gnawing of the canker that must ever abide in his heart, instead of staining my hands with his blood? Freely would I have abandoned every hope of pleasure in the world to have washed his blood away!

"When I arrived in Philadelphia, with a heavy heart, I sought a quiet hotel, not daring to confront my uncle with such a tale of wo and crime. For several days I remained in my chamber without seeing any one but the servant that brought my food. At length I asked for a New York paper. For more than an hour after it was brought I could not summon courage to peruse the hated tragedy. Finally

I snatched up the sheet convulsively and glanced along the columns. When my eyes rested upon the paragraph I was in quest of, I sprang to my feet in ecstasy. The wound had not been fatal! Wold still lived!

"In a twinkling I was dressed and on my way to my uncle's residence. Nothwithstanding there was a dreadful epidemic in the city, and hearses and mourners were passing every few minutes, I felt within a buoyancy that defied the terrors of disease and death.

"But it seemed that disaster and desolation were fated to attend me whithersoever I turned. A gloom brooded upon my heart when I approached my uncle's mansion, and found the badge of mourning at the door. I paused and asked the servant who was dead. He informed me that my uncle alone remained. His wife and children, all had been consigned to the tomb the day before, and he himself now lay writhing with the fell disease. I rushed in and entered the sick chamber. It was the chamber of death. My uncle pressed my hand and died. I followed him to the grave, the chief and almost only mourner.

"I returned and shut myself up in the mansion, bewildered and stupefied. I was now the possessor of immense wealth. But I was unhappy. I knew not what to do to enjoy life. Gradually the pestilence abated and disappeared, and by degrees the gloom that oppressed me subsided. At the end of a few months, I was informed by my young Virginian friend that Wold had entirely recovered. I likewise received a letter from Mrs. Arras, stating that Judge —— had sought out Laura, (who had been enticed to an obscure part of the city,) and, as her misfortune had been kept a profound secret among the few, he forgave the offence, and once more extended to her a father's love and a father's protection. I need not say that a blissful thrill bounded through my veins. Wold was living, and Laura not irrecoverably lost. Yet I did not then deem it possible that I could, under such circumstances, ever desire to possess the once adored, but since truly fallen, Laura. But I experienced a sweet gratification to be thus informed of the prospect of her being reinstated in society. My love was not yet wholly extinguished!

"When it was generally known that I possessed great riches, a crowd of flatterers and sycophants hovered around me. I was a distinguished guest at the mansions of the fashionable and great, and had in turn many brilliant parties at my residence. But among the tinsel and glitter of the gay world I sought in vain for peace and happiness. Many beautiful and bewitching belles lavished their sweetest smiles upon me, but they could not re-ignite the smothered flame in my bosom. Wine could only exhilarate for a moment, to be succeeded by a gnawing nausea. Cards could only excite while I lost, to be succeeded by irritability and disgust.

"Thus my time was spent for twelve months, when I suddenly conceived the resolution to seek a union with the ill-fated Laura, notwithstanding all the obloquy the world might attach to the act. I still loved her in spite of myself. I could not live in peace without her, and I determined without delay to offer her my hand, heart, and fortune. I set out for Boston, and on my arrival instantly proceeded to the residence of Judge ——. Again my evil star was in the ascendant. Desolation and death presided in Judge ——'s family. The ominous badge of mourning greeted me at the threshold; Laura's mother had just been consigned, broken-hearted, to the cold grave. The venerable Judge bowed his hoary head to the blows that Providence inflicted. He could not speak to me. His reply to my offer in relation to his child was only a flood of tears. He then retreated into his library and locked the door. An aged domestic told me all. Laura had abandoned her parental roof, and voluntarily entered one of those sinks of pollution that so much degrade human nature! I stood upon an awful abyss. The whirlpools of deceit, ingratitude, indifference, and calumny, howled around me, and the dark floods of sensual corruption roared below. Turn whithersoever I might (alas, I thought not of heaven!) gloom, discord, and misery seemed to be my portion.

"I hurried back to Philadelphia, and strove to mitigate my grief in the vortex of unrestrained dissipation. I lavished my gold on undeserving and unthankful objects. I cared not for life, much less for fortune. I was the victim of a frenzy that rendered me reckless, and bereft me of calm meditation. My frantic laughter was heard at the gaming-table, and my plaudits were boisterous at the theatre, but I was a stranger to enjoyment. There was no pleasure for me. My brawling companions swore I was the happiest and noblest being on earth. But I knew too well there was not a more miserable fiend in hell.

"At length disease fortunately arrested my demoniac career before my wealth was expended. It was my good fortune to secure the services of a distinguished and skillful physician. He was a benevolent and universally esteemed *Quaker*. His attention was not only constant, but soothing and parental. His earnest and tender tones often made me weep. When I recovered, I resolved to amend my life. This *friend* had applied a healing balm to my aching heart. I determined to prosecute my profession, and before a year elapsed my exertions began to be crowned with success.

"I was a frequent attendant at the lectures, and on terms of the closest intimacy with the professors. Indeed, I had a prospect of a professorship myself. I devoted my attention particularly to the anatomical department of my studies, which I preferred; and it was in this department of the institution that I would probably be installed in a few months. The gentleman who occupied that chair was about to resign, and, being my friend, used his influence to procure my election.

"My medical friend invited me one evening to be present at a dissection, which promised to be one of extreme interest. He described the subject as one that had elicited the admiration of the class. He said it was a female of perfect proportions, but who had recently been an inmate of a brothel of the lowest description. She had, in a state of beastly inebriation, fallen into the fire. Yet, with the exception of a small but fatal orifice in the side, her form and features remained unaltered. I consented to meet him at the hour appointed, and made my arrangements accordingly.

"That evening there were many more persons in the dissecting-room than usual. I had now become much more cheerful, and enjoyed the frank greetings of my many friends with a relish and an ardour that had hitherto been unknown to me. Many flippant remarks and careless observations were exchanged in relation to the business before us. We had become accustomed to such scenes, and habit had rendered us callous to the reflections and impressions generally produced when gazing upon the cold lineaments of the dead. Dissection was an indispensable act. It had been resorted to under the deliberate conviction that it was necessary to the perfection of science, and in a great degree redounded to the welfare and preservation of the living. To us the pale inanimate limbs, and the attenuated, insensible bodies of the dead brought no disagreeable sensations. We cut and sawed them with the same composed indifference with which the sculptor hews the marble.

"'This is a beautiful subject we have to-night, Glenn,' observed one of my friends, as we approached the dead body. He then threw up the white cloth, and exposed the corpse, the head being still obscured. A breathless silence reigned, while all gazed at the lifeless form in admiration. She was a perfect Venus! Not having been wasted and shrivelled by disease, the symmetry of her lineaments was preserved in all the exactness of life and health. Her bust was full, plump, and the skin of the most exquisite whiteness, except where it had been marred by the fire that caused her death. Her limbs surpassed any model I had ever beheld, round and tapering, smooth and white as ivory. Her ankles were most admirably turned, and her feet of the smallest dimensions. Her handsome and gently swelling arms were covered with a slight gauze of short, dark hair, through which the snowy whiteness of her skin was displayed to greater advantage. Her hands were extremely delicate, and indicated that she had been accustomed to ease and luxury.

"I was requested to open her breast and exhibit to the students the formation and functions of the heart. She was lying on her back, on a long narrow table, around which the students stood gazing at her fair proportions. Some reflected in sorrow that so beautiful and lovely a being should die and be conveyed to the dissecting-room; while others joked and laughed in a light unfeeling manner. When about to make an incision with the sharp glittering steel in my hand, for the first time since I had graduated, I confessed that my nerves were too much affected by the sight of the subject to proceed, and I begged my friends to be patient a few minutes, during which I would doubtless regain my accustomed composure.

"'What was her name?' I inquired of the friend who had accosted me on my entrance.

"'Haven't you heard?' said he, smiling—'I thought you all knew her. Nearly every person in the city has heard of her, for she was the most celebrated and notorious "fallen angel" in the city—celebrated for her unrivalled beauty and many triumphs, and notorious for her heartless deceit and reckless disregard of her own welfare. She has led captive many an unguarded swain by a passing smile in the street, and then unceremoniously deserted him to join some drunken and beastly party in an obscure and degraded alley.'

"'Her name—what was her name?' I again asked, once more taking up the knife, my nerves sufficiently braced by the above recital.

"'Anne R——,' he replied; 'I thought,' he continued, 'no one could be ignorant of her name, after hearing a description of her habits.'

"'*All* of us,' I continued, rallying, 'are not familiar with the persons and names of the "fallen angels" about town. But let us look at her face.' Saying this, I endeavoured to lift the white cloth from her head, but finding that the resurrectionist had tied a cord tightly round the muslin enclosing her neck and head, I desisted.

"'Her face is in keeping with her body and limbs,' said my merry friend; 'she was a perfect beauty. I have seen her in Chestnut Street every fair day for the last six months, until she got drunk and fell in the fire.'

"I now proceeded to business, but my flesh quivered as my knife penetrated the smooth fair breast of the subject. Soon the skin and the flesh were removed, and the saw grated harshly as it severed the ribs. When the heart was exposed, all bent forward instinctively, scanning it minutely, and seemingly with a curiosity to ascertain if it differed from those of others whose lives were different.

"When the operation was over, my anxiety to see her face returned. After an ineffectual effort to untie the cord, I became impatient, and seizing the knife that lay on the table, ripped open the muslin that hid her features! My God! The knife dropped from my hand, and penetrating the floor, quivered upright at my feet, while every member of my body trembled in unison with it! I raised my hands

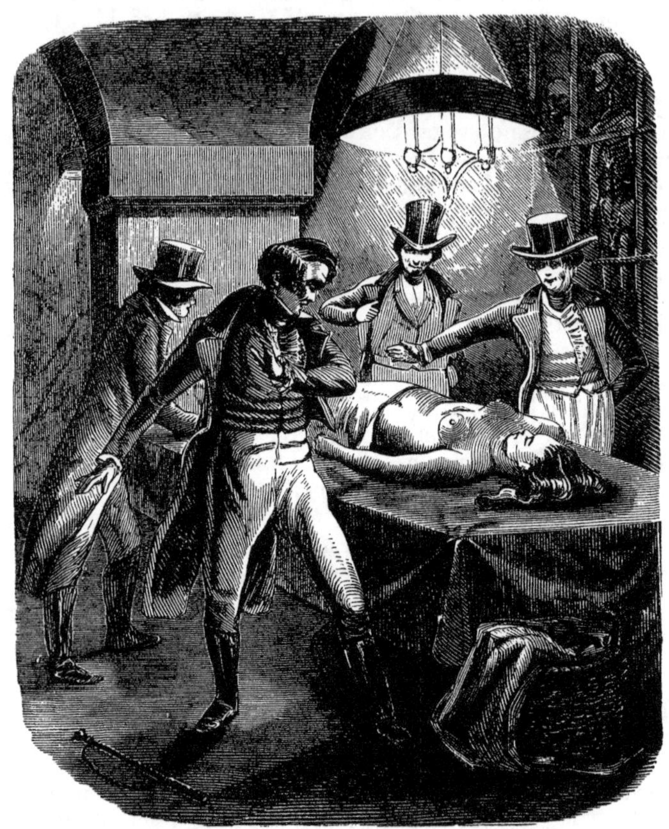

It was Laura, the loved, adored Laura!—P. 221.

with my fingers spread out to the utmost tension. My mouth fell open, and my eyes felt as if they were straining to leap from my head. *It was Laura*—the loved, adored Laura—*my* Laura! My friends heard me repeat the name, and marked with surprise and concern my inexplicably miserable condition. They gathered round me, and endeavoured to divert my attention from the dead and now gory body. It was in vain. I heeded not their words, but gazed steadfastly at the sad features of Laura, with my hands still uplifted. I was speechless, deaf, and immovable. No tear moistened my eyes, but burning thoughts rushed through my brain. My heart was cold, cold. Ah, I remembered how I had loved her once! I thought of the time when I was happy to bow down at her feet, and in good faith attribute to her many of the pure qualities pertaining to *risen* angels. And this was her end! The beautiful and innocent—the loving and beloved—the high born and wealthy—the light and joy of fond and indulgent parents—had been beguiled by the infernal tempter to make one step aside from the straight and narrow path of duty—and this was the result! The sensitive and guileless girl became an incarnate fiend, callous to every modest and virtuous impulse—scorned by the honest and good, and hating and undermining the redeeming principles of her species—rushing from the high station which her ancestors had arduously laboured for generations to attain, and voluntarily taking up her abode in the dens of squalid misery and indelible pollution—closing her eyes to the might and majesty of a merciful God, beckoning her to his eternal throne in heaven, and giving heed to the fatal devices of the enemy of mankind, till she was dragged down, down to the innermost depths of a raging and roaring hell! Such was the fate of Laura. Such is the fate of thousands who willingly err, though it be ever so slight, for the sake of enjoying an impious gratification. Poor Laura! Oh, how I loved her! But it is bootless to think of her now.

"I was gently forced from the dissecting-room by my friends, and conducted to my home in silence—in silence, because I had no words for any one. I pressed their hands at the door of my mansion, and bowing, they departed for their homes to muse over the incidents of the evening I entered my silent chamber, but not to rest. I threw open the casement and gazed out at the genial rays of the moon. The dark green leaves of the linden trees were motionless, and the silvery rays struggling through them cast a checkered and faint tint of mingled light and shade on the pavement beneath. The cool fresh air soothed my throbbing temples. I sank back in my seat and gazed up at the innumerable stars in the boundless sky. I thought the stellar host glittered with unusual brilliance, as if there were a joyous and holy revelry going on in heaven. My heart grew calm. I felt a conviction that true happiness, and purity of thought and purpose were inseparable. I knew that the contaminations of the world had overthrown many a righteous resolve, and linked the noblest minded with infamy. I thought of Laura. The seductions of the world had literally prostrated an angel before my eyes. I determined to *leave* the world, if not for ever, at least as long as its temptations to err, in the remotest degree, were liable to beset my path. I came hither."

When Glenn finished his narrative, Roughgrove rose in silence, and producing a small Bible that he always carried about his person, read in a low, but distinct and impressive tone, several passages which were peculiarly applicable to the state of their feelings. Glenn then approached the couch where William slumbered peacefully. A healthful perspiration rested on his forehead, and a sweet smile played upon his lips, indicating that his dreams were not among the savage scenes in which he had so lately mingled. Mary, who had fallen asleep while seated at his side, overcome with silent watching, yet rested with her head on the same pillow, precisely in the same attitude she reclined when Glenn began his recital. Roughgrove took her in his arms, and placing her softly at her brother's feet, bestowed a kiss upon her brow, and retired with Glenn to rest.

CHAPTER XVI.

Balmy spring—Joe's curious dream—He prepares to catch a fish—Glenn —William and Mary—Joe's sudden and strange appearance—La-u-na —The trembling fawn—The fishing sport—The ducking frolic—Sneak and the panther.

It was now the first week in May. Every vestige of winter had long since disappeared, and the verdure of a rich soil and mild temperature was fast enrobing the earth with the freshest and most pleasing of colours. Instead of the dreary expanse of ice that had covered the river, its waters now murmured musically by in the early morn—its curling eddies running along the sedgy shore, while the rising sun slowly dissipated the floating mists; and the inspiring notes of all the wild variety of birds, contributed to invest the scene with such charms as the God of nature only can impart, and which may only be fully enjoyed and justly appreciated by guileless and unsophisticated mortals.

Glenn rambled forth, and, partaking the harmony that pervaded the earth, air, and waters, his breast swelled with a blissful exultation that can never be known amid the grating voices of contending men, or experienced in crowded cities, where many confused sounds vibrate harshly and distracting on the ear. He stood in his little garden among the flowers that Mary had planted, and watched the humming-birds poised among the trembling leaves, their tiny wings still unruffled by the dew, while their slender beaks inhaled the sweet moisture of the variegated blossoms. Long he regarded the enchanting scene, unconscious of the flight of time, and alike regardless of the past and the future in his all-absorbing admiration of the present, wherein he deemed he was not far remote from that Presence to which time and eternity are obedient—when his phantasm was abruptly and unceremoniously put to flight by his man Joe, who rushed out of the house with a long rod in his hand, yawning and rubbing his eyes, as if he had been startled from his morning slumber but a moment before.

"What's the matter?" demanded Glenn.

"It was a wapper!" said Joe.

"What was?"

"The fish."

"Where?" asked Glenn.

"I'll tell you. I dreamt I was sitting on a rock, down at the ferry, with this rod in my hand, fishing for perch, when a thundering big catfish, as long as I am, took hold. I dreamt he pulled and I pulled—sometimes he had me in the water up to my knees, and sometimes I got him out on dry land. But he always flounced and kicked back again. Yet he couldn't escape, because the hook was still in his mouth, and when he jumped into the river I jumped to the rod, and so we had it over and over——"

"And now have done with it," said Glenn, interrupting him. "What are you holding the rod now for?"

"I'm going to try to catch him," said Joe, with unaffected simplicity.

"Merely because you had this dream!" continued Glenn, his features relaxing into a smile.

"Yes—I believe in dreams," said Joe. "Once, when we were living in Philadelphia, I had one of these same dreams. It was just about the same hour——"

"How do you know what hour it was you dreamt about the fish?" again interrupted Glenn.

"Why—I——," stammered Joe, "I'm sure it was about daybreak, because the sun rose a little while after I got out."

"That might be the case," said Glenn, "if you were to dream about the same thing from sun-down till sun-up. And I believe the fish was running in your head last night before I went to bed, for you were then snoring and jerking your arms about."

"Well, I'll tell you my other dream, anyhow. I dreamt I was walking along Spruce Street wharf with my head down, when all at once my toe struck against a red morocco pocket-wallet; I stooped down and picked it up and put it in my pocket, and went home before I looked to see what was in it."

"Well, what was in it when you did look?" asked Glenn.

"There was a one thousand dollar note on the Bank of the United States, with the president's and cashier's names on it, all genuine. Oh, I was so happy! I put it in my vest-pocket and sewed it up."

"But what have you done with it since?" asked Glenn.

"I—Hang it! it was only a dream!"* said Joe, unconsciously feeling in his empty pocket.

"But what has that dream to do with the fish?" pursued Glenn.

"I'll tell you," said Joe. "When I got up in the morning and discovered it was a dream, I slipped on my clothes as quickly as possible and set off for the wharf. When I got there, I walked along slowly with my head down till at length my toe struck against an oyster-shell. I picked it up, and while I was looking at it, the captain of a schooner invited me on board of his vessel to look at his cargo of oysters, just stolen from Deep Creek, Virginia. He gave me at least six dozen to eat!"

"And this makes you have faith in such dreams?" asked Glenn, striving in vain to repress his laughter.

"I got *something* by the dream," said Joe. "I had a first rate oyster-breakfast."

"But what has all this to do with the fish?" continued Glenn; "perhaps, instead of the fish, you expect to catch a *frog* this time. You will still be an Irishman, Joe. Go and try your luck."

"St. Patrick forbid that I should be any thing else but an Irishman! I should like to know if an Irishman ain't as good as anybody else, particularly when he's born in America, as I was? But the dream in Philadelphia *did* have something to do with a fish. Didn't I catch a fish? Isn't an oyster a fish? And it had something to do with *this* fish, too. I've been bothering my head ever since I got up about what kind of *bait* to catch him with, and I'm sure I never would have thought of the right kind if you hadn't mentioned that *frog* just now. I recollect they say that's the very best thing in the world to bait with for a

* Thousands have had similar dreams about similar notes since Joe's dream.—*Printer's Devil.*

catfish. I'll go straight to the brook and hunt up a frog!" Saying this, Joe set out to execute his purpose, while Glenn proceeded to Roughgrove's house to see how William progressed in his studies.

The intelligent youth, under the guidance of Roughgrove, Glenn, and his unwearying and affectionate sister, was now rapidly making amends for the long neglect of his education while abiding with the unlettered Indians. He had already gone through the English grammar, and was entering the higher branches of study. The great poets of his own country, and the most approved novelists were his companions during the hours of relaxation; for when the illimitable fields of intellect were opened to his vision, he would scarce for a moment consent to withdraw his admiring gaze. Thus, when it was necessary for a season to cease his toil in the path of learning, he delighted to recline in some cool shade with a pleasing book in his hand, and regale his senses with the flowers and refreshing streams of imaginative authors. And thus sweetly glided his days. Could such halcyon moments last, it were worse than madness to seek the wealth and honours of this world! In that secluded retreat, though far from the land of his nativity, with no community but the companionship of his three or four friends and the joyous myriads of birds—no palaces but the eternal hills of nature, and no pageantry but the rays of the rising and setting sun streaming in prismatic dies upon them, the smiling youth was far happier than he would have been in the princely halls of his fathers, where the sycophant only bent the knee to receive a load of gold, and the friend that might protect him on the throne would be the first to stab him on the highway.

A spreading elm stood near the door of Roughgrove's house, and beneath its clustering boughs William and Mary were seated on a rude bench, entirely screened from the glaring light of the sun. A few paces distant the brook glided in low murmurs between the green flags and water violets over its pebbly bed. The morning dew yet rested on the grass in the shade. The soft sigh of the fresh breeze, as it passed through the motionless branches of the towering elm, could scarce be heard, but yet sufficed ever and anon to lift aside the glossy ringlets that hung pendent to the maiden's shoulders. The paroquet and the thrush, the bluebird and goldfinch, fluttered among the thick foliage and trilled their melodies in sweetest cadence Both the brother and sister wore a happy smile. Happy, because the innocence of angels dwelt in the bosom of the one, and the memory of his guileless and blissful days of childhood possessed the other. Occasionally they read some passages in a book that lay open on Mary's lap, describing the last days of Charles I., and then the bright smile would be dimmed for a moment by a shade of sadness.

"Oh! poor man!" exclaimed Mary, when William read of the axe of the executioner descending on the neck of the prostrate monarch.

"It is far better to dwell in peace in such a quiet and lonely place as this, than to be where so many cruel men abide," said William, pondering.

"Ah me! I did not think that Christian men could be so cruel," said Mary, a bright tear dropping from her long eyelash.

"But the book says he was a tyrant and deserved to die," continued the youth, his lips compressed with firmness.

"He's coming!" exclaimed Mary, suddenly, and the pitying thought of the unfortunate Charles vanished from her mind. But as she steadily gazed up the path a crimson flush suffused her smooth brow and cheek, and she rose gracefully, and with a smile of delight, welcomed Glenn to the cool and refreshing shade of the majestic elm.

"You have come too late. William has already said his lesson, and I'm sure he knew it perfectly," said Mary, half-reproachfully and half-playfully.

"Mary don't know, Mr. Glenn; because I am now further advanced than she is," said William.

"But what kept you away so long this beautiful morning?" continued the innocent girl. "Don't you see the dew is almost dried away in the sun, and the morning-glories are nearly all closed?"

"I was lingering in the garden among the delicate flowers you gave me Mary; and the green and golden humming-birds charmed me so that I could not tear myself away," replied our hero, as he sat down between the brother and sister.

"I shall go with brother William on the cliff and get some wild roses and hare-bells, and then all your humming birds will leave you and stay here with me," said Mary, smiling archly.

"But you will be the prettiest bird among them, and flower too, to my eyes," said Glenn, gazing at the clear and brilliant though laughing eyes of the pleased girl.

"If that were the case, why did you linger so long in the garden?" asked the maid, with some seriousness.

"I should not have done so, Mary, but for Joe, who, you know, will always be heard when he has any thing to say; and this morning he had a ludicrous dream to tell me."

"I like Joe a great deal—he makes me laugh every time I see him. And you must tell me what he said, and how he looked and acted, that I may know whether you did right to stay away so long," said the thoughtless and happy girl, eager to listen to the accents of the one whose approach had illumined her features with the mystical fires of the heart.

Glenn faithfully repeated every word and gesture of his dialogue with Joe, and the unsophisticated girl's joyous laugh rang merrily up the echoing vale in sweet accompaniment with the carols of the feathered songsters.

When the narration ended, they both turned with surprise to William, who, instead of partaking their hilarity as usual, sat perfectly motionless in deep thought, regarding with apparent intensity the straggling spears of grass that grew at his feet. The book he had taken up, which had dropped from Mary's lap when she hastily rose at the approach of Glenn, now fell unobserved by him from his relaxed hand. His face became unusually pale. His limbs seemed to be strangely agitated, and the pulsations of his heart were audible.

"What's the matter, dear brother?" cried Mary, in alarm.

"La-u-na—LA-U-NA!" he exclaimed, and, sinking softly down on his knees, applied his ear close to the ground in a listening attitude.

"Dear brother William! *do* tell Mary what ails you! What is La-u-na!" said the startled and distressed girl, with affectionate concern.

"*La-u-na*—THE TREMBLING FAWN!" cried William, pantingly.

"Listen" said Glenn, checking Mary when she was about to repeat her inquiry. A plaintive flute-like sound was heard at intervals, floating on the balmy and almost motionless air down the green-fringed vale. At times it resembled the mournful plaint of the lonely dove, and then died away like the last notes of the expiring swan.

Before many minutes elapsed another sound of quite a different character saluted their ears. This was a rustling among the bushes, heard indistinctly at first, while the object was far up the valley, but as it approached with fearful rapidity, the rushing noise became tremendous, and a few moments after, when the trembling sumachs parted in view, they beheld Joe! He dashed through the briers interspersed among the undergrowth, and plunged through the winding brook that occasionally crossed his path, as if all surrounding obstacles and obstructions were contemptible in comparison with the danger behind! Leaping over intervening rocks, and flying through dense clusters of young trees that ever and anon threatened to impede his progress, he at length reached the spot where the little group still remained seated. Without hat or coat, and panting so violently that he was unable to explain distinctly the cause of his alarm, poor Joe threw himself down on the earth in the most distressed and pitiable condition.

"What have you seen? What is the cause of this affright?" asked Glenn.

"I—oh—they—coming!" cried Joe, incoherently.

"What is coming?" continued Glenn.

"I—Indians!" exclaimed he, springing up and rushing into the house.

"They are friendly Indians, then," said Mary; "because the hostile ones never come upon us at this season of the year."

"So I have been told," said Glenn; "but even the sight of a friendly Indian would scare Joe."

"It is La-u-na!" said William, still attentively listening.

"What is *La-u-na?*" interrogated Mary, again.

"The *Trembling Fawn!*" repeated William, with emphasis, in a mysterious and abstracted manner. Presently he stood up and intently regarded the dim path overshadowed by the luxuriant foliage that Joe had so recently traversed, and an animated smile played upon his lips, and his dark, clear eyes sparkled with a thrill of ecstasy.

A slight female form, emerged from the dark green

thicket, and glided more like a spirit of the air than a human being towards the wondering group. Her light steps produced no sound. In each hand she held a rich bouquet of fresh wild flowers, and leaves and blossoms were fantastically, though tastefully, arranged in her hair and on her breast. A broad, shining gold band decked her temples, but many of her raven ringlets had escaped from their confinement, and floated out on the wind as she sped towards her beloved.

"La-u-na! La-u-na!" cried William, darting forward frantically and catching the girl in his arms. He pressed her closely and fondly to his heart, and she hid her face on his breast. Thus they clung together several minutes in silence, when they were interrupted by Roughgrove, whose attention had been attracted by the sudden affright of Joe.

"William, my dear boy," said the grieved old man, "you must not have any thing to do with the Indians—you promised us that you would not ——"

"Leave us!" said the youth, sternly, and stamping impatiently.

"Do, father!" cried Mary, who looked on in tears, a few paces apart; "brother won't leave us again—I'm sure he won't—will you, William?"

"No, I will not!" exclaimed the youth. The Indian girl comprehended the meaning of his words, and, tearing away from his embrace, stood with folded arms at his side, with her penetrating and reproachful eyes fixed full upon him, while her lips quivered and her breast heaved in agitation. All now regarded her in silence and admiration. Her form was a perfect model of beauty. Her complexion was but a shade darker than that of the maidens of Spain. Her brows were most admirably arched, and her long silken lashes would have been envied by an Italian beauty. Her forehead and cheeks were smooth, and all her features as regular as those of a Venus. The mould of her face was strictly Grecian, and on her delicate lips rested a half-formed expression of sad regret and firm resolution. Her vestments were rich, and highly ornamented with pearls and diamonds. She wore a light snowy mantle made of swan skins, on which a portion of the fleecy down remained. Beneath, the dress was composed of skins of the finest finish, descending midway between her knees and ankles, where it was met by the tops of the buckskin moccasins, that confined her small and delicately-formed feet. Her arms, which were mostly concealed under her mantle, were bare from the elbows down, and adorned at the wrists with silver bands.

"Why, hang it all! Was there nothing running after me but this squaw?" asked Joe, who had ventured forth again unobserved, and now stood beside Glenn and Mary.

"Silence!" said Glenn.

"Oh, don't call *her* a squaw, Joe—she's more like an angel than a squaw," said Mary, gazing tenderly at the lovers, while tears were yet standing in her eyes.

"I won't do so again," said Joe, "because she's the prettiest wild thing I ever saw; and if Mr. William don't marry her, I will."

"Keep silent, Joe, or else leave us," again interposed Glenn.

"I'll go catch my fish. I had just found a frog, and was in the act of catching it, when I saw the sq—— the— *her*—and I thought then that I would just run home and let you know she was coming before I took it. But I remember where it was, and I'll have it now in less than no time." Saying this, Joe set off up the valley again, though not very well pleased with himself for betraying so much alarm when there was so little danger.

"La-u-na, I am no Indian," said William, at length, in the language of her tribe, and much affected by her searching stare.

"But you were once the young chief that led our warriors to battle, and caught La-u-na's heart. I heard you were a pale-face after you were taken away from us; and I thought if you would not fly back to La-u-na, like the pigeon that escapes from the talons of the eagle and returns to its mate, then I would lose you—forget you—hate you. I tried, but I could not do it. When the white moon ran up to the top of the sky, and shone down through the tall trees in my face, I would ever meet you in the land of dreams, with the bright smile you used to have when you were wont to put your arm around me and draw me so gently to your breast. I was happy in those dreams. But they would not stay. The night-hawk flew low and touched my eyes with his wings as he flapped by, and I awoke. Then my breast was cold and my cheeks were wet. The katydids gathered in the sweet rose-bushes about me and sung mournfully. La-u-na was unhappy. La-u-na must see her Young Eagle, or go to the land of spirits. She called her wild steed to her side, and, plucking these flowers to test his fleetness, sprang upon him and flew hither. He is now grazing in the prairie at the head of the valley; and here are the blossoms, still alive, fresh and sweet." The trembling and tearful girl then gently and sadly strewed the flowers over the grass at her feet.

"Sweet La-u-na!" cried William, snatching up the blossoms and pressing them to his lips, "forgive the young chief; he will still love you and never leave you again."

"No—no—no!" said the girl, shaking her head in despair; "the pale face youth will not creep through the silent and shady forest with La-u-na any more. He will gather no more ripe grapes for the Trembling Fawn. He will not bathe again in the clear waters with La-u-na. He will give her no more rings of roses to put on her breast. The Trembling Fawn is wounded. She must find a cool shade and lie down. The dove will perch over her and wail. She will sing a low song. She will close her eyes and die."

"Oh, no!" cried William, placing his arms around her tenderly, "La-u-na must not die, or if she does, she shall not die alone. Why will not La-u-na dwell with me among my friends?" The girl started and exhibited signs of mingled delight and doubt, and then replied—

"The pale maiden would hate La-u-na, and the gray-head would drive her away."

"No, La-u-na," said William; "they would all love you, and we would be so happy! Say you will stay with me here, and you shall be my wife, and I will have no other love. My sister is sweet and mild as La-u-na, and my father will always be kind."

The dark eyes of the girl assumed an unwonted lustre, and she turned imploringly to Mary, Glenn, and Roughgrove.

"Oh!" cried William, in his native tongue, addressing his white friends; "let La-u-na dwell with us! She is as innocent as the lily by the brook, and as noble as a queen Father," he continued, stepping forward and taking Roughgrove's hand, "you won't refuse my request! And you,

"Oh, no!" cried William, placing his arms around her tenderly; "La-u-na must not die; or, if she does, she shall not die alone. Why will not La-u-na dwell with me, among my friends?" The girl started, and exhibited signs of mingled delight and doubt.—P. 232.

sister Mary, I know you will love her as dearly as you do me. And you, my friend," said he, turning to Glenn, "will soon hear her speak our own language, and she will cull many beautiful flowers for you that the white man never yet beheld. Grant this," added the youth, after pausing a few moments, while his friends hung their heads in silence, "and I will remain with you always; but if you refuse, I must fly to the forest again."

"Stay! Oh, brother, you shall not go!" cried Mary, and rushing forward, she threw her arms round his neck. The Indian girl kissed her pale brow, and smiled joyfully, when the youth told her that Mary was his dear sister.

"He loves her, and her affection for him is imperishable!" said Glenn.

"And why may they not be happy together, if they dwell with us?" asked Roughgrove, pondering.

"There is no reason why they should not be. Let us tell them to remain and be happy," said Glenn.

When fully informed that she might abide with them and still love her Young Eagle, La-u-na was almost frantic with ecstasy. She looked gratefully and fondly on her new friends, and pressed their hands in turn. She seemed to be more especially fond of Mary, and repeatedly wound her smooth and soft arms affectionately about her waist and neck.

William led his Indian bride to the seat under the spreading green tree, and signified a desire to commune with her alone. When seated together on the rude bench, the maiden's hand clasped in William's, Mary fondly kissed them both and withdrew in company with Roughgrove and Glenn. Roughgrove prostrated himself in prayer when within the house. Mary ran up to the top of the beetling cliff to cull flowers, and Glenn directed his steps down the valley towards the river, whither Joe had preceded him with the frog he had succeeded in capturing.

Glenn was met about midway by Joe, who was returning slowly, with peculiar marks of agitation on his face. He had neither frog, rod, nor fish in his hand.

"I thought you were fishing," remarked Glenn.

"So I am," replied Joe; "and I've had the greatest luck you ever heard of."

"Well, tell me your success."

"I had a bite," continued he, "in less than three minutes after I threw in my hook. It was a wapper! When he took hold I let him play about awhile with a slack line, to be certain and get it well fixed in his mouth. But when I went to draw up, the monster made a splash or two, and then whizzed out into the middle of the river!"

"Where was the hook?" asked Glenn.

"In his mouth, to be sure," replied Joe.

"And the line?"

"Fast to the rod."

"And the rod?"

"Fast to the line!" said Joe, "and following the fish at the rate of ten knots, while I stood on the bank staring in utter astonishment."

"Then, where was your great success?" demanded Glenn.

"It was a noble *bite*," said Joe.

"But you were the *bitten* one," remarked Glenn, scanning Joe's visage, which began to assume a disconsolate cast.

"If I'd only been thinking about such a wapper, and had been on my guard," said Joe, "splash me if he should ever have got my rod away in that manner—I'd have taken a ducking first!"

"Have you no more lines?" asked Glenn.

"No," replied Joe, "none but your's."

"You are welcome to it—but be quick, and I will look on while you have your revenge."

Joe sprang nimbly up the hill, and in a few minutes returned with fresh tackle and another frog that he found on his way. They then repaired to the margin of the river; but before Joe ventured to cast out his line again he made the end of the rod fast to his wrist by means of a strong cord he had provided for that purpose. But now his precaution seemed to have been unnecessary, for many minutes elapsed without any symptoms of success.

Glenn grew impatient and retired a few paces to the base of the cliff, where he reclined in an easy posture on some huge rocks that had tumbled down from a great height, and lay half-imbedded in the earth. Here he long remained with his eyes fixed abstractedly on the curling water, and meditated on the occurrence he had recently witnessed. While his thoughts were dwelling on the singular affection and constancy of the Indian girl, and the probable future happiness of her young lord, his reflections more than once turned upon his *own* condition. The simple pleasantries that had so often occurred between Mary and himself never failed to produce many unconscious smiles on his lips, and being reciprocated and repeated day after day with increased delight, it was no wonder that he found himself heaving tender sighs as he occasionally pictured her happy features in his mind's eye. He now endeavoured to bestow some grave consideration on the tender subject, and to think seriously about the proper mode of conducting himself in future, when he heard the innocent maiden's clear and inspiring voice ringing down the valley and sinking in soft murmuring echoes on the gliding stream. Soon his quick ear caught the words, which he recognised to be a short ballad of his own composing, that had been written at Mary's request. He then listened in silence, without moving from his recumbent position.

THE CRUEL MAIDEN.

I.

She heard his prayer and sweetly smiled,
Then frown'd, and laughing fled away;
But the poor youth, e'en thus beguiled,
Still would pray.

II.

He'd won her heart, but still she fled,
And laugh'd and mock'd from dell and peak
While his sad heart, that inward bled,
Was fit to break!

III.

Where the bright waters lead adown
The moss-green rocks and flags among,
He paused—and on his brow a frown
Darkly hung!

IV.

A shriek came down the peaceful vale,
Full soon the maid was at his side,
Her ringlets flowing, and cheeks all pale,
A *willing* bride!

Glenn long remained motionless after the sounds died away, as if endeavouring to retain the soothing effect of the ringing notes that had so sweetly reverberated along the jutting peaks of the towering cliff!

"I've got a bite!" exclaimed Joe, bending over the verge of the bank and stretching his arms as far as possible over the water, while his line moved about in various directions, indicating truly that a fish had taken the hook.

"Hold fast to the rod this time, Joe," remarked Glenn, who became interested in the scene.

"Won't I? Its tied fast to my wrist."

"Is it not time to pull him up?" asked Glenn, seeing that the fish, so far from being conscious of peril, inclined towards the shore with the line in quest of more food.

"Here goes!" said Joe, jerking the rod up violently with both hands. No sooner did the fish feel the piercing hook in his mouth than he rose to the surface, and splashing the water several feet round in every direction, darted quickly downwards, in spite of the strenuous efforts of Joe to the contrary.

Nevertheless, Joe entertained no fears about the result; and the fish, as if apprized of the impossibility of capturing the rod, ran along parallel with the shore, gradually approaching the brink of the water, and seemingly with the intention to surrender himself at the feet of the piscator. But this was not his purpose. When Joe made another strong pull, in the endeavour to strand him in the shallow water, the fish again threw up the spray (some of which reached his adversary's face,) and, turning his head outwards, ran directly away from the shore.

"Pull him back, Joe!" said Glenn.

"I am trying with all my might," replied Joe, "but he's so plaguy strong he won't come, hang him!"

"He'll get away if you don't mind!" continued Glenn, evincing much animation in his tones and gestures.

"I'll be drenched if he does!" said Joe, with his arm, to which the rod was lashed, stretched out, while he endeavoured to plant his feet firmly in the sand.

"He'll have you in the water—cut the rod loose from your wrist!" cried Glenn, as Joe's foothold gave way and he was truly drawn into the water.

"Oh, good gracious! I've got no knife! Give me your

hand!" cried Joe, vainly striving to untie the cord. "Help me! Oh, St. Peter!" he continued, imploringly, as the fish drew him on in the water, in quick but reluctant strides. "Oh! I'm gone!" he cried, when the water was midway to his chin, and the fish pulling him along with increasing rapidity.

"You are a good swimmer, Joe—be not alarmed, and you will not be hurt," said Glenn, half inclined to laugh at his man's indescribable contortions and grimaces, and apprehending no serious result.

"Ugh!" cried Joe, the water now up to his chin, and the next moment, when in the act of making a hasty and piteous entreaty, his head quickly dipped under the turbid surface and disappeared entirely. Glenn now became alarmed; but, when in the act of divesting himself of his clothing for the purpose of plunging in to his rescue, Joe rose again some forty paces out in the current, and by the exertion of the arm that was free he was enabled to keep his head above the water. The current was very strong, and the fish, in endeavouring to run up the stream with his prize in tow, made but little headway, and a very few minutes sufficed to prove that it was altogether unequal to the attempt. After having progressed about six rods, Joe's head became quite stationary like a buoy, or a cork at anchor, and then, by degrees, was carried downward by the strong flow as the fish at length became quite exhausted.

"Now for it, Joe—swim towards the shore with him!" cried Glenn.

"He's almost got my shoulder out of place!" replied Joe, blowing a large quantity of water out of his mouth.

"I see his fin above the water," said Glenn; "struggle manfully, Joe, and you will capture him yet!"

"I'll die but I'll have him now—after such a ducking as this!" said Joe, approaching the shore with the almost inanimate fish, that was no longer able to contend against his superior strength. When he drew near enough to touch the bottom, he turned his head and beheld his prize floating close behind, and obedient to his will.

It required the strength of both Glenn and Joe to drag the immense catfish (for such it proved to be) from its native element. It was about the length and weight of Joe, and had a mouth of sufficient dimensions to have swallowed a man's head. It was given to the ferrymen, who had witnessed the immersion, and were attracted thither to render assistance.

"I suppose you have now had enough of the fish?" remarked Glenn, as they retraced their steps homeward.

"I'll acknowledge that I'm satisfied for the present; but I was resolved to have satisfaction!" replied Joe.

"Yes, but you have had it with a vengeance; and I doubt not that your apparent contentment is but cold comfort," continued Glenn.

"I'm not a bit cold—I shan't change my clothes, and I'm ready for any other sport you like," said Joe.

"If you really suffer no inconvenience from the wet—and this fine warm day inclines me to believe you—we will take our guns and walk out to the small lakes on the borders of the prairie."

"Splash it"—began Joe.

"No—*duck* it," interrupted Glenn.

"Well, I should like to know exactly what you mean—whether you are in earnest about going to the ponds, or whether you are joking me for getting *ducked*—as there's nothing in them now to shoot but *ducks*, and it may have popped into your head just because I had the *ducking*," said Joe.

"I am in earnest," said Glenn; "I do not wish to annoy William, or to meet Roughgrove and Mary until their domestic arrangements are all completed."

"That's strange," said Joe.

"What's strange?" asked Glenn, quickly.

"Why, your not wanting to meet Miss Mary. I say it is most mysteriously strange," replied Joe.

"Say nothing more about it, and think less," said Glenn, striding in advance, while a smile played upon his lip.

"But I can't help dreaming about it—and my dreams all come true," said Joe.

"What have you been dreaming—but never mind—bring out the guns," said Glenn, pausing at the gate of the inclosure, and not venturing to hear Joe recite the dream about himself and Mary.

When possessed of the necessary implements, they set out towards the groves that bordered the prairie, among which were several lakes of clear water, not more than fifty or sixty paces in diameter, where the various wild fowl, as well as the otter and the muskrat, usually abounded. Our hero had previously anticipated some sport of this na ture, and constructed blinds on the verge of the lakes, and cut paths through the clustering bushes to reach them stealthily. The lake they now approached was bounded on one side by the green meadow-like prairie, and fringed on the other by hazel thickets, with an occasional towering elm that had survived the autumnal fires.

The morning breeze had subsided, and a delightful calm prevailed. A thousand wild flowers, comprising every hue, filled the air with delicious fragrance, while no sound was heard but the melody of happy birds.

"I think I see a duck!" whispered Joe, as they moved slowly along the path in a stooping posture.

"Where?" asked Glenn, as they crept softly to the blind and cast their eyes over the clear unruffled water.

"I thought I saw one on the muskrat house; but he must have gone to the other side," responded Joe, now looking in vain for it, and closely scanning the little hillocks that had been thrown up in the lake by the muskrats.

"You must have been mistaken," said Glenn; "suppose we go to the other lakes."

"No, I wasn't mistaken—I'd swear to it—be quiet and keep a bright look-out, and we'll see him again in a minute or two," replied Joe, who stood in an attitude of readiness to fire at an instant's warning.

"What is that?" asked Glenn, just then actually observing a small brown object moving behind the hillock.

"Wait till I see a little more of it," said Joe, with his finger on the trigger.

"Don't fire, Joe! its a man's *cap!*" exclaimed Glenn, detecting under the dark brim the large staring eyes of a human being, apparently evincing a sense of imminent peril; and the next moment the muzzle of a gun pointing above their heads came in view.

"Dod rot it, look up that tree!"

The smile that began to play on our hero's features on recognizing the voice of Sneak was quickly dispelled and succeeded by horror when he cast his eyes upward and beheld an enormous panther, stooping, and on the eve of springing upon him!

"Oh!" exclaimed Joe, letting his gun fall, and falling down himself, bereft alike of the power of escape and the ability to resist.

"Be quiet!" said Glenn, endeavouring to raise his gun, which had become entangled in the bushes; but before he could execute his purpose Sneak fired, and the ferocious animal came tumbling down through the branches and fell at his feet.

"Ugh! Goodness!" exclaimed Joe, his hat stricken down over his eyes by the descending panther, and, leaping over the frail barrier of bushes into the water, he plunged forward and executed a series of diving evolutions, as if still endeavouring to elude the clutches of the carnivorous beast, which he imagined was after him.

"Dod—come out of the pond! Its dead—didn't you hear *me* shoot?" said Sneak, who had by this time paddled a little canoe in which he had been seated to the shore. But Joe continued his exercises, his crushed hat not only depriving him of sight, but rendering him deaf to the laughter that burst from Glenn and Sneak. Sneak ran round to the opposite side of the lake to a point that Joe was approaching, (though all unconscious of his destination,) and remained there till the poor fellow pushed his half-submerged head against the grass, when he seized him furiously and bore him a few paces from the water, in spite of his cries and struggles.

"*I* ain't the painter!" said Sneak, at length weary of the illusion, and dragging Joe's hat from his head.

"Ha! hang it! ha!" cried Joe, staring at Sneak and Glenn in bewilderment. "Where is it?" he cried, when in some degree recovered from his great perturbation.

"Didn't you hear *me* shoot? Of course its dead!" replied Sneak.

"Which do you prefer, Joe, *ducking* or *fishing?*" asked Glenn.

"I never saw a feller *duck* his head so," said Sneak.

"Ha! ha! ha! you thought I was frightened, and trying to get away from the panther! But you were *much* mistaken. I was chasing a muskrat—I got wet in the river, and was determined to see ——"

"You couldn't see your own nose!" interrupted Sneak.

He plunged forward, and executed a series of diving evolutions. — P 240.

"If I couldn't see, I suppose I could hear him run!" replied Joe.

"You couldn't 'ave heard thunder!" said Sneak.

"Did you ever try it?" asked Joe.

"No," replied Sneak.

"Then you don't know," replied Joe; "and now I'm ready to kill a duck," he continued, looking up at a number of water-fowl sailing round and awaiting their departure to dip into the water.

"I will leave you here, Joe. When you hear me fire at the other lake, you may expect the ducks that escape me to visit you," observed Glenn, and immediately after disappeared in the bushes.

"And I'll take the painter's hide off," said Sneak, going with Joe to the blind, where he quietly commenced his labour, that Joe's sport might not be interrupted.

Several flocks of geese and ducks yet flew round above, and gradually drew nearer to the earth, but still fearful of danger and cautiously reconnoitering the premises.

"Suppose I pink one of them on the wing?" said Joe, looking up.

"I don't believe you *kin*," said Sneak, as he tugged at the panther's hide.

"Wait till they come round the next time, and I'll show you—so look out," said Joe.

"I'll not look—there's no occasion for my seeing—*I'm* not after a muskrat," responded Sneak, stripping the skin from the animal, and laughing at his own remark. When the ducks came round again, Joe fired, and sure enough one of them fell—descending in a curve which brought it directly on Sneak's cap, knocking it over his eyes.

"Dod rot it! hands off, or I'll walk into you!" exclaimed Sneak, rising up in a hostile attitude.

"Good! that's tit for tat," cried Joe, laughing, as he loaded his gun.

"You didn't do it a purpose," said Sneak, "nor I won't jump into the water nother."

"Yes I did!" continued Joe, much pleased at the occurrence.

"You didn't do any sich thing—or we'd have to fight; but nobody could do sich a thing only by accident. You'd better load your gun, and be ready by the time the next comes," added Sneak, again tearing asunder the panther's skin.

"I thought I *had* loaded," said Joe, forgetting he had performed that operation, and depositing another charge in his old musket.

Presently Glenn's gun was heard, and in a few minutes an immense flock of geese and ducks, mingled together, flew over the bushes and covered the face of the lake. Joe very deliberately fired in the midst of them, and the rebound of his gun throwing him against Sneak, who was still in a stooping posture, they both fell to the ground.

"I did that on purpose, I'll take my oath—I knew you had put in two loads," said Sneak, rising up.

"Yes, but I ain't hurt—falling over you saved me, or else I'd a thrashed you or got a thrashing," replied Joe, his good humour recovered on beholding some fifteen or twenty dead and wounded ducks and geese on the surface of the water. By the time he had collected his birds, by means of Sneak's canoe, Glenn, who had met with the like success, emerged from the bushes on the opposite verge of the lake, bearing with him his game. Being well satisfied with the sport, he and Joe retraced their steps homeward.

CHAPTER XVII.

The bright morning—Sneak's visit—Glenn's heart—The snake hunt—Love and raspberries—Joe is bitten—His terror and sufferings—Arrival of Boone—Joe's abrupt recovery—Preparations to leave the west—Conclusion.

THE sun rose the next morning in unusual glory. Not a breath of air stirred the entranced foliage of the dark green trees in the valleys, and the fresh flowers around exhaled a sweet perfume that remained stationary over them. The fawn stood perfectly still in the grassy yard, and seemed to contemplate the grandeur of the enchanting scene. The atmosphere was as translucent as fancy paints the realms of the blest, and quite minute objects could be distinctly seen far over the river many miles eastward. Nor were any sounds heard save the occasional chattering of the paroquet in the dense forest across the river, a mile distant, and yet they appeared to be in the immediate vicinity. The hounds lay extended on the ground with their eyes open, more in a listless than a watchful attitude. The kitten was couched on the threshold (the door having been left open to admit the pure air,) and looked thoughtfully at the rising sun. The large blue chanticleer was balanced on one foot with an eye turned upwards as if scanning the heavens to guard against the sudden attack of the far-seeing eagle. Nature seemed to be indulging in a last sweet morning slumber, if indeed not over-sleeping herself, while the sun rose stealthily up and smiled at all her charms exposed!

"Hillo! ain't you all up yit? Git up, Joe, and feed your hosses," cried Sneak, approaching the gate on the outside, and thus most unceremoniously dispelling the charm that enwrapped the premises.

"Who's there?" cried Joe, springing up and rubbing his eyes.

"It's me—dod, you know who I am. Come, open the gate and let me in."

"What's the matter, Sneak? Are the Indians after you?" said Joe, running out, but pausing at the gate for an answer before he drew back the bolt.

"No—I thought you had sense enough by this time to know no Indians ain't going to come this time a-year. Let me in!" added he, impatiently.

"What are you doing with them long sticks?" asked Joe, opening the gate and observing two hickory poles in Sneak's hand. "Are you going to try your luck fishing?"

"No, nor *ducking* nother," replied he, sarcastically.

"Plague it, Sneak," said Joe, deprecatingly, "never mind that affair; you were mistaken about my being frightened. The next chance I get I'll let you see that I'm not afraid of any thing."

"Well, I want you to go with me on a spree this morning that'll try you."

"What are you going to do?" asked Joe, with some curiosity in his looks.

"I'm going a *snaking*," said Sneak.

At this juncture the dialogue was arrested by the appearance of Glenn, whose brow was somewhat paler than usual, and wore an absent and thoughtful cast; yet his abstract meditations did not seem altogether of a painful nature.

"Joe," said he, "I want you to exercise the horses more in the prairie. They are getting too fat and lazy. If they cannot be got on the boat when we leave here, we will have to send them by land to St. Louis."

"Dod—you ain't a going to leave us?" cried Sneak.

"Well, I thought something was in the wind," said Joe, pondering? "but it 'll break Miss Mary's——"

"Pshaw!" replied Glenn, quickly interrupting him; "you don't know what you are talking about."

"Well, I can't say I do exactly," said Joe; "but I know its a very mysterious matter."

"*What* is such a mysterious matter?" asked Glenn, smiling.

"Why, you—Miss Mary"—stammered Joe.

"Well, what is there mysterious about us?"

"Hang it, *you* know!" replied Joe.

"Pshaw!" repeated Glenn, striding out of the inclosure, and descending the path leading to Roughgrove's house, whither he directed Joe to follow when he had galloped the horses.

"Have you got any licker in the house?" asked Sneak, staring at the retreating form of Glenn.

"No—its all gone. Why do you ask?" returned Joe.

"Becaise that feller's drunk," said Sneak, with a peculiar nod.

"No he ain't—he hasn't drunk a drop for a month."

"Then he's going crazy, and you'd better keep a sharp look-out."

"I know what's the matter with him—he's in love!" said Joe.

"Then why don't he take her?" asked Sneak.

"I don't know," replied Joe; "maybe he will, some day. Now for a ride—how are you, Pete?" he continued, opening the stable door and rubbing the pony's head that was instantly thrust out in salutation.

"I'll ride the hoss," said Sneak.

"Will you? I'm glad of it," said Joe, "for that'll save me the trouble of leading him."

"That's jest what I come for," said Sneak, "becaise this hot morning the snakes are too thick to fight 'em on foot."

"Can you see many of them at a time?"

"Well, I reckon you kin."

"Won't they bite the horses?"

"No, the hosses knows what a snake is as well as a man, and they'll keep a bright eye for 'emselves, while we stave out their brains with our poles," said Sneak.

In a few minutes the companions were mounted, and with the fawn skipping in advance, and the hounds in the rear, they proceeded gayly out toward the prairie on a *snaking* expedition.

The sunlight was now intensely brilliant, and the atmosphere, though laden with the sweet perfume of the countless millions of wild flowers, began to assume a sultriness that soon caused the horses and hounds to loll out their tongues and pant as they bounded through the rank grass Ere long the riders drew near a partially barren spot in the prairie, where from some singular cause the grass was not more than three inches high. This spot was circular, about fifty paces in diameter, and in the centre was a pool of bright water, some fifty feet in circumference. The grass growing round this spot was tall and luxuriant, and terminated as abruptly at the edge of the circle as if a mower had passed along with his sharp scythe.

"Sneak, I never saw that before," said Joe, as they approached, while yet some forty paces distant. "What does it mean?"

"You'll see presently," said his companion, grasping more firmly the thick end of his rod, as if preparing to deal a blow. "When I was out here this morning," he continued, "they were too thick for me, and I had to make tracks."

"What were too thick for you?" asked Joe, with a singular anxiety, and at the same time reining in his pony.

"Why, the *snakes*," said Sneak with much deliberation

"I was a-foot then, and from the style in which they whizzed through the grass, I was afraid too many might git on me at a time and choke me to death. But now I'm ready for 'em; they can't git us if we manage korect."

"I won't go!" said Joe.

"Dod, they ain't pisen!" said Sneak; "they're nearly all *black racers*, and they don't bite. Come on, don't be such a tarnation coward; the rattlesnakes, and copperheads, and wipers, wont run after us; and if they was to, they couldn't reach up to our legs. This is a glorious day for *snaking*—come on, Joe!"

Joe followed at a very slow and cautious pace a few steps farther, and then halted again.

"What're you stopping for agin?" asked Sneak.

"Sneak, the pony ain't tall enough!"

"That's all the better," replied Sneak; "you can whack 'em easier as they run—and then they can't see you as fur as they kin me. I'll swap hosses with you."

"No you won't!" replied Joe, whipping forward again. But he had not advanced many seconds before he drew up once more. This time he was attracted by the unaccountable motions of the fawn, a short distance ahead. That animal was apparently striking some object on the ground with its feet, and ever and anon springing violently to one side or the other. Its hair stood erect on its back, and it assumed a most ferocious aspect. Now it would run back toward the men a moment, and, wheeling suddenly, again leap upon the foe, when its feet could be heard to strike against the ground; then it plunged forward, and after making a spring beyond, would return to the attack.

"Here, Ringwood! Jowler!" cried Joe, and the hounds ran forward to the spot pointed out to them. But no sooner had they gone far enough to see the nature of the enemy that the fawn was attacking, than they turned away affrighted, and with their tails hanging down retreated from the scene of action.

They rode up and surveyed more closely the strange battle. The fawn, becoming more and more enraged, did not suspend hostilities at their approach. They paused involuntarily when, within a few feet of the object, which proved to be a tremendous rattlesnake, some five feet in length, and as thick as a man's arm. It was nearly dead,

It grew weaker and weaker, and finally turned over on its back.--P 247

Its body, neck, and head, exhibited many bloody gashes cut by the sharp hoofs of the fawn. Every time the fawn sprang upon it, it endeavoured in vain to strike its fangs into its active foe, which sprang away in a twinkling, and before it could prepare to strike again, the fatal hoofs would inflict another wound on its devoted head. It grew weaker and weaker, and finally turned over on its back, when the infuriated deer, no longer compelled to observe cautionary measures, soon severed its head entirely from the body and stood over it in triumph.

"Pete can do that if a deer can!" said Joe, somewhat emboldened at the death of so formidable a reptile, and beholding the fixed though composed gaze of the pony as he stood with his head turned sideways towards the weltering snake.

"Sartinly he kin," said Sneak, standing up in his stirrups, and stretching his long neck to its utmost tension to see if any snakes were in the open area before them.

"Do you see any, Sneak?" asked Joe, now grasping his rod and anxious for the fray.

"I see a few—about forty, I guess, lying in the sun at the edge of the water."

"Sneak, there's too many of them," said Joe.

"Dod—you ain't a going to back out now, I hope. Don't you see your pony snuffing at 'em? He wants to dash right in among 'em."

"No he don't," said Joe—"he don't like the smell, nor I either—faugh!"

"Why, it smells like May-apples—I like it," said Sneak; "but there ain't more than one or two copper-heads there—they're most all racers. Come on, Joe—we must gallop right through and mash their heads with our sticks as we pass. Then after a little while we must turn and dash back agin—that's the way to fix 'em."

"You must go before," said Joe.

The number that Sneak mentioned was not exaggerated. On the contrary, additions were constantly made to the number. The surface of the pool was continually agitated by the darting serpents striking at the tadpoles and frogs, while on the margin many were writhing in various fantastic contortions in their sports. Nearly all of them were large, and some could not have been less than eleven feet long. They were evidently enjoying the warm rays of the sun, and at times skipped about with unwonted animation. Now one of the largest would elevate his black head some four feet from the ground, while the others wrapped themselves around him, and thus formed the dark and horrid spectacle of a pyramid of snakes! Then falling prostrate with their own weight, in less than a twinkling they were dispersed and flying over the smooth short grass in every direction, their innumerable scales all the time emitting a low buzzing sound as they ran along. Every moment others glided into the area from the tall grass, and those assembled thither rushed towards them in a body to manifest a welcome.

"Now's the time!" cried Sneak, rushing forward, followed by Joe. When Joe's eyes fell upon the black mass of serpents, he made a convulsive grasp at the reins with an involuntary resolution to retreat without delay from such a frightful scene. But the violence of his grasp severed the reins from the bit, and the pony sprang forward after the steed, being no longer subject to his control! There was no retreating now! Sneak levelled his rod at a cluster just forming in a mass two feet above the ground, and crushed the hydra at a blow! Joe closed his eyes, and struck he knew not what—but Sneak knew, for the blow descended on his head—though with feeble force. In an instant the horsemen had passed to the opposite side of the area and halted in the tall grass. Looking back, they beheld a great commotion among the surviving snakes. Some glided into the pool, and with bodies submerged, elevated their heads above the surface and darted out their tongues fiercely. Others raced round the scene of slaughter with their heads full four feet high, or gathered about the dead and dying. and lashed the air with their sharp tails, producing sounds like the cracking of whips. The few copper-heads and rattlesnakes present coiled themselves up with their heads in the centre in readiness to strike their poison into whatever object came within their reach.

So sudden had been the onset of the horsemen that the surprised serpents seemed to be ignorant of the nature of the foe, and instead of flying to the long grass to avoid a recurrence of bloodshed, they continued to glide round the pool, while their number increased every moment.

"What'd you hit me on the head for?" asked Sneak, after regarding the snakes a moment, and then turning to Joe, the pony having still kept at the heels of the steed in spite of his rider's efforts to the contrary.

"Oh, Sneak," cried Joe, in tones somewhat tremulous, "do, for goodness' sake, let us go away from here!"

"I sha'n't do any such thing—what'd you hit me on the head for?"

"I thought I was a killing a snake," replied Joe.

"Do I look like a snake?" continued Sneak, turning round, when for the first time he discovered the condition of his companion's bridle.

"Sneak, let's ride away!" said Joe.

"And leave all them black sarpents yander poking out their tongues at us? I won't go till I wear out this pole on 'em. Ha! ha! ha! I thought you hadn't spunk enough to gallup through 'em on your own accord," said Sneak, looking at the pony, and knowing that he would follow the steed always, if left to his own inclination.

"Come, Sneak, let's go home!" continued Joe, in a supplicating tone.

"Come! let's charge on the snakes agin!" said Sneak, raising the rod, and fixing his feet in the stirrups.

"Hang me if I go there again!" said Joe, throwing down his rod.

"You're a tarnation coward, that's what you are! But you can't help yourself," replied Sneak.

"I'll jump off and run!" said Joe, preparing to leap to the ground.

"You jest do now, and you'll have forty sarpents wrapped round you in less than no time."

At that moment two or three racers swept between them with their heads elevated as high as Joe's knees, and entered the area.

"Oh goodness!" cried Joe, drawing up his legs.

"Git down and git your pole," said Sneak.

"I wouldn't do it if it was made of gold!"

"If you say you'll fight the snakes, I'll git it for you—I'm a going to stay here till they're all killed," continued Sneak.

"Give it to me, then—I'll smash their brains out the next time!" said Joe, with desperate determination.

"But you musn't hit me agin!" said Sneak, dismounting and handing up the weapon to Joe, and then leaping on the steed again.

"Sneak, you're no better than a snake, to bring me into such a scrape as this!" said Joe, leaning forward and scanning the black mass of serpents at the pool.

In a few minutes they whipped forward, Sneak in advance, and again they were passing through the army of snakes. This time Joe did good service. He massacred one of the coiled rattlesnakes at a blow, and his pony kicked a puffing viper to atoms. Sneak paused a moment at the pool, and dealt his blows with such rapidity that nearly all the black racers that survived glided swiftly into the tall grass, and one of the largest was seen by Joe to run up the trunk of a solitary blasted tree that stood near the pool, and enter a round hole about ten feet from the ground.

But if the serpents were mostly dispersed from the area around the pool, they were by no means all destroyed; and when the equestrians were again in the tall grass, they found them whizzing furiously about the hoofs of their horses. Once or twice Sneak's horse sprang suddenly forward in pain, being stung on the ham or shoulder by the tails of the racers as they flew past with almost inconceivable rapidity.

"Oh! St. Peter! Sneak!" cried Joe, throwing back his head, and lifting up his knees nearly to his chin.

"Ha! ha! ha! did one of 'em cut you, Joe? They hurt like fury, but their tails ain't pisen. Look what a whelk they've made on the hoss."

"Sneak, why don't you get away from this nasty place! One of them shot right over the pony's neck a while ago, and came very near hitting me on the chin."

"You must hit 'em as they come. Yander comes one —now watch me!" Saying this, Sneak turned the steed so as to face a tremendous racer about forty paces distant, that was approaching with the celerity of the wind with its head above the tall grass. When it came within reach of his rod, he bestowed upon it a blow that entirely severed the head, and the impetus with which it came caused the body to fly over the steed, and falling upon the neck of the pony, with the life yet remaining (for they are constrictors,) instantly wrapped in a half dozen folds around it! Pete snorted aloud, and, springing forward, ran a hundred paces with all the fleetness of which he was capable. But being unable to shake off the terrible incumbrance, with his tongue hanging out in agony, he turned back and ran directly for the horse. When he came up to the steed, he pushed his head under his neck, manifesting the greatest distress, and stamping and groaning as if becoming crazed.

"Dod! let me git hold of him!" cried Sneak, bending forward and seizing the snake by the tail. The long headless body gave way gradually, and becoming quite relaxed fell powerless and dead to the earth.

"Oh, Sneak, let's go!" said Joe, trembling, his face having turned as pale as death while Pete was dashing about in choking agony under the tight folds of the serpent.

"Smash me if I go as long as there's a snake left!" replied Sneak, striking down another huge racer; but this one, having its back broken, remained stationary.

Thus he continued to strike down the snakes as long as any remained on the field; and, as they became scarce, Joe grew quite valorous, and did signal service. At length the combat ceased, and not a living serpent could be seen running.

"Sneak, we've killed them all—huzza!" cried Joe, flourishing his rod.

"Yes, but you didn't do much—you're as big a coward as ever."

"Oh, I wasn't *afraid* of them, Sneak," said Joe; "I was only a little cautious, because it was the first time I ever went a snaking."

"Yes, you was mighty cautious! if your bridle hadn't broke, you'd have been home long ago."

"Pshaw, Sneak!" said Joe; "you're much mistaken. But how many do you think we've killed?"

"I suppose about a quarter of a cord—but I've heard tell of men's killing a cord a day, easy."

"You don't say so! But how does it happen so many are found together? When I go out I can never find more than a dozen or so."

"There's a *snake den* under that clear place," said Sneak, "where they stay all winter—but its not as big a den as some I've seen."

"I don't want to see more than I have to-day!" said Joe, whipping past the steed as they started homewards, having mended his bridle. But as he paced along by the decayed tree mentioned above, he saw the glistening eyes of the large racer peering from the hole it had entered, and he gave it a smart blow on the head with his rod and spurred forward. The next moment, when Sneak came up, the enraged serpent sprang down upon him, and in a twinkling wound himself tightly round his neck! Sneak's eyes started out of his head, and being nearly strangled he soon fell to the earth. Joe looked on in amazement, but was too much frightened to assist him. And Sneak, unable to ask his aid, only turned his large eyes imploringly towards him, while in silence he vainly strove to tear away the serpent with his fingers. He thrust one hand in his pocket for his knife, but it had been left behind! He then held out his hand to Joe, and in this dumb and piteous manner begged him to lend him his knife. Joe drew it from his pocket, but could not brace his nerves sufficiently to venture within the suffocating man's reach. At length he bethought him of his pole, and opening the blade thrust it in the end of it and cautiously handed it to Sneak. Sneak immediately ran the sharp steel through the many folds of the snake, and it fell to the ground in a dozen pieces! The poor man's strength then completely failed him, and he rolled over on his back in breathless exhaustion. Joe rendered all the assistance in his power, and his companion soon revived.

"Dod rot your skin!" exclaimed Sneak, getting up and seizing Joe by the collar.

"Hang it, it wasn't *me!* it was the *snake!*" said Joe, extricating his neck from his companion's grasp.

"What'd you *hit* the sarpent for?"

"Why, I wanted to kill him."

"Then why didn't you help me to get it away from my neck?"

"You didn't *ask* me," said Joe, with something like ingenuousness, though with a most provoking application.

"I couldn't speak! The tarnation thing was squeezing my neck so tight I couldn't say a word. But I *looked* at you, and you might 'ave understood me. Never mind, you'll git a snake hold of you some of these days."

"I'll keep a sharp look out after this," said Joe. "But Sneak, I'll swear now you were not born to be hung."

"You be dod rot!" replied Sneak, leaping on the steed, and turning towards the river.

"I would have cut him off myself, Sneak," said Joe, musing on the odd affair as they rode briskly along, "if I hadn't been afraid of cutting your throat. I knew you wasn't born to be hung."

"Ha! ha! ha! that was the tightest place that ever I was in," said Sneak, regaining his good humour, and diverted at the strange occurrence.

"Didn't he bite you?" asked Joe.

"No, a black snake can't bite—they havn't got any fangs. If it had been a rattlesnake or a viper, I'd been a gone chicken. I don't think I'll ever leave my knife behind again, even if I wasn't to go ten steps from home. Dod—my neck's very sore."

The companions continued the rest of the way in silence. When they reached home, and returned the horses to the stable, they proceeded down the path to Roughgrove's house to report their adventure.

Glenn and Mary, William and La-u-na, were seated under the spreading elm-tree, engaged in some felicitous conference, that produced a most pleasing animation in their features.

Mary immediately demanded of Joe a recital of his adventures that morning. He complied without reluctance, and his hearers were frequently convulsed with laughter as he proceeded, for he added many embellishments not narrated by the author. Sneak bore their merriment with stoical fortitude, and then laughed as heartily as themselves at his own recent novel predicament.

La-u-na asked Sneak if he had been bitten by any of the poisonous snakes. Sneak of course replied in the negative, but at the same time desired to know the name of the plant that was used by the Indians with universal success when wounded by the fangs of the rattlesnake. The girl told him it was the *white plantain* that grew in the prairies.

"I'll go and get some right straight," said Joe, "because I don't know what moment I may be bitten."

"Never mind it, Joe," said Glenn, rising. "We are now

going to gather wild raspberries on the cliff south of us, and we want you and Sneak to assist us."

"Well—I like raspberries, and they must be ripe by this time, if the chickens havn't picked them all before us."

"Dod—if the chickens have ett 'em can that make 'em *green* agin?" replied Sneak to Joe's Irishism.

"You'd better learn how to read before you turn critic," said Joe, taking up the baskets that had been brought out of the house. He then led the way, quarrelling all the time with Sneak, while Glenn, placing Mary's arm in his, and William imitating the example, followed at a distance behind.

When the party reached the raspberry thicket, they found truly that the fowls were there before them, though quite an abundance of the delicious berry still remained untouched. A few moments sufficed to drive the feathered gatherers away, and then without delay they began to fill their baskets.

Many were the hearty peals of joyous laughter that rang from the innocent lovers while momentarily obscured by the green clustering bushes. Ere long they were dispersed in various parts of the thicket, and Glenn and Mary being separated from the rest, our hero seized the opportunity to broach a tender subject.

"Mary," said he, and then most unaccountably paused.

"Well," said she turning her glorious dark blue eyes full upon him.

"I have something of moment to say to you, if you will listen attentively—and I know not a more fitting time and place than this to tell it. Here is a natural bower surrounded by sweet berries, and shielded from the sun by the fragant myrtle. Let us sit on this mossy rock. Will you listen?" he continued, drawing her close to his side on the seat in the cool retreat.

"Have I ever refused to listen to you? do I not love to hear your voice?" said the confiding and happy girl.

"Bless you, Mary—my whole heart is yours!" exclaimed our hero, seizing a rapturous kiss from the coral lips of the maiden. Mary resisted not, nor replied; while tears, but not of grief, glistened on her dark lashes.

"You will not reject my love, Mary? Why do you weep?"

"It is with joy—my heart is so happy that tears gush out in spite of me!"

"Will you then be mine?" continued Glenn, winding his arm round her yielding waist.

"Forever!" she replied, and, bowing her head slightly, a shower of dark silken tresses obscured her blushing face, and covered our hero's panting breast. Thus they remained many moments in silence, for their feelings were too blissful for utterance.

"Are you always happy, Mary?" said Glenn, at length, taking her little white hand in his.

"No!' she replied, with a sigh.

"Why?"

"When you are away, I sometimes fear the Indians—or a snake—or—or something may harm you," said she, falteringly.

"I thank thee, Mary, for thinking of me when I am away."

"I always think of thee!" said she.

"Always, Mary?"

"Ay, by day—and thou art ever with me in my dreams."

"And I *will* be with thee always!"

"Do!" said she.

"But dost thou not sometimes repine that thy life is thus spent in the wilderness far from the busy world?"

"I sometimes wish I could see the beautiful cities I read of—but when I think of the treacheries and miseries of the world, I look at the pure fresh flowers, and list to the sweet birds around me, and then I think there is more happiness to be enjoyed here than anywhere else."

"And such is truly the case," said Glenn, pondering "But then, Mary, we all have obligations to discharge. We were created for society—to associate with our species, and while mingling with kindred beings, it is our duty to bestow as many benefits on them as may be within the scope of our power."

"You think, then, we should leave our western home?" she asked, with undisguised interest.

"Wilt thou not consent to go?"

"If you go, I will go!" said she.

"And now I declare I will not go unless thou art willing."

"But is it a *duty?*" she asked.

"Your fa—Mr. Roughgrove says so."

"Then let us go! But why did you not say *father?*"

"He is not your father."

"No!" exclaimed the maid, turning pale.

"I will tell thee all, Mary." And Glenn related the story of the maiden's birth. "Now, Mary," he continued, "thou knowest thine own history. Thou art of a noble race, according to the rules of men—nay, thy blood is royal—if thou wouldst retract thy plighted faith (I should have told thee this before,) speak, and thy will shall be done!"

"Oh! Charles! I am thine, THINE ONLY, were I born an angel!" she cried, throwing herself into his arms. At this juncture a violent rustling was heard in the bushes not far distant, and the next moment Joe's voice rang out,

"Oh me! Oh St. Peter! Oh murder! murder! murder!" cried he. Instantly all the party were collected round him. He lay in a small open space on the grass, with his basket bottom upward at his side, and all the berries scattered on the ground.

"What is the matter?" asked Glenn.

"Oh, I'm snake-bitten! I'm a dead man! I'm dying!" cried he, piteously.

"That's a fib," said Sneak, "bekaise a dead man can't be a dying."

"Let me see," said William, stooping down to examine the place on which Joe's hands were convulsively pressed. With some difficulty he pulled them away, and tearing down the stocking, actually saw a small bleeding puncture over the ankle bone!

"What kind of a snake was it?" asked Glenn in alarm

"A rattlesnake—Oh!"

"Did you *see* it?" continued Glenn, knowing Joe's foible, though it was apparent he suffered from some kind of a wound.

"I heard it rattle. Oh, my goodness! I'm going fast! I'm turning blind!"

La-u-na told him to run to the house and cover the wound with salt, and remain quiet till Sneak could obtain some plantain leaves from the prairie. Joe sprang up and rushed down the hill. Sneak set out in quest of the antidote, and the rest directed their steps homeward.

When they reached Roughgrove's house, they found Joe lying in the middle of the floor on his back, and groaning most dolefully. He had applied the salt to the wound as directed, and covered it and his whole leg so plentifully with bandages that the latter seemed to be as thick as his body.

"How do you feel now, Joe?" asked Glenn.

"I'm a dead man!" said he.

La-u-na told him not to be alarmed, and assured him there was no danger.

"But I'll die before Sneak can get back!"

"Your voice is too strong to fear that," said William; "but do you suffer much pain?"

"Oh, I'm in agony!" said he, rolling back his eyes.

"Where does the pain lie?" asked Glenn.

"Oh, St. Peter! all over me! In my toes, ankles, legs, arms, heart, throat, mouth, nose, and eyes! Oh, I'm in tortures! I'm blind—I can't see any of you!"

At this moment Roughgrove, who had been over the river on a visit to Boone, entered the apartment with the renowned hunter at his side. When fully informed of the circumstances, Boone stooped down and felt Joe's pulse.

"The strokes are irregular," said Boone.

"Oh heaven!" exclaimed Joe.

"But that may be caused by fright," continued Boone.

"Oh goodness! it ain't that—I'm a dying man!"

"Is the leg much swollen?" asked Boone, endeavouring to ascertain without taking off the bandages.

"Oh! oh! don't do that! it'll kill me in a minute—for its swelled fit to burst!" cried Joe, shrinking from Boone's grasp.

"All the cases of snake-bite that I have seen differ from this. I have always found the swollen limb nearly devoid of feeling. Did you kill the snake?"

"No—Oh!"

"Tell me precisely the place where you were standing when it bit you—there is a mystery about it that I must solve."

"Oh—it was—I can't speak! my breath's going fast! Oh! Paternoster——"

William then described the spot to Boone in such precise terms that the old woodman declared he would immediately repair thither and endeavour to find the snake. He accordingly set out in the direction indicated without further delay; while Roughgrove, believing that poor Joe was really on the verge of eternity, strove to comfort his departing spirit with the consolation that religion affords.

"Oh! that ain't the right one!" exclaimed Joe, pushing away the Episcopal prayer-book held by Roughgrove.

"Then here is one you cannot object to," said Roughgrove, opening the Bible.

"Oh, that's not it, either!" cried Joe, in great distress. "Is there no priest in this region? I'm a Roman Catholic —oh!"

"Can you not confess your sins *directly* to God—the God who is everywhere, and governs all things?" said the aged man, impressively, and with animation.

"I have prayed," said Joe; "but now I want the ointment!"

"Your body, which must be placed in the damp cold earth, needs no oil. It is far better to purify the soul, which perishes not," said Roughgrove, in fervent and tremulous tones.

"Oh!—Oh! Ugh!" cried Joe, in a deep guttural voice, and turning over on his face. His fears had evidently been increased by the solemn tone and look of Roughgrove.

"Don't be alarmed, Joe," said Glenn, turning him again on his back. "Sneak will soon be here, and La-u-na says the plantain will be sure to cure you. William tells me that he has seen the Indians permit the snakes to bite them for a mere trifle in money, so certain were they of being restored by the plant. And indeed he never knew a bite to terminate fatally."

"But I'm afraid Sneak won't come in time," replied Joe, somewhat comforted.

"Pshaw! he won't loiter in a case of this kind—he knows it is no joke," continued Glenn.

"But suppose he can't *find* any plantain—then I'm dead to a certainty! Oh me!"

"Does the pain increase much?" asked Mary.

"Oh, yes! its ten times worse than it was ten minutes

ago? I'm going fast—I can't move either leg now," he continued, in a weak utterance.

Glenn grew uneasy. Joe was pale—very pale, and breathed hard.

Boone entered, with a smile on his lip.

"Have you got the plantain?" asked Joe, in feeble accents, with his languid eyes nearly closed, thinking it was Sneak.

"Sit up and tell me how you feel," said Boone, in vain striving to repress his smile.

"Oh, St. Peter! I haven't strength enough to lift my hand," said Joe, his eyes still closed.

"Did you find the snake?" asked Glenn.

"Yes," replied Boone. Joe groaned audibly. "I will tell you all about it," he continued; "I found the spot where Joe had been gathering the berries, and tracked him without difficulty to every bush he visited by the bruised grass under his foot-prints. At length I came to the cluster of bushes where he received the wound. I stood in his tracks and saw where he had plucked the raspberries. When about to cast down my eyes in quest of the snake, suddenly I felt a blow on my own ankle!"

"Did the same snake bite you?" asked Mary, quickly.

"Yes," replied Boone, still smiling. Joe opened his eyes, and after gazing a moment at Boone, asked him if he did not suffer much pain.

"Fully as much as you do—but hear me through. I sprang back with some violence, I admit, but I did not run away. Lifting my cane, I returned with a determination to kill the snake. I stooped down very low to ascertain the precise position of its head, which was concealed by a large mullen leaf—I saw its eyes and its *bill*——"

"What!" exclaimed Joe, rising up on his elbow with unwonted vigour, and his eyes riveted on the speaker.

"Yes, its *bill*," continued Boone. "And while my cane was brandished in the air and about descending on its devoted head, a low clucking arrested my arm, and approaching closer to it than before, and gazing steadfastly a moment, I lowered my cane to its usual position, and fell back laughing on the grass among the raspberries you had dropped."

"Mr. Boone—Mr. Boone!" cried Joe, springing up in a

sitting attitude, and seizing the hand of the veteran, "for Heaven's sake tell me what it was?"

"It was an old SITTING HEN!" said Boone.

"Upon your honour?" continued Joe, leaping upon his feet, and staring the aged hunter in the face, while his eyes gleamed with irrepressible hope and anxiety.

"It was nothing else, upon my honour," replied Boone, laughing in concert with the rest.

"Huzza! huzza!! huzza!!!" shouted Joe, casting the bandages hither and thither, and dancing nimbly over the floor. "Fal-de-lal—tider-e-i—tider-e-o—tider-e-um!" he continued, in frenzied delight, and, observing Sneak at the door with an armful of plantain (who had returned in time to witness his abrupt recovery, and now continued to regard him with wonder and doubt—at times thinking he was delirous,) skipped up and held out both hands, as if inviting him to dance.

"Dod rot it, your leg ain't swelled a bit!" said Sneak.

"Don't use that bad word, Sneak," said Mary.

"I won't—but dod—he's had me running all over——"

"Tider-e-i—tider-e-um!" continued Joe, still dancing, while the perspiration streamed over his face.

"Have done with this nonsense, Joe!" said Glenn, "or else continue your ridiculous exercises on the grass in the yard. You may rejoice now, but this affair will be sport for others all your life. You will not relish it so much to-morrow."

"I'd rather all the world would laugh at me alive and kicking, than that one of you should mourn over my dead body," replied Joe, leaping over Sneak, who was sitting in the door, and striding to the grass plot under the elm, where he continued his rejoicings. Sneak followed, and, sitting down on the bench in the shade, seemed to muse with unusual gravity at the strange spectacle presented by Joe.

This was Joe's last wild western adventure. The incident was soon forgotten by the party in the house. Serious and sad thoughts succeeded the mirthful scene described above. Roughgrove had brought Boone thither to receive their last farewell! The renowned woodman and warrior wore marks of painful regret on his pale features. The rest were in tears.

"William," said Roughgrove, "listen to a tale concerning thy birth and parentage, which I feel it to be my duty to unfold. Your sister has already learned the story from your friend, who sits beside her. But I will repeat it to all present. You who are the most interested can then determine whether it shall ever be disclosed to other ears. The secret was long locked in my bosom, and it was once my purpose to bury it with my body in the grave. I pondered long on the subject, and prayed to Heaven to be instructed. I have satisfactory evidence in my own heart that I have acted correctly." He then related the history of the twins, as we have given it to the reader. When he concluded, La-u-na, who had betrayed much painful interest during the recital, threw her arms round William's neck, and wept upon his breast.

"Why do you weep, La-u-na?" asked the youth.

"La-u-na must die!" said she; "her William will leave her and forget her. The wild rose will bend over her grave—the brook will murmur low at her cold feet—the rabbit will nip the tender grass by her tombstone at nightfall—the katydid will chirp over her, and the whippor-will will sing in vain. William will forget her! Poor La-u-na!"

"No—La-u-na! no! Thou shalt go with me and be my bride, or else I will remain with thee! Death only shall separate us!" said the youth, drawing the slight form of the Indian maiden closer to his heart, and imprinting a rapturous kiss on her smooth forehead.

"We will all go together," continued Roughgrove, "save our beloved friend here, who tells me that no earthly consideration could induce him to dwell in cities among civilized men."

"True," said Boone; "I would not exchange my residence in the western wilds for the gorgeous palaces of the east. Yet I think you do right in returning to the society which you were destined to adorn. I shall grieve when I miss you, but I will not persuade you to remain. Every one should act according to the dictates of his conscience. It is my belief that Providence guides our actions. You, my friends, were fitted and designed to move in refined society, and by your example and influence to benefit the world around you. The benefits bestowed by *me* will not be immediate, nor altogether in my day. I am a PIONEER, formed by nature. Where I struggle with the savage and the wild beast, my great grandchildren will reside in cities. I must fulfil my mission."

At this moment Joe and Sneak appeared at the door.

"There's a covered flat-boat just landed down at the ferry," said Joe.

"It is from the island above," said Roughgrove, "and the one I have had constructed for our voyage down the river."

"Are we going, sure enough?" asked Joe.

"Yes; to-morrow," said Glenn.

"Dod—are you *all* going off?" asked Sneak, rolling round his large eyes, and stretching out his neck to an unusual length.

"All but me, Sneak," said Boone.

"And you won't be any company for me. Dod—I've a notion to go too! If I could foller any thing to make a living in Fillydelfa——"

"If you go with us, you shall never want—I will see that you are provided for," said Glenn.

"It's a bargain!" said Sneak, with the eager emphasis characteristic of the trading Yankee.

"But poor Pete—the horses!" said Joe.

"There are stalls in the boat for them," said Roughgrove.

"Huzza! I'm glad. Huzza!" cried Joe.

* * * * * * *

The next morning beamed upon them in beauty—and in sadness. The sun rose in majesty, and poured his brilliant and inspiring rays on peak and valley and plain. But the hearts of the peaceful wanderers throbbed in sorrow as they gazed for the last time on the scene before them. Though it had been identified with the many perilous and painful encounters with savages, yet the quivering green leaves above, the sparkling brook below, and the soft melody of happy birds around, were intimately associated with some of the most blissful moments of their lives.

La-u-na retired to a lonely spot, and poured forth a farewell song to the whispering spirits of her fathers. Long her steadfast gaze was fixed on the blue sky, as if communing with the departed kings from whom she descended. At length her tears vanished like a shower in the sunshine, and a bright smile rested upon her features, as if her prayer had been heard and all she asked were granted! Prophetic vision! While the race from which she separated is doomed to extinction in the forest, the blood she mingled with the Anglo-Saxon race may yet be destined to sway the councils of a mighty empire.

William mused in silence, guarding at a distance the bride of his heart, and not venturing to intrude upon her devotions. The past was like a dream to him—the present a bright vision—the future a paradise!

Glenn and Mary were seated together, regarding with impatience the brief preparations to embark. Boone, Roughgrove, Sneak, and Joe were busily engaged lading the vessel. Sneak had hastily brought thither his effects, and without a throe of regret abandoned his *house* for ever to the owls. Joe succeeded with but little difficulty in getting the horses on board. The fawn, the kitten, the hounds, and the chickens were likewise taken along.

And now all was ready to push out into the current. All were on board. Boone bid them an affectionate adieu in silence—in silence, but in tears. The cable was loosened, and the boat was wafted down on its journey eastward. William and La-u-na sat upon the deck, and gazed at the receding shore, rendered dear by hallowed recollections. Glenn and Mary stood at the prow, and as they marked the fleeting waters, their thoughts dwelt on the happy future. Roughgrove was praying. Joe was caressing the pony. Sneak was counting his muskrat skins. And thus we must bid them adieu.

THE END.

www.ingramcontent.com/pod-product-compliance
Lightning Source LLC
LaVergne TN
LVHW010215110826
845151LV00004B/1091